First published 2024

First printed edition published 2024 by Drollery Ltd.

Copyright © Alice Coldbreath, 2024

ISBN 978-1-916736-12-2

I0611326

More books available by Alice Coldbreath:

The Vawdrey Brothers Series:

Book 1: Her Baseborn Bridegroom

Book 2: His Forsaken Bride

Book 3: An Ill-Made Match

The Brides of Karadok Series:

Book 1: Wed By Proxy

Book 2: The Unlovely Bride

Book 3: The Consolation Prize

Book 4: Her Bridegroom, Bought and Paid For

Book 5: An Inconvenient Vow

Book 6: The Favourite

The Victorian Prizefighter Series:

Book 1: A Bride for the Prizefighter

Book 2: A Substitute Wife for the Prizefighter

Book 3: A Contracted Spouse for the Prizefighter

This book is dedicated to my talented friend Francesca.
Your beautiful art is hanging in my office.

1

Bath

The elegant carriage came to a halt outside number ten, and Jeremy Vance, fifth Viscount Faris, leaned out of the window to look expectantly at his footman.

"Not dignifying them with your presence today, then?" Colfax asked from his perch.

"God no. There's only so much of the Arbuthnots I can take in one calendar month," Jeremy replied dryly. "Kindly retrieve my heir."

"They'll be disappointed," Colfax commented sotto voce as he climbed down. *Let them*, thought Jeremy callously. He did not care for the Arbuthnots and intended to do everything in his power to sway his son's partiality for their society as soon as possible.

He watched Colfax ascend the steps to ring the bell, but the door was whisked open before his fingers had closed around the pull cord. Judging by the way the housemaid blushed and giggled, Jeremy didn't think *everyone* was disappointed by his nonappearance.

Observing the twitch of the parlor curtains, Jeremy looked away. He knew his son considered Arthur Arbuthnot the best of his old school friends, but he found he could not abide another meeting with the boy's mother, not even for Teddy's sake. He was sure it was her elaborately ringleted head he'd caught a glimpse of at the window. *Ghastly woman.*

Mercifully, Teddy did not take long to emerge this time. Was it too much to hope that Arthur Arbuthnot's charm might have waned somewhat in his fickle affections? Jeremy scanned his son's face as he made his way down the steps toward him. As he did so, his heart sank a little. Nine-year-old Teddy had a speculative look on his deceptively angelic face. Oh God, what was he after now?

Jeremy threw open the door as Colfax made his way unhurriedly back down the steps.

"Good evening, Papa" Teddy caroled as he climbed into the carriage.

"Did you have a pleasant afternoon?" Jeremy enquired politely.

"Yes, thank you," he replied promptly.

"What was it this time?" he asked. "A Punch and Judy show? A new puppy?"

Teddy shook his head as he settled onto the seat opposite his father. "No, for Arthur's mother wanted us to sit quietly with her today. She said Arthur must remember that I am convalescing," he said, "and must not expect me to play nasty boys' games."

Jeremy shot him a surprised look. "I was not aware that you and Arthur had been indulging in any rough and tumble," he said, revising his opinion of staid, bespectacled Arthur.

"Oh, we haven't," Teddy said blithely, "but Arthur has a new cricket set and asked if Simpson could take us to the park with it. His mama said no, and that he must bring down some books for me and his train set instead."

Jeremy eyed his son with some puzzlement as Colfax climbed atop the carriage. Teddy had an air of suppressed excitement about him that a staid afternoon in the Arbuthnots' parlor did not account for. Knowing his son's frequently and strongly expressed feelings about occupying himself quietly with books, he could not imagine that Mrs. Arbuthnot's suggestion was met with any enthusiasm by Teddy.

Reaching up, Jeremy rapped the roof to signify they should drive off. "Well, I imagine you were both disappointed," he ventured as the carriage lurched into action, "but perhaps it was for the best. Dr. Reid did say no physical exertion for at least six weeks."

Teddy, who had been complaining nonstop about intolerable boredom for the past month, nodded philosophically. "And if we had not remained indoors, then I should never have heard about Miss Ballentine, would I, Papa?"

"Of whom?" Jeremy was startled by the air of import that Teddy attached to the name. Startled, also, by the blast of associated emotion with that same name. Surely, *surely* he did not say what Jeremy *thought* he had said.

His son gazed back at him with disapproval. "Miss Ballentine," he repeated sternly. When Jeremy continued speechless, Teddy rolled his eyes. "Arthur's mother told me all about her. They came out in the same season, but Miss Ballentine's father was 'an awful cit.' What's *an awful cit*, Papa?"

Jeremy considered this as his thoughts raced. "A cit, my boy, is someone who makes his money in the city. A self-made man of business, usually. A most entrepreneurial and resourceful fellow. Certainly nothing to be ashamed of, as Mrs. Arbuthnot seems to have given you the impression."

"Oh." Teddy appeared to digest this. Then he turned a forbidding glower upon his father. "Arthur's mama," he said severely, "said Miss Ballentine used to turn very red when you came to parties, and you used to make everyone laugh by dancing with her."

Jeremy paused. "I used to do what?" he asked, turning cold. Feigning deafness to stall for time seemed the best course of action. Why in hell would the Arbuthnot woman think it was appropriate to relay such tales to his own son?

"Arthur's mother said you used to wink at your friends after you asked her to dance, and they all used to laugh up their sleeves at her."

Damn the woman. Jeremy straightened up in his seat. "I'm afraid Mrs. Arbuthnot is laboring under a misapprehension," he said firmly. "If I asked this Miss—?" He bent a quizzical look on Teddy, as though he had forgotten her name.

"Ballentine," he supplied helpfully.

"Miss Ballentine to dance with me," Jeremy continued smoothly, "then it would have been because I *wished* to dance with her. If I winked to my friends, it must have been because I was feeling particularly proud of myself."

Teddy's shoulders relaxed slightly. "So…you weren't making fun of her, then?" he asked, his blue eyes very intent.

"That would have been very bad form indeed," Jeremy answered smoothly. "I would hope you would have a better opinion of your papa." He felt strangely winded by the exchange. *Emmeline Ballentine*. He had not permitted himself to think of her for years. Suddenly, he seemed to catch a faint and surely phantom scent of orange blossoms.

"You liked her, then?" Teddy persisted. "You must have, if you wanted to dance with her."

"If I asked her to stand up with me at parties, then obviously I liked her," Jeremy confirmed crisply, ignoring the fact he had done a good many selfish and cruel things over the years. His conscience stirred uneasily. The damn thing had been inactive for eons, until it had slowly limped forth, sometime in the past eighteen months, to trouble him. Sometimes he wished it would go back to malfunctioning. Things had been so much easier when he had been an unprincipled swine.

Previously, he had dealt with such stirrings with a stiff drink. That seemed to obliterate such feelings of guilt, but that was no longer an option. He could not be divorced *and* a drunkard. That was simply too much to weigh against him in the balance. He may have been considered unprincipled in his salad days, but he had never been a social outcast.

"That's good," Teddy said, looking relieved now that matter had been cleared up. "That should make things easier."

"Things?"

"You marrying her, I mean."

Jeremy's eyes bulged. "Marrying?" he repeated faintly.

"Yes," Teddy confirmed before turning a reproachful gaze upon him. "You told me, did you not, that you would not get married again without my approval," he reminded his father.

"I did," Jeremy agreed, "and yet, forgive me, my son, I envisaged your part as more of a final veto. Not the actual selector of my bride."

Teddy leaned against the cushioned seat and closed his eyes. "I'm quite worn out," he sighed dramatically. "Arbuthnot's mother talks *a lot*. She's rather like a buzzing fly when one's trying to sleep." He frowned. "I'm glad my mama was not like that, even though she did shout and scream and hit the servants."

"Your mama had her faults," Jeremy mused, "but a crushing bore, she was not."

"How soon before you procure my next one?" Teddy enquired.

"Next what?"

"Mama."

Jeremy blinked. "Well, er, these things take time, my boy. It has not been a full twelve months since my divorce, and—"

"That's nearly a year," Teddy pointed out critically.

"Maybe so, but people have strong opinions on divorce, which only the passage of time can assuage."

"Mama has remarried, has she not? That French man who owns the gambling den in Paris."

Jeremy winced. "Who told you that? Besides, he's Italian."

"Mrs. Oxley," Teddy responded promptly.

"Mrs. Oxley, our cook at Vance Park?" Jeremy asked carefully.

Teddy nodded. "Well, she wasn't telling me, precisely," he admitted. "She was telling Iverson the undergardener. I just happened to be under the kitchen table at the time, eating a treacle tart."

Jeremy closed his eyes briefly. "Of course you were."

"She said Mama's papa may have been an earl, but she was *no better than she ought to be*."

Jeremy thought it best not to comment on this damning indictment of his ex-wife's morals. "Mrs. Oxley makes a very good treacle tart, does she not?" he murmured instead.

"The best," Teddy agreed. "Gosh, they didn't serve desserts like that at Paverton Hall," he said, naming the select boarding school that he had once attended. He looked suddenly wistful. "I just bet I could eat one of Mrs. Oxley's tarts about now," he said sadly.

Jeremy was just glad Teddy was not about to turn teary-eyed over his old school. His son had despised the place when he had been there but recently, he had turned somewhat sentimental about that period of his life. Doubtless it was all part of his depressed spirits following his illness. "It's a good sign your appetite is returning," he said aloud. "Shall we stop at the bakery and pick up some iced buns?"

Teddy shook his head. "I don't care for them," he said irritably. "They always taste stale from Fritton's."

"How about the bakery on Gideon Street?" Jeremy suggested.

Teddy pulled a face. "They're even worse."

"Then, what do you say to getting an ice from Marshall's?"

Teddy's expression wavered. He had a weakness for strawberry ices. "No," he sighed. "In any case, they would be shut at this hour."

Jeremy reached for his pocket watch and was forced to concur. "Tomorrow, then," he suggested. "We could go for luncheon there."

"Arthur invited me to his house again tomorrow," Teddy said without any great enthusiasm.

"I think not," Jeremy said swiftly. "We could not possibly impose on the Arbuthnots' kindness anymore. You have already spent three afternoons under their roof in the past week. What is your papa supposed to do with himself all day with no society? I will grow lonely."

"You could come along. Mrs. Arbuthnot said to tell you that you were always welcome."

Jeremy suppressed a shudder. "Surely you and Arthur have caught up on all your reminiscences by this point. Good lord, you were only at Paverton Preparatory for nine months!"

Teddy shrugged, looking suddenly washed-out. A flicker of enthusiasm lit up his disinterested gaze. "We could call on Miss Ballentine," he suggested, and Jeremy had to work to keep his expression unruffled.

"It must have been some ten years or so ago that we were acquainted, my son. It is more than likely that Miss Ballentine is no more."

"She's not dead, Papa!" Teddy responded with spirit, clearly suspecting his father of trying to wriggle out of the obligation. "Arthur's mother said she has lodgings in Winkworth Street!"

"I meant," Jeremy explained painstakingly, ignoring the strange skip in his chest at hearing she was in Bath, "that after all this time, the lady is more than likely married already."

"Oh no," Teddy said, shaking his head. "No, she's not. Mrs. Arbuthnot said her papa could not bring anyone up to scratch, even though he was rich as Jesus in those days."

Jeremy cleared his throat, concentrating on his son's words, rather than his strange reaction to them. He doubted very much that a Galilean carpenter's wealth equated that of a wealthy cit. "Is it possible you mean 'Croesus'?" he enquired politely.

"It's possible," Teddy conceded generously. "In any case, her papa's not rich anymore. Arthur's mother said he lost it all on the 'change."

"The Exchange," Jeremy corrected him absently. That would make sense, for the direction of Winkworth Street eluded him. Most likely it was not in a fashionable quarter of town.

"Yes," Teddy agreed. "So, Mrs. Arbuthnot says she does not *even have to 'knowledge her anymore.*"

"Acknowledge," Jeremy supplied.

"Yes, what does that mean, Papa?"

"It means, my boy, that Mrs. Arbuthnot has quite appalling manners. I do not think we should consider her a reliable source when it comes to Papa's past behavior. Are we agreed?"

"What about Miss Ballentine?" Teddy asked, a mutinous cast to his features.

"Naturally I shall look up my old acquaintance, Miss Ballentine, whilst we are in Bath," Jeremy responded coolly. "It would be most remiss of me not to."

Just for a moment, he allowed himself to remember Emmeline Ballentine as she had been on that last evening. Plump, pretty Emmeline in her frilly white gown, with her curling red-gold hair done up and framing her face in ringlets. Orange blossoms, yes, of course. Hawford's conservatory. *Shall I give you something to remember me by, Ballentine?*

Not his finest hour. Then, other memories, less pleasant, seeped from the breached vault, making him wince. Her openly admiring gaze across a ballroom. The offhand comments he would make to the other young bucks, the barely hidden smirks and laughter. He had made Emmeline a figure of fun that season, for entirely selfish reasons. He wanted nothing more than to forget how he had behaved. *Didn't he?*

He sat back in his seat, breathing deeply. Then why had he just promised his son that he would renew the acquaintance? And why was his pulse racing so damn fast at the prospect of seeing her again? He was sure she would be a good deal older and wiser now, despite the fact she had never married.

She was certainly far less likely to be receptive of his attentions. Not after that announcement that same night as the conservatory and the orange blossoms and…all the rest of that wretched business.

Would she still be the same sweet girl he had known, and would she play along and reassure his child that he had not acted like the worst kind of cad toward her? He had no idea, but he knew one thing. He wanted to find out. Badly.

*

Fritton's Bakery, Bath

The queue at Fritton's was longer than usual for this time of day. Seeing the assistant turn obligingly to the man to her left, Emmie leaned against the counter, letting her mind wander back once more to the worrying letter she had received that morning from Mr. Hardiman, the senior clerk at her father's firm.

It had been plaguing her ever since, and her stomach turned over once again as her thoughts returned queasily to the doom-laden words. Mr. Hardiman was a quiet, cautious sort and not given to exaggeration of any kind. If he was using phrases like "dire straits" in connection with her late father's business concerns, then things *must* be bleak indeed.

But, if that was the case, then why on earth had Humphrey not been in touch? Even more worrying, whatever would she do for income if the business really was in trouble? The amount she received from her father's shares had dwindled alarmingly in the past eighteen months. She and Pinky had already downgraded their lodgings in Bath twice in the past year.

"Is all well, dear?" her companion and friend, Hannah Pinson, asked timorously. She tipped her head to one side in her typically birdlike fashion. "You look quite peaky. Indeed, I have been wondering all day if you might not be a little under the weather."

"I'm fine, Pinky dear," Emmie assured her bracingly, and turned back to face front. Poor Pinky would be a nervous wreck if she knew they were staring potential ruin in the face. The last thing Emmie wanted to do now was heap more worries onto those narrow shoulders, not until it was strictly necessary.

"Now, have you decided in which delicacy we shall partake?" Emmie asked brightly, her eyes scanning the pastries on offer. Today was the last Friday of the month, which meant Emmie had received her banker's draft and they always had some indulgence treat for tea.

Pinky, for that was what Emmie had called her since childhood, peered shortsightedly over the counter. "Oh dear," she fretted. "I am sure coconut tarts did not used to be so expensive. And as for those cherry cakes, why, you used to get two for that price and I am sure they used to be twice the size!"

Emmie shot a sidelong glance at her friend. Perhaps Pinky was not so sweetly oblivious to their financial plight after all. "We can afford a little splurge on the day I receive my stipend, dear," she said bravely, trying not to think of how small this month's payout had been.

"Well, in that case…" Pinky hesitated. "Perhaps the iced buns?" she suggested, naming the cheapest thing available. "I have always had a decided weakness for them."

"My favorite!" Emmie lied, feeling vastly relieved for her, even though she knew for a fact that cream horns were her friend's true weakness. They beamed at one another reassuringly, and having procured a paper bag of iced buns, exited the shop, and proceeded cordially down the street together arm in arm.

"Did you have any books to return to the lending library?" Emmie asked, as she once again fretted over the fact she had not received a letter from Humphrey in, oh, it must be some three or four weeks now. He was not just her fiancé, but also the man running her late father's firm, Ballentine's Trading Company.

The profits had never soared, not once in the ten years since her father had passed. Humphrey, his able second-in-command, had always been viewed as "safe hands" rather than brilliant. Emmie suppressed a sigh now, thinking of her father's last words. Had Father, once so instinctive about matters of business, been entirely wrong about trusting all to Humphrey?

She had clung doggedly to her father's instruction, despite the dwindling income. She had seen it not only as a matter of loyalty to her fiancé, but also her father's memory, but perhaps after all, she should have hired someone new for the position after the downward trend of profits in the first five years. Things had not improved as Humphrey had sworn they would if they just had faith and weathered the storm. Instead, they had gotten steadily worse.

"Emmie?" Pinky touched her sleeve, jolting her out of her gloomy reverie. "What is it? Have you—have you had bad news? Is it…Humphrey?"

"Humphrey?" Emmie was startled by the question. "Good gracious, no. I have not heard from him in weeks." Instead of looking reassured by this confidence, her friend looked even more disturbed. Emmie took a deep breath. "I'm so sorry, dear. I was woolgathering, do not pay me any heed. Now, tell me, how are you getting on with *Love's Innocence Fled* and how is beleaguered Josephine faring? I'm simply itching to know."

Josephine was the heroine in the novel Pinky was currently reading. Since they had moved from London eight years ago, their social circle had vastly reduced. As an heiress to her father's fortune, living in a large London house, Emmie had friends and acquaintances galore. They had been invited to dinner parties, soirees, and coffee mornings every week.

A shabby gentlewoman and her companion, living in straitened circumstances in Bath, simply did not possess such a social circle. These days she and Pinky had one another to rely on. Novels were heaven-sent. They read them avidly and spoke of their plots as though they were present events in their lives, and the characters within their pages as people they actually knew. It greatly enriched their rather colorless day to day.

"Did she find her beloved Fernando at the Venice Opera House as the mysterious note intimated, or was it all a cruel ruse by that scoundrel, the count?" Emmie persisted.

Pinky brightened. "Now, how *did* you guess?" she marveled. "I was never so shocked as when poor Josephine took the amulet to the appointed meeting place only to find herself confronted by that wicked Count Stefano!" Pinky tutted. "I tell you, the lengths that villain will go to simply to get poor Josephine in his clutches, you would hardly credit it, my dear."

"I daresay I would not," Emmie murmured, thinking that her own fiancé could scarcely cobble a letter together for her these days, despite the fact she had not seen him since New Year's. Briefly, she wondered what it might be like to be pursued by a man like Stefano, who would jump through so many hoops in pursuit of his beloved.

It was no good, she simply could not imagine it. Perhaps because she had no experience of being the fair pursued. Even in the early days of their courtship, she could never describe Humphrey as being anything other than terribly polite in his wooing.

"Alas," Pinky sighed sadly, "poor Fernando is so unworldly, dear man, that he simply does not realize the peril Josephine faces as a beauteous and virtuous maiden quite alone in the world." A tear sprang to Pinky's eye. "His devotion to his art, though noble, blinds him at times to her plight."

"Perhaps she would be better off with Stefano," Emmie replied without thinking. "At least he is not so oblivious to her struggles and promises to drape her in all manner of luxury if she would only succumb to his wicked lures." Emmie could not quite keep the envious note from her voice. She could do with a few worldly goods about now. She had been forced to sell her own diamond brooch three winters ago.

Pinky gasped. "Oh no, dear! That would not do at all! Count Stefano is a man quite *steeped* in sin with the very worst of reputations attached to his name. Indeed, no one in polite Venetian society would allow him to darken their doorstep. As his wife, Josephine would *never* receive any invitations to parties and routs and all those masked balls they always seem to have in that part of the world."

"Yes, I suppose that *would* count against him," Emmie replied doubtfully. "Though why should Josephine care if all of polite society bars their doors against her? Married to the count, she would have her own ballroom to dance in, and her own staff to load her dining table with delicacies, would she not?"

"Yes, but there would be no one to dine with at the dinner table, and no one to dance with, save for the wicked count himself," Pinky pointed out with a shudder.

"True, but Stefano might be a very good dancer," Emmie speculated. "In my experience, the Fernandos of this world tend to tread on toes." Fleetingly, she imagined Humphrey, stolid, dependable Humphrey, in the role of Fernando. Quite ludicrous really, as Humphrey did not have an artistic bone in his body, and moreover quite despised unworldly types. He *was* a lamentably poor dancer though, with no sense of timing or rhythm.

Casting the role of the wicked count was distressingly easy, even after all these years. She didn't have to think about it. The honorable, or should she say dishonorable Jeremy Vance sprang to mind immediately, in all his despicable glory. He had been such a beautiful dancer though! So graceful and…*oh*, Pinky was talking again. She gave her head a quick shake to dismiss her errant thoughts.

"There may be something in what you say," Pinky was musing. "One of the rectors at my father's church was a most proficient country dancer, and then later, it turned out that he had a dreadful weakness for gambling hells and would visit them every time he traveled to Tunbridge Wells."

The idea of gambling hells in Tunbridge Wells sounded so incongruous that Emmie blinked. "Was this the rector who drank too much elderberry wine one Christmas, and outraged your cousin Winifred, or the one who loathed cats?" she asked.

"Oh no, dear, it was *quite* another one to both of those. We had dozens of rectors trooping through the doors of St. Wulstan's," she sighed. "Such happy times." She dabbed a handkerchief to the corners of her eyes.

Recollections of her childhood always turned Pinky sentimental. Her parents had had her very late in life and as a consequence, she had lost them both young. "Now, what were we saying?" Pinky asked, having lost the thread of the conversation.

"You were speaking of the den of iniquity that is Tunbridge Wells," Emmie replied gravely.

"Oh! Oh, dear me, no, I did not mean to imply that Tunbridge Wells was anything less than wholesome. I had a great-uncle who resided there for many years, most happily. My uncle Randolph. I daresay, it was merely a game of cards the rector used to indulge in within the parlor of some gentleman acquaintance," she reflected. "But you see, Mama always referred to Mr. Anstruther as frequenting 'gambling hells,' though whether it was in jest, or out of naivety, I really could not say after such a passage of time."

Emmie laughed and squeezed her friend's arm. "I expect she said it in fun," she said, "to tease your father, the vicar."

Pinky's eyes turned misty. "Yes," she agreed. "They were always *so* fond of one another, always. Everyone remarked upon it, even my aunt Harriet. To be as devoted after forty years married as you were on your wedding day must be a wonderful thing."

Emmie tried to imagine how she would feel about Humphrey after forty years. In truth, she had felt surer of him ten years ago than she did now. She sighed. "A feat indeed," she agreed. They walked the rest of the way in near silence, both lost in their own thoughts, until they reached the peeling green door of number six, where they rented rooms on the second floor.

Florrie, the maid of all work who belonged to their landlady who lived on the ground floor, opened the door at once. "Here you are at last, Miss Ballentine!" she said excitedly, ushering them inside. "Almost thought you'd got lost, you been gone such an age."

Pinky tutted, for she did not approve of Florrie's manner, but she did it so faintly that the smart little maid barely noticed. Not that she'd care, for Florrie thought Pinky a poor, drab creature.

"Are we late?" Emmie asked in surprise, reaching for the watch she'd pawned two weeks ago. Her fingers closing on thin air, she turned instead to glance at the grandfather clock stood solidly in the hallway. "It is a little after five, Florrie. We are not so very late."

"You've 'ad a caller, miss, *ever* such a gent, 'e was," Florrie gabbled excitedly. "Lovely calling card all edged in gilt and *such* manners." She sighed ecstatically.

"Humphrey?" Emmie asked, pausing in the act of removing her hatpin.

"Not 'im!" Florrie burst out in disgust. "This one tips!"

"Perhaps if you presented his calling card that might clear up the confusion," Pinky suggested mildly.

Florrie regarded Pinky with narrowed eyes a moment, as though imagining some slight. Then, grudgingly, she reached into her apron pocket to retrieve the card. She glanced at it one last time, then sighed, and handed it over.

Viscount Faris, Emmie read in elegant copperplate beneath an elaborately embossed crest. Who the deuce was that? She turned it over to read the elegant scrawl on the back.

Dear Miss Ballentine, I have recently come to Bath, for my son's convalescence. If it would be convenient for me to call on an old friend one morning this week, I would be grateful for the opportunity to introduce the two of you and renew our acquaintance. J.V.

If anything, Emmie's bafflement grew. She was sure she had never met a Viscount Faris in her life! "Er, thank you, Florrie," she murmured, unsure how else to respond, and turned toward the stair.

"What about your answer, then?" Florrie demanded indignantly.

Emmie swung back around. "Did he leave some direction for it?"

Wordlessly, Florrie crossed to the hall window and lifted the lace curtain. Greatly puzzled, Emmie walked over to join her and stood gazing out in growing astonishment. Somehow she and Pinky had entirely failed to notice a luxurious-looking carriage parked on the opposite side of the street.

"Whoever is it, Emmie?" Pinky asked in hushed tones, appearing suddenly at her elbow.

"I hardly know," Emmie confessed. "If this was one of our novels, Pinky dear, it would be a rich and heretofore unknown uncle, come to—" She broke off her words abruptly as the carriage door swung open, and an elegant figure stepped out.

Emmie gasped, and for a moment, time stood still as she remained frozen, a hand to her throat and her mouth hanging open. *Surely, that could not be...* Just then, the late afternoon sun appeared from behind a cloud, and its rays struck his impeccably styled hair, making it gleam as gold as a newly minted guinea.

The spell was broken, and she could finally move. "Oh dear," Emmie quavered, slumping against the wall. She felt quite weak and shaken. "*Count Stefano.*"

"What?" Pinky gasped, her head whipping around. Emmie wasn't attending. Instead, she remained where she was, her eyes glued to the immaculate vision unhurriedly crossing the street. He was every bit as devastatingly handsome as she remembered him.

Jeremy Vance had appeared from her past, like some bad fairy she had conjured by foolishly speaking his name aloud. *Speak of the devil and he shall appear.* Her common sense immediately rebelled. This was *nothing* to do with the fact she had allowed herself to think of him this afternoon! It was just some...horrible coincidence.

Besides, she told herself uneasily, she had *not* actually spoken his name. She had been speaking of wicked Count Stefano, which was an entirely different thing. The three women watched transfixed as he approached their front steps, seemingly oblivious to the fact he was being avidly observed.

Oh God, Emmie thought, dry-mouthed. All this time, she had told herself he could not possibly be so good-looking. It just wasn't fair, she thought, her bosom swelling with indignation, that the passage of time had not marred his appearance in any way. If anything, he had grown even more attractive. It was monstrously unjust!

Drawing herself up, she turned to Florrie. "Allow Miss Pinson and myself three minutes to reach our sitting room, and then show him up," she instructed with as much dignity as she could muster. Florrie nodded fervently as Emmie turned to her friend. "Come along, Pinky dear."

Pinky made haste to comply, even managing to hold her tongue as they hurried up the stairs to their own rooms. Moving swiftly, they hung their bonnets on their pegs, and set their reticules and gloves down on the rickety side table used for that expressed purpose.

Only once they were comfortably seated did Pinky lean forward to whisper urgently, "You are alright, dear, aren't you?"

Emmie nodded but mercifully there was no chance to speak further, for Florrie was knocking on the door. She flung it open, cleared her throat, and announced importantly, "Count Stefano!"

Jeremy Vance, or rather, Viscount Faris as he was apparently now known, paused, a faint pucker appearing between his brows. Still, he advanced into the room, assured as ever, his eyes on Emmeline's face as she rose to give him her curtesy.

"Miss Ballentine," he said, his own bow grace itself. "It has been too long, and yet, I would have recognized you anywhere."

"You are too kind. Allow me to present my friend and companion, Miss Hannah Pinson."

He turned at once to Pinky. "I am delighted to meet you," he said with a charming smile. Emmie was glad that Pinky was on her guard, or she might have been completely taken in by such beautiful manners. As it was, her friend merely curtseyed, her eyes wary, her face tight with concern.

"Please be seated, my lord," Emmie said, gesturing toward a spoon-back armchair, which was their best and did not match the rest of the room, since it was a relic from more affluent times.

Lord Faris hesitated slightly before seating himself. "I hope I have not come at an inopportune time," he said. "It appears you are expecting someone else's company at present." When they gazed blankly back at him, he said, "A certain Count Stefano?"

Pinky went off into a coughing fit and Emmie felt a hot flush start crawling up her neck.

"That was a simple misunderstanding only," she said hastily. "I do apologize. It was my fault; Florrie mistook my meaning."

He waved this off. "So long as my poor company is not a crushing disappointment in his stead."

"How could it be?" Emmie said brightly. "You are a count yourself, are you not? A viscount no less, and no longer a mere honorable."

He opened his mouth, then closed it again, a gleam appearing in his eye. What had he been about to say? Emmie found herself wondering. Likely, something about never being honorable in his life, she guessed. Then, something seemed to occur to him, and the laughter abruptly vanished from his eyes. "The title," he said softly, "you did not realize who I was." He shot her a look of disconcerting frankness. "Am I still welcome, Emmeline? Now that you know it is me."

Emmie's stomach lurched. *Emmeline?* She did not dare look at Pinky, who was doubtless scandalized by such familiarity. She was shocked herself. No one called her Emmeline. He had certainly not done so during her London season. Instead, he had called her "Ballentine," a form of address equally improper, though more contemptuous than overfamiliar.

Still, the unaccustomed look on his face as he asked made her feel quite unequal to upbraiding him. He looked *almost* unsure of himself. She plastered a smile to her face. "Of course you are welcome!" Emmie declared. "You have certainly grown a good deal more modest in the past decade it seems. Pinky," she said, turning to her friend, "during my brief time as a debutante, Viscount Faris, or rather, the Honorable Jeremy Vance as he was known then, was quite the most eligible bachelor of my season."

Pinky's eyes widened and she nodded, looking from Emmie to Lord Faris. "How interesting," she said politely.

"I don't know that I would put it quite in those terms," he said with a rueful smile.

"On the contrary, that is *exactly* how you put it," Emmie corrected him. "In fact, those were the very words you used to me, on the occasion of our first dance at Lady Barwood's ball. 'Ballentine,' you said, 'I am sure our host has informed you, but should she have neglected the fact, you happen to be dancing with the most eligible man in London.'"

She had meant to put him to the blush, but unfortunately, halfway through the anecdote, Emmie realized she was confessing she had memorized his every word. *How embarrassing.*

Lord Faris stared at her, his lips parted and his breath coming fast. The air in the sitting room seemed strangely oppressive somehow. Never had Emmie been so grateful for the fact she had a chaperone. She had the oddest feeling Pinky's presence was the only thing keeping the situation from falling apart completely.

Suddenly, he laughed. "What an insufferable blackguard I must have been. Could you ever find it in your heart to forgive me, do you think?"

Nonsense, of course, to imagine the flippant words meant anything to him. "Whatever could there be for me to forgive, my lord?" she asked, opening her eyes wide and matching his light tone. "You spoke nothing but the truth in any case. Several people had already apprised me of that same fact over the course of the evening. I was profoundly grateful you deigned to notice me, and single me out for a dance. It was the highlight of my evening, I assure you."

His eyes held hers for a breathless moment, until finally, he inclined his head. "You are too gracious, Miss Ballentine. It *is* still Miss Ballentine, I take it?"

"Miss Ballentine is engaged to be married, my lord," Pinky interjected firmly, surprising them both. She then ruined this by adding, "And has been anytime these past ten years."

"Ten years?" His tone was faintly incredulous, his brows, surprisingly dark for his golden hair, shot up.

"Yes," Emmie agreed in a choked voice. "Dear Humphrey resides in London and is busy running my late father's business there. Alas, we have had to put our marriage plans on hold."

"Is that so?" His tone was polite, but it still stung somehow.

"And how is your lady wife?" Emmie heard herself ask with a faint edge to her voice. Amanda Liversedge had been one of the most beautiful girls she had ever met. Beautiful and remote. Emmie doubted very much that she would ever deign to visit.

"Ah, you have not heard that news either, it seems," he replied. "Amanda is no longer my wife."

"No longer...?"

He met her gaze. "We are divorced." Pinky gasped, sparing Emmeline the necessity. "Yes," he agreed, without looking away from Emmie's face, "shocking, is it not?"

Emmie blinked. "How fortunate you have a title now, and your reputation can survive such an infamous thing."

He laughed again. "Fortunate indeed, for me."

Finding herself a little unnerved, Emmie decided the best thing to do was not allow any uncomfortable silences. "You mentioned a son, I think?" she said, clearing her throat. "In your note."

"Yes, I have a son. Edward. He recently turned nine."

"And desirous of an introduction to me apparently?"

His smile grew. "You think this strange?"

"A little," she confessed.

Again, he seemed to consider his words before speaking. "My son was most unwell three months ago with scarlet fever."

In spite of herself, Pinky could not help from uttering, "Oh dear, the poor child!"

Viscount Faris flashed her a grateful smile. "We were fortunate that Teddy was spared. At one point the doctor feared he might contract pneumonia, but he has a strong constitution, and slowly recovered his strength. His spirits, though, have been somewhat depressed by the experience. I find he lacks his customary vivacity. I hoped that bringing him to Bath might restore the color in his cheeks."

Emmie nodded politely, though she still could not see what this had to do with her. "You have been reminiscing with your son, perhaps of your own youth?" she hazarded, though it seemed a strange thing for him to do.

He blanched slightly. "Good God no! I do not take him for my confessor!"

"I admit that did seem rather odd to me," Emmie said without thinking as Pinky bridled slightly at the casual blasphemy. Jeremy—or rather, Lord Faris, as she should think of him now—smirked instead of taking offence.

"I have been indulging Teddy's every whim since we hit Bath," he admitted. "Whatever tickles his fancy. Sadly, his latest caprice is a fondness for the company of one Arthur Arbuthnot, who was briefly a school friend. We bumped into him at the botanical gardens, and they have been joined at the hip ever since." His tone was dry.

Emmie kept a vague smile on her lips, though the name frankly conveyed nothing to her. "It seems you do not care for young Arthur?" she ventured.

"Arthur, a slightly dull and adenoidal child, is not the problem. His mother, however, is quite a different matter. She was a Skellern."

A ripple of unease ran up Emmie's spine. "A Skellern," she repeated, immediately remembering someone of that name from her debut. A pretty yet spiteful face sprang to mind, giving her pause. "As in…Lily Skellern?"

"I forget her Christian name," he answered with a shrug. "A wholly unremarkable woman, save for her marked lack of tact and discretion."

"I came out in the same season as Lily Skellern," Emmie confided, keeping her tone carefully expressionless. "She resides now in Bath, I believe, and is married to a banker." She shot a look at Pinky to whom she pointed out Lily Skellern on more than one occasion, when their paths had crossed. Every time, she had been pointedly and exaggeratedly ignored by that lady. Pinky's lips formed an O of understanding.

"Ah. That sounds the very one," Lord Faris replied. "You were debutantes together? You have my profound sympathy. I have avoided her wherever possible these past five days. Her conversation is execrable. Sadly, in my absence, she has seen fit to regale my son with questionable tales from my past." He sent Emmie a significant look, and she tensed slightly.

"I see," she muttered, feeling her color rise. She dared not look at Pinky, who had not been a fixture in her life during her disastrous season. Her father had dismissed poor Pinky as far too dowdy and unfashionable to act as Emmie's chaperone. Instead, she had been accompanied by the well-connected Mrs. Laverdale, who had been a good deal laxer in her duties.

Perhaps if Pinky had been there, Emmie would never have acted like such a fool and... She gave a little gasp and shook her head to dispel such unpleasant memories. She opened her mouth to ask what sort of thing Lily Skellern had been saying but found she did not really want to know.

Silly to feel humiliated about such an inconsequential thing, especially when she had far more pressing problems these days. "I dread to think what nonsense she has been telling your son," she heard herself say with an empty laugh. It did not come out as convincing as she had hoped it would.

"Just a lot of spite and nonsense," he said after a heavy pause. "I realize this is a severe imposition, Miss Ballentine, and I have no right to ask this of you, but I was wondering—"

"If I would meet with young Edward and assure him we were always the best of good friends?" she supplied brightly.

He did not speak for a moment, then said, "Precisely."

Emmie felt a burning surge of indignation rise up in her chest. *Rise above it, Emmie,* she told herself. It was all water under the bridge. This pretty, spiteful person had no power to hurt her anymore. *Be the better person.* Besides, it was a chance for her to rewrite an embarrassing episode of her past that did not reflect well on her.

She rose from her seat, holding her hand out to him. "But of course I will!" she said, plastering a smile to her face.

For a moment, he looked a little taken aback. Then, he, too, stood up and accepted her proffered hand in a tentative shake.

"You are generous, Miss Ballentine," he murmured, and she whipped her hand away before he could do something like lift it to his well-formed lips.

"Not at all, Lord Faris," she replied briskly, only too aware that she had offered him scant hospitality and nothing at all by way of refreshment. "It would not inconvenience me in the slightest to reassure your son on that score. Now, if you do not mind, Miss Pinson and I have plans this evening…"

"Of course," he answered swiftly.

"I hate to rush you out of our door," she said insincerely.

"You have been more than generous with your time," he assured her. "As to time and place, I have a suggestion. How would tomorrow morning suit you?"

Emmie suffered an unpleasant jolt that she could only hope did not show on her face. She would not get a wink of sleep tonight with such a prospect in front of her. Then again, she reflected, perhaps it would be better to get the ordeal over with at once, rather than delaying it. "Tomorrow morning would suit admirably."

"We could meet you here at…ten o'clock?" he suggested.

"Ten o'clock?" she repeated blankly.

"I thought we could go for a walk in the park."

Emmie quickly considered this. Yes, it was a good idea. Neutral territory. She need never have him intrude on her ever again. Then, too, it would spare her the necessity of having to provide some elegant repast for their visit. "A walk in the park would be very pleasant." She turned to Pinky. "Do you agree, Hannah?" Pinky hesitated, then nodded, looking from Emmie to Lord Faris and then quickly back again.

With a sinking heart, Emmie realized Pinky was picking up on the underlying tension. She smiled reassuringly at her and then turned back to accompany Lord Faris to the door. He took his leave of her with punctilious politeness and instead of watching him descend the flight of stairs with his elegant tread, she turned and closed the door firmly behind her.

"Well," she said lightly, "that was certainly unexpected."

"Shall I fetch the tea things?" Pinky asked, clearly feeling in need of a fortifying cup.

"Yes, please," Emmie concurred, though she had never felt *less* like tucking into an iced bun.

*

Emmie turned in early, after fending off Pinky's gentle quizzing over supper. Her friend was clearly agog with curiosity but far too delicate in her sensibilities to prod more than lightly. Emmie found herself profoundly grateful for Pinky's tact, for what could she even say by way of explanation? It was all such foolish stuff and hardly worth the fuss and pother her nerves were making of it. She was quite cross with herself.

She knew full well that she had made an utter cake of herself all those years ago. She had always known, even at the time. She had just not cared in the dizzy moment. The Honorable Jeremy Vance had been the most glamorous and dazzling figure in what was, for her, a very dismal London season indeed.

No one else had wanted to pass the time with the dumpy, ill-connected daughter of a cit. Even her paid sponsor, Mrs. Laverdale, had scarcely hidden her embarrassment at the distasteful task of foisting Emmie on polite society. If it had not been for the honorable Jeremy, she would barely have stood up for a dance.

She had been under no illusions, despite what her fellow debutantes had whispered to one another behind their fans. Emmie had known the whole time that he was only playing with her, but she had not cared. Not one bit.

Jeremy Vance had been quite the most charming and certainly the most beautiful creature she had ever beheld, and when he was whirling her about the dance floor, it had been so easy to forget how excruciating the whole miserable charade of her London season was.

When she had been escorted about a hot ballroom on his arm, she had simply not cared how horribly out place she was, among all those daughters of the peerage. Indeed, she had not even felt out of place in those moments, for nothing had touched her.

She had felt surrounded by a warm glow in his presence. Her step had felt light and dainty, and her heart had felt fluttery in her chest. She had beamed at his every remark, and she was sure she had craned her neck for a glimpse of him at every miserable assembly room she had been herded into.

Her patron, Mrs. Laverdale, had felt compelled to warn Emmie that she was being made a fool of, and that his intentions were not serious. Her warning had been wholly unnecessary. Emmie had not the smallest expectation Jeremy Vance ever offering for her. Such a notion was laughable. She could not even begrudge the barely suppressed titters. Not really.

Thinking of it now, Emmie did wince. She must have looked like such a little idiot, hanging off his every word but the fact was that if it had not been for those snatched moments, her societal debut would have been pure, unalleviated misery. He had enlivened her horrible London season, and she had never begrudged him his fun, even though it had been at her expense.

Of course, she had felt terribly low when she heard of his subsequent marriage to Lady Amanda Liversedge, and their honeymoon in Florence at the end of the season. The least said about her, the better. Lady Amanda had matched the honorable Jeremy in both beauty and rank, and that was all these dreadful society people cared about.

Emmie had wrapped up the dance cards he had written his name on, so boldly and so often, in tissue paper along with a pair of gloves that had touched his arm and an ivory fan that he had once taken out of her hand to wave in her reddened face. Placing them in a rosewood box, she had consigned them, and him, firmly to the past.

Until he showed up at her front door.

Oh God, she hoped she had managed to preserve some semblance at least of a calm, placid front, though inside she had been a churning mess. It was perhaps not surprising that Pinky should suspect something was amiss. After all, Pinky had known her since she was a sticky five-year-old.

Then, too, there had been that indiscreet comment she had made about Count Stefano. So stupid to blurt that out like that! No wonder Pinky was eyeing her askance after she had named Lord Faris after the villain in Pinky's latest novel. She could kick herself, really!

She washed and undressed for bed, her stomach still fluttering, and her face flushed. As she tied the ribbons on her nightgown, she hoped and prayed that her cool smiles were fooling Jeremy Vance. The thought of him being aware of her inner turmoil was just too humiliating to be borne!

Climbing into bed, she comforted herself that she would just have to bear up through this meeting with his child, and then the ordeal would be over. Lord Faris could ride away to his life of privilege, and she would be left to her own of increasing privation.

Then suddenly, it struck her. She had not thought once of Mr. Hardiman's letter since Jeremy Vance had crossed the street and knocked on her front door. No, nor of Humphrey. She sucked in a breath. The break from constant money worries would have been more beneficial if it had not been chased away by other uncomfortable recollections. *How about I give you something to remember me by, Ballentine?* Unbidden, the words sprang into her mind, making her ears burn from memory alone. She ought to have slapped him, not trotted after him like an eager spaniel into that dratted conservatory.

The nerve of him. The absolute *nerve*! And then to expect her collaboration in hoodwinking his innocent child into believing him entirely blameless? Shameless. Clearly, he had not changed one bit. Oh, she would do it alright. Anything to be rid of the wretched man.

Anything to expunge the sense of shame and embarrassment she felt over that last disastrous night at Lady Hawford's ball. Maybe this little interlude would help her rewrite her role, even if it was only in her own mind? To recast herself as fellow conspirator, instead of lovesick little fool.

He's laughing at you; can't you see that? But Mrs. Laverdale's warning had come too late. Clasping the pillow to her head, Emmie rolled over and tried to quiet the clamoring memories and block them out of her poor head.

2

Emmie awoke early the next morning, ridiculously early, her stomach knotted with dread. Before she had even opened her eyes, she had remembered who was coming to the house this morning at ten. Viscount Faris. She lay tossing and turning for half an hour and then decided she might as well get up.

She dressed with care in her mauve walking dress, which would be ideal for the park. Then she kept herself busy by going downstairs and preparing a light breakfast for herself and Pinky. Checking the meagre contents of their personal cupboard, she boiled them an egg apiece and toasted the end of their loaf to disguise the fact it was rather stale.

Sadly, the butter dish was empty, and she had been sure they had a scraping of butter left from the previous day. Emmie wondered if the Startrites, the family occupying the third floor, might have helped themselves to the last of it. That was the worst part of sharing a kitchen. Ruefully, Emmie reflected that until three years ago she had truly had no notion about such things as shared kitchens. What a privileged life she had led!

She climbed the stairs now, bearing the heavy tray laden with the tea set and breakfast plates. As she neared the top, Pinky's small, neat figure appeared there.

"Oh, Emmie!" she exclaimed with dismay. "I was just on my way down. You know it is my turn today. How wickedly indulgent of you to let me sleep in!"

"Nonsense," Emmie answered briskly. "You know I like to do it."

Pinky bit her lip. "Was your sleep troubled, dear?"

"Not at all," Emmie lied smoothly. "Why? Do I still look peaky this morning?"

"Oh no! Of course not!" Pinky murmured, following close on her heels. "You look charming. You always look so pretty in that mauve gown. I remember your father remarking on it one time."

Emmie was surprised to hear that, remembering her father's usually critical words about her appearance. *Well, Emmie, after all, you can't make a silk purse out of a sow's ear.* "Did he? I do not recall. I suppose I have had this gown a few years now." She glanced down, wondering if it looked dated and shabby.

"Oh, I did not mean…" Pinky trailed off awkwardly. "That is, it still looks very smart, I am sure."

"Your grandmama's brooch looks nice," Emmie answered, nodding to Pinky's lace collar. She always thought the pretty pink cameo looked so much nicer than the ugly jet mourning brooch Pinky habitually wore.

"Oh! Thank you, dear." Pinky flushed. "I thought as we were walking out with company today, I might wear it." She hurried after her as Emmie made her way into their parlor and set down the tea things on the tiny table in the corner which the two of them dined upon.

Pinky fetched the napkins and silver from a rather cumbersome corner cabinet which was frankly too large for the current room it found itself in. She would have to sell it, Emmie thought, before they moved again. They really did not need anything so large and ostentatious these days. Especially as most of the silver and all the good china had already been sold.

Pinky was still wearing a worried look on her face as they laid the table. Emmie made a concerted effort to look cheerful. "Well, we have fine weather this morning. Blue skies," she observed, glancing toward the window as she pulled out her seat. "How fortuitous to have a little sunshine for our walk in the park."

"Oh yes," Pinky agreed dutifully as they sat down opposite one another. "Very lucky."

Emmie held up the plate of toast and extended it toward her. "I'm afraid there is no butter to be had today."

Pinky helped herself to a slice immediately. "For my part, I sometimes think butter tastes a little rich when paired with an egg yolk," she insisted. *Dear Pinky,* Emmie thought with a surge of affection. Whatever would she have done without her? "Oh, this egg is perfect, Emmie. Just as it should be, with a runny yolk and a nice, firm white."

Emmie smiled. Thus had Pinky praised her when she was a young girl still learning her lessons. She was just lifting toast to her mouth when they heard a knock on the door. Emmie's heart flew into her mouth. It could not be later than quarter past nine! Her wide eyes met Pinky's across the table. Surely Viscount Faris would not be so early?

"Miss Ballentine?" It was Florrie at the door.

"Come in," she answered. They heard the maid's quick step in the hallway.

"You've got a visitor." Emmie's racing heart calmed a little when she saw Florrie's sour expression. There was no excitement there today. Perhaps it was not him?

"Who is it, Florrie?"

"It's that Mr. Stockton," the maid sniffed. "And 'e looks a right state! Not fit to be seen in decent company."

Humphrey? Emmie dragged back her chair at once. Stolid, respectable Humphrey looking "a right state"? This did not sound good. Immediately, Emmie's thoughts turned to the business. Oh Lord, things must be in bad repair. "No, do not let this interrupt your breakfast," she said quickly as Pinky set down her spoon. She did not want Pinky troubled with such matters until it was strictly necessary.

"I will see him downstairs in the reception room if it is available?" she said, addressing the question to Florrie.

Florrie nodded. "Oh yes, it's quite free this morning."

"Thank you. You stay and finish your egg, Hannah," she said firmly as Pinky's expression wavered.

She made her way downstairs, following closely behind Florrie, who kept up a stream of chatter about how shocked and disapproving Mrs. Chalfont would be if she could see the state of their gentleman caller. Emmie's thoughts were far too disordered for consideration of her landlady to ruffle her.

"Yes, thank you, Florrie," she said in dismissal as soon as she reached the door to the reception room. Florrie flounced away and Emmie let herself into the room, closing the door behind her.

"Humphrey, this is unexpected…" she began before she had even turned, then broke off abruptly when she did. "Humphrey!" she exclaimed weakly. "My dear, whatever is wrong?" While not as disheveled as Florrie's words had led her to expect, he did not look well at all.

Though his sober gray suit was tidy as ever, his eyes were red-rimmed and his usually immaculate hair practically standing on end. He threw up a hand when she started toward him.

"No, do not attempt to…to comfort me, Emmie," he said in a choked voice. "You must allow me some room in which to unburden myself. *Please*."

She stilled, taking in his agitation. "Very well," she conceded carefully. "I will take a seat here," she said, motioning to a wing-backed seat at some distance from the fireplace where he stood, practically vibrating with suppressed emotion.

"Something dreadful has happened," he started and then swallowed, as though past a lump in his throat. "I hardly know how to tell you, in truth, it is so very—" He bowed his head, then turned abruptly to brace his shaking hands against the mantel. "I need a minute," he gritted out, flinging back his head.

When nothing was forthcoming over the loud tick of the carriage clock, Emmie cleared her throat. "Humphrey," she said gently, "is it the business?" His shoulders tensed. "I know things have been—"

"It's gone under!" he burst out, removing one hand from the mantel to cram a fist into his mouth.

"Gone under?" she repeated blankly.

"Hit the wall, smashed, gone bust," he said, turning to face her with a sob. "Ballentine's Trading Company is no more. It has collapsed in on itself."

Collapsed? Emmie raised a hand to cover her mouth. This was even worse than she had feared.

Humphrey flung himself into the chair opposite her, driving his fingers into his hair. No wonder it was standing on end, she thought distractedly.

"So, we must cease trading with immediate effect?" she asked quite horrified. "Will there be—"

He jerked upright. "Cease trading? That is the least of our worries!" he said with a bitter laugh.

"The least of our worries?" Emmie was confused. Surely the loss of the business was tragedy enough. "How can that be?"

His color drained, leaving him pale as milk. "Not only has the company folded," he uttered hoarsely, "but there is also a mountain of debt to make reparation for."

Debt? Emmie's stomach sank. *Oh no.* "Debt?" she whispered. "How much debt?"

"I hardly know by this point," he admitted wretchedly. "At first, we borrowed to make up the shortfall, and then I—I took some risks— Your father, he always speculated, and I thought—" he groaned and buried his face in his hands.

She waited, while a cold feeling crept up her spine. *Risks?* Steady Humphrey took some risks? He must have been desperate indeed. "I cannot pretend this is not a severe blow," she said numbly when he did not speak for another full minute. "But we—we must—find a way forward together."

Oh heavens, she thought suddenly, what of their employees? Mr. Hardiman had worked for the firm for over thirty years! Then there was old Mr. Rigby, and at least five others. Were they to be out of a job without any severance package to ease their way?

Her head span. She needed to say something, *anything*. Humphrey looked in a flat despair. He was frightening her a little. "Perhaps, if we combined our household expenses then we could make some saving—" she started desperately.

He sprang from his chair and started pacing in front of the fireplace. "No, you do not understand."

"I realize that bankruptcy is hardly the best start to married life but—"

"There can no question of our combining households or of marriage," he said flatly. "You see, not only have I ruined your family business, but I have been on the verge of ruining *you* for years as well."

"Ruining *me*?"

He nodded. "Oh God, I can hardly tell you this. You see, I cannot marry you, Emmie. That—all that must be at an end." He swept an arm in a most un-Humphrey-like gesture.

Emmie was speechless. She regarded him with some concern. "Won't you take a seat, Humphrey?" she asked gently. "You are clearly under some strain and—"

"I cannot marry you, Emmie," he repeated with emphasis. "Clara will not let me."

"Clara?" Emmie echoed in bewilderment. She had never heard him mention a Clara before. "Who, pray, is Clara?

Humphrey gulped. "Clara is my wife," he said hoarsely.

"*Your wife?*" Emmie repeated dumbly, not quite believing her ears. "You—but when—?"

"My wife of twelve years," he confessed shakily, jerking at his necktie as though to give himself room to breathe.

"*Twelve years*," Emmie cried. "But we have only been engaged for ten!"

"I know." He winced. "My marriage predates our engagement."

Emmie blinked up at him. "Forgive me, I do not understand," she said, groping for the arm of her chair and clutching it.

"I was married to Clara at nineteen. We had already been married for two years when I met you."

Emmie heard a rushing in her ears and wondered for a moment if she might actually faint. "I don't—but how—*why*? Why would you do this to me, Humphrey?" she asked in horrified wonder. "Why in heaven's name would you propose marriage to me when you were not in the position to do so?"

He dropped into a chair. "God, I don't know," he moaned, scrubbing his eyes with his palms. "I was so flattered when your father started inviting me to dine at your big house in Porchester Square. I—I was dazzled. I hoped for promotion, and I wanted to ingratiate myself." He threw her a desperate look. "Can't you try to understand, Emmie? Your father was such a force of nature. When he suggested marriage to you, I was too intimidated to object."

"Intimidated?" she repeated. "Intimidated or ambitious?"

He flushed hotly. "Both, I suppose," he admitted wretchedly. Then after a pause said fervently, "How you must hate me now!"

"Hate?" she said shakily. "In truth, I feel too numb for so strong an emotion." Humphrey's eyes dropped from hers. Silence reigned for a minute or two until Emmie heard herself ask inconsequentially, "How is it you arrived in Bath so early?" It was surely too early for the stagecoach to have arrived from London.

"I arrived last night," he answered. "Stayed in a hotel nearby. I set out a dozen times to see you but could not face the interview until this morning."

"Does Clara know about me?" she asked, abruptly changing the subject. He nodded. "Always? Has she always known?"

He gulped. "Yes."

"And yet she—?"

"Please try to understand, Emmie," he appealed to her. "We wanted to get out of her mother's house. To get a little place of our own. She wasn't happy about the deception but—"

"Ten years you let me wait for you," she interrupted. "*Ten whole years!*"

"The time just never seemed right. You see, we needed to save a little nest egg," he gabbled, "and then the baby came—"

"Get out, Humphrey!"

He rose shakily to his feet. "I realize that at this moment you must—"

"Please just *leave!*"

Resolutely, Emmie covered her ears with her hands and closed her eyes tight shut. She huddled down in the chair and stayed like that for as long as she dared. She wished she could sit there all day. She wished she could stop time for another ten years or no—turn it back. Turn it back ten years and then tell Humphrey Stockton to go to hell with his offer for her hand.

She was not sure *how* long she sat there, willfully unseeing and unhearing of the world. It must have been a couple of minutes at least. Before opening them, she told herself she would see everything quite differently now. She was an older and more jaded woman.

She was a woman who had been jilted at the altar. Nay, not quite that. A woman, then, who had been snared by a bigamist! But even that was not quite true. Humphrey was not a bigamist for his Clara had not let him become one. What was she, then, she wondered, aside from bankrupt?

As her blurred vision swam back in view, she found, to her astonishment, that the chair opposite her was still occupied. It was no longer Humphrey who sat there, looking distressed and pale. Instead, it was Jeremy Vance, who looked as beautiful and wicked as ever, clad immaculately in a pale gray lounging suit. "Good morning, Emmeline," he said.

"Not for me," she replied hollowly.

He nodded. "You have suffered a nasty shock," he said. "Two shocks, in fact. But life goes on all the same."

She sat up straighter in her seat. *He knew! But how?* She cast a quick look at the door and found it open, considerably more than a crack. "You heard all that?" she croaked.

"I did," he agreed conversationally. "The maid Florence allowed me to sit just outside to await you but alas, the door to this room does not shut all the way. The catch must be broken."

She regarded him for a moment quite speechless. How long had he sat there looking at her hunched over with her eyes squeezed shut? She almost shuddered at the spectacle she must have made of herself. Besides this debacle even her ignominious time as a debutante paled into insignificance. "A man with nice manners would not have sat there listening!" she pointed out at last with dignity.

His smile grew. "Ah, but I am not a nice man, as well you know."

Hot color crept into her cheeks. "You must have turned up unforgivably early for our walk!"

He nodded. "Oh, I did. I did not feel sure of you, you see. I do now though."

She did not quite care for the glint in his eye. "What do you mean, you did not feel sure of me?"

"I could not feel easy in my mind. That you would corroborate my blamelessness in our past dealings, I mean. So, I came early to persuade you that I had turned over a new leaf."

"Oh." She eyed him curiously. "And why is it you now feel sure I will cooperate?"

"Because, my dear Ballentine, I now have the means to bargain with you."

Emmie watched him with some horrified fascination. It was like ten years had not even passed since she had last seen him. She felt like a mouse frozen in front of a snake. It had all the qualities of a bad dream.

Seeing he was still closely watching her, she roused herself. "Means?" she repeated with a frown. She could not even pretend to understand him.

"Yes, for you are in a pretty pickle and so am I. Let us consider for a moment if we cannot come to one another's aid."

She really was lost by this point. Lifting a hand to her brow, she asked helplessly, "How is it you are in a pickle, my lord?"

"I am recently divorced," he reminded her. "My respectability is tarnished. My social standing, on shaky ground. Even my nine-year-old son suspects my past is not as honorable as it should have been." He sighed, and for some reason this made her narrow her eyes.

"I hardly think your pickle, I mean, predicament, compares to mine."

"Well, it is all a matter of perspective, is it not? You did not actually make it down the aisle."

"No, and if I had, it would have been a criminal offence!" she said with spirit.

"Let us be grateful, then, that dear Clara prevented it."

Emmie stiffened. He really *had* heard everything. "At least you have not been saddled with horrendous debt," she said bitterly.

"Actually, Amanda frequently incurred considerable gambling debts, which I settled in a quiet and discreet fashion. I could do the same with yours, given the right enticement."

Emmie gasped. "What on earth?" She stared at him. His blue gaze was steady. "We—we do not even know the sums involved!" she pointed out. "In any case, you are not in earnest."

"I assure you that I am."

"Why on earth would you?" she spluttered.

"A man does, for his wife."

She blinked at him uncomprehendingly. "Then the enticement you speak of…?"

"Marriage, my dear Emmeline," he said urbanely. "You and me. How about it?"

3

A horrified gasp from the doorway had them both turning their heads. It was the mousey companion from yesterday, Jeremy realized. What was her name? *Munsen? Pinkerton?* Whatever it was she had lousy timing.

"Pinky!" Emmeline blurted, starting up out of her chair. "It's not... That is, Viscount Faris arrived early for our walk and—" She turned an agonized look upon him.

Jeremy came to his feet, wondering why she felt the need to bleat excuses to her paid companion. It was not as though she had walked in on them *in flagrante delicto*. "Good morning, Miss Pinkerton," he started politely, sketching her a bow.

"It's Pinson," Emmeline corrected him swiftly.

"My apologies, *Miss Pinson*. I came by a little early, encouraged by the blue skies. I hoped to persuade Miss Ballentine to partake of the morning sunshine before the showers."

"I see," murmured Miss Pinson, two spots of bright pink in her cheeks. *That is not the only thing you thought to persuade her of,* that outraged maiden's gaze seemed to convey. She was not as old as he had originally thought, closer in years to forty than fifty. "And your little boy?" she asked, lifting her chin. Her expression showed she no longer remotely believed in the child's existence.

"Alas, not feeling up to the exertion this morning," he lied smoothly.

"I see," she repeated tightly. Her gaze darted to Emmeline, and she took a deep breath. "I think we must—"

"Miss Ballentine has agreed to accompany me to Royal Victoria Park, but I will return her to you in time for luncheon, never fear." Miss Pinson looked alarmed but could not seem to summon a response to this. He turned to Emmeline and proffered his arm. "Shall we?"

Swallowing, she took his arm and they made for the door together. Miss Pinson fled into the hallway before them. "Your hat and coat, Emmie," she squeaked. "You cannot possibly—"

Seeing the curious maidservant's approach, Jeremy turned to her. "Ah, this most obliging young woman will fetch them for us, I am sure." He certainly was not about to let Miss Pinson snatch Emmeline out of his clutches.

"Yes, milord." Clearly remembering his generous tip from yesterday, the maid instantly hastened to climb the stairs in search of them.

"Oh dear, she will not know which gloves to bring," Miss Pinson fretted. "Please excuse me," she said, hurrying up after her.

"Poor Pinky," Emmeline muttered. "We have given her the most horrendous shock."

It was on the tip of his tongue to mention the time a companion of hers had walked in on something far more shocking between them, but it was too soon. Besides, this was not the same companion. That one had borne a more worldly air.

"She will recover presently, I have no doubt," he assured her. Emmeline was looking pale and the hand which still rested on his arm had a decided tremor running through it.

"It's not too cold out," he assured her, despite knowing that was not the reason she was shivering. He should take her for some refreshment. Sweet tea was meant to be good for shock as well as fortifying the spirits, though she would derive more benefit from a splash of brandy. No doubt she would cavil at hard liquor at this time in the morning.

Jeremy doubted very much that she carried smelling salts upon her person. Emmeline was a healthy, well-built woman and not at all the type for swooning. If she had been, she would not have lasted her season. Not with the way he had been after her.

He would take her to Hutton's, he decided, in spite of her shabby dress. He didn't care if people did stare, he would enjoy squiring her about, even if she wasn't presented to her best advantage. He eyed the faded velvet of her gown. It did not detract from her charms one bit. How could it, with that magnificent figure?

He was profoundly glad her reduced means had not wasted away her pleasing person. Emmeline had been plump and pretty at eighteen and she was still delightfully full-figured at twenty-eight, maybe even a little more so. The turn of her cheek remained rounded and dimpled. He still wanted to corner her and kiss those cherry ripe lips, though they looked a little bloodless at present.

As though becoming aware of his scrutiny, Emmeline stirred and self-consciously withdrew her hand from his arm. He could not hold back his own murmur of discontent, which seemed to startle her, for her gaze fell away from his and she took a step back. Thankfully the maid was coming back down the stairs bearing a cape and a wide-brimmed poke bonnet about five years out of style.

"Thank you, Florrie," Emmeline said, making haste to don them with the maid's assiduous help. From the surprised look on Emmeline's face, Jeremy deduced Florrie was not usually so attentive.

"Miss Pinson said you'd want your tan gloves on a day like this," Florrie pronounced loudly, handing them over. Jeremy handsomely tipped her as Emmeline drew on her gloves and he whisked her out of the front door without more ado, ushering her in the direction of his carriage.

Colfax sat up with a surprised look and hurriedly discarded the cigarette he was smoking.

"St. John Street," Jeremy called, opening the door for Emmeline himself and helping her in.

"I thought we were going for a walk in the park," she remarked as soon as she settled onto the seat.

"Change of plan."

"Oh."

"Your companion does not trust me at all," he remarked, shutting the door fast behind them.

"No," she agreed absently, "I'm afraid that's my fault."

The coach wheels turned, and Jeremy regarded her with some surprise. "And why is that?" When she did not speak, he asked slyly, "Have you been reminiscing, Emmeline?"

Emmeline's cheeks turned pink, and she would not meet his eye. "C-certainly not!" she said breathlessly. "It is merely because, well, because we are both avid novel readers, I'm afraid."

He waited but she did not elaborate, instead turning her head to stare fixedly out of the window, her expression stony.

"Your latest novel features a wicked viscount?" he hazarded, taking the chance to appreciate her profile. She had a perfect retroussé nose, he reflected. He would like to own a cameo depicting it.

She turned even pinker. "Something like that," she admitted uneasily, making him laugh.

"Count Stefano," he guessed softly, and Emmeline's hands flew to cover her cheeks.

Her astonished face whipped around. "How on earth did you—?"

"Lucky guess." She looked so dismayed he had a terrible impulse to tease her and really that was the last thing he ought to be indulging in right now. He needed to ruthlessly press his advantage, not sit here dallying with her like some infatuated swain. "What is the title? I will make sure to pick up a copy." *Shut up, Jeremy.* He couldn't seem to help himself.

Emmeline shook her head, then met his eyes full on. He held his breath. "If we really do this thing…get married I mean, you will let me keep Pinky, I mean, Hannah Pinson, won't you?" she asked hoarsely.

He was startled. "Your companion?"

"Yes."

He paused. "You wish to retain her services *after* we are married?"

She nodded. "Yes, you see, she is not just—" She made a vague hand gesture, then started again. "She is my very best friend in all the world," she said gravely. "I cannot imagine being without her."

Jeremy felt an unpleasant sensation that he had to examine a moment to even identify. Jealousy. *How strange.* It was not an affliction he had ever suffered from before, and Amanda had taken several lovers in the collapsing days of their marriage. He was jealous of a dowdy spinster companion. "She must have been in your employ for some years."

"Yes, for she was my governess before she was my companion. She has been in my life since I was five years old. By this point she is more like family."

He frowned. "She was not your companion during your season though."

"No," she agreed uncomfortably. Any mention of her season seemed to discompose her. "My father did not think her sufficiently smart for a London season. He dismissed poor Hannah, and I came out under the aegis of Mrs. Barbara Laverdale. She was the widow of a captain of the dragoon guards. I expect she is the one you remember." She swallowed, still avoiding his gaze.

Why? he wondered. In truth, he could hardly remember the Laverdale woman. She had obviously been remiss in her duties, for Emmeline had been far from well-guarded. If she had, he would not have been able to impose on her as he had.

"Poor Hannah suffered a twelvemonth in the employ of a family in Yorkshire who had four rambunctious children and three boisterous dogs," she continued after an uncomfortable pause.

Jeremy considered his options. He did not want Miss Pinson guarding Emmeline against him at every turn, an inconvenience in his own home. She seemed a tiresome, fussy little woman who would fling herself in front of her charge whenever she felt it her duty to shield her from life.

However, by denying Emmeline's first request, he felt it would set an unfortunate tone to their new arrangement. He knew only too well how such a decision could sour things. "Perhaps Miss Pinson could use her governess skills to help out with Teddy," he conceded graciously at last.

"Teddy?"

"My son."

"Oh!" She winced. "She is rather terrified of boys, in truth."

By great restraint, he managed not to roll his eyes. "It probably won't be for long. He will have to go to school at some point," he said vaguely.

She bit her lip, likely not reassured with this, but it was as much as he was willing to give. "And where is that you principally reside these days?" She clutched her hands together. "London?" she asked almost fearfully.

"Cornwall," he corrected her. "Have you ever visited? My family estate is there."

"Oh!" She brightened a little. "No, I have never been. I have heard that coastline is very beautiful."

"I am prejudiced but yes, I believe so." The carriage was slowing down now, and Jeremy waited only for it to stop before climbing out and turning to help her down. It was not his custom to hover over ladies but he felt strangely proprietary and wanted to do all the handing in and out when it came to Emmeline.

"Hutton's?" she said, seeing he was towing her in the direction of that fashionable tea shop. "It looks very busy this morning," she said with some misgiving. "Why do we not go instead to that little place opposite?"

"Why, Emmeline," he said, "are you afeared you might see someone you know?"

"Hardly! My purse does not extend to such an establishment," she hissed. "But you may likely bump into some acquaintance, and they will wonder that you are accompanied by—by an unaccompanied female!"

"Affianced couples can usually dispense with a chaperone on such an innocent occasion," he answered lightly.

"But we are not formally—" She bit off her words when the bell jingled as he opened the door for her. She pressed her lips together and entered before him.

"Table for two," Jeremy instructed the hovering waiter. "In the window, I think."

"Alas, sir, there are none currently available," the waiter replied, his eyes passing over Emmeline's faded bonnet.

"That couple over there in the window seem as though they are about to leave," Jeremy replied without looking once in that direction.

The waiter gave him a swift appraisal and seemed to revise his opinion. "Of course, milord. Right away."

"I can't see anyone on the point of leaving," Emmeline murmured as the waiter hurried away. "There is a little table over in that far corner that looks to be free," she said, pointing it out.

"We do not hide away in corners, Emmeline," he said grandly. "We are the Vances of Vance Park."

"Vance Park?" She looked blank.

"My country seat in Cornwall."

She gave a quick glance about them. "We should not really speak of this as though it is all settled, you know," she said, suddenly earnest. "For it is not. Not by a long chalk." He liked the way she lowered her voice and leaned toward him, he realized, disregarding her obstinate words. It reminded him of the old days when she had been eager for his attention.

Whatever tiresome society function he had turned up to, a bored latecomer, he knew she would be there, scanning the room for him, her aspect brightening at the mere sight of him. She had not been able to hide it. Toward the end, he had scarcely bothered to even greet his hosts or get a drink before seeking her out.

How reckless he had been. Reckless with her reputation and reckless with his heart. It had not been until Italy, on his honeymoon, that he had realized the depth of his own feeling. What a fool he had been. Blind as well as reckless.

"Ah, here we are," he said out loud, seeing the waiter was making for them. This time he was wreathed in obliging smiles. They followed in his wake and were directed to a prime spot in front of the window. Jeremy attended to the removal of her cloak himself. He passed it to the waiter, and saw she was comfortably seated before taking the chair opposite her. "Will you take tea or coffee?" he asked.

"Tea, please."

"Tea for the lady, coffee for me, and a selection of your finest cakes." He turned back to Emmeline. "Have you breakfasted?" he asked quietly. "Shall I order sandwiches?"

"I have eaten," she said quickly, and the waiter disappeared with their order. Emmeline fidgeted with the buttons on her gloves before leaning forward over the table. "In truth, my lord," she said in hushed tones, "you cannot offer for me until you know the full amount of debt the company has incurred—"

"I have already offered for you," he corrected her. "And moreover, you have as good as said yes."

"Still," she persisted grimly, "the sensible course of action would be to wait until we have a clear picture of the sum involved."

He shook his head. "I am rarely sensible. Besides, it won't matter."

"What do you mean?"

"Whatever the sum involved, I will pay it." Seeing her astonished expression, he added, "I warn you, if you try to pull out now, I will sue you for breach of promise."

"I wish you would be serious."

"In any case, I doubt very much the banks have allowed your previous fiancé to run up anything too steep. If it had been your father negotiating the loans, then yes, considerable funds might have been involved, but *this* fellow..." He gave a contemptuous shrug.

Emmeline seemed surprised he knew of her father's reputation as a formidable man of business. "But if they have?" she persisted doggedly.

"If they have, I'm sure I can still bear the expense. By the way, did you determine which hotel your erstwhile suitor was staying at in Bath?"

She blinked at the rapid change in subject. "Oh. No." Her face fell. "I should have, shouldn't I? I was not thinking straight."

"It is of no matter. You will have to give me his direction in London though. And that of the offices of your late father's business." He retrieved his calling card case from his pocket, extracted a card, and passed it to her along with his pencil in its engraved silver holder. "Will you write it on the back of this card, along with Humphrey's full name?"

Emmeline paled at this more businesslike approach. "Yes," she agreed in stifled tones and bent over the card. "There are at least seven employees I'm afraid. They will all need some sort of recompense for the loss of their living."

He nodded. "I can see to that." Once she had written a few lines, she handed it back to him along with his pencil. He glanced it over. *Stockton*. So that was the bastard's name.

"Mr. Thomas Hardiman is the oldest and most trusted of my father's clerks. He wrote to me last month and tried to warn me…" She trailed off guiltily. "Poor Mr. Hardiman."

"Poor Hannah, poor Mr. Hardiman," he mocked softly as he tucked the card away for safekeeping. "What about my poor Emmeline?"

She drew in a sharp breath. "I'll be fine!" she said bravely. "At least, I will now *you* have stepped into the fray." She struggled a little over the last sentence.

"Will you though?" he asked softly. "Is it not a case of out of the frying pan and into the fire?" He did not really want the role of savior. Count Stefano was much more in his line.

"You would be a better judge of that than I," she responded hotly, and Jeremy could not hold back his laughter. She looked so much better with a little color in her cheeks.

"We will do very well together, Ballentine, I have no doubt."

Their drinks and cakes arrived at this point, so the conversation ceased while their fare was laid out before them.

"What a treat," Emmeline said in dazed accents as her eyes traveled over the array of cakes. "Hannah would love this. Cream horns are her favorite."

"Teddy likes the Genoese fancies. Maybe we should take some back for them?"

Her eyes lit up at his suggestion. "Oh yes, we could take back what we do not eat," she suggested frugally.

He frowned. "I can easily buy more. What are your favorites?"

"Whatever's cheapest," she responded, then flushed. "I have a great eye for a bargain."

She would have no need of this skill once they were wed, he thought, but did not voice. "What about when you lived in London?" he asked, thinking this must have been before she had monetary woes. "What sort of cake did your father used to buy you for a treat?"

"My father? He always thought I needed to reduce my waistline and as such discouraged my eating cake at all." Jeremy swiftly revised his impression of Ballentine's father, from doting papa to that of monstrous tyrant. "Do you often buy such treats for your little boy?" she asked with a flicker of interest.

"All the time," he admitted. "Why not?"

"You are a fond parent?" She looked encouraged by this notion.

He inclined his head. "I am. I hope you will be too, Emmeline."

A small pucker appeared between her brows as she lifted the teapot. "Do you think Edward will be well-disposed toward a stepmother?" she asked hopefully, though he had not only been thinking of Teddy when he said it.

"Certainly, he has intimated as much. He thinks a year is too long for me to languish without a wife."

This made her pause, but all she asked was "Will you not choose a cake?"

"You choose first."

After some deliberation she took a madeira tartlet. "Thank you." She took a dainty bite.

"I will head to London this afternoon to set the wheels in motion," he decided, helping himself to an almond slice.

"You will? And by that, you mean…?"

"The usual things." He shrugged. "Put an announcement in the *Times*, procure a special license…"

"Visit Ballentine's Trading Company?" she suggested, setting her cake down on its plate.

He nodded, lifting his cup to his lips and taking a sip. That was the most pressing matter after all. "We could pick out a ring after this," he suggested. "There's a decent jeweler close by in Abbey Lane."

Emmeline glanced down at her still-gloved hand. "I quite forgot to give Humphrey back his ring," she said in a stricken voice.

"I can return it for you."

Setting down her teacup, she drew off her glove at once and slid an inconspicuous ring from her third finger. It pleased him that she did not look at it, just handed it over to him wordlessly before picking up her drink again.

Jeremy gave it a quick glance before pocketing it. It was an unprepossessing affair, an opal surrounded by a ring of garnets. Under such circumstances it was unlikely that Humphrey Stockton would expect its return, not after she had fruitlessly worn it for a decade. Still, he did not want her to keep it for a keepsake, so let the fool have it back and be done with it.

They partook of their refreshment a moment in silence. "I have heard opals are unlucky," he mused aloud. "Are you, Emmeline, a proponent of the language of gemstones?"

She shook her head. "I know nothing about it, unless you mean those acrostic rings that spell out secret messages."

"Secret messages?"

"You know, like 'regard' or 'dearest.' Each stone spells out a letter. So 'dear' would be a band set with a diamond, an emerald, an amethyst, and a ruby."

Privately Jeremy thought such a clash of colored stones would look extremely ugly, but he nodded politely. "You would like something like that?"

"Oh no, I did not mean—"

"What secret message could we share?" he pondered.

"I rather dread to think," Emmeline answered, making him laugh.

"How about Stefano?" he suggested, making her blush. "Sapphire, topaz, emerald—" he began, ticking off his fingers.

"I wish you would not joke so," Emmeline said in a choked voice. "It—it makes me nervous and quite on edge."

This gave him pause. "How so?"

She bit her lip. "It makes me fear that once again, this is all just a grand jest to you," she said in a low, trembling voice, "and that I am once more the butt of the joke. That you, my lord, are not remotely in earnest."

"Once again?" he queried, and Emmeline's color drained as she set her cup and saucer carefully down.

"I'm terribly sorry, my lord, but I think I made a mistake coming here with you," she started, pushing back her chair.

He reached across to grip her hand in his. "Emmeline. Don't," he said. "Don't bolt. What can I say to convince you that I am completely in earnest?" Her hand trembled in his and she was breathing fast. Suddenly he wished he had not brought her to a respectable place like Hutton's. He wished he could drag her into his lap and persuade her with a kiss or two.

"Have I not spoken of practicalities? Of the settlement of debts?" he coaxed reasonably. "Would it be more convincing if I spoke to you of personal attraction? I could, you know. I could easily speak of such things if it would carry more weight with you."

"No," she said quickly, tugging at her hand. Grudgingly, he allowed her to extricate herself. "I do not wish to hear anything of that kind, thank you," she said firmly. "That kind of thing does not hold any water with me anymore. It is not real."

Jeremy frowned. There were depths of feeling here that he had not fathomed. He wanted to argue the point with her but did not quite dare. She was poised for flight even now, he realized. "Very well, we will not speak of it, then," he said lightly. "Instead, we will stick to plain statement of fact." He leaned forward in his seat. "I mean to marry you, Ballentine," he said slowly and decisively, "to settle your debts and make you my viscountess. Make no mistake about that. I do not speak remotely in jest."

She stared at him a moment, then swallowed, inclining her head. "Because you want a quiet, convenient match, after your contentious divorce. I understand that part," she reasoned, "but you see, marrying me will not make your reentry into society any easier. I have no social standing, no dowry, and by the time my season was over—"

"I had practically ruined you," he cut in smoothly.

Emmeline gasped and shrank back into her seat. Clearly, this plain speaking was too much for her. "My lord!" she protested feebly, glancing about her in embarrassment.

"Well, which way do you want it, Emmeline? Sugar-coated or not?" he asked softly.

She hesitated, then took a deep breath. "Well…let us have plain-speaking for just this moment and then have nothing but politeness between the two of us forever after," she blurted.

Jeremy felt the laughter bubbling up inside him but knew it would be a mistake to let it out. God, he had forgotten how much he liked *talking* with her. It was so strange how she still had the ability to make him feel like the world was a better place simply by being in her presence.

"Very well, let me make myself plain," he said slowly, while his brain scrambled for whatever the hell it would take to convince her. He remembered her nervous question about London. "You will be precisely the kind of wife I require because you have no great love of London," he started, "and possess little desire to make a splash in high society.

"My first marriage was not a success," he continued grimly. "Neither of us were happy and certainly neither of us behaved well. In truth, my old and venerated family name has been dragged through the proverbial mud and I now mean to clean it up. I want a wife who will be happy to spend most of her time in Cornwall, mending relations with my neighbors and tenants, and strengthening our ties with the local community.

"I want the sort of wife who joins committees and espouses charities," he lied. In reality, Jeremy could not care less about such things, but he knew lots of respectable ladies liked to dabble in worthy causes. Likely, after being powerless and without influence for so long, Emmeline would enjoy throwing her weight around in such a fashion.

I want another child, trembled on his lips but bearing his seed might not appeal to her currently, so he quashed that thought. "I want someone who will embark on several projects around the estate," he improvised. "I want *domesticity*," he concluded at last. "In short, I've had a wife who was the toast of London, and I loathed her. My second wife will need to be quite a different kettle of fish."

What a complete and utter load of old horseshit, he thought wryly. Still, his words had done their job, and the fear was fading fast from Emmeline's eyes. *Thank God.*

Wordlessly, she pointed a finger to her chest. "Me," she mouthed soundlessly. He nodded. "You think I could be all those things?"

"All those things and more." Emmeline gulped, then picked up her teacup and took a fortifying swig. "Do you think you could uphold your end of such a bargain?" he asked lightly. If not, he would have to think up some other bunch of conditions that she *would* find acceptable. Anything, he suddenly realized, to convince her, he could swallow. Except for lovers. He would never permit that. Not for Emmeline.

"Very well," she said bravely, lifting her chin. "I will do it."

He breathed out, finally allowing a smile to curl his lips. "Good," he said.

"Lord Faris!" a surprised voice interrupted them. "I heard you were in town but could hardly credit it, as I know your scathing opinion of Bath." The speaker gave a jovial laugh and shot a curious glance at Emmeline before dismissing her as beneath his notice. "As a matter of fact, I'm glad I ran into you, old chap, I wanted to ask your opinion on the favorite for the next race meet."

Jeremy stood up. "How are you, Henry?" he asked, not really caring about the answer. "Miss Ballentine, allow me to introduce you to an old acquaintance of mine, Lord Fulsham." Henry looked surprised by the introduction and turned and bowed. Emmeline came to her feet and bobbed a curtsey, her face a polite blank.

"Actually…" Jeremy tipped his head to one side. "Now that I come to think on it, you two have probably already met."

Emmeline gave a brittle smile and Henry's eyebrows shot up into his top hat. "Good lord, really? When would this have been?" he asked, shooting a puzzled look at Emmeline.

"Oh, it was a long time ago now," she replied readily. "You will not remember, Lord Fulsham, and I am sure I do not blame you."

"It would have been during the London season, ten years ago," Jeremy volunteered.

"Is that so?"

"As a matter of fact, you can offer us your felicitations, Henry. Miss Ballentine has just agreed to marry me."

"Good grief! The devil you say!" Henry forgot all about horse racing tips. Congratulations were proffered and accepted. "Good lord, m'sisters will be excited to hear this news," Fulsham proffered, moving hurriedly off with a decided gleam in his eye.

"Why on earth did you have to tell him?" Emmeline hissed across the table once he was out of earshot. The door jangled as he left the shop.

"Oh, is it a secret engagement?" Jeremy asked innocently. "I did not realize."

Emmeline glanced out of the window and paled. "He has just met up with a large group of fashionable-looking people," she muttered, "and they are all *staring* in at us!"

"Dear me, how ill-bred," Jeremy tutted, taking a sip of coffee. "Yes, now I come to think of it, old Fulsham is a bit of a gossip," he lamented. "I suppose it *was* indiscreet of me but at least this way, when the *Times* announcement hits the streets, there will be some tidbit in circulation regarding how and when we met." At her disbelieving stare, he added, "It shows our association is one of long-standing, and not the result of wild impulse alone."

"From what I remember, you are decidedly prone to wild impulses!" she retorted, then looked stricken.

Jeremy could not hold back his laughter. "That's all in the past now, Ballentine," he assured her, nudging the plate of cakes toward her.

"The events of this morning would seem to refute that claim!"

"Let us return to more pressing matters," he suggested placatingly. "Your engagement ring for one. I rather like sapphires…"

4

Emmie shut the door behind her and leaned back against it. She closed her eyes and took several deep breaths, summoning the courage to face Pinky with her shocking news. Her engagement to Humphrey was broken. She was instead now engaged to Lord Faris. They were going to be married in a matter of days. They would all be moving to Cornwall.

What in God's name was she doing?

Too late for that. Instead, Emmie fortified herself with the thought of Thomas Hardiman and the other clerks receiving generous compensation for their job losses. There was also the comfort that her late father's name would not be dragged through the mud as his company fell apart. Moreover, she and Pinky were no longer facing the possibility of being put out on the street.

Pushing away from the door, she made for the parlor, where she found her friend stood before the unlit fireplace wringing her hands. "Oh, Emmie!" Pinky blurted on catching sight of her. She took three steps toward her, scanning her face. Whatever she saw there caused her to promptly freeze on the spot.

"I have wonderful news, dear," Emmie began brightly, ignoring her friend's reaction. She walked into the room with a firm tread. "Our money worries are over," she declared. Pinky's mouth dropped open. "Also, we have cakes for lunch and likely for supper too," she said, carefully setting down the box she had been clutching on the occasional table. "Lord Faris insisted on buying us ever so many."

"Oh, er, most generous," Pinky twittered distractedly. "How kind."

"Yes," Emmie agreed. "He has been all that is considerate." She reached up to carefully extract her hatpin and remove her bonnet. Upon setting this down, she pulled off her gloves, revealing the large gold ring set with five matched sapphires which she now wore on her left hand. It felt somewhat cumbersome, and she flexed her hand self-consciously, darting a look at Pinky as she did so. Pinky's gaze, however, remained riveted to her face. "Do sit down, dear, there is something I need to tell you."

"Shall I fetch the tea tray first?" Pinky enquired in failing accents.

Emmie shook her head. "Let me tell you my news first. Then tea."

Pinky nodded and, after a moment's dithering, sat in her usual chair. Emmie lowered herself into her own seat opposite. "As you know, Humphrey visited first thing this morning," she began. "I'm afraid he bore rather ill tidings." She took a deep breath. "Ballentine's Trading Company is no more. The whole concern is now quite sunk without hope of revival."

Pinky raised a shaking hand to cover her mouth. "Oh *no*!" she gasped, her eyes filling with tears. "Oh, *Emmie*!"

Emmie nodded. "Collapsed and buried under, well, under a pile of debts I'm afraid. Also…" Emmie swallowed, rushing on before she lost her nerve. "Humphrey told me he can no longer marry me," she continued with a slight wobble in her voice.

"You mean because of the debt?" Pinky whispered in horror. "But surely—"

"No, not because of the debt," Emmie interrupted her. For an instant, she considered not telling her friend the full extent of Edward's perfidy. It was so *lowering* to admit all. *Ten whole years* wasted. Then she thought better of it. Pinky deserved to know the whole truth.

"You see, it turns out Humphrey was never in a position to offer me marriage," she said quietly. "In short, he already has a wife. He's had one for these past twelve years."

Pinky blinked at her uncomprehendingly. "I beg your pardon, Emmie? I think I must have misheard you."

"A Mrs. Clara Stockton, apparently," Emmie persisted doggedly. "I think he even made mention of a child toward the end of our interview, but I confess I was struggling to take in any more by that point…"

Pinky's pale face flushed hectically with color. "Are you in earnest?" she asked, sitting up straighter in her seat. "You tell me that Mr. Stockton was *already married* when he entered into an engagement with you ten years ago?" Pinky's hand fluttered at her throat. "Why, I can hardly comprehend such…such *wickedness*!"

A martial gleam entered Pinky's watery eyes and she sprang out of her chair. "You poor, poor dear!" she exclaimed with feeling, her slight bosom heaving as she hurried over to clasp one of Emmie's hands between her own. In her agitation, she did not seem to notice the sapphire ring at all.

"He is fortunate indeed that you do not possess a brother to defend your honor," she rambled on distractedly. "Why, if I was a man, I am not sure I would not challenge him to duel myself!"

Emmie gave a startled gurgle of laughter; she could not help it. The idea of her dainty Pinky sallying forth with a dueling pistol clasped in her lace-mittened hands was an absurd one. "I am sure I could have no nobler defender of my honor," she said placatingly.

"I have never been so deceived in a man's character in my life!" Pinky exclaimed. "Mr. Stockton seemed like such an estimable young man. Yet for him to have acted thus…" She broke off to shake her head and tut vigorously. "If your papa had only known, he would surely have had him horsewhipped!"

"Papa always thought himself a sound judge of character," Emmie reflected. "He believed Humphrey safe, solid, and rather dull if truth be told. He simply thought I could not do any better, matrimonially speaking."

Pinky hardly seemed to hear her. "How dreadful for you to have learned these awful truths all alone, Emmie," she fretted. "How I wish I had been there to support you in your hour of need." Pinky's eyes filled with tears and her narrow shoulders drooped.

"It is perhaps just as well you were not," Emmie answered gravely. "As his words might have inspired you to violence."

"I am sure none could have blamed you if you had slapped his face," Pinky announced with such a hopeful look on her face that Emmie could not help but give another weak laugh.

"No, I did not slap him," she admitted. "I would make a very bad heroine of the novels we read, Pinky dear. I was just…terribly shocked and rather hurt. I wanted to shrink into myself." To her surprise, she felt her own eyes fill with tears at the humiliating memory.

"It must have been dreadful for you, dear, just dreadful," Pinky repeated with vehemence. "I am most vexed at Mr. Stockton. Most vexed indeed. What in the world could he have been *thinking*—" She broke off her words noticing the expression on Emmie's face. "But there, what is the point in fruitless speculation? Hot tea, that is what you need. Hot tea with plenty of sugar. Oh dear, I hope we have some sugar left," she murmured, dropping Emmie's hand and heading for the door.

"It does not matter if we do not, for we have sugary cakes," Emmie reminded her, but Pinky was already halfway across the hall by this point.

As a rule, Pinky avoided using the shared kitchen wherever possible, for she dreaded running into the other tenants and felt having to use communal resources was rather vulgar. However, her blood was up at this point, and even if she should encounter their least favorite neighbor, the contentious Mrs. Bridgholme, Emmie felt certain her friend was equal to the occasion.

Emmie took the opportunity of her absence to bolster her nerve before delivering her last revelation. She put away her hat and gloves and tidied her hair, which looked rather windblown. In truth, it did not take much for her hair to look blowsy for it had a strong wave and inclination to untidiness, which frequently dismayed her. She was sitting back in her seat, composed and tidy, by the time Pinky returned with the tea tray five minutes later.

"We did not have any sugar," Pinky admitted guiltily. "But as I am convinced the Startrites regularly help themselves to ours, I took two spoonfuls from their tin."

Emmie directed a look of astonishment at her friend, who was usually scrupulously honest in her dealings. Pinky's expression was unrepentant. "Our need is far greater, and you are to have *both* spoonfuls mind. I *insist!*"

"I think it is you who needs to prepare yourself for a shock," Emmie warned her apologetically. "I have a second piece of news which is no less disquieting than the first."

"Let me pour before you give it," Pinky implored. "I am sure we are both in need of fortification. There now," she said as she passed over a brimming cup. "Take two sips before you so much as speak a word."

Emmie complied, then lowered the cup into its saucer. "Pinky dear, I am still to be married, and very soon. As soon as a special license can be procured."

Pinky nodded briskly. "Yes, to Lord Faris," she said bracingly. At Emmie's startled look, she added with a little cough, "I did hear his offer of marriage to you this morning, dear, if you recall? When I came downstairs to check on you." She averted her eyes tactfully and took another sip of tea.

Emmie felt the hot color flood back into her face. *How about it?* That was what he had said. Hardly the most formal and flowery of proposals. She dreaded to think what Pinky, always so upright and proper, would have made of such an offer. "Yes," she said lamely. "He also offered to pay off any debts Papa's company has incurred and to award compensation to the employees who will now find themselves out of a job."

Pinky inclined her head. "Now that was nicely done of him," she conceded. "And must have held a great deal of sway in your decision to accept his suit."

"Well...yes," Emmie admitted.

Pinky took a deep breath. "You acted as you saw fit, my dear, and I am sure no one could blame you. You must not worry about what will happen to me. I have my profession to sustain me, and I am sure—"

"No, no, Pinky, you must not think of leaving me," Emmie said quickly. "I have already spoken to Lord Faris, and you are to accompany us to Cornwall."

Pinky blinked owlishly. "Cornwall?" She faltered.

"Yes, for that is where his seat lies."

Pinky set down her cup and saucer with a rattle. "Am I to understand my services will be retained?" There was a wobble in her voice, and she made haste to retrieve a handkerchief from her sleeve as emotion overcame her.

"I cannot part with you after all this time," Emmie said gently as Pinky dabbed at her watery eyes. "You are not just my closest friend but must count as family by this point."

"Oh, Emmie!" Pinky quavered.

"I am afraid you will have to take up some governess duties to Lord Faris's son, for a while at least," Emmie admitted in a rush. "But with me around, I hope it will not prove too onerous a task. In any case, it seems he will be going away to school at some point in the not-too-distant future."

"Oh! So, there *is* a son," Pinky murmured, looking momentarily surprised. "I had supposed…" Her words trailed off and something else seemed to occur to her. "There is only the one boy, I take it?" she asked in faltering tones.

"Yes. Master Edward Vance, aged nine years."

Pinky gulped. "I am sure I can manage," she said bravely. "And Cornwall is meant to be so very beautiful. Perhaps I could take up my watercolors again," she said, perking up.

Emmie smiled perfunctorily. "Perhaps you could tutor young Edward in the art?" she suggested. "And you could take little field trips together to find the best scenery?"

Pinky blanched a little at the thought of venturing out of doors with her young charge. "Er, yes," she agreed nervously. "Perhaps you could even accompany us on occasion, Emmie dear? I am sure the fresh air would be greatly beneficial."

"Perhaps," Emmie agreed cautiously, for she had never been any good at painting. She was just glad to see her friend, who always suffered greatly at any change in circumstances, making plans. It heartened her and made her feel a good deal better about the choices she had made.

It was not that she had expected outright condemnation, but she *had* anticipated a shocked and quiet sort of disapproval from her. It would have been only natural. Pinky was such a cautious and proper person, and this wedding was going to proceed with almost indecent haste.

Emmie felt the greatest relief that her friend was being so philosophical about it all. "Shall we open the cakes?" she suggested, despite having no appetite.

"Oh yes," Pinky agreed, though Emmie was not sure she would manage a whole cake due to her nervous energy. "Oh my!" she blurted on lifting the lid and seeing just how many cakes the box contained.

"I did warn you," Emmie replied. "I told Lord Faris of our Friday tradition of treating ourselves, and he seemed determined to indulge us."

"These would last us a whole week!"

"Look at this," Emmie said, extending her left hand. The sapphires flashed. "I think going overboard might be a personality trait where he is concerned."

Pinky gaped at the ring. "Good lord!" she uttered faintly. "It must be worth a fortune!"

Emmie looked down at it. "Yes," she agreed quietly. It still did not seem real to her. Not one bit. Then a horrible thought flashed into her mind. What if it was all some horrible sort of hoax? Like Jeremy Vance seeking her out at all those debutante balls and dancing with her, giving her his attention and then... She gasped, and balled her hands into fists so hard her nails bit into her palms.

She had known all along that he was making a May game of her, but she had gone along with it anyway, because the giddy pleasure of dancing with him had almost made the misery of her social debut worth it. Goodness gracious, what a little fool she had been! Was she still a complete fool where he was concerned? A nasty feeling lurked in the pit of her stomach, telling her it was so.

"Emmie?" Pinky was leaning forward and pressing her hand. "You look a little green around the gills, dear. Are you feeling well?"

"It's nothing. Just, well, this morning I woke up engaged to one man, and tonight I go to bed affianced to another," she said unevenly.

Of course it was not an elaborate hoax, she told herself sternly, feeling the weight of his ring on her finger. He had ulterior motives in marrying her, just as she had for accepting him. He wanted her to help clean up his tarnished image. She needed him to discharge her debts. They would have a perfectly sensible marriage of convenience. That was all.

She was no longer a stupid, naïve girl of eighteen whose heart raced whenever the Honorable Jeremy Vance entered the room. A decade had passed since that unfortunate incident in Lady Hawford's conservatory. Her cheeks still burned to think of it. Resolutely, she thrust the memory away.

He probably did not even remember it. Doubtless he had kissed dozens of girls before *and* after his marriage to the beauteous Lady Amanda. She had no illusions as to his dissolute character. Only fancy, kissing her on the night his own engagement had been announced! Nay, worse than that, mere moments before the official announcement was made! She felt her face turn pink with indignation.

"Ah, you have a little color returned," Pinky said with satisfaction. "For a moment, I thought I would have to fetch my smelling salts."

Emmie forced a smile. "Nothing so drastic, I assure you. There is another cup left in the pot. Will you have it?"

"No, you help yourself, dear. I will have one of these excellent cakes instead," Pinky said, peering once again into the box.

5

Against her expectation, Emmie slept soundly that night. Really, she must have been emotionally wrung out by the events of the day, for when she awoke the next morning, she spent a few disorienting moments unsure where she even was, let alone who she was marrying.

A quiet knock on the door proved to be Pinky, who was not only up and dressed but had also apparently been down to the kitchen to fetch cans of hot water for their morning wash. "You are up far too early!" Emmie protested, still in her threadbare dressing gown. "Do not dare to stir another step downstairs for I mean to do my part."

"Nonsense!" Pinky replied roundly. "You made our breakfast yesterday, so it is only fair that I should take over this morning. Do not delay in your wash, for your jug of water will grow cold."

She disappeared before Emmie could press the matter, so she made for the bathroom instead. Emmie was back in her room, washed, dressed, and just pushing in her last hairpin when she heard a knock at their outer door. *Pinky's hands must be full with the breakfast tray*, she thought, hurrying out into the hallway to throw it open.

To her surprise it was not her friend bearing their morning meal, but instead a large, muscular man in footman's livery. Standing next to him was a small golden-haired boy clad in a sailor suit complete with a matching hat sat atop his curls. She looked from one to the other in lively astonishment. "Good morning," she said on finding her tongue.

"Good morning," replied the child, looking up at her soulfully.

"Good morning, miss," the footman said hurriedly. "I deliver this with the compliments of Viscount Faris."

Emmie noticed at this point that he held out a thick-looking envelope. She took it from him with thanks and could not forbear looking once more at the boy. He was a vastly pretty child with golden locks and very blue eyes.

"Am I right in thinking you are Master Edward Vance?" she guessed.

"I am. Are you Miss Emmeline Ballentine, of whom I am so curious to meet?"

"I am Miss Ballentine," she admitted. "Though no one ever calls me Emmeline."

"My father does," he corrected her.

"Well, yes, yes *he* does," she was forced to concede. "But I wish he would call me Emmie as my friends and particular acquaintances do."

He seemed to consider this. "I suppose I will soon be expected to call you Mama," he observed sagely. The footman coughed loudly. "I wish you would not step on my toe, Colfax!" the child complained loudly. Colfax, who was good-looking and fair-haired himself, turned rather red.

Seeing Florrie's face bobbing over the banister, all agog to learn who the visitors were, Emmie took a step back. "Perhaps you would like to come inside?" she heard herself offer hesitantly.

Master Edward's expression brightened at once. "I *would* like that, yes," he agreed, evading the footman's sudden grab, and slipping past her into their rooms.

"You little—!" the footman muttered, then cleared his throat. "I beg your pardon, miss," he said in a more respectful tone. Emmeline gestured to him to come inside and after a pause, he followed. "Lord Faris only instructed me to deliver the envelope," he said with misgiving. "And Master Edward promised that if I let him accompany me, he would be satisfied with just a glimpse at you!" Colfax sounded aggrieved. When agitated, his accent sounded a good deal more cockneyfied. "I might have known he would play me some trick," he said bitterly.

"Well, there is no harm done," Emmeline placated him as she led him into the parlor, where young Master Edward was looking about him with great interest.

"Papa promised me I could meet with Miss Ballentine yesterday, and then he went back on his word," Edward pointed out. "So, it is only fair that I should spend some time with her today." He directed a lofty look at Colfax as he sauntered over to the window to peer out at the street view below.

Seeing the footman visibly seethe, Emmie said apologetically, "The original plan *was* for us all to walk together in the park. Unfortunately, I had some…some rather bad news which meant I was not up to it that day."

Colfax frowned and moved toward the window. Edward nimbly crossed the room to stand in front of the unlit fireplace. "What is this thing?" he asked, reaching up to fiddle with the tassels on the decoration over the mantelpiece.

"It is called a mantel scarf. My friend Miss Pinson made it. She is excessively fond of lace. Do you not have any like that in your own home?"

He thought about it for a moment. "No," he said at last. "Except maybe in our housekeeper Mrs. Cheviot's room. She has a small fireplace like this one, and she likes to put doilies under everything," Edward explained artlessly.

"Ah," Emmie responded. "It sounds as though they might have similar tastes."

"What about you?" the boy asked with interest. He leveled a serious look at her. "Do you like frilly things?" There was a faint note of disapproval in young Master Vance's tone.

"I do," she concurred. "I like a good many pretty and frivolous things."

"What about kittens?"

"Adore them, don't you?"

He ignored this, shooting a speculative look at her through his eyelashes. "What about my father?" he asked. Colfax let out a warning grumble from his throat which startled Emmie more than the boy.

She paused. "I imagine you are better placed to know his opinion of cats than I, Edward," she responded calmly.

"I wish you would call me Teddy," the boy said plaintively. "I am only called Edward when I am in disgrace."

Emmie's lips twitched; she could not help it. The child was incorrigible. "Very well, Teddy," she said, moving toward the door, for she heard Pinky's tread outside and the tinkle of tea things. "Ah, here you are, Hannah," she said, quickly warning her friend, who had a nervous disposition. "We have visitors this morning."

Pinky's step into the room faltered. "Oh!" she exclaimed in stricken accents, freezing to the spot, her hands clutching the breakfast tray in a deathly grip. Her startled gaze flew from Colfax's intimidating bulk to Teddy's slight frame clad in nautical garb. She quivered and the contents of the tray started rattling.

"Allow me, miss," the footman said smoothly and moved so swiftly that before they knew it, he had taken the tray from her hands and deposited it gracefully onto the small dining table tucked into the corner.

"Th-thank you," Pinky stammered, though her gaze could not meet Colfax's. "Most, er, most kind."

"Hannah," said Emmie bracingly, "this is young Master Vance, who is paying us a visit with Colfax this morning." The large footman bowed. "Teddy, this is my best friend in all the world, Miss Hannah Pinson."

Pinky could always fall back on impeccable manners and managed a graceful curtsey. Teddy stepped forward to courteously shake her hand. "Pleased to meet you, Miss Pinson," he said, staring up at her friend with undisguised curiosity.

Oh dear, thought Emmie. The kindest thing she could do was to draw the child's attention away from Pinky, who was clearly a mass of nerves. At that moment, Colfax caught her eye. To her surprise, the footman was also staring hard at poor Pinky.

Emmie cleared her throat, and Colfax seemed to remember where he was, immediately averting his eyes from her stricken friend, his expression turning carefully blank.

Teddy skipped over to the table. "Is this your breakfast?" he asked, examining the tray which held two boiled eggs and two pieces of unbuttered bread.

"It is," she answered cheerfully as Pinky's hand fluttered to her throat. Poor Pinky looked quite mortified at the exposure of their meagre breakfast. "Will you join us for a cup of tea this morning?"

"Yes, I will," Teddy answered with assurance. "Though I do not want an egg for I have already eaten." Which was just as well, Emmie reflected, for she was not sure they had any spare.

"Wait till you're asked," Colfax growled, and Emmie realized he would recognize the signs of straitened circumstances far better than his young charge.

Teddy ignored him, pulling out the third chair and sitting himself on it with all the dignity of a young prince upon his throne. Emmie crossed to the corner cupboard, set down the envelope to read later, and took out three sets of cups and saucers.

She threw a quick questioning glance at Colfax, for the footman's role did not seem to be that of mere attendant, but he had retreated to the window again. He looked so stiff and formal; she thought better of offering him refreshment.

"Shall I pour, Pinky?" Emmie asked gently, sliding into the chair behind the teapot.

"Pinky?" repeated Teddy, looking immediately intrigued.

"Oh, a childish form of address," Emmie explained with some momentary embarrassment. "Hannah and I have been together since I was five years old, and I sometimes fall back on calling her that."

"I'll pour, dear," Pinky said with a small smile and picked up the milk jug.

"I'm afraid we do not have any sugar this morning," Emmie said, anticipating Pinky's next crisis. "Though we do have a good deal of cakes. Shall I go down to the kitchen and fetch you one?"

"No thank you," Teddy answered promptly. "I don't have much appetite these days," he sighed. "I used to eat lots and lots."

"Because of your recent illness?" Emmie enquired.

"Yes, they don't know if I will ever fully recover," Teddy answered tragically. There was a snort heard from the direction of the window. "Some children *die* from scarlet fever," he pointed out, throwing a cold look Colfax's way before continuing sadly. "I may remain a semi-invalid for the rest of my life."

"Oh, you poor child!" Pinky gasped. Evidently, Teddy's angelic appearance was starting to win her over, despite his maleness.

"You must look to rebuild your strength," Emmie said gravely, for clearly Master Teddy had a mind to play up to his convalescent status.

"You must take my egg, Master Edward," Pinky fussed, pushing her plate his way. "No, I insist. They are most nutritious, and I am sure it will do you good."

"Hannah, Teddy has already breakfasted," Emmie protested, and she thought she heard another grumble of disapproval from Colfax.

"I could not eat a thing," Pinky assured her, and noticing her agitation, Emmie believed her. It did not take much to spoil her friend's appetite.

"It is too bad, you must certainly eat a cake for elevenses, Hannah."

Pinky made a quick dismissive gesture, her eyes on Teddy, who, despite his previous words, was now tucking into her boiled egg. She looked gratified. "There now, that's a good child."

Emmie was not so sure.

"Do you not eat butter?" Teddy asked, eyeing next the piece of dry bread.

"Oh, er," Pinky twittered in confusion.

"I'm afraid we are out of butter today," Emmie interjected smoothly.

"Butter *and* sugar," Teddy commented in his high childish voice. "I think you need to go shopping, Miss Ballentine."

Emmie turned a deaf ear to Colfax's hissed breath.

"I was so *sure* we had some butter left," Pinky said, shaking her head as she passed her piece of bread to Teddy. "Those Startrites…"

"What's a Startrite?" Teddy asked, picking up the bread and taking a bite of it.

"They occupy the floor above us," Emmie said, pointing a finger to the ceiling. "We all share the kitchen and bathroom facilities, you see."

Pinky's cheeks turned even pinker at the mention of this. "So vexing," she muttered. "Things wander so. That cake of rose hip soap, my dear," she said, turning to Emmie, then clearly decided it was highly improper to discuss such things before a gentleman, even if he was only nine years old. She coughed.

"Did they pinch it?" Teddy asked through a mouthful of bread.

"I think I misplaced it," Emmie said tactfully. "It was my own fault for not putting it away."

"I bet they did pinch it," Teddy said darkly. "When I was at boarding school, someone stole my best dip pen. It was made of mother-of-pearl and my godfather gave it to me for a present."

"That is a good deal too bad," Pinky clucked.

"Yes, for Lord Atherton said he would not buy me another," Teddy recalled bitterly. That particular name from the past gave Emmie quite a jolt. Tall and arrogant, Lord Atherton had been Jeremy's closest crony in those days. Of course, he *would* be Teddy's godfather. "He said I probably lost it and would not even listen to a word I said." His voice rose with indignation.

Pinky looked shocked and dismayed by this. "I am sure you would never be so careless with a treasured possession, dear boy," she said firmly.

Teddy looked smug. "Never," he agreed, and took a sip of unsweetened tea. Emmie saw him struggle to conceal his grimace. She was impressed he made the effort. "Will you come around to call on us this afternoon?" Teddy asked. "We are staying in The Royal Crescent."

Emmie opened her mouth to decline this kindly, if improper offer, but Colfax was already clearing his throat portentously.

"Miss Ballentine has an appointment this afternoon," he said uncompromisingly.

"An appointment?" She turned in her chair to look at the footman in surprise.

"You have not read your letter, miss," he said with some reproach. *Oh yes, the letter.* Emmie cast about for it, before remembering she had placed it in the corner cupboard. She went to retrieve it and wondered once more at its thickness.

No sooner had she broken the seal than the mystery was solved. The envelope was stuffed with banknotes. Emmie stared down at them uncomprehendingly. It looked to be a small fortune! She looked up and met Colfax's impassive gaze.

"His lordship said you would need to purchase bride-clothes," he said.

"At such short notice?" Emmie objected faintly. "Wherever could I find—?"

"He has already booked you in with a modiste on Jerwin Street. One o'clock this afternoon. I'm to bring the carriage round for you."

"Did he not take his carriage to London?" Emmie asked in surprise.

Colfax shook his head. "Wanted the horses to be well-rested before returning to Cornwall. He hired a conveyance to take to London."

"Oh." One of the sheets of paper was not money, Emmie noticed. It looked like a letter. She drew it out and unfolded it, with some trepidation.

Ballentine,

You will oblige me by attending an appointment with Madame de Flores at one o'clock on Monday 15 to arrange your trousseau. I have left the direction with my man, Colfax, and he will collect you accordingly.

Make use of the carriage during this time to say your farewells and run your errands. Colfax will call on you every morning to take instruction from you. Label any furniture that you want transported to Cornwall. He will see it is done.

You have two weeks, so use them wisely. Return your books to the lending library, hand your notice to your landlady, pay your bills, pack your bags. Above all else, prepare yourself, for at the end of these two weeks I will return, and you will be mine.

Jeremy

Emmie let out a shaky breath. "He seems to have thought of everything," she said, lowering the letter.

Colfax nodded matter-of-factly. "Any instructions for me to carry out this morning?" he asked.

"I will need to confer with Pink—with Miss Pinson, I mean," she corrected herself swiftly. "And we will compile a list." *The pawnbrokers*, she thought suddenly. "Actually…"

"Yes, miss?" He must have seen the light spring to her eyes, for he looked curious.

"Would you be so good as to redeem some valuable items I have had to—to send to *the menders*," she said with emphasis, sending a meaningful look toward Teddy. "The one on Wainfleet Road. My Vienna clock, a French-style mirror, and a full set of lead crystal glasses are all there currently."

"Of course, miss, nothing could be simpler."

"Thank you so much, Colfax," she enthused as she hurried from the room to find the slips. There were actually a good deal more of them stuffed into her empty jewelry box than she had remembered. Her watch and her gold gate bracelet had also been pawned, though she had sold her good quality jewelry long ago.

She hurried back to Colfax with the slips balled up in her fist. He accepted them wordlessly and she retrieved the envelope of money. She realized that just one of the banknotes would redeem the whole lot. Passing it to Colfax, she thanked him profusely and returned to the table.

"Come along, then, Master Edward," he said. "Say your farewell to the ladies."

Teddy dragged his feet over the leave-taking and clearly did not wish to return to his father's lodgings. "For there is no one there for me to talk to," he lamented.

"You have that nurse his lordship hired for your stay here," Colfax reminded him.

"Nurse Jopling is so dull," he complained. "She makes me drink horrible draughts and wear woolen undergarments."

"She is devoted, I am sure, to your recovery," Pinky opined.

"We have run out of conversation," Teddy grumbled. "All she ever talks about is her old patients, most of whom are dead!"

Even as Colfax marched him downstairs, they could hear Teddy's voice drifting back up toward them. "Well, but *why* can't I come with you to fetch Miss Ballentine's clock back from the menders? I tell you; I'm fed up lying on a sofa all day!"

"Oh dear," muttered Pinky as they made their way back into their rooms. "Of course, Colfax cannot explain to him the sordid reality of a pawnbroker's establishment."

Emmie thought Colfax looked more than equal to the task but kept this to herself. "Well, he is certainly an interesting child," she reflected. "Plenty of spirit and opinions of his own."

"Indeed," Pinky agreed. "Though delicate, of course, both in constitution and of mind."

Emmie gave her a sidelong look. "Do you think so?" she murmured. "Curious, I thought him quite reassuringly robust."

"I hope he will still partake of his luncheon," Pinky continued absently. "And I did not spoil his appetite by letting him eat my egg. Meat, you know. As I understand it, men must eat a lot of it in order to maintain their health." Hannah always spoke of the opposite sex as though they belonged to an entirely different species.

"In any event, I *am* glad we do not have to return to the pawnbroker's," Emmie admitted as they resumed their seats in the parlor.

"Oh yes, indeed!" Pinky agreed with a small shudder. "Such a dreadful place! It really is providential we need never set foot there again."

"It certainly is, I had no idea what we could even hock next," Emmie said, her glance flitting around the room. The things she still owned were all big, heavy pieces and she had no notion how they could have carted them as far as Wainfleet Road.

Would she have her own suite of rooms as Lady Faris? She knew some grand residences did have separate quarters for family members. And even if she did, would she have any need of her hefty bow-fronted cabinets, and the mahogany sideboard? It seemed unlikely.

"We must make a list of things we need to do in the next two weeks," she said, thinking of Jeremy's letter. "There's a lot to organize, and only two weeks left to do it."

"Two weeks, dear me," Pinky uttered. "We must certainly hurry and finish our latest novels before we return them."

"Yes," Emmie agreed. "We cannot leave Josephine languishing. We must see her safely returned to the arms of her beloved Fernando." Pinky paused and gave her a funny look. "What?"

"Oh, nothing, dear," Pinky said quickly.

"No, tell me," Emmie insisted.

"Well, it is just I have been considering if you were not right in what you said previously."

"What did I say?"

"About, well, Count Stefano perhaps being the better choice for Josephine."

"When did I—? Oh, that!" Emmie found herself suddenly extremely embarrassed. "That was just a nonsensical conversation, dear, I was not in earnest."

"Well, I think, in hindsight, you made some salient points," Pinky insisted. "Though, now that I come to consider it…" Her expression grew thoughtful. "I suppose that really Humphrey is the villain of the piece and Lord Faris, the hero."

Emmie spluttered. "You think Lord Faris would make the better Fernando now?" She could think of nothing *less* appropriate, save for that of Humphrey cast in the role of a wicked mustachioed villain. "I cannot see it somehow!"

She wondered briefly what Pinky would think if she knew how Jeremy Vance had toyed with her back in the day. Perhaps it was better not to speculate. "You will come with me this afternoon, won't you?" she said. "I shall need your help choosing wedding garments, and if it is the establishment I am thinking of, then it looks very smart and intimidating."

"Of course, my dear."

"And afterward we might even go to dinner somewhere nice?" she suggested, brandishing the envelope full of money. Their morning passed swiftly, and the carriage duly collected them for Emmie's appointment and set them down on Jerwin Street.

The fabrics and trimmings were selected for Emmie's wedding gown and few others besides. Leafing through the swaths of white silk, organza, and crepe gave her unfortunate recollections of her presentation dress, and she was determined that this time, she would have no train and wear no feathers.

Madame de Flores was insistent that only shades of white would do, so a fine duchess satin in ivory was settled on. Pinky fervently agreed her friend must follow in Queen Victoria's footsteps and brought a veil to her attention that was embellished heavily with elaborate silk flowers.

Understanding that it was to be a daytime ceremony, she and Pinky had agreed that a high neckline and long sleeves were a necessity, but Madame de Flores shot this idea down at once.

"No, no, his lordship wishes for you to wed in a gown most elaborate. He wishes for you to wear the pearls and the orange blossom." She snapped her fingers and fashion plates were brought forward showing highly trimmed gowns with low-cut bodices and puffed sleeves.

"These look more like evening dresses," Emmie protested, "and besides, I do not own any pearls! Not anymore."

Madame gave her a look. "You are to be a viscountess, mademoiselle. *Certainement*, there will be pearls."

"Oh, you mean an heirloom necklace?" Pinky said with dawning understanding. "We did not think of that."

"I'm confused," Emmie admitted in a low voice as Madame clapped her hands for refreshment to be brought in for them. "I wonder if he means for us to be married here in Bath and then travel down to Cornwall, or if he means for us to be married at Vance Park."

"I suppose with a special license," Pinky replied, "you can really be married anywhere his lordship pleases."

Moments later, Madame was sketching designs with delicate décolleté necklines. Emmie winced over them, only too aware that her own figure looked nothing like the wispy, waiflike maidens of Madame's imaginings.

With this in mind, she firmly vetoed the elaborate swathing of tulle over any part of her, deaf to Madame's protests. Despite its popularity, Emmie felt it added bulk, and bulk was neither necessary nor desirable to either her already ample bosom, or her not-so-slender waist.

"But ze neckline it will be indecent without ze tulle!" Madame protested, tape measure in hand.

"No, it will not, for you will not cut it so low as to expose too much," Emmie responded firmly.

As for the full skirt, it was already a bell shape with its stiffened petticoats, and she did not want further rows upon rows of frills to make it even bigger. Madame was disappointed but Emmie was resolute.

This time around, she would not be forced into silhouettes that did not suit her. She wanted clothes that would flatter her and make her feel pretty, not a spectacle. Quite frankly, she did not care if she was wearing the latest fashion or not.

"Will it truly be ready for two weeks' time?" Emmie asked doubtfully as Madame had her assistants carry the bolts of fabric away.

"Most assuredly. I have hired extra hands on his lordship's instruction. You must come back every day at the same time until that time."

"Every day?" Emmie was startled and not pleasurably so.

Madame nodded emphatically. "Tomorrow we will look at fitting the bodice toile. We have the measurements now to start the calico pattern and will make any necessary adjustments tomorrow. The team is sat in the back room now, starting work on your gown."

Emmie was impressed if not a little intimidated by this efficiency. As a reward, after the appointment, she and Pinky went for a very nice meal and made the most of it. Emmie's mood veered wildly over the three courses, from grimly determined to cautiously optimistic and back again.

It would be so nice not to have to worry about money ever again! It wore on one so and tainted almost every experience when you never knew if you would be able to afford next month's rent.

Of course, these days she had other concerns lurking at the back of her brain. Namely what manner of bridegroom she had agreed to marry, but she refused to let herself dwell on this overlong. She had done what she needed to do, that was all. Accepting Lord Faris's suit had been a necessary evil, nothing more.

Over the next two weeks, their days were full and busy. Colfax called every morning and on the third morning, he returned their formerly pawned items. He was apologetic when informing Emmie that her gold bracelet had been sold, for the six-month waiting period had passed. Emmie bore the loss stoically, for she had sold pieces she had liked far better.

The morning after that, they received a hamper of sugar, eggs, jam, and pastries piled high and tied up with a ribbon, sent with the compliments of Master Teddy. Pinky was quite overcome. "So thoughtful!" she exclaimed. "Really, quite a dear little boy."

"He's hanging out for another invitation to breakfast," Emmie laughed. "But we are far too busy to entertain at present, and besides, we have half-packed boxes and trunks lying open in every room."

They started attaching labels to the various pieces of furniture on the second week. Any item Emmie thought she could live without would send Pinky into flat despair. "Oh, you surely cannot part with that, Emmie!" she would protest, her eyes filling with tears. "It is so grand, and do you not remember how *handsome* it used to look in the sitting room at Porchester Square?" It seemed Pinky could only bear to part with the cheaper items they had bought in recent years to fit into smaller spaces.

In the end, Emmie simply resigned herself to the fact they were taking several unwieldy pieces and devoutly hoped Vance Park could accommodate them. Thinking of Lord Faris's luxurious carriage and immaculate clothes, she felt some misgivings on the subject. If his home was half as smart as he was, then he would take a poor view of having to house several out-of-date pieces of furniture.

Emmie eyed the comfortable, if rather shabby, mismatched armchairs and wondered if Pinky would have a room of her own large enough to contain them. She knew housekeepers often had their own sitting rooms. Would Lord Faris's generosity extend to such a thing for his governess? She could but hope.

Every afternoon Emmie was collected by Viscount Faris's crested carriage and taken to Jerwin Street where she had pattern pieces pinned to her. Once they were satisfied with the fit of her bridal gown, then more sketches were brought forth for walking gowns, day dresses, house dresses, frilly wrappers, and elaborate evening gowns.

"But Madame," Emmie objected. "There is surely not enough time for all of these gowns to be made up."

"No," she agreed with alacrity. "But if we get the pattern pieces fitted to you, then the finished gowns can be sent on afterward to Vance Park."

Emmie supposed she could see the sense in that. Madame was quick to veto Emmie's habitual shades of green, navy, and brown. "It is spring, and you are a bride, mademoiselle. You must pick out the pretty colors."

She was encouraged instead to pick from a bewildering variety of pinks and pale blues. "I have not worn such colors for years," Emmie admitted. Practical considerations such as how things would wash, and durability had been prioritized of late.

"You were in mourning," Pinky agreed. "And then…" They exchanged a look which said, *And then money became tight*, but neither of them voiced this thought aloud. "Oh, this would look so pretty on you, Emmie!" Pinky exclaimed, leaning forward to touch a bolt of delicate material. "You always looked so well in shades of pink."

"You do not think it might be a little too…young for me?" Emmie prevaricated.

But Madame de Flores would not hear of this and by the end of the session, Emmie had completely lost track of precisely what garments were being made, let alone how many of them. She would simply have to keep to her daily appointments and leave the rest to providence.

It was on the twelfth day that Madame de Flores announced the dress was ready and they were to have a full-dress rehearsal. To Emmeline's astonishment, they had a girl ready to dress her hair as well as the regular attendants. Silk stockings, long gloves, and embroidered slippers which matched her veil were all laid out ready for her.

"I had not realized we were doing this today," she protested as the team of young women carried her off to be dressed and pampered. Even Pinky did not escape their attention, for when Emmeline emerged in her finery, her friend was trying on a selection of bonnets which had been brought out for her inspection. This seemed quite odd for the establishment was not a millinery.

"I hardly know," Pinky was dithering. "I am sure I have plenty of wear left in my black crepe. Oh, *Emmie!*" Pinky cried, catching sight of her, her hand flying to her mouth. "Oh, *don't* you look a picture!"

"Do you think so?" Emmie asked self-consciously. "You don't think it is, well, a little *too much*?"

"Oh *no!*" Pinky said earnestly. "You look like a fairy-tale princess."

This was not exactly reassuring. At eighteen, Emmie would have been delighted to hear this, but at twenty-eight... She hastened toward the full-length mirror to gape at her dazzling reflection. "I'm not sure about this veil now my hair has been dressed in all these fancy hair pins. When I picked out this elaborate one, I thought my hair would be quite plain, not all swept about and dressed like this."

"But the pins are so pretty!" Pinky enthused. "Why, when they catch the light, they glitter like diamonds!"

"They do, don't they?" Emmie agreed uneasily. "They must be made of a new kind of glass for Madame has not charged me any new exorbitant amount. And look at these shoes," she said, sticking one foot out from under her white satin skirts.

"Oh!" Pinky gasped again. "Such exquisite embroidery. They match your veil, Emmie."

"Yes, and that's not all," Emmie said, lowering her voice. "You should see my drawers!"

Pinky's hand flew to her throat. "Oh," she said faintly. "Perhaps a French notion?" Anything slightly risqué Pinky always thought must be French. She had better not mention her corset, Emmie thought. Even she had been scandalized by the lack of whalebone. The stays she had worn during her London season had been so constricting they had creaked. These were so light; they did not pinch her at all.

Realizing she had left her handkerchief in the other room, Emmie made for the door, practically colliding with another person coming in.

"I'm so sorry—" she started to apologize when she looked straight into Jeremy Vance's blue eyes. "Oh!"

"Ah, Ballentine, what providential timing," he said, his hands lightly clasping her elbows as he steadied her.

Oh dear, thought Emmie. *Oh dear, oh dear*. Being in his arms was horribly familiar. She felt herself turn puce. "Were you, er, coming to find me?" she croaked foolishly, for what other reason would he be visiting a lady's dressmaker's?

"I was," he answered with a slow smile. He still hadn't lowered his arms, she realized, glancing about them. She wished he would. Two of the seamstresses bustled down the corridor past them and giggled. Doubtless, everyone would think he was embracing her.

"My lord!" Emmie blurted in astonishment. "You said two weeks, and it has only been twelve days!"

"My keenness lent an urgency to my task, and I swept all before me," he said, dragging her into the room. Once there, he held her hands out to her sides, and swept an appreciative gaze down her body. Emmie's breath stuck in her throat. As usual, his presence seemed to have sucked all the air out of the room. Her head swam.

"My God," he murmured. "I knew you would make a beautiful bride, but this is almost too much."

"Too much?" Emmie repeated in alarm.

"Too much for me to take," he clarified, lifting one of her hands to press it to his chest. "My heart is threatening to beat right out of my chest."

Emmie stared at him. He was joking, of course. She heard Pinky's breathing hitch and forced herself to respond sensibly. "Thank you, my lord," she replied, "but you are too effusive in your praise. And in any case, you should not see me before the wedding day."

He glanced down at himself and then looked back at her. Belatedly, Emmie noticed he was wearing wedding attire of pale gray trousers, a silk waistcoat, and pale blue coat.

"You—you mean—?"

"Why that today is to be our wedding day, of course. We are due at St. Matthew in the Avon within the hour."

"What?" Emmie squeaked, wheeling around to locate the clock.

"It is to be a three o'clock wedding," he clarified, "and tomorrow we will set off for Vance Park." As Emmie's jaw dropped, he sauntered over to where Pinky sat among all the hatboxes. "Allow me, Miss Pinson. It must be this one, I think," he said, lifting a silky lavender confection from some tissue paper and presenting it to her friend with a small bow. "I thought how well that shade would become you as soon as I saw it in London. I had gray gloves trimmed with matching buttons and an umbrella sent also. They must be here somewhere, I fancy." His gaze traveled over the pile to pull out a flat pale blue box done up in ribbon. "Here." He dropped it into her lap. "With my compliments."

Pinky's mouth dropped open. "For me? Oh, my lord, I—I couldn't—"

He smiled at her. "Of course you must. You are to act as Emmeline's witness, I presume?" He turned with a look of query in his eye.

"Of course," Emmie said at once. "I could have none other." Despite his high-handedness, Emmie felt touched by this attention to her friend. Perhaps he had understood her feeling on this matter after all. Pinky turned crimson, accepting the gifts with tears in her eyes. "So kind," she murmured in confusion.

Emmie hastened to her friend's side. "What a becoming bonnet, Hannah," she said soothingly. "You must let us see you wear it."

Hannah moved over to the mirror and drew it on. It did suit her with its pretty pleats and ribbon, though her friend would never have picked it out for herself. "You do not think it a little youthful for my years?" she quavered.

"You cannot be a day over thirty," Jeremy interjected gallantly, which embarrassed Pinky greatly for she was fully forty years old.

"It looks so well with your coat too," Emmeline said loudly, reassuring her friend and simultaneously shutting down the subject of age.

"It does complement it, does it not?" Pinky allowed cautiously. "Let me try it with the gloves," she said shyly, unfastening the ribbon to the box.

"Here," Jeremy said, passing two velvet boxes to Emmie. At her quizzical glance, he added, "Something old and something new is customary for brides, is it not?" The first box contained a long string of perfectly matched and lustrous pearls, far finer than the ones she had used to own. "These have been in my family for a while now. They were my great-grandmother's and have been sitting in the bank for the past twelve months. Now they are yours."

He took them from the silk-lined box, twisting the strand so that it was doubled and then clasped them around her neck. He nodded to the smaller box. "I bought you that in London." Emmie opened it and gasped aloud at the fabulous diamond bracelet within. "Colfax told me you lost a bracelet to the pawnbroker's, so now I have replaced it."

"It was nothing to compare to this one," Emmie said weakly as he clasped it about her wrist. He gave her an absent smile and then his eye fell on a long package which he pounced on and passed to Hannah. "The missing umbrella," he explained, "to complete your ensemble."

As her friend unwrapped and exclaimed over the handsome umbrella with its lavender trim, Jeremy turned back to Emmie. "Now, is there anything else we must attend to?"

"What about the clothes I wore here, Pinky's old bonnet and gloves?" Emmie asked, glancing around for those items.

"Leave them, Madame will see they are parceled up and sent on to us." He paused for a moment. "We set off for Cornwall tomorrow at noon."

"Tomorrow!" Emmie was aghast at such short notice. She was not sure she had attended to every detail she should have.

"Do not worry," he assured her with a smile. "If you have overlooked anything, I can see it is attended to after our departure."

She regarded him doubtfully but at that moment, Pinky broke into her thoughts.

"Oh, I have it!" she exclaimed, looking up quickly. "It is something borrowed we have forgotten! A bride must always wear some borrowed token, must she not? Would you accept something from me, Emmie?"

"With pleasure," she answered, smiling.

Pinky promptly unfastened her grandmother's pink cameo brooch and approached her. "I know how much you admire it. How lucky I am not wearing the jet one today!"

"Thank you," Emmie said, indicating a spot on her neckline.

"If you wanted to pin it to your petticoats out of sight, I would not be offended," Pinky assured her.

"Nonsense! I want it in full view."

Pinky carefully pinned the little brooch to Emmeline's decolletage. "Now that just leaves something blue," she commented. "And a sixpence in your shoe."

"I already have something blue," Emmie pointed out, holding up her left hand. "My engagement ring."

"I'm sure Teddy will happily supply the silver sixpence," Jeremy said confidently. "And he will appreciate being part of proceedings. Now, the carriage awaits; shall I settle up with Madame and meet you ladies outside?"

6

By the time Jeremy paid up his account with Madame de Flores and joined the others outside, Emmie was safely ensconced in the carriage with Miss Pinson. Teddy was waiting for him beside it, in his best velvet suit and lace collar, his golden curls shining in the afternoon sun.

"I gave Miss Ballentine my silver sixpence, Papa," he volunteered eagerly.

"It was my silver sixpence, as I recall!" Colfax countered, opening the door to the carriage.

"Very well, it was Colfax's sixpence for I spent mine," Teddy admitted, looking back over his shoulder as he scrambled in. "But what I want to know is this, who is going to give away the bride, Papa?"

Jeremy passed Colfax a golden guinea as he climbed in behind his son. "Consider the debt repaid," he said. Colfax's frown disappeared in a trice. He shut the door behind them and swung up to sit up top beside Juggins.

"By rights it should be me," Teddy continued as Jeremy dropped into the seat beside him.

"What should be you, my son?" Jeremy asked absently. Looking at Emmeline sitting opposite in that dress drove all else from his mind.

"It should be me that walks Miss Ballentine down the aisle," Teddy reiterated. "For she was my choice, was she not, Papa? I chose her for your next wife."

Noticing the close attention Emmeline was paying to his words, Jeremy cleared his throat to cut off his son's prattle. "Let us ask Miss Ballentine who she wishes to accompany her down the aisle," he suggested.

She looked first rather intently at Teddy and then back at him. "I have no objection to it being Teddy," she said quietly. The boy was immediately all smiles.

"You will also be carrying our rings," he told his son, presenting another velvet box and drawing back the lid. "This one is mine, and this one is for Miss Ballentine."

Teddy took the box from him, puffing out his chest. "I'm probably the most important person at this wedding," he observed with satisfaction.

"Carry on, Juggins," Jeremy called up to the driver, and they were on their way.

They managed to disembark from the carriage with only minor difficulties involving the length of Emmeline's veil. Miss Pinson caught it up at the back like a bridesmaid to avoid dirtying it in the street.

Emmeline hitched up her wide skirts and they were just maneuvering her through the church gate when his friend Atherton walked around the side of the church, top hat at a jaunty angle atop his head of gleaming black hair. He was smoking with one hand and carrying a box of spring flowers in the other.

"Picked them up as arranged," he drawled, thrusting the flowers under Jeremy's nose. "Apparently, it's a little early in the season for orange blossom."

"You remember Atherton, I'm sure," Jeremy said, taking the flowers and passing the bouquet to Emmeline, and a nosegay to Miss Pinson.

"Er, yes," Emmeline agreed, looking far from thrilled to be reacquainted. "Lord Atherton." She dipped a curtsey and Atherton waved his cigarette and gave her an ironic bow.

"God, it's been years," he replied, blowing out a plume of smoke. He looked Emmeline up and down critically. "You've worn well, Miss Ballentine," he said, discarding his cigarillo as Jeremy passed him a flower for his lapel.

"This is Miss Pinson, Emmeline's oldest friend."

Atherton's eyebrows rose but he bowed again, simultaneously fastening the peony to his coat. "Delighted," he drawled.

Miss Pinson, her hands full of flowers, umbrella, and veil, still managed a passable curtsey.

"Hello, Teddy, you repugnant brat," Atherton commented, his eyes falling on his godson.

As Jeremy was pinning a peony to his lace collar, Teddy's response was restrained. "Hello, revolting godfather," he sang out.

Atherton turned to Jeremy. "Shall we go in?"

"You go ahead, I'll join you in a moment."

"Oh, very well, be like that." Atherton shrugged and took off with his long-legged stride. "See you inside," he said with an airy wave.

Jeremy turned back to Emmeline. "Could you spare me a flower from your bouquet?"

She extracted one and obligingly pinned it to his coat. "Is Lord Atherton acting as your groomsman?" she asked, a slight wobble in her voice.

"He is." Suddenly, it occurred to him that she might not have the fondest recollection of his friends. He opened his mouth to ask if she had any objection but then closed it again. After all, it was a little late in the day for that.

Instead, he took her cold hands in his. "I have seen to all your business in London, Emmeline," he told her in a low voice. "Should I have brought you proof that I have discharged all obligations honorably? I have it and can fetch it now if you deem it necessary."

"No, of course not!" she said quickly, color rushing into her cheeks. "I did not doubt that for one minute."

"Then why...?" he started to ask but did not have the courage to continue. *Why do you suddenly look so full of misgivings?* Damn it, maybe bringing London folk had been a mistake, but he had not wanted to marry her in an underhand fashion, as though he had something to hide.

"It will be easier all around if we are legally wed before I carry you off to the wilds of Cornwall," he murmured, squeezing her hands lightly. "For traveling purposes, your reputation and mine."

Her eyes looked searchingly into his and Jeremy steeled himself to look honorable and dependable, two ideals he had never aspired to live up to.

"Of course," she agreed, but he could see her heart wasn't in it. He felt a pang in his own. "You had better go inside," she said. Jeremy hesitated. She would not bolt, would she? Suddenly, he was the one flooded with doubt. Emmeline held out her hand to Teddy and they clasped hands. "We won't be far behind you," she reassured him with a brave smile.

Jeremy gazed at her intently, found he believed her, and only then turned and headed up the church steps.

The ceremony went off without a hitch, though his bride's fingers clutched sporadically at his sleeve, and she did not look so much blooming, as frozen stiff. Jeremy found himself profoundly grateful that Emmeline spent the whole time facing forward and did not gaze about at the strange mix of guests he had assembled. He was wondering now about the wisdom of that.

It could not last, of course. As Jeremy whisked her out to his waiting carriage, he was sure she was afforded many glimpses of the assembled company. He saw her nod at Fulsham beaming ear to ear and accompanied by his two gossiping sisters, and how her eyes widened at the huge plumage of feathers atop the hat of Jeremy's sour-faced godmother, Lady Wickford.

He helped Emmeline inside their carriage and climbed in behind her, slamming the door shut as the window was pelted with rice. "The Guild Hall, Juggins!" he called and the carriage lurched off. He held a hand up and smiled at their well-wishers.

"Is that *Lily Skellern*?" Emmeline asked in a dazed voice, staring out of the window.

"Technically her name is Arbuthnot now," Jeremy reminded her. Lily Arbuthnot looked as though she was suffering from indigestion. Jeremy smiled at the memory of delivering her invitation. He had been sure to give that one by hand. She had looked as though she might pass out from the shock.

"And who is that stood next to her?"

"Her husband, the banker probably."

"No, the other woman!" Emmeline said wildly. "She looks somehow familiar, but I cannot quite place her…"

Jeremy glanced out of the window. "Ah, you mean Mrs. Laverdale, your neglectful London sponsor." Emmeline made a choking sound in her throat. "You haven't swallowed any rice, have you?" he asked in sudden concern.

She ignored this, dragging her veil out of her face. "What on *earth* is she doing here in Bath?"

"Naturally, I invited her to witness the fruition of our little romance. After all, the majority of it was conducted under her nose, was it not?"

Emmeline sank back into her seat, an expression of horror on her pretty face. "My lord, you *didn't*!" she uttered faintly. "How could you *do* such a thing?"

"You must call me Jeremy now," he said firmly. "And naturally I wanted all interested parties invited. Is that so strange?"

"But she always—" She bit off her words, turning red.

"She always discouraged you from allowing my attentions?" he suggested lazily.

Emmie huffed but would not answer. At least her color had returned. "What about Hannah? We have left her behind and she knows no one."

"I hired a second carriage. Atherton will escort her and Teddy to the wedding breakfast."

She looked for a moment rather mutinous, opening her mouth and then shutting it again.

"Is it the mention of Atherton or the wedding reception that offends you so?" he asked lightly.

"I am not offended," she said, though if Jeremy was any judge of character, she was far from pleased. Two spots of color were burning in her cheeks and her eyes were bright. "Though if Lord Atherton is rude or sarcastic to my dearest friend, I will never forgive him!"

Jeremy paused. Had Atherton acted thus to her all those years ago? The inference was clear. "There is a vast difference between nineteen and twenty-nine, Emmeline. Gervais was—we were both callow youths at your coming out. Neither one of us conducts ourselves now as we did then."

She gave a brief nod and turned her head to gaze steadfastly out of the window. Once again, Jeremy found himself wondering uneasily if a quiet ceremony in Penarth would have been the better choice. They duly arrived at the Guild Hall, and he led Emmeline inside. Attendants escorted them to the grander of the function rooms which he had hired for the purpose.

Glancing around, he gave his nod of approval seeing all had been arranged as he had ordered. The elaborate three-tiered cake had arrived and was sat pride of place at the high table, the silverware and best china shone under the glittering chandeliers, and large arrangements of flowers matching the bridal bouquet had been placed strategically about the room.

"What do you think?" he asked Emmeline.

"It all looks vastly elegant, my lord," she answered, peering up at the Queen's state portrait in her coronation robes.

"Shall we welcome our guests here?" he asked, glancing around at the backdrop the heavy velvet curtains made. Emmeline hurriedly agreed as they both turned, hearing approaching footsteps. It proved to be Atherton, escorting Miss Pinson and Teddy. Fortunately for his marital accord, they all seemed to be getting along famously.

"Oh, how beautiful this all is!" Miss Pinson exclaimed, looking around the room, pink-cheeked with excitement.

Jeremy was gratified. "Have you seen the cake, Miss Pinson?" he asked. "The icing is inscribed with our entwined initials."

"Oh, it's wonderful," Miss Pinson breathed. "Why, it's the tallest one I've seen, and what are those figures sculpted along the edges?"

"Cherubim and seraphim," Jeremy explained.

"Signifying our union is blessed by heaven above?" Emmeline hazarded, a faint note of sarcasm in her voice.

"Exactly."

"You must stand here next to me, Miss Pinson," Atherton informed her when she looked as though she would wander off for a closer look at the cake. "As part of the bridal party we must welcome the guests together."

"Oh, of course, Lord Atherton," she said, hurrying back to stand in their line.

"I will hold your umbrella, Miss Pinson," Teddy volunteered.

"Oh, would you?" She handed it over at once, not suspecting that it would be instantly transformed into a lance or a rapier blade. "So kind."

Jeremy eyed his son suspiciously, but Teddy gazed back, his eyes wide and innocent. Experience had taught him this was when to be most on his guard where his son was concerned.

"Lord and Lady Faris will receive their guests through here," they heard a voice announce portentously, and the doors were thrown wide. The string quartet set up in the far corner struck up a tune.

Truth be told there were only about forty guests, so it was far from a large affair. Fulsham's sisters were the most amiable for they were thrilled to have been invited. In Bath for their mother's health, they had not expected a wedding to brighten their stay.

One of them was not even out yet and the other only twenty-one. They were in raptures over Emmeline's embroidered veil and quite convinced that April was the finest month of all for weddings, despite the ever-present threat of rain.

"I hope I meet someone in my first season that never forgets me," Miss Dorothea confided as she sighed over Emmeline's engagement ring. "I hope you do not mind, but Lawrence told us all about it." She sent a fleeting glance at her brother.

"We thought it was wonderful," her older sister added quickly when Emmeline looked startled by this remark. "How you ran into one another again in Bath a decade later and reignited old flames."

"Oh, er, quite," Emmeline replied in a strangled voice.

"How could I ever forget her?" Jeremy asked, his eye on Emmeline's flushed profile.

"Oh look, Amabel!" Miss Dorothea exclaimed. "The wedding band also has stones set directly into the gold band."

The sisters bent over Emmeline's hand. "A diamond, a sapphire, and another diamond," puzzled Miss Amabel. "Is there a special significance, my lord?"

"Sapphires signify love, or so my jeweler informed me, and diamonds forever," he supplied.

"Ohhhh," the young ladies caroled.

After they had moved along, shepherded by their brother, it was the Arbuthnots' turn to felicitate them. "Ah, here you are," Jeremy greeted them. "*So* glad you could make it. It just would not have been the same without Mrs. Arbuthnot in attendance, after she was so instrumental in bringing the two of us back together." He passed a proprietary arm about his bride.

Mr. Arbuthnot seemed surprised by this news. "Is that so, Lily?" he asked, turning to his wife.

Lily's fixed smile looked as though it pained her by this point. "It was nothing, really," she said shrilly.

"I assure you it is true," Jeremy continued heartily. "If not for our kind benefactress here, I would never have dreamed that my Emmeline was in the vicinity and, lucky for me, still unwed."

"Well, you've remedied that situation, by Jove!" Arbuthnot said and laughed jovially. His wife gripped his arm so tightly he winced. "Well, congratulations," he added lamely, and they moved along the line to be quizzed by Teddy on why their son had not accompanied them.

Next up was Jeremy's godmother, who was still stiff with affront that the wedding had not taken place in London. She offered her best wishes without thawing and the only time she cracked a smile was when informing him with malicious glee that she had told Lady Tipton she was attending the ceremony today.

"Is she still in London?" he asked breezily. "I would have thought family matters might have taken her to the Continent."

Lady Wickford's eyes gleamed with appreciation. "I believe she has sent her sister to try and mitigate matters there," she said before moving off. Jeremy shot a quick look at Emmeline, but she did not appear to be attending.

Luckily the line of well-wishers was not very long, and the next dozen or so passed along without incident. Then Jeremy heard Emmeline draw in a quick breath.

"Ah, Mrs. Laverdale," he greeted the lady as she gave her curtsey. She took great pains to explain she had recently remarried and was accompanied by her new husband, a Major Smith. Presumably the woman had a thing for military men. Introductions were made all around.

Smith looked like a bounder of the first order with his huge sideburns and air of forced gaiety. Jeremy was not sure if it was Emmeline's decolletage he was ogling or her pearls. "Still not sure how it is you all know each other," Smith admitted after giving his bow. "Not related, the wife tells me."

"No," Jeremy answered firmly. "Most assuredly not. You see, your wife was entrusted by the late Mr. Ballentine to oversee my wife's introduction to polite society. Ensure she was not exposed to any undesirable elements, that sort of thing."

Major Smith gave a gusty laugh. "That's a good one, Mariah!" he joked. "Hard to imagine you in the role of protectress. I expect you were off flirting when you should have been standing guard!"

Mrs. Smith née Laverdale forced a rather mirthless laugh. "I was little more than a girl myself at the time," she insisted, though to Jeremy's reckoning she must have been at least thirty. "Little did I know that I would attend Miss Ballentine's wedding ten years later," she said, sending a fleeting glance Emmeline's way. "I hardly dreamed…" Her words trailed off. "Well, how could I?"

"This must be quite a trip down memory lane for you, seeing the two of us together again," Jeremy said, reaching across to brush a wayward lock of hair from Emmeline's face. "Quite like old times, is it not?"

"As you say, my lord," Mrs. Smith agreed after an awkward pause. "You were always sure to, well, pay your little *attentions* to Miss Ballentine, as it were."

Jeremy's smile broadened. "I certainly was," he agreed. "I'm sure you were not the only one to notice my partiality."

"Of course, if I had realized the serious nature of them, I would have encouraged them at the time," she replied defensively.

"Well, you certainly did not *discourage* them as far I was concerned," Jeremy answered, making her bridle. "I scarcely remember your presence. Except perhaps for that one time," he said, frowning with the effort of remembrance. "Now let me think, when was it. Ah! I have it. The occasion of the Hawfords' ball. I was coming out of the conservatory, and I recall opening the door and you practically fell in a heap at my feet. You must have been searching for Emmeline, I suppose."

Mrs. Smith turned quite crimson. Unfortunately, so did Emmeline.

"I expect you were peeping in at the keyhole, eh, Mariah?" Major Smith joked, jostling his wife in the ribs.

"George!" Mrs. Smith expostulated crossly.

"It was all such a long time ago," Emmeline said, coming into the fray. "I am sure I do not know how we can be expected to remember such things. So much water has passed under the bridge since then."

Mrs. Smith said with an awkward laugh, "Oh, I quite agree, Lady Faris!"

"Well, well, all turned out as it should have," Jeremy reflected philosophically. He picked up Emmeline's hand and carried it to his lips. "Fortunately for me."

"You are enjoying this a bit too much," Emmeline murmured as the Smiths moved away. She reclaimed her hand. "Kindly stop torturing our guests."

"I? You wound me. Have I not laid on every comfort and indulgence for their entertainment?"

Emmeline smiled and nodded at the next in line. "Thank you so much," she murmured in response to their congratulations. "So kind." As they drifted away, she whispered in an undertone, "Just because you ply them with champagne and lobster salad does not mean you can be unpardonably rude!"

"My dear Emmeline, there is also mayonnaise of salmon and veal and ham pie! Pray do not minimize my efforts to provide for our guests."

"I am sure there is also jelly and blancmange!" she retorted with spirit, "but that does not mean you are at liberty to—!"

Atherton leaned forward at this point and interrupted them. "Lord, is that the last of them?" he asked with a shudder. "Far be it from me to comment on your choice of wedding guest, but *really*, Faris."

"Just consider yourself fortunate that you are seated at the high table with the likes of Miss Pinson," Jeremy replied.

"Believe me, I do!" Atherton responded with feeling. He turned to Emmeline's friend. "Shall we go and find our seats, Miss Pinson?" he asked, presenting his arm. "I am convinced we are stood in a draught here and shall catch our deaths if we linger any longer."

"*I* am escorting Miss Pinson, not you!" piped up Teddy, sounding aggrieved. "After all, I am the one carrying her umbrella!" As he dropped it twice whilst arguing, Jeremy could not help but feel his son failed to prove his point.

"We can *both* escort Miss Pinson," Atherton replied firmly, and they moved away, one on each side of her, with poor Miss Pinson doing her best to avert a full-blown row.

"I think I have the beginnings of a headache," Emmeline said faintly.

"You are likely just thirsty," Jeremy said. "Come, let us be seated." He towed her in the direction of the high table and saw her comfortably seated. Miss Pinson and Teddy were sat to his left and Atherton was sat to Emmeline's right. Seeing the wan smile Emmeline bestowed upon his friend, he wondered if he should have balked tradition and insisted the bridal couple were seated separately to the rest of the wedding party.

"Fetch us some lemonade for this table," he instructed a server who had just finished handing around several glasses of champagne.

"Some water also," Emmeline requested quickly. "I'm afraid I am not fond of lemonade."

"It's not for you, it's for me," he said, passing her a glass of champagne.

"I don't really like champagne either," she admitted. "Water will do very well for me."

"All the more champagne for myself and Miss Pinson," Atherton commented, toasting them both with his glass.

"Miss Pinson and I believe ginger beer is the superior drink," Teddy announced. "Do you like ginger beer, Miss Ballentine?"

"She is not Miss Ballentine any longer, you loathsome brat," Atherton pointed out affably. "You must henceforth address her as Mama."

"I would by no means insist on such a form of address so soon," Emmeline put in hastily. "If your father is agreeable, then I would be glad if you would call me Emmie."

Teddy looked at him inquiringly and Jeremy nodded in assent. "You do not call her Emmie though," his son pointed out. "You call her Emmeline."

"A force of habit. She will always be Emmeline to me."

Emmeline frowned but did not argue the point. The waiter reappeared with carafes of water and lemonade and Emmeline drank her water while Jeremy stood up to formally welcome their guests and bid them eat.

Large decorated platters of roasted fowl and garnished tongue were brought out and set alongside the salads. The guests started conversing among themselves and Jeremy urged Miss Pinson to sample the dishes widely, and not limit herself only to his son's favorites.

Deducing Miss Pinson was not a lover of ginger beer, whatever his son might say, Jeremy set her untouched glass aside and called for another which he filled from his own pitcher of lemonade. Miss Pinson was pathetically grateful for the attention, and Jeremy turned back to his bride to hear Atherton explaining who Lady Wickford was.

"She lives in Grosvenor Square. Husband's a Member of Parliament. He's not here today though," Atherton said, glancing around. "Probably couldn't drag him away from London."

"She's by way of an aunt of mine. My father's younger stepsister," Jeremy said, interrupting their conversation. "Wickford's damnably careful of his reputation so you probably won't meet him until we've been married a decade, and any scandal died down."

"Oh," Emmie whispered.

"As for Aunt Louisa"—he pulled a face—"she made her feelings on the matter plain. A member of the family must be present to legitimize the union. She saw it," he said grandly, "as a matter of duty."

"Is she your only family?" Emmeline asked. "I'm afraid I have none to bring to the table myself, not even a long-lost cousin."

"No," he answered. "I have a sister, who I would far rather have here, but Mina has not long had a baby so she would not venture far from home at this time. She lives in Cornwall; you will meet her there."

The lavish spread was partaken of, and Jeremy was pleased to see that Emmeline had a good meal, trying some of everything on offer and tucking in heartily to her plate. Dishes were replenished all around them and once the savories were done, they were replaced with sweets such as savoy cake, meringues, and cream trifle.

"*I* have a cousin now," Teddy was telling Miss Pinson in his high, carrying voice. "His name is really Baby James, but my uncle Nye always calls him Jimmy."

Miss Pinson nodded. "Just as your name is Edward, I suppose, but everyone calls you Teddy."

"'Zackly," Teddy agreed through a mouthful of Bavarian cream.

"I did not realize just how hungry I was," Emmeline said at last, sitting back in her seat with a sigh.

"Will you have some cheese?" he asked, drawing her attention to a platter of various varieties surrounded by an arrangement of wafer biscuits. "I wish I had grapes for you, but it is too early. Still, we grow them in the hothouse at Vance Park so you will have them in late summer."

"Grapes for me?" she asked, looking startled.

"Yes, for I remember you had a fondness for them."

Emmeline blinked at him. "When did I—?"

"It was at some party." He shrugged. "They had bunches of Black Hamburg, and you were excited to try them."

She gave a short laugh. "No doubt displaying my gaucheness to one and all," she said lightly.

"I did not find it gauche."

"Yet you probably laughed at the time."

"Probably," he agreed after a pause, refilling her water glass, for she had not touched her champagne. "Are you sure I cannot tempt you to try some of this syllabub? Or some of this rhubarb compote? You have not yet sampled all the desserts on offer."

"I do not think I could fit in any more," she said regretfully. "You were right, you provided a veritable feast for your guests."

He smiled at her. "And yet I thought only of you, Emmeline," he admitted in a low voice, making her blush.

"Dear me," drawled Atherton, "I suppose it must be about time for speeches."

7

Emmie suffered agonies throughout the speeches. Despite the fact that both the groom's and Lord Atherton's groomsman's speeches were nothing but highly complimentary toward her, she felt on tenterhooks the whole time, as though waiting for the axe to fall.

If their tone should turn mocking, she felt with increasing dread, it would destroy her. And then what should she do? She could hardly flee from the reception room, a stumbling, incoherent mess. She had not even done that ten years ago.

No, she had stood there, frozen with humiliation, her lips still swollen from his kisses as Jeremy Vance had announced his engagement to another woman. God, she could still remember now how utterly shattered she had felt. For a moment, it had been a close thing that she would not faint at the foot of Lady Hawford's staircase. Her head had certainly swum, and her ears had rung. Wouldn't that just have been the crowning indignity? Thank heaven she had managed to keep her head.

She would just have to do the same today, she told herself. Keep breathing and keep sane, even while he lifted his glass to her and pronounced himself proud to call her his wife. *Proud.* As if she could ever believe such a thing. How *could* she have put herself in such a situation again? she wondered with mounting panic as the toast was echoed by all and sundry. *"To Emmeline."*

What a joke. Even the name. No one called her that. No one had *ever* called her that. Yet her father had been insistent that for her coming out, she would be known by her christened name "among all the fine folk." He had not anticipated all the tittering behind fans that her rhyming name would cause. *Emmeline Ballentine.*

Sounds rather like a nursery rhyme character was what Lord Atherton had announced once at a garden party in his well-bred, bored voice. Everyone had laughed and Emmeline had pretended not to hear him. *Like someone who lives in a shoe or rolls down hills or something equally absurd.*

Then Emmie had been subjected to a lot of very silly comments for weeks, like *Have you any wool?* or *Sitting in the corner again, Miss Ballentine? I vow your name should be Jack Horner!* Of course, it had not been Lord Atherton who had carried on the jest. In his aloof way, he most likely had been barely aware of it. He had certainly thought her beneath his notice for the most part.

He had spawned such comments though, and she blamed him for the whole debacle. Remembering how heartily she detested his supercilious manner and unspeakable hauteur, she felt rather sick. Would she be expected to mingle with him on a regular basis now she was Lady Faris? Horrible thought!

Stupid of her not to anticipate such social obligations as part of her new role. Lord Atherton had always been thick as thieves with her new husband. Somehow, though, the way Jeremy had spoken of his tarnished reputation, she had imagined him quite estranged from his former circle of elites.

No doubt his former wife was the one ostracized, she reflected darkly. She had not received a good impression of Amanda Liversedge during their debut. The glittering beauty had seemed cold and standoffish, and Emmie did not think she had bothered to exchange a single word with the daughter of a city trader.

Still, she had not gone out of her way to persecute Emmie, which was something she could not say of her former husband. Emmie's husband now. Oh God, what *had* she done? It had been bad enough all those years ago, but at least she had youth then to excuse her arrant stupidity. This time around she did not even have that! She felt like the worst kind of fraud sat among all this company decked in satin, diamonds, and pearls.

She was a fraud! Half the people here thought her a cossetted bride. God only knew what the other half thought. Perhaps they thought her father's brass had finally bought her a title? Or would they be only too aware of the sad demise of Ballentine's Trading Company?

Lily Skellern certainly knew, or whatever she was called nowadays. Emmie had seen her about the streets of Bath many times and been summarily snubbed by her at any time these past two years. Lily would certainly not keep any secrets for her sake. She would glory in telling anyone who asked.

Then again, the likes of Fulsham's sisters might find that heightened the romance, with her being swept off her feet and rescued from poverty. So perhaps Lily would not tell people after all. They would likely *not* find it romantic how she had been engaged for years to a married man though, she thought with a sudden clarity.

What if the likes of Lily Skellern ever found out about Humphrey? a nasty, cold little voice whispered in her head. What if people found out that Emmie had been strung along for *years* by a man who had never harbored the smallest intention of marrying her? A cold shiver passed down her spine. That certainly would be humiliating.

Then again, it was unlikely that Jeremy would have told even Atherton about that. At least, she hoped to God he had not. The fewer people who knew about that the better. A smattering of applause broke out, and Emmie realized she had not been attending to the close of Atherton's speech.

Her eyes sought out Pinky, who was still smiling and nodding, so it could not have been anything to her detriment. In fact, it seemed the speeches were finally at an end, thank goodness. The murmur of conversation started up and the quartet started to play once more. She jumped when Jeremy's hand slid over hers to cut the first slice of the wedding cake.

"You feel cold, Ballentine," he murmured as they cut into the firm plum cake. For some reason, the fact he still called her that was strangely comforting. Everyone clapped, and attendants stepped forward to take over the distribution of the cake. "Hopefully the dancing will warm you up."

"Dancing?"

"I have requested a couple of waltzes to start. I don't know why you look like that, you were always a good dancer," he had the nerve to say.

Emmie did not see how that could be true when she had been so oblivious the whole time to her own footwork. She had a nasty suspicion she had spent the whole time staring at his face filled with equal parts terror and happiness. Lord, how she wished she could just forget her former folly.

"I have not had much occasion for dancing these past few years," she admitted as he led her into the middle of the room. Their guests were all drifting now in that direction to watch them.

"Well, if you permit yourself to be led by me, I will be content," he answered with a smile. Emmie felt all of a jitter. It was like the years had fallen away. All day she had had one foot in the past and one in the present. Dancing with him again seemed to really compound the sensation. She steeled herself as he passed his arm about her.

"Well, this takes me back," he said with a decided glint in his eye. Emmie did not respond; her eyes were darting about the circle of people forming around them. "Forget them," he said softly. "Ready?" She gave a terse nod, and they began to glide around the floor. "You see?" he encouraged her. "You are still as light on your feet as ever."

"Well, I have not yet trampled on yours if that's what you mean," she said dampeningly.

His smile broadened. "It's been too long since I held you in my arms, Ballentine."

"Now you sound *very* like Count Stefano," Emmie told him. "Next you will tell me you like a woman with spirit."

He laughed. "Why not? For all his failings, I daresay you preferred the wicked count to that milksop Fernando."

Emmeline almost missed her step. "You have not—? No, you could not have…" She faltered.

"Read it? But of course I have. I went straight to the bookshop and secured a copy. I read it avidly every night during my London sojourn. I made notes to discuss it at great length with you."

"You did not!" Emmie protested. "How could you even have deduced the title?"

"Are you impressed? It was not so very hard once I had the villain's name."

"Well…I suppose I am a little taken aback that you would go to such trouble."

"It was no trouble at all. I would go to much greater lengths, I assure you. Besides, we must have something I can discuss amicably with Miss Pinson during our four-day journey to Penarth. I can see she still distrusts me, and I need to win her over."

"I don't know about that," Emmie answered without thinking. "She told me the other day that she now considers you more in the light of a Fernando."

Jeremy gave a choked laugh. "Me? The tortured artist?"

"I think it was more that she now considers Humphrey a villain," she confessed in low tones.

"Ah, I *see.*" He nodded. "Yes, that makes more sense. So, I am redeemed by comparison alone."

"I told her she had it all quite wrong," she said dismissively.

His eyebrows rose. "So Humphrey, then, is *not* a villain in your book?" he asked.

Emmie shot a quick look about them. "My lord!" she protested, though mercifully, other couples were now taking to the floor and diverting attention away from them.

He did not take his eyes from her face. "Answer the question, if you please."

"Neither of you are remotely Fernando-like, as far as I am concerned," she said, pressing her lips firmly together.

"I suppose that is fair," he said. "In any case, you are quite right, this is not a fit topic for our wedding day." He glanced across the floor. "Just a warning, you will need to prepare yourself. Your next dance is with Atherton."

Emmie managed to keep her expression a careful blank. "Yes, so I supposed," she lied. She had not even considered the possibility.

He gave a short laugh. "Careful, Ballentine, you will make me jealous. I'm starting to think you dislike him more than you do me."

She struggled a moment to answer, and then gave up altogether, staring instead at his cravat until the number ended.

"I believe we must swap partners now," Atherton interrupted them, and Emmie was surprised to see he had been dancing with Pinky. She scanned her friend's face but was relieved to find no signs of discomfort in her expression.

"Of course," Jeremy responded, standing aside, and offering his hand to Pinky. "Miss Pinson."

"Lord Faris," Pinky responded, curtseying.

"Lady Faris," Atherton said. Emmie accepted Lord Atherton's gloved hand and the next number began. "Well, well," he said at last, perhaps realizing she was not going to break the silence. "Here we are again." His lips twisted. "Another waltz. Another dance floor."

"I do not believe we have ever danced together before, my lord," Emmie answered truthfully.

"You can hardly be surprised at that."

She sent a rather cool look up at him. "Because I was such a wallflower, you mean?" It was true, her dance card had been far from crowded in those days. Still, it was pretty rude of him to bring that up now.

"Because I did not wish to get my neck wrung," he answered laconically. "Perhaps you are unaware of Charlie Symond's fate."

Emmie considered this. "I do vaguely remember a Mr. Symonds," she admitted. "He had very curly hair did he not? And perhaps an older sister married to a sir someone or other...?"

Atherton gave a short laugh. "Ask your husband to refresh your memory about him sometime."

Emmie narrowed her gaze at him suspiciously. "You are annoyingly tall, my lord," she said at last. "I am going to get a crick in my neck trying to converse with you and maintain eye contact at the same time."

He smirked. "You clearly prefer a partner of only middling height," he commented. "Fortunate considering your choice of husband."

What choice? thought Emmie. Mind you, Humphrey was not a tall man either, so maybe he did have a point. "You are Teddy's godfather, I understand?" she asked, casting about for something to say.

"I am, for my sins."

"Do you often visit Vance Park?" she asked, gazing over his left shoulder. *Please say no. Please say no. Please say…*

"Not as often as I should," he admitted. "Jeremy's last viscountess made the prospect a chore. Perhaps you will make the occasion a less onerous one."

"How did she…?" Emmie bit her lip. Good manners dictated that she should not ask.

"Oh, tantrums, mostly," Atherton replied vaguely. "And the occasional indecent proposition. She quite put me to the blush at times." Emmie beheld him speechlessly. "Quite so," he said with a faint smile, as though she had voiced her astonishment aloud. "I must confess your union after all this time seems almost too good to be true."

"Does it really seem that way to you?" she asked in surprise.

"Of course. And to Faris it must seem providential that you have landed in his lap this way." Emmie stiffened with suspicion; she could not help it. "Let us face it, his partiality for you was always decidedly indecent."

"I'm sure I don't know what you mean, my lord!" Emmie spluttered.

"Don't you?" He sounded faintly surprised. "Do you mean to tell me you thought his conduct in those days was in any way permissible in polite society? Pursuing you in that marked manner, I mean."

Emmie had to take a steadying breath before answering. "Honestly?" she enquired calmly. "I thought he was dallying with me. Gentlemen do sometimes, as I understand it."

"Dallying?" Atherton gave a short laugh. "I suppose it might have counted as dalliance the first or second time he sought you out," he said judiciously, "but by the fourth or fifth occasion? I think not."

"Mrs. Laverdale always maintained he was toying with me," Emmie said with unaccustomed frankness.

"Laverdale? Was that your chaperone?" he asked with a faint frown. "I must say, I vastly prefer the one you have these days."

"Mrs. Laverdale was my sponsor during my season only."

"Well, whoever she was, she was most remiss in her duties," Atherton said damningly.

"Perhaps she thought I deserved a little excitement to get me through the ordeal of it all," Emmie said with a brittle smile.

"If she thought anything, it was that putting Jeremy in his place was above her pay grade," he answered dryly.

"Well," Emmie said briskly. "It is all in the past now in any event."

"Is it?" He gave her a keen look.

"We are married now," she pointed out doggedly. "So, his past intentions hardly seem to matter."

"If that were the case then you would not be holding him at arm's length, now, would you?"

Emmie pressed her lips together. She ought not to answer him. The whole conversation was most improper. Instead, she heard herself ask quietly, "Do you blame me?"

"No," he admitted. "Not for that."

"So, then you *do* lay some fault at my door?" she said accusingly.

He paused. "Perhaps. Do you think me unfair?"

"I do!" she said forthrightly. He gave a short laugh. "But then, you are his friend, are you not? So, I suppose it is perfectly natural that you would take his part."

He did not answer immediately, but when he did, he surprised her. "I believe I should like to stand your friend, too, someday, if you would ever allow it," he said, sounding a little surprised about the fact himself.

"Really?" She was startled. "Why?"

"At the end of the day, I find I quite like you," he answered with a shrug. "Despite my initial feelings on the matter."

"And by that, I suppose you mean that ten years ago you thought me a vulgar upstart?"

A smile tugged at his lips. "I cannot deny it. I was a detestable youth. Besides, I was alarmed by my friend's reaction to you. He completely lost his head over you. I see now that it was wrong of me to blame you for that, but at the time…" He shrugged.

"At the time you did not hesitate to lay the blame at my door."

"I did not," he admitted. "In my youthful arrogance, I felt entirely justified. Of course, now I see you were just as much a victim as he." Emmie huffed incredulously but before she could speak, he carried on smoothly. "It was hardly your fault that you embodied his every physical ideal. It was just an unfortunate circumstance."

"His every—?" Emmie stared at him.

"Of course. Do not tell me you still stand in ignorance of this fact because I will not believe you. He was attracted to you, like a moth to the flame, and I believe you were in much the same condition." When she looked as though to deny this, he gave her a dry look. "You always lit up like a beacon whenever you clapped eyes on him."

Emmie closed her eyes briefly. "Well, I was young and…"

"In love?" he suggested.

"Unaccustomed to hiding my feelings," she corrected him primly.

He nodded, "To one such as Jeremy, it must have been a heady combination. I never suspected it as a callow youth, but I think he has always been…" His mouth twisted as he searched for the word.

"What?" Emmie asked, unable to resist.

"Left out in the cold, as it were," Atherton concluded whimsically.

Emmie found this hard to believe. "By whom?"

"Oh…everyone. You never met his father, did you?"

"No."

"No, he buried himself in Cornwall most of the time. He was the taciturn type. Always glowering and snarling at everyone. Jeremy took after his departed mother in looks and his father never quite forgave him for it."

She did not know how to respond to this. Her own father had always been disappointed Emmie had not been a dainty beauty like her mama. She *had* taken after her father's side of the family, but he had not liked her any better for it.

"Well, in any case, things have worked out for the best, much the same as if the natural conclusion had been drawn all those years ago."

"Natural conclusion?" Emmie's mouth was dry. Her voice sounded like a croak at this point. He could not be saying what she thought he was saying. That Jeremy had been just as taken by her as she had been with him? Her head whirled. This could not be true. She was misconstruing his words, surely?

"Why, that you would have been married ten years ago, of course."

Emmie was just reflecting that Lord Atherton was as alarming nowadays as he had ever been when Jeremy reclaimed her. After ascertaining she did not wish to join the quadrille, he led her back to the table where Teddy was sat rubbing his eyes. "You are tired, my son," Jeremy said, peering into his face.

"No, I'm not," Teddy responded, trying to smother a yawn.

"He has been taking early nights since his illness," he explained as an aside.

"Very sensible," Emmie responded promptly.

"I think we shall have to get him back to his bed."

"I'm not tired," Teddy insisted irritably.

Jeremy shot a level look at her. "You would not object to us cutting our celebrations short?"

"Of course not. We cannot have Teddy suffering a setback in his recovery." It suddenly occurred to her that she had no idea what the plan was for their wedding night. Would she sleep at her own lodgings or accompany him to his? And what of Pinky? Was she to return to Winkworth Street alone?

"Give me one moment," Jeremy said, and Emmie saw that Atherton and Pinky were also exiting the dance floor. He and Atherton had a quick discussion as Pinky took a seat next to Emmie.

"The child looks very flushed," she whispered in concern.

"Yes, his father is just arranging to take him home."

Pinky nodded with approval as Jeremy returned to Emmie's side. "You and Miss Pinson are to take my carriage back to Winkworth Street and I will join you later. First, I mean to take Teddy back and see him settled. Come, we will walk down together."

Emmie and Pinky both rose and followed behind as Jeremy lifted his still-protesting son and carried him across the room. Emmie noticed that Teddy's protestations did not last long, and by the time they had navigated the corridors and stares, his head lolled against his father's shoulder.

Emmie was profoundly grateful that no great leave-taking was expected of the bride and groom and that slipping away early was considered perfectly natural newlywed behavior.

"Emmie, you have no cloak," Pinky whispered as they retrieved her coat from the attendants below.

"This veil is just as voluminous as a cloak," Emmie responded. "Don't worry." Still, there was a decided nip in the air when they emerged into the street outside.

They soon spotted the carriage, and made for it, Colfax climbing down from beside the driver to open the door for them.

"Get a rug from under the seat for Lady Faris," Jeremy instructed. Teddy was now fast asleep in his arms. Colfax retrieved a blanket and set it on the seat before handing first Emmie and then Pinky into the carriage. "Wrap it around your shoulders," Jeremy advised, looking in. He watched Pinky help swath her in the blanket before turning back to Colfax. "Make sure you see them both inside," he said and then stepped back.

The carriage pulled away and Emmie turned her head to watch her new husband walk toward a second carriage with Lord Atherton. "He said he will join me later," Emmie said into the darkness of the carriage.

"Oh! At Winkworth Street?" Pinky sounded a little startled but then, quickly added, "After all, well, it *is* your wedding night, dear."

"Yes," Emmie agreed.

"And am I right in thinking we embark on the journey to Cornwall tomorrow?"

"Yes, tomorrow?" Emmie agreed hollowly. "Everything is moving so fast. I hope we have not overlooked anything too important."

"I said the same to Lord Atherton," Pinky admitted. "But he said we must not worry for—"

"*He* is not coming with us, is he?" Emmie asked in dismay, interrupting her.

Pinky blinked. "I do not think so," she said. "At least, I did not form that impression. Is everything alright, dear?"

"Oh yes, of course," Emmie hastened to assure her. "It's just been such a busy day. I daresay I did not take everything in."

"That is perfectly understandable, under the circumstances," Pinky replied. "I am sure my head is all of a whirl, so I cannot even begin to imagine how yours must spin! But it was such a lovely reception," she carried on wistfully. "So elegant and refined, and his lordship really thought of everything, did he not?"

"He did," Emmie agreed weakly.

Pinky gazed down at her new umbrella and gloves. "And he seems a very conscientious parent," she continued thoughtfully.

"Oh yes." Emmie was more confident in that reply.

"It is very touching to see such a bond exist between father and son."

Emmie agreed and before long they were pulling up at Winkworth Street. It was a little after nine, so they had to use Pinky's latch key to open the door. "Oh," she said, turning to Colfax. "I had better give you this for his lordship, as Florrie will have retired for the night."

Pinky turned rather red as she said this, but Colfax took the key from her wordlessly standing to one side as they entered the building. "Good night," Pinky called after him as the door closed. She still looked rather flustered. "Oh dear, I hope I did not make him feel awkward."

Emmie did not reply, for as they were climbing the stairs, she was starting to wonder if she had misheard her new husband's intention. Perhaps he had not said he would come tonight? After all, he had not repeated any such intention as the carriage had pulled away.

If they were leaving for Cornwall tomorrow, would it not make more sense for them all to have an early night? And why on earth would he want to spend a night at her lodgings, which were now barer and less welcoming than ever. Most of the furniture had been shipped and a good deal of her possessions were packed away into trunks and cases.

"Will you help me out of this gown?" she asked her friend once they were inside their rooms.

Pinky hesitated. "Will you not keep it on for your groom?"

Emmie blinked. The thought had not even occurred to her. "Do you think I should? I must own I would much rather get comfortable."

"I'm sure you know best, dear," Pinky said brightly. "I just thought, as he had so clear a vision of the dress that he might, well…" Her words trailed off.

"Want to remove it himself?" Emmie asked, realizing her friend's meaning.

Pinky coughed. "Well, I don't know that I would put it quite that way, dear," she said delicately.

Emmie pulled a face. "This is not his first wedding," she reminded Pinky. "He has done all this before, so I do not think he will be too disappointed. Who knows, once he reaches his lodgings, he may find himself too tired to drag himself back across town."

Pinky looked doubtful but held her tongue, and together they managed to unfasten and remove Emmie's layers of finery until she stood, freshly scrubbed and barefoot in her worn cotton nightdress, her fancy hair arrangement undone and any vestiges of glamor long gone.

"Go and ready yourself for bed now, Pinky dear. We have so much to do tomorrow and I can see you are trying not to yawn."

Pinky kissed her cheek good night and, picking up one of the candles, made for her own room. Emmie pulled on a wrapper that was a little shabby now around the cuffs and walked over to her dresser to apply some face cream. Fortunately, they had left their bedroom furniture to be sent on last, so she was not sleeping on a mattress or living out of a packing case in this room at least.

Should she have left her hair up? Emmie wondered, gazing at her reflection. She was sure she had never dressed it half so well herself. She had always had very abundant hair, though it was sadly wayward and seldom did as it was told.

Marie, the hairdresser Madame had hired, had used a slick of pomade on her flyaway hairs and given her hair, which had a sad tendency to frizz, a semblance at least of silkiness, while the many glass hair pins had managed to keep the arrangement in place.

Now she and Pinky had removed them all, her hair was returning to its habitual cloud of reddish gold. The strong wave meant it had always grown outward rather than downward. She patted it and wondered if she should try sprinkling some water on it or plaiting it into a braid.

Then she heard it, the sound of a key turning. Picking up her candlestick, she opened her bedroom door and peered out into the corridor. Her heart thudded. It was him. He spotted her at once, a smile breaking out on his face as he approached her. She took a step back to admit him into her bedchamber.

"I changed into my nightgown," she blurted out a little defensively as she shut the door behind them.

"Very sensible of you," he answered at once. "I like this," he said, gesturing to his own shoulders.

"My hair?" she guessed after a moment's hesitation.

He nodded, his eyes wandering over her head and shoulders. "It's very luxuriant."

Luxuriant? "Oh, thank you."

"I almost wish I had not bothered to buy you all those diamond hair pins now."

"Diamond—?" Emmie shot an alarmed glance at the pile of pins she had carelessly heaped on her chest of drawers. *They were diamonds?*

"I always wondered what it would look like out of its confines," he murmured, coming closer. "May I?"

Emmie regarded him wide-eyed. "Of course," she said, though she had no idea what he was asking.

He reached out to hesitantly touch her springy mass of curls, a fascinated look in his eye. "How do you maintain it?"

"Maintain it?" She gave a short laugh. He stood practically toe-to-toe with her and was only a head taller than she. "It grows this way," she admitted.

"I suppose this effect would take hours to achieve with a curling tong and papers," he mused, running his hand lightly over her head.

"I would not know. Pinky achieves her ringlets with rags, but I've never needed to encourage mine to curl."

His hand slid around to cup her cheek. "Have you completed your toilette?" he asked, glancing toward her dresser.

"Yes," she said, if by that he meant had she cleaned her teeth and applied some cream on her face. She had bought some new lotion now her purse was plumper, but she did not have half the ladies' preparations she used to own in more affluent times. "Do you need me to give you some space to undress?" He was probably used to having his own dressing room and valet.

"No," he said, immediately divesting himself of his frock coat.

"You did not bring anything to change into?" she asked, glancing around for a bag.

"No," he repeated, tugging at his cravat. "I was far too keen to attend to such trivialities."

Emmie blinked but as he seemed unconcerned at the prospect of wearing his formal clothes again on the morrow, why should she fret? She *should* be more concerned about what he would wear to bed, she realized as he stripped off his shirt.

"Can I fetch you anything? Something to drink? Water?" she suggested, hovering near the door.

He glanced at the pretty glass bedside carafe filled with water. "You already have water," he pointed out.

"Well, yes, but there is only one glass."

"I don't mind sharing with you."

Bereft of anything else to do, Emmie retreated to the far side of the room to unfasten her wrapper. Jeremy had commandeered the only chair for his clothes, so she hung it up before turning around clad just in her nightgown. She sucked in a breath, finding Jeremy already sitting in her bed, covers drawn up to his waist.

"Don't run away, I'm entirely harmless, I swear it." He lifted his hands to show her his palms. Instead of answering, she approached the bed and drew back the covers, climbing in beside him, cheeks aflame. "Your bed isn't very wide," he commented, shifting even closer.

"I've always found it sufficiently roomy," she answered. "Though I suppose I never had a man in it before." She cleared her throat as his thigh came to rest against her own.

"Haven't you, Ballentine?" he asked quietly, but something about his tone made her turn her head and look at him. When she did not speak, he added, "After all, ten years is a long time to be engaged to someone. I won't judge if you—"

"I haven't. We didn't," she interrupted him, facing forward again. "Humphrey was not—" *Keen*, she thought. Humphrey was not keen. He had never asked to touch her hair, let alone climb into her bed. She had never really admitted this to herself, let alone anyone else. "Well," she continued lightly. "I suppose he was not such a villain as all that." Jeremy's expression hardened but he did not reply. "I was starting to wonder if I had misheard you," she said, suddenly desiring a change of subject. "And that I would not see you until morning after all."

"What?" He looked stunned.

"Well, we have a long journey ahead of us. You said it would take four days in a carriage at least. I would not have been surprised if—"

"Emmeline," he said heavily, "wild horses could not drag me from your bed tonight."

Emmie stared at him. "Oh," she said, but suddenly it was Lord Atherton's words about her embodying Jeremy's every physical ideal that echoed in her brain. He could not possibly have been telling the truth, could he?

Jeremy turned fully toward her, his movements slow and careful as the mattress shifted. "Do you remember that night at the Har—?"

Oh God no. Not Lady Hawford's ball again! "I don't want to remember!" she blurted. "Not tonight. I would much rather we made some new memories between us." Seeing his surprised expression, she decided to be reckless and press her advantage.

8

Jeremy was not really sure *what* was happening. One minute, he had been treading oh so carefully in an attempt not to startle his surprisingly virginal bride. The next, she had knocked him flat on his back, pounced on top of him, and was kissing him with an abandonment that quite took his breath away. His hands crept up to graze first her hips and then clasp tightly the slight dip of her waist.

My God, he thought. This was the Emmeline Ballentine he remembered, the one who wanted him wholeheartedly and could not hide the fact. *Thank God.* Thank God he had not lost her. He had been so afraid that eager girl was gone.

Their connection was still there, that was all that mattered. She still wanted him and he—oh God, he was still absolutely *desperate* for her. He groaned against her mouth, then made a noise of protest when she tore her lips from his. She rolled off him and lay on her side, panting and trying to catch her breath. "My God, who taught you how to kiss like that?" he had to ask, shifting forward so their bodies touched.

It was stupid to feel both scorchingly jealous and wildly appreciative at the same time. But there was not a single chance in hell it had been that cold fish Stockton. Had there been some other man with the good sense to corner her over the last ten years? If so, he wanted to kill him and shake his hand at the same time.

She gave him a funny look. "I thought we agreed not to—to mention that night," she said. He opened his mouth to point out he had agreed to nothing, she had simply bowled him over. Then the realization hit him. Was she saying that *he* was the one who had tutored her in the art of kissing, and him alone?

He reached out to her, catching her chin and gently turning her face toward him. "*Me?*" he asked with sudden urgency. "Just me, and no one else?" When she remained silent, he urged, "Tell me." Emmeline pressed her pretty lips together. She would not meet his gaze but when he did not release her, she finally relented and gave a short nod of assent.

A fire blazed in his chest. *"Emmeline,"* he whispered, feeling profoundly shaken. Pulling her back into his arms, he lowered his head and kissed her, sealing his lips to hers gently and sweetly, giving her all the care and solicitude his kisses had lacked during that stormy embrace neither of them had forgotten.

For all that they were tender, they left him no less affected than the kisses that came before, and he was sure she must be only too aware of the fact. After all, he was entirely naked, and her nightgown was worn and thin. Through its cotton, he could feel the glorious press of her rounded thighs so she could be in no ignorance of his hard, eager cock or the brazen way it pressed into her soft belly.

His hands skimmed her back before sliding around to her front, where he paused to check she made no objection before lightly cupping her full breasts. He groaned and simultaneously Emmeline let out a breathy sigh. "Can I undo this?" he asked, his fingers already settling on the uppermost button.

"Yes." Her answer was mercifully swift, and he made short work of the six mother-of-pearl buttons, slipping his hand inside the bodice and running his palm over the plump swell of her breasts.

"Oh, Emmeline," he said hoarsely, kissing her again as he made out their shape. She made a noise in her throat, part surprise, part something else. "Do you like that?" he asked, pulling back to feast his eyes on her in the candlelight.

"Yes," she murmured, half opening her eyes. "Do not stop."

He felt the smile curve his lips as he kneaded her generous breasts. Her face was flushed, and her glorious hair spread across the pillow. He would have liked to stroke the tumbled tresses if he could bear to remove his hands from her bosom.

He could not, however. So instead, he traced their peaks until his fingertips found her hardened nipples. These were just as delectable as the rest of her. She was gorgeous, he thought dazedly, like the most splendid Renaissance painting he had ever seen.

And the wonder of it was, she was still half-dressed in her dowdy nightgown. It was all wrong. She should be wearing sumptuous silk draperies, not practical cotton. He tugged down the neckline until her breasts jutted out, freed from the bodice but framed by the frilled fabric and ribbon, as though presented to him as an offering.

Emmeline gave a muffled squeak, glancing down. "Should I just take it off?" she asked, struggling up onto her elbows.

"No," he said huskily. "I like seeing them like this."

Her face was a picture. "Wh-what?"

"They look almost gift-wrapped for me," he mused, running his fingertip over her deep pink nipples. "Like a present." Emmeline's face flamed, and she looked as though she was struggling to find words. "Has anyone ever told you your breasts are magnificent, Ballentine?"

"Of course not!" She sounded scandalized, her breath coming short and fast, making her chest heave.

He bit his lip, his eyes roaming greedily over the spectacle. "Well, that's almost criminal," he lamented. "But I confess I'm selfish enough to be glad of the fact." She stared at him, all rosy and confused. "I want to suck on them. May I?"

Her mouth fell open but no sound came out. He guessed Miss Pinson's education had never covered such eventualities.

"How about we try it first, and then you decide?" he suggested, his mouth already watering at the prospect.

"Er, y-yes, very well," she assented stiltedly, her gaze sliding away. He could almost feel the heat radiating from her face.

"Brave Ballentine," he murmured with approval and flicked a nipple with his thumb. She made that startled noise in her throat again and he lowered his head to bestow soft kisses, first down the valley between the globes of her breasts, and then around their crested peaks, teasing the nipples liberally with his tongue.

Emmeline squeaked and wriggled beneath him, which only added to his pleasure. He rolled more firmly atop her, pinning her in place and rubbing his hips against hers, letting her know what was in store for her. He had never felt so hard in his life. His hands encircled her breasts, crudely squeezing as he feasted on them in turn, sucking the nipples deep into his mouth and moaning against them.

Emmeline's muffled, breathy sounds in his ears spurred him on and on until he realized he was in imminent danger of spilling against the friction of her nightgown and the warmth of her belly. He had never felt so voracious, so utterly consumed with a woman. It would all be over if he did not exercise some control.

Tearing his mouth from her, he rested his forehead against hers, breathing raggedly and praying for strength. "My God, Emmeline," he started shakily, "I knew it would be good between us but *this*. It surpasses everything. I can't wait, forgive me, my darling."

"Yes," she murmured. Yes, she forgave him for his haste? His thoughts were scattered and lust-filled as he gazed down searchingly at the blissful expression on her face. Her eyes were half shut and her lips parted. Christ, she was exquisite. He had known this at nineteen, so why had it taken him a decade to rediscover her?

Giving his head a quick shake, he shoved the disordered blankets aside and reached down for the hem of her nightgown, drawing it up and over her plump thighs. His hand trembled as he uncovered her to his gaze, still breathing hard. The hair on her pussy was an even redder gold than that on her head.

His mouth was watering again, but he did not have the forbearance to last through another round of delights at this point. He would have to postpone that pleasure. "Open your legs for me, Emmeline," he begged, his voice thick with desire.

Emmeline's legs fell apart, and Jeremy caught his breath. *Please be—* "Wet," he groaned as his fingers sought out her drenched slit. "Fuck," he enunciated distinctly, then remembered his manners. "Emmeline, you are so, so ready for me." Thank God, he thought with a rush of gratitude. Thank God that fool Stockton had not taken what was his. "Wider," he said huskily. "Bend your knees."

She did not even hesitate. Jeremy stared at the sight his fingers made, embedded in her pink, plump pussy. He felt an almost dizzying rush of blood to his head. He pumped his fingers inside her and thumbed her clitoris, spreading the wetness there.

Emmeline shifted beneath him restlessly. "Tell me what pleases you," he demanded.

"Y-you do," she whimpered. Her eyes were closed, her breathing hitched as she arched up into his fingers. God, she was responsive.

"There?" he asked, concentrating his efforts in that precise area. She bit her lip and gave a stifled moan. "Yes, I think that is the spot," he murmured, lavishing her stiff clitoris with attention. He felt a gush of wetness against his fingers.

"Oh!" she gasped. "Oh, *Jeremy*!" She stiffened, her eyes opened wide, and she stared at him as her limbs started trembling violently, her slick sheath pulsing tightly around his two fingers.

"That's it," he grunted as she came apart beautifully with a low, husky moan. *Fuck*. It was the most arousing thing he had ever seen in his life.

"Ohhhhhh!" she cried. Her cheeks were poppy red by this point and her shining eyes spilled over as she slumped in his arms, breathing hard. "Oh," she whispered again, sounding dazed.

"I like it when you say my name when you come, Ballentine," he whispered, kissing her brow. "I want you to do it again."

"Jeremy," she murmured obediently.

He smiled, hearing the languorous satisfaction in her voice, and slid his fingers out of her. They were wet with her essence, and he tasted first one and then the other before sucking them fully into his mouth. "You taste good," he observed with a groan. "I look forward to pursuing that at some later point." Emmeline blinked up at him, seemingly lost for words. "Right now, though, I am absolutely at my limit," he continued regretfully. "I, er, need my cock inside you now, if that is agreeable with you."

Emmeline's mouth opened and closed again. She could not possibly get any redder. "Oh, of course," she said in a strangled voice.

He shifted over her, letting her feel more of his weight, though he kept his hands braced on either side of her. "Emmeline," he whispered. She was delightfully warm and cushiony beneath him. Her eyes fluttered open, big, brown, and lustrous. God, she was beautiful. "Have I ever told you how much I like your eyes on me and only me?" he asked, sounding tortured even to his own ears.

"I think you did once," she said in a whisper. "Though I think you were slightly foxed at the time."

Christ, had she realized that even then? "Keep your eyes on me now," he ordered, "and your hands."

She met his eyes and slipped her arms around his back. The motion jostled her breasts against him, distracting him. Should he let her put them away? He didn't want to. Not at all. Strangely, he liked the fact her nightgown was still intact, though hitched indecently around her waist. It lent a certain something to proceedings.

"I was more than slightly foxed all the time in those days," he admitted hoarsely. "If I had not been…" He could not continue his train of thought as he slid his cock through her wet folds, slicking himself up on her. He was watchful for any sign of nervousness, but Emmeline showed none, lying pliant and warm beneath him.

His nostrils flared as he restrained himself from pushing into her. His body wanted to rut but what was left of his thoughts reminded him that she was untouched but for him. "I hope I do not hurt you," he said as the unpleasant thought occurred to him.

"It does not hurt at this moment," she answered, her voice sounding strange.

"No, but the next part might," he said, reaching down to position his cock against her warm, moist entrance. He had to bite back a moan as he felt his cockhead notch just right and start to sink into her. She was so warm and delightfully wet. Emmeline took a sharp breath, and he froze at once. "Too much?" he asked.

"No, no, all is well," she urged, squeezing her arms tight around his back.

"My brave Ballentine," he murmured, then he adjusted his hips and thrust right into her.

Her cry was drowned out by his own grunt of satisfaction as he closed his eyes to savor the feeling. He shuddered. God. It was good. It was almost too good. He could come at this moment, he realized with surprise. It would be almost a relief to just come in a rush, then lie in her arms.

He could not allow such a thing, of course. Unless she would rather it was over with. He opened his eyes and beheld her. "Emmeline?" he whispered.

Her eyes were bright with tears, but they did not fall. Instead, she gave him a shaky smile and he felt something stir in his chest. Something that had lain dormant for a long, long time. Maybe for as long as ten years.

"It only hurts a bit," she whispered, "but I do not mind it at all."

Fuck. That was all it took. He lowered his head with a gasp and came hard, emptying himself into her like a green boy with his first fuck. *What the hell?* God, the relief of it though. He could have wept. Instead, he lay there feeling dazed and oddly grateful.

After a moment, he felt Emmeline's hand hesitantly brush across his shoulder blades. He should move off her, he realized, instead of lying slumped over her like a felled oak. He *should*, but he did not want to. Not remotely. Emmeline's flesh was so soft and welcoming. He wanted to luxuriate in her forever and never to part. Still, his spent body must be heavy, and no doubt she was uncomfortable, though she voiced no objection.

At last, he mustered the strength to withdraw and roll off her, stretching out beside her on the mattress. Neither of them spoke for a long while. Then Emmeline stirred, sat up, and started rearranging her nightgown into a more decent state. "I am going to have to take a wash," she whispered almost apologetically as she did up her buttons. "Do you want to come along? I could show you where the bathroom is. It's a shared one, I'm afraid, though we should not bump into anyone at this hour."

This talk of shared bathrooms was oddly jarring. He was sorely tempted to tell her to undo her buttons and like back down again. She wanted to wash between her legs, he guessed and felt…strange about it. Still, he did not want her uncomfortable or to see her leave the room without him.

"You will have to lend me your robe," he said, "as I did not bring anything." This seemed to take her aback, but she did fetch him a velvety garment with mercifully few flounces. He guessed in the dark it might be taken for a man's. He rose from the bed, still feeling giddy and light-headed after the strength of his orgasm.

He slipped the robe on and tied the belt as Emmeline donned her slippers and a shawl and collected a drawstring bag. "Come here," he said, picking up the candle which had practically guttered and holding his other hand out to her. She took it and together they crept along the hall, unlocked the door, and then went out into the corridor beyond.

"It's this one," she whispered, halting before a door. "Will you go in first?" she asked awkwardly, for all the world as though he were her guest rather than her husband.

"I am not leaving you out here in a draughty corridor, Ballentine," he said, pulling her in behind him and fastening the door.

Emmeline seemed a little shy about sharing the contents of her toiletry bag with him, which was ridiculous considering they had just shared their bodies. Still, he did not really mind, he realized as he sniffed her rose-scented soap and inspected her face flannel as she filled the basin on the washstand from a large jug on the windowsill. There were five lined up there all in a row.

"The water's cold, I'm afraid. The copper in the scullery won't be lit until tomorrow morning."

"I'll survive a little cold water," he assured her, though the prospect of dousing himself in it was far from enticing. He wondered if she and Miss Pinson were obliged to run up and down the stairs with jugs of water to fill the bath.

There were three leaning against the wall, ranging in size. He wandered over to them, inspecting the smallest one which looked to be no more than a Parisien sponging bath, while the largest was a tub of decent size.

"Did you want to use the sponge bath?" Emmeline asked, turning her head.

"No, you're right, it's too cold right now. I should like to see you use it, though not today."

"Me?" She lowered her washcloth to stare at him in surprise.

He nodded. "Crouched over it with your hair pinned high on your head. You would look just like a bathing Venus," he said, imagining her pouring water over her plump curves, her eyes half-closed as they had been while he pleasured her with his fingers. Not in this cold, tiled bathroom though. Such a scene deserved a more luxurious setting. His own private bathroom perhaps, at Vance Park.

Emmeline colored hotly and returned to her much more practical ablutions. When she was done, he replaced her at the sink as she brushed and tamed her hair into a braid which hung over her shoulder. He watched her in the mirror as he completed his own wash.

Then they retraced their steps, the candle burning very low at this point. When Emmeline turned the key in the door to her rooms, it seemed very loud, and they exchanged a conspiratorial look, no doubt hoping they had not woken Miss Pinson.

Once they had climbed back into her bed, he reached for her at once, drawing her into his arms and brushing a stray lock of her hair from her face. He let his fingers trail down her cheek and neck, lightly tracing her rounded shoulder.

"What color would you say your hair is?" he asked in a low voice. "Sometimes it looks dark gold and other times it looks quite coppery."

"A reddish sort of light brown, I suppose," she murmured, making him frown.

"It's no such thing. It is some shade that lies between Titian red and Venetian blond," he corrected her. "Light brown indeed! When we get to Vance Park, I must show you my collection of Venuses." He looked thoughtful. "Some of them resemble you very much."

"Venuses?" He nodded. "Are they very fleshy?" she asked suspiciously, surprising a laugh out of him.

"That's the way I like them," he answered with perfect truth, sitting up to blow out the candle. He did not think he had ever been entirely honest about that before though, even to himself. Emmeline pulled a face. "I'm glad you're back in my life, Ballentine," he said impulsively. "I missed you."

Just before he extinguished the candle, he had time to register Emmeline's reaction, first surprise, then a quickly veiled disbelief. "You don't believe me?" he asked, settling back down beside her. She did not answer for a moment.

"If Lily Skellern had not mentioned me in passing to your son, I daresay you would scarcely have remembered my name," she said wistfully.

"That is simply not true," he replied, feeling stung. "And she did not 'mention you in passing.' She took great relish in telling my son of my misconduct toward you. That is an entirely different thing."

"Hmm," Emmeline murmured noncommittally.

"Had you forgotten me?" he demanded. Again, she held her tongue. "I never forgot you," he stressed. "I was just married to another woman. I assumed you would be married too." He hesitated. "You *should* have been married, by rights. But all the same," he softened his voice, "I am glad you were not."

She was so quiet, he could almost believe she had drifted off to sleep. Almost. "What position do you sleep in?" he asked her quietly, deciding to let her get away with her rebelliousness this once. Wordlessly she rolled over to face away from him and he curled around her back, settling against the warmth of her body. The physical closeness consoled him for the sudden emotional distance. He would have to bridge that gap at some later point. For now, he thanked his stars to have her in his arms once more. It was enough, he told himself. For now.

9

Jeremy slept deeply until around five in the morning when he woke and could not get back off to sleep. Finally, he gave up all attempt and rose, careful not to wake the other occupant in the bed. Emmeline was a sound sleeper it seemed, for she did not stir, even as he dressed and let himself out of her bedroom. Unless she was pretending again, of course.

He found the bathroom from the previous evening, had a quick wash and brush up and headed down the stairs, feeling somewhat disheveled in yesterday's attire. Fortunately, not even Florrie was around at this hour to let him out of the front door.

He emerged into the empty street below. Only the odd tradesman was starting his round as Jeremy started his brisk walk across town, his thoughts dwelling pleasurably on his newly married status. He had her at last. She was his and no man could put them asunder.

There had been moments in the past few weeks when he had worried that Emmeline did not feel for him as she once had. That her partiality for his company, once so obvious to all, had faded and her desire for him quite fled. But no, last night had reassured him that she still wanted him.

Her heated kisses had proved she still longed for him, even if she had learned mannerly restraint these past ten years. Restraint be damned. Jeremy wanted her to be always open and frank with him. Open and passionate and holding nothing back, like she had been that day in the conservatory when he had lost his head and thought to seize the moment with her.

God. It had nearly killed him when she had been so receptive to his kiss, so clinging and ardent when he knew as soon as it stopped that he would have to walk away from her and make that bloody announcement. No, he would not remember such bitter regret now, not when everything had finally turned out right.

What was it that Emmeline had said last night? That she would rather they made new memories? She was right. The bitter aftermath of that first kiss had likely tainted that for her, however much he treasured it. They needed to move on from the past and forge their way into the future.

Of course, he thought, his steps slowing, there *had* been that moment before the candle went out, when he had seen the doubt spring into Emmeline's eyes. She did not believe that he had missed her all these years. He supposed it might seem a strange thing to claim when he had made no attempt to contact her in a decade.

In his defense, he had been married. Unhappily married but that was beside the point. He could offer her nothing respectable, and at the end of the day he *had* respected her, even as a rakehell of nineteen. Or as near an approximation of respect that one such as he could muster.

At that moment, an inconvenient memory arose. He seemed to remember a drunken conversation with Atherton that had involved his determination to seek her father out and make the man a dishonorable offer for his daughter. He winced. Admittedly, that had been far from respectful.

Thank God, his friend had managed to dissuade him from it, pointing out her father would hardly have borne the expense of a London season for his daughter to end up a kept woman. At least he could count on Atherton to keep his mouth shut about the whole disgraceful episode.

In all fairness, he could hardly blame Emmeline for doubting his dependability. Even the manner in which he had secured her hand in marriage had been, well, *slightly* disreputable if looked at in a certain light. He frowned, considering the matter. It was true, he had not coerced her exactly, but he *had* bribed and cajoled her into it.

Would it be so very surprising if she did not wholly trust him? He acknowledged to himself that it would not. Quite frankly, she had afforded him a lot of grace, considering his past conduct toward her. He would just have to work on building Emmeline's confidence in him.

She was by nature affectionate and warm, so that was a point in his favor. He would just have to trust that, with time, she would come to trust him and that, where she was concerned, he could be depended on. His mind made up, his step once again gathered speed and before long he had reached his rented house in The Crescent.

He did not have to worry about rousing the household, for Colfax's hulking presence was already haunting the front step, dressed immaculately in his powder blue livery. Initially, Jeremy suspected the fellow was indulging in a crafty smoke, but as he drew closer, he realized he had done him wrong.

No, in fact, his footman seemed deep in thought, staring off into the distance. Jeremy had a hand to the gate before he appeared to notice him. Once he did, he straightened up with a polite "Milord."

"Good morning, Colfax. Thought I'd caught you smoking there for a minute," he added.

His footman eyed him reproachfully. "I'd step out back for that, milord. What do you think I am, some kind of savage?"

Jeremy laughed. "Well, in any case, I am glad you are not outraging our neighbors," he said flippantly. "I was informed yesterday that the lady next door is sister to a duke, no less."

Colfax lifted an eyebrow. "Oh yes," he said in noncommittal tone, but his attitude conveyed he was not remotely impressed.

"I'm starting to think our neighbor has offended you, Colfax," Jeremy observed as his footman opened the door for him.

Colfax sniffed. "It's no business of mine how your neighbors conduct themselves, milord," he answered coolly, his words dripping with disapproval.

Jeremy deduced that the duke's sister had fallen short somehow in Colfax's estimation of what constituted a "real lady." Colfax had a strange attitude when it came to that sort of thing, which sat at odd variance with his usual attitude in life.

For instance, Jeremy knew full well his footman had been raised in an East End slum and had had several brushes with the law before he had entered Jeremy's service. At the time he had hired him, he had not considered this a disadvantage, for it was useful to have a man who could back him up in a tight spot.

Living the life Jeremy had in his twenties, it had been a decided bonus to have a footman who could comfortably deal with whatever debt collectors or enraged husbands turned up at his bachelor rooms demanding an audience.

Those were the days before he had succeeded to his father's title and estate. In those days, Jeremy had existed on an allowance which often did not stretch the whole month. During that time, Colfax had been an invaluable member of his household; ingenious and resourceful, he had ensured the lines of credit were extended until the bills could be paid.

If not for Colfax, Jeremy would have lived half the month without candles for light or coal for the fire. It was true, he did not much care about the empty cupboards, for he could reasonably exist on the invitations out to dine, but no doubt his valet and coachman had appreciated the fact they were fed and watered on a daily basis.

Then had come his disastrous marriage, and Colfax had really proved he was worth his salt. For he had not liked Amanda. Moreso, the handsome footman had proved entirely impervious to Amanda's alluring beauty. His dislike had been covered at all times with a veneer of politeness, but even Amanda, arrogant as she was, could not fail to pick up on it.

In the beginning, Jeremy had thought it might prove a problem, for she had believed Colfax a challenge to overcome. She had turned the full force of her charm on the footman, showering him with her attention, flattery, and trusted confidences.

When this did not move him, she had been by turn teasing and then coldly aloof. It made no difference. Colfax was indifferent and would not partake in her games. Mercifully at this point, Amanda had decided to be amused by it all. She called Colfax a puritan. She talked loudly of his disapproval of her in front of her friends, and they all laughed about it. She wanted him to dance with her when she was drunk.

It had been at this point that Jeremy had become aware of Colfax's strange feeling on the matter, for he had asked him outright. Did he want to leave his service? Were things becoming too much for him, now Jeremy's living arrangements had changed? No, and no. Then, in a lowered tone, did he loathe his mistress?

Colfax had cleared his throat. It was not his place to judge Lady Amanda's character. Jeremy had insisted. "Indulge me this one time. I won't dismiss you for a little plain speaking just this once." Colfax had been silent for such a long moment that Jeremy had almost given up on a response, when he had said quietly, "She ain't no lady, not as I see it. Not in the real sense of the word. Not how it counts."

And that had been when Jeremy had found out Colfax's peculiarity. Despite being rough around the edges himself, he liked respectable women, not fast ones. Amanda could throw her arms around his neck, half spilling out of her gown, demand he carry her to her bedchamber and ravish her, and Colfax would always respond with the utmost restraint and correctness. Hell, she could have danced naked in front of him, and Colfax would not have batted an eyelash.

It had been an astonishing revelation. Jeremy was not a fool. He knew Amanda had made a play for his closest friend Atherton, just as he knew Atherton had rejected her. However, Atherton would have done so out of a sense of loyalty to him, while Colfax had not even been tempted.

For a man who had been forced to lose at least one friend, a couple of acquaintances, and even his son's tutor over his wife's affairs, his footman's disdain was a breath of fresh air. It had cemented Colfax's position of importance with him.

Jeremy had increased his already generous wages, secure in the knowledge he need not feel unduly concerned when Amanda made another of her scenes. It was not a case of Colfax remembering his position, or where his duty lay. He simply was not attracted to her.

They were walking through the house now; Jeremy noted the neatly packed trunks and cases piled in the hallway. Colfax clearly had their move to Cornwall well underway.

"That Nurse Jopling's left already," Colfax commented as Jeremy started up the stairs.

Jeremy swung back around. "So early?"

"Her next post is in Hampshire, so she was eager to be off."

"Ah, well, I don't think Teddy will miss her somehow. They never seemed to really hit it off."

Colfax mounted the stairs after him, clearing his throat. "Is that Miss Pinson going to be Master Edward's new nurse?" he enquired, adding with just a trace of self-consciousness, "If I might make so bold as to ask."

Jeremy sent a quick look at Colfax's carefully blank face. Who had taught him that piece of politeness? Maybe it had been Garraway. The butler at Vance Park was always at pains to smooth Colfax's rougher edges.

"Well, I'm hoping he is now well enough to dispense with a nurse altogether," he answered. "Miss Pinson is an experienced governess, so the idea is that she can tutor him until I have decided what to do about his schooling."

Colfax looked skeptical and Jeremy could not really blame him. It must be two years since Teddy attended Paverton Hall. Jeremy had not wanted to send him to boarding school in the first place, and when an outbreak of tuberculosis had occurred, he had likely been the first parent to send for his child's return.

Teddy was young for his age, he had told himself. Then, too, with his parents' divorce, scarlet fever, and now his remarriage, the boy had had a lot to contend with.

"He'll run rings round her," Colfax predicted gruffly.

"Most likely," Jeremy agreed. "But as I say, it will be little more than an interim measure."

"And then what?"

Jeremy halted before his bedroom door. Colfax was being surprisingly tiresome this morning. "As I said," he responded irritably. "It'll be a case of either a new school or tutor."

"I meant for her," Colfax said, glancing away.

"What?" Jeremy was startled.

"Miss Pinson," Colfax persisted doggedly.

"Oh. Well, she'll make her home with us at Vance Park, I suppose." Jeremy shrugged. "The new Lady Faris has made her feelings on the matter clear."

Colfax was looking at him rather hard, but Jeremy was bored of the conversation by this point. "Send my valet to me, would you?" he said, effectively putting an end to it. "I need a shave and a change of clothes."

Strange to say, once he was leaning back in his dressing room, a hot towel wrapped around his face, Jeremy found himself pondering Colfax's words. After all, had he not raised a rather salient point? What *was* to become of Miss Pinson? It had been made quite apparent to him that she was no mere paid companion.

Emmeline was considerate of her, relied on her, and turned to her quite naturally for companionship when Jeremy would much rather she turned to him instead. Would having Miss Pinson on the premises mean that Emmeline would continue to do so?

The thought was not a welcome one. Was there anyone else he could fob her off on? he wondered idly. The vicar was always trying to find new tutors for his hellions. Would Miss Pinson be able to restore order to Penarth vicarage? That was rather a good idea.

Then he remembered Emmeline had claimed the unworldly Miss Pinson was not fond of boys. Afraid of them, in fact, was the wording she had used. That was no good, then, for the vicar had two of them. He couldn't remember their names. Was it George and Freddie? No, that wasn't right.

Giving up on the names of the vicar's progeny, Jeremy thought instead of Emmeline's spirited defense of her erstwhile governess. He remembered her heartfelt words about "poor Pinky" winding up with some boisterous family somewhere up north. She had sounded so indignant. No, the vicarage was not a suitable place for the delicate Miss Pinson.

Where then was? Suddenly, he thought of the recently vacated cottage of one of his gamekeepers. His estate manager, Wallis, had mentioned it in his letter of two days ago. Somerton had been dissatisfactory all round and his disappearance one night was no great loss though he had left a slew of bad debts and disgruntled neighbors in his wake.

How should Miss Pinson like to become one of his tenants? He could easily claim that the governess position came with a cottage, and then simply let her remain there when Teddy went off to school. A place of her own would surely be desirable to one who had only ever had a room under her employer's roof.

Yes, he rather liked that idea. Miss Pinson dealt with, he dismissed her summarily from his thoughts, sitting up as Carver approached, brush and shaving soap in hand. Before long he was washed, clean-shaven, and dressed in a new suit of sober hue, offset with a gold silk waistcoat and burgundy cravat.

He was inspecting himself in the looking glass when Atherton strolled into his dressing room. "Thought I had better come and bid you a fond farewell," he said breezily. "I need to get back to London." He cast a critical eye over Jeremy's outfit. "Rather formal for a day's traveling, aren't you? I would have thought tweeds were more appropriate."

"You're one to talk."

Atherton looked down fondly at his own gray pinstripe. "Well, I have a certain reputation to maintain. What is your reasoning?"

"That I'm not in the country yet and it's still early days with Emmeline," Jeremy replied, straightening his cuffs.

Atherton nodded thoughtfully. "You mean to distract her with good looks. Wise. One cannot flaunt one's beauty in tweeds."

"Why do you need to get back to London?" Jeremy asked. "Your uncle expecting you to dance attendance on him again?"

Atherton leaned a hip against a convenient dressing-bureau. "Sadly no, the old boy's cut off my line of credit again. Didn't I tell you?"

Jeremy adjusted his cravat. "No, what happened this time?"

Atherton sighed. "I refused his bride of choice, the bottled fruit heiress. Now he reckons he'll marry her himself and beget a new heir."

Jeremy turned to face him. "Inconvenient. You have the title, but he has all the money."

Atherton gave a murmur of agreement. "I would gladly swap our circumstances but alas, such a thing is not possible. In any case, I have other fish to fry at present. Carstairs asked me to go into partnership with him on a gentleman's establishment."

"What kind of gentleman's establishment?"

"Officially, a gin palace. Unofficially, a gambling den."

"Won't you need capital to invest in such a venture?"

Atherton cocked his head. "A certain sum, yes. But it would not be primarily money I would bring to the table. I would bring the prestige."

Jeremy smirked. "Man cannot live on prestige alone. I could always—"

Atherton threw up his hands. "Do not say it, Faris. I do not borrow money from my friends."

"Who said anything about borrowing?"

"Very well, then. I do not accept handouts from my friends."

"It would hardly be a handout. You were one of the original investors in my stable, don't forget. Bucephalus is still winning cups and looks set to do so for another couple of years at least."

"I do not forget," Atherton said lightly. "But I do not mean to draw any money from that pot just yet."

Jeremy picked up his watch and slipped it into his pocket while threading the chain through a buttonhole. "Well, you know it is there should you need it."

Atherton nodded. "Besides, I mean to come and sponge off you in a month or so in the summer, so you need not imagine you will miss me."

"You are always welcome at Vance Park, as I think you know."

Atherton nodded. "Oh, I know. But I think you need both time and space to court your bride. Re-insinuate yourself into her good graces as it were."

"Noticed that, did you?" Jeremy asked with a wry twist of his lips. "I have some ground to recover, it is true. Any recommendations?"

"If you have not already, I would write and have Garraway take down your previous wife's portrait in the blue sitting room *tout suite*," Atherton said promptly.

Jeremy snorted. "It was consigned to the attics months ago," he assured his friend.

"I would have thought a bonfire more appropriate."

Jeremy shot him a look. "She is Teddy's mother at the end of the day," he said mildly. "The only vestige I had of my own growing up was her portrait. It may be that someday, when I am dead and buried, Teddy or one of his offspring may want to hang it in the long gallery with the rest of their ancestors."

"How maudlin."

Jeremy smiled. "You might feel differently if your own title had been accompanied by such things."

"Very likely," Atherton agreed without rancor. "However, as it did not, we will never know. Uncle George inherited all the ancestral portraits along with the sense of familial piety. Consequently, I am entirely footloose and fancy-free."

"Well, there are decided advantages to that, I am sure."

"If I was you," Atherton continued, ignoring this and picking up the previous thread, "I would offer her free rein over redecorating at Vance Park. Amanda's tastes were rather extravagant. It may be that Emmeline would rather not write her letters in a sitting room masquerading as an Egyptian tomb."

Jeremy winced. "It is not quite as bad as that, and besides, the décor of the viscountess's sitting room is nothing compared to that of her bedroom."

"Do tell."

"Her inspiration was the seraglio in an Ottoman palace, complete with wall hangings, ceramic tiling, and Turkish carpets."

Atherton blinked. "Good grief. Please tell me you have had the rooms stripped bare in readiness for their new occupant."

"I have not," Jeremy admitted. "There has hardly been time, but I am happy for my bride to redecorate at will." He thought fleetingly of Emmeline's rooms at Winkworth Street. Doubtless they had been furnished with thoughts of economy in mind, rather than personal taste.

Even so, he suspected that given a choice, her fancy would not run to the extravagances of the ancient world. He wondered idly what setting she would choose for herself if money was no object. He knew what he would choose for her, of course. Aphrodite's bower, complete with attendant cupid statues, but doubtless she would think that just as opulent and inappropriate as his previous viscountess's choice.

"What *are* you thinking of?" Atherton asked curiously.

"The Birth of Venus," Jeremy answered unthinkingly.

Atherton laughed. "You mean to have her sleep in a scallop-shaped bed?" he enquired. "Dressed with sheets of seafoam green."

"Why not? I'd rather like that."

"I just bet you would," Atherton said, shaking his head, "but I suspect your bride's tastes run along more conventional lines."

The same suspicion had crossed Jeremy's mind, but it annoyed him hearing his friend say so. "You scarcely know her," he pointed out irritably. "She is a great reader of novels and likes a good many fanciful things."

A bookroom, he thought suddenly. That was what he should have installed at Vance Park. A bookroom which he could fill with all the latest novels so she would not miss the lending library here in Bath. His mood lightened. He would do it. It would be one way to woo and win her over, and he would think of several more.

"I take it inspiration has struck," Atherton said dryly as Jeremy strode to the doorway and called for Colfax.

"You were right," Jeremy admitted. "The viscountess's suite at Vance is in dire need of redecoration. I can't think why it never occurred to me before."

When Colfax appeared, he gave him brief instructions to have letters written to several prominent designers and decorators in London. "Have it stressed it is a matter of urgency and that they must come to Cornwall immediately if they accept the commission."

Colfax accepted the task without complaint, despite having several more pressing matters in hand at present, including their imminent vacating of the premises. "Very well, milord," he said, and disappeared again, intent on his task.

Jeremy turned back to Atherton, who was watching him with an amused look on his face. "What?" he asked, narrowing his eyes.

"Oh nothing," his friend assured him. "I was just wondering where your viscountess is going to camp out while you have her rooms made ready for her."

"I would have thought that was obvious," Jeremy responded with a raised brow.

"However *shall* you bear the inconvenience?" Atherton drawled.

Jeremy could not quite hide his answering smile, however hard he tried.

10

It was past lunchtime by the time Jeremy's carriage pulled into Winkworth Street. The ladies were ready for departure, and when he entered the hall, they were at the top of the stairs dressed in their hats and cloaks and laden down with overnight bags.

"Good morning," Emmeline called down to him, shifting her bulky dressing case into her left arm and almost dropping her reticule.

By this point, Colfax had bounded up the stairs, and with a swift "I'll take that, Lady Faris," divested her of her dressing case, tucking it under his left arm, while simultaneously scooping Pinky's walnut writing box out of her friend's arms and tucking it under his right.

"So kind," twittered Miss Pinson, turning on the step. "I'll just go back up and fetch down my—"

"No need, Miss Pinson," Jeremy called up from the foot of the stairs. "I have two burly fellows here employed to carry down your things. Please come down and join me." He smiled up at Emmeline, who looked shy and flustered this morning, though she was trying to hide the fact.

The maid, Florrie, and even the landlady, an officious woman, seemed determined to get in the way this morning and by the time he had disentangled his bride, and managed to bundle her and her friend into the carriage, Emmeline looked both harried and apologetic.

"Will your men really be able to oversee the last of the packing?" she asked anxiously, peering out of the carriage window to where a wagon stood waiting for the last few bits of furniture.

"Undoubtedly. Do not give it another thought."

She heaved a great sigh of relief and settled back into her seat. "Well," she said brightly, "we have never made a move with so little fuss and botheration, have we, Hannah?"

Her friend agreed. "It was so easy that I feel almost *un*easy, if that makes sense," Miss Pinson admitted, glancing over her shoulder at the disappearing view of Winkworth Street.

"Have you moved lots of times?" Teddy asked, stirring with interest from where he sat on the seat beside his father. He had not ventured into number six, and he looked pale and wan, as though yesterday's excitement might have taken a toll on his recovering health.

"Oh yes, we're quite old hands by this point," Emmeline answered lightly. "Last time we had to push a handcart through the streets of Bath with our cases and trunks. Do you remember, Hannah? It was difficult to steer but fortunately we had only moved ten minutes away."

Miss Pinson shuddered at the memory, but Teddy looked intrigued. "I bet I could have steered it," he put in with confidence. "Have you still got it?"

Emmeline shook her head and smiled. "We only hired it for that morning's work."

"I have a pony and a gig of my own at Vance Park," Teddy boasted. "I drive it all around the estate, but Papa says I cannot go down to Penarth unaccompanied, so I have to take a groom."

"What a very lucky boy you are," she responded. "I should have loved such a thing at your age."

"I could take both of you for a ride, if you like," Teddy offered generously. "It would have to be one at a time though, as the gig only fits two people." Emmeline thanked him but Miss Pinson looked hesitant, so Jeremy assured them his son was quite proficient and could be trusted in the driver's seat.

The next few hours passed amicably enough. Teddy was an enthusiastic conversationalist and displayed his tendency to monopolize any subject, however obscure. When he finally grew quiet, Jeremy suggested he put his feet up on the seat and a cushion behind his head, but he spiritedly refused this and grew quite fractious, insisting he was not an infant in need of such things.

Jeremy accepted this without argument, but when his son's eyelids began to droop, he was quick to maneuver him into a prone position, unlace his boots, and drape a blanket over him. "Fast asleep," he murmured. "I knew he would succumb before long." Emmeline returned his smile, her eyes soft as she looked at the sleeping boy.

"His illness must have been hard on you both," she commented.

"Yes, but he is generally moody and difficult when he is tired," he admitted. Seeing Miss Pinson gulp, he was quick to draw her attention to Teddy's angelic appearance in sleep.

"He is a beautiful child," she quavered, still looking rather anxious.

"Now we can have some adult conversation at last," he said, settling back into his seat. Emmeline shot a quick alarmed glance toward her friend, and he lifted his brows at her. "And by that, I mean that we can finally have a cozy discussion of *Love's Innocence Fled*," he said with relish, rubbing his hands together.

"Oh!" exclaimed Miss Pinson, turning toward him excitedly. "Do not tell me that you have read it, my lord!"

"I have," he responded gravely. "I read it avidly from cover to cover in the space of three nights."

"Three nights!" Miss Pinson was impressed. "Enthralling, was it not? Fortunately, Emmie managed to finish it just before we had to return it to the lending library."

"I am very glad to hear it," he said, turning back to Emmeline. "Now tell me, what was your favorite passage?"

Emmeline regarded him suspiciously. "What was yours?" she asked, clearly doubting he had so much as cracked open the cover.

"That's easy," Jeremy replied at once. "It was the chapter which dealt with the thrilling escape from the count's secret lair in the country. When Josephine was forced to masquerade as a shepherdess."

"That was very resourceful of her," she agreed. "I, too, liked that part, but I think I preferred when she had to rescue Fernando from the count's dungeon and they saw the ghost."

"Oh, that part made me suffer agonies of anxiety," Miss Pinson said breathlessly. "I was so sure they would be caught."

"What, then, was your favorite, Miss Pinson?" Jeremy asked politely.

"Oh, I can hardly decide," she wavered, pushing her pince-nez further up her nose. "Perhaps when they discovered the ghost was really the count's henchman causing mischief." She shivered slightly. "The accounts of the spectral clanking of chains and the agonized moans of a soul in torment were quite dreadful. I vow I could hardly sleep after reading of them."

Jeremy gave a murmur of agreement. "I am always profoundly thankful that our ghosts at Vance Park are benign." Miss Pinson gave a little shriek.

"You have a ghost?" Emmeline asked, sounding rather thrilled.

"Two actually. Two ancestresses of mine who haunt the grounds on special occasions."

The ladies exchanged glances. "Did some great tragedy occur?" Emmie asked, lowering her voice.

Jeremy nodded. "In Tudor times, two sisters fell in love with the same suitor. Before he could decide between them, he died of dysentery."

"Such an unromantic disease," Miss Pinson said sadly.

"What happened to the sisters?" Emmeline asked.

"One died of a broken heart," Jeremy said, "and the other dwindled into spinsterhood. The trouble is it is hard to differentiate between the two. Hardly anyone can ever be sure which ghost they saw, Lady Frances or Lady Mary. They look very similar. One betokens impending misfortune, and the other matrimony. Mixing them up can be most disappointing."

"Oh, I see…" Miss Pinson broke in excitedly. "Which one betokens good fortune? The spinster? Then bad fortune would be the one who died prematurely. After all, the spinster probably found the time to do a lot of rewarding good works."

Jeremy shook his head. "Not a single one," he said. "She scorned charitable works till the end of her days. She was entirely self-serving, like most Vances. It is the Lady Mary who warns of marriage."

Miss Pinson looked taken aback. "Oh," she said faintly.

"In any case," Emmeline interjected, "I don't believe the other died of a broken heart. That very rarely happens in real life as I understand it, though," she added conscientiously, "I know it often happens in novels."

"You think it was likely dysentery too?" Jeremy asked with interest. "I have heard it is catching."

Seeing her friend's horrified reaction, Emmeline hastened to change the subject. "Tell me, my lord, which character did you think had the most rewarding development over the course of the story?"

Her willingness to debate the topic pleased him more than he could say. "Which do you?" he asked, genuinely curious.

"I think perhaps Fernando," she said after a moment's pondering. "For Josephine was already perfection from the first page, but as a hero, Fernando had a lot of maturing to do, did he not?"

"Oh!" chimed in Miss Pinson, her enthusiasm for the subject sweeping her shyness away. "I thought Fernando's growing disillusionment with his fellow man rather sad, but then I suppose that comes to us all in time," she said, shaking her head.

"I disagree with you both," Jeremy said staunchly. "I think the wicked count had the greatest journey, and quite redeemed himself in the end, by sacrificing his life to save the young lovers."

"It was wholly due to his machinations that they were poised on that perilous rooftop in the first place!" Emmeline pointed out indignantly.

"True," Jeremy conceded. "But he saw the light at the eleventh hour, you must admit. Moreover, I believe that Josephine rather missed him by the end of the book. I was not convinced by that closing paragraph about how much she savored the peace and quiet as Fernando's devoted helpmeet. I suspect the atmosphere at the artist's cottage left a lot to be desired."

"Oh, but their cottage sounded so picturesque, surrounded as it was by jasmine and honeysuckle and lemon tree groves," Miss Pinson rhapsodized. "I am sure that Fernando must have produced some truly wonderful paintings in surroundings so fertile to his artistic sensibilities."

"You are fond of cottages, Miss Pinson?" Jeremy asked, immediately thinking of the scheme that had occurred to him that very morning, to offer her the vacant gamekeeper's cottage.

"Oh yes," she enthused. "Though in my eyes an English cottage is vastly superior to an Italianate one, with larkspurs and dianthus and perhaps a little plum tree in the garden." Her face beamed at the pretty picture she had described.

"How fortunate," Jeremy pronounced. Both ladies looked at him with surprise.

"Fortunate, how so?" asked Emmeline.

"Well, you see, the position of governess comes with a cottage attached," he said smoothly. "It lies on my estate, a twenty-minute ride from the house."

"A cottage?" breathed Miss Pinson, turning very pink. "Am—am I to understand—?" Words seemed to fail her, and she dropped her handkerchief and then fumbled with the clasp of her reticule. "Oh dear," she mumbled, turning incoherent as she groped for her pince-nez.

"But Pinky is only occupying that position on a temporary basis, you said," Emmie put in. "You surely do not expect her to take possession of this cottage, only to suffer the inconvenience of having to move back out again after a couple of months when Teddy goes to school?" Facing him as she did, Emmie did not see the way her friend's face fell.

"*Oh!* Oh, dear me, yes, for a minute I had quite forgotten," Miss Pinson said, turning back to face him, quite crestfallen. She assumed a brave smile, though Jeremy could see she was quite crushed by this reminder.

"But why should Miss Pinson have to vacate the cottage?" Jeremy asked. "When he is back for the holidays, Teddy will require Miss Pinson's supervision, and, if he is anything like me, to study to re-sit the exams he fails each and every term."

Emmeline took a deep breath. "Even if that is so, Teddy's age would mean it was still only a temporary arrangement," she insisted. "And as such—"

139

"Why temporary?" Jeremy interrupted her. "God willing, we will have more children in need of educating, and besides"—he shrugged—"it is not unusual for nannies to stick around and help out the family in other ways when the children outgrow the nursery."

Emmeline's eyes had grown very wide at his words, but this last point seemed to snap her out of her surprised state. "Hannah is *not* a nanny!" she said with dignity.

"No, but her position is just as trusted," he countered. "It would be good for you to have her living at such close proximity to us."

Emmeline bit her lip, though he could see she wanted very much to insist on having her friend far closer and living under the same roof.

"So, does that mean I am to have the cottage after all?" Pinky asked timidly, her hands clasped tightly together in her lap.

Jeremy saw the way Emmeline's head turned sharply at the hopeful note in her friend's voice. Finally, it seemed to dawn on her that Miss Pinson was neither terrified nor upset at the notion of living independently. He saw the flash of hurt in Emmeline's eyes before she quickly recovered herself.

"You would like to take this cottage, Hannah?" she asked carefully.

"Oh yes," Miss Pinson breathed. "A little place of my own? Why, it would—" She swallowed. "It would be like a dream come true," she concluded in a tremulous voice.

"Well," Emmeline said after a moment's pause. "Then you must certainly have it, if it is truly to be yours." She turned back to Jeremy with a slight challenge in her voice.

"Certainly, I could make it over to Miss Pinson for the duration of her days," he answered coolly.

"So kind," Miss Pinson said in a choked voice, dabbing at her eyes with a handkerchief. "And truly generous. Though, you must not do so, my lord, until I have completed a trial period, and you have had the opportunity to judge if my methods are agreeable to yourself and the dear child." She cast a fearful look at Teddy's sleeping form.

Jeremy smiled. "But I have already had adequate opportunity to judge your *results*, Miss Pinson," he said, his eyes dwelling fondly on Emmie. "And it is the results that count in these matters."

Both ladies fell silent at this point and Emmeline remained quiet for the rest of the afternoon. Miss Pinson roused herself to prattle away, pointing out place names, such as Shepton Mallet, where she believed there was a famous market, or Barton St. David, where a good friend of hers once spent the summer with friends.

Jeremy suspected that Emmeline was only too well acquainted with these tales, for though she nodded her head and smiled in encouragement, agreeing that oh yes, she remembered hearing her friend speak often of Miss West, she did not ask many questions or evince any great curiosity in these themes. As for Jeremy, he responded with the utmost civility and was rewarded for his efforts, for by the time dinnertime rolled around, Miss Pinson no longer seemed quite so nervous around him.

He proposed that they stop for an hour to dine and then press on, for Jeremy wanted to reach the coaching inn at Ilminster by nightfall. As they had started so late, he did not think they would now manage this before nightfall.

The ladies were agreeable, so they duly stopped at The George, a well-kept inn where they were led into a private dining room and served a decent meal of mulligatawny soup, followed by roast beef with redcurrant sauce and Yorkshire pudding.

Teddy was tired and fractious and ate very little of his dinner, despite coaxing from the adults, as he pushed his food around his plate. When dessert was served, it was quite a different matter. Teddy ate two helpings of syrup sponge, and then finished off Miss Pinson's portion, which she had barely touched. None of them cared to linger over coffee, so he paid the bill and they left to resume their journey.

By the time they reached their first layover, three hours later, Teddy was not the only one smothering his yawns. Both ladies looked weary, and Jeremy proposed that they shared a room, while he and Teddy bunked in together. Emmeline looked grateful for the suggestion though deep down he would have preferred her to be disappointed by such sleeping arrangements.

Still, he contented himself with the thought that once they reached Vance Park, he would have her all to himself. He would be generous and allow her these last few days with her precious companion. He slept indifferently despite the comfortable bed, and Teddy woke very early and talked his ear off until it was time for breakfast. They descended to the private parlor to find Emmeline and Miss Pinson already in residence and drinking tea.

After a good breakfast, they met Colfax and Juggins in the courtyard and the second leg of the journey was undertaken. Teddy was a good deal more cheerful, and everyone enjoyed the morning's scenery, which included the Blackdown Hills, which Miss Pinson seemed particularly taken with.

Emmeline explained to Jeremy that her friend had artistic inclinations, something Miss Pinson blushed and protested about. She grew very flustered at Jeremy's assertion that he would like to see her sketches someday. Teddy made sure to boast about his own skill with a pencil, and drawing lessons were discussed and settled on, which seemed to please everyone.

They took lunch at Combe Raleigh before pressing on to Exeter, where they were due to change their team of horses. The second night was spent at a coaching inn called The Lucky Hayrick, where once again, Jeremy shared his bedchamber with his son, who complained the mattress was lumpy and kicked and talked a good deal in his sleep.

Jeremy was up in the night, dosing his son with medicine, and he made sure the boy drank his tonic the next morning, disregarding Teddy's complaints that it tasted nasty. A relapse was the last thing he wanted, especially since Nurse Jopling was no longer with them. He wondered now if he would need to hire another and could not be easy in his mind about it.

The third day was not so leisurely, for their fresh horses meant they could press on to Plymouth, so they set off at a lively pace, making good progress and stopping briefly only for luncheon where they all agreed they would delay their next meal and take a late supper once they had reached their accommodations for the night.

The ladies were very taken with the Devon scenery, but Teddy was quick to inform them that Cornwall was far superior in every way. Jeremy explained the rivalry of the neighboring counties, his son chiming in with supporting evidence, before Teddy's eyes grew heavy-lidded, and he curled up in the seat and could scarcely be roused to eat his supper before bed.

The fourth and final day of their travels dawned fair and bright, and Jeremy woke with profound relief that they would soon be home. Teddy had slept better but still seemed flushed and a little sluggish. Jeremy felt his brow throughout the day to check he was not feverish.

After three days of being cooped up together in the carriage, everyone's nerves seemed a little frayed. The ladies appeared jittery, though whether this was with excitement or anxiousness, it was hard to tell. They talked quickly or not at all, and there were several long periods of heavy silence, as they all fell prey to their own thoughts and distractions.

To try to allay the tension, Jeremy spoke at length of what they would find at Vance Park. He described the house, neoclassical in style and built in 1715 to replace the original Tudor seat which burned down during the reign of Edward VI. He explained that the Vance family had lived there since at least 1480, though they had not been raised to the peerage until Queen Anne's reign.

He described his own addition to the estate, the extensive stables, and his champion racehorses. Teddy joined in here and there, and it was not until he was describing the maze and the formal gardens that he realized Emmeline was looking more intimidated than anticipatory regarding her new home.

"You will want to make changes of course," he said swiftly. "And put your own stamp on the place. I have invited designers down to discuss the redecoration of your suite. They should start responding soon and you can start your plans."

If anything, Emmeline's eyes grew even wider at this. "I see," she said doubtfully and turned to Miss Pinson as though for support. Miss Pinson, however, was deeply occupied with thoughts of her own. Jeremy suspected she was busy daydreaming about country cottages.

Noticing them both looking at her, she said distractedly, "I always think foxgloves look so charming gathered around a cottage gate."

"Oh, I quite agree," he responded politely, and Emmeline narrowed her eyes at him. Night was fast falling by the time they reached St. Ives. "Not long now," he consoled Teddy, who was once again fretful and complaining. "This is the nearest town to us," he directed at the ladies. "It has some very fine beaches and several shops." Emmeline and Miss Pinson pressed their noses to the windows despite the failing light to appreciate what they could see of the scenery. "We are only about an hour away from home now," he added.

"Home," Miss Pinson echoed wistfully and gave a little sigh. Emmeline looked rather queasy, though she had not suffered from travel sickness before this point. He wished he could pull her into his lap, but one could hardly settle one's wife on one's knee with others present, even if they were only family. Instead, he consoled himself with the thought she would sleep under his own roof tonight.

The place was in complete darkness by the time they swept up the drive. A pity, for the long avenue of trees was particularly impressive, and he was strangely keen that she should admire her new home. As they neared the house, he saw several lighted torches and was pleased to see the household was roused and primed for their arrival.

Clearly the messages Colfax had sent on his behalf to prepare everyone for their return had been received. Still, he was surprised to see the number of staff hurrying down the steps to line up to greet their new mistress. He had not expected quite such a formal greeting.

"It looks as though Garraway has herded everyone out for your inspection," he said, casting Emmeline a quick apologetic glance. "Garraway is our butler," he added, seeing her blank look.

"What a lovely welcome," Emmeline said determinedly, sitting up very straight in her seat and straightening her bonnet. "I hope you will introduce me to everyone."

"Oh dear." Miss Pinson faltered, looking down first at her own rather travel-worn gown, and then at Emmeline's. "We are not looking our best for first impressions. My skirts are quite crushed."

"They will understand," Jeremy said, dismissing such concerns gallantly, though, privately he agreed with her. Both ladies' faces looked tired and wan peering out of their bonnets and their drab traveling ensembles had clearly seen better days.

Springing down from the coach, he turned around to hand down first his bride, and then Miss Pinson. Finding Teddy fast asleep, he glanced around for Colfax and found his footman at his elbow. "Carry Master Teddy inside, would you, Colfax? And take him straight up to his bedroom. I will look in on him presently."

Colfax nodded and made haste to carry the child inside.

Turning back to Emmeline, Jeremy offered her his arm. "I had thought to usher you in quietly," he confessed, "but perhaps it would be better to get the formalities out of the way."

Miss Pinson fell in step behind them, and they moved toward the elderly butler, who puffed out his chest. "My dear, allow me to introduce you to Garraway, who is quite an institution here at Vance."

11

Emmie woke in the early hours and lay a while, feeling disorientated and ill at ease. These feelings were not unfamiliar after spending the last few days on the road. This time, however, recalling where she was did not allay her anxiety one bit. She shivered slightly in her bedsheets. Vance Park seemed to her an austere and grand place. The task of making it feel like home was already daunting.

Recollections of the night before flitted back through her mind, the house with all its columns and Palladian windows, and those huge stone lions guarding its front steps. Once inside there had been the entrance hall with its marble relief sculptures of heroes and monsters, its gold-painted ceiling all decorated with gods. None of it seemed comforting or remotely welcoming.

Emmie had never cared much for the Greek gods, or did she mean Roman? She always got them mixed up. Darling Pinky had never thought their shenanigans suitable for the schoolroom. They were always doing such cruel and extraordinary things, even the ones who were supposedly beneficent.

Rolling onto her side, Emmie tried to make out the layout of the room in the early morning light, but the truth was, she had not had a good enough look at it the night before to map it out. No, instead of appreciating her luxurious new quarters, Emmie had taken a bath, then crept under the covers and extinguished the light. She had been tired and dispirited, and this morning she still felt the same way.

It was no good, she had to face facts. She was in the bedroom of Viscountess Faris, lying in her bed, and the truth of it was, she felt like an imposter. What on earth was she doing here? she asked herself despairingly. She must have been mad to accept Jeremy's proposal! How in the world was she supposed to conduct herself now she was his wife?

This great big house with its army of servants bewildered her. It was true, she had lived in a fancy London townhouse before, though that seemed a lifetime ago and hardly compared with an estate like *this*. She would not even have Pinky beside her to help navigate the pitfalls, she reflected glumly, for Jeremy seemed determined to deprive her even of that familiar comfort.

She hoped Hannah was alright. She did not know precisely where her friend was at this moment. That housekeeper had borne her off last night. Colfax had carried Teddy off to his nursery, and as for her husband, well, he had disappeared, too, after informing her he had his own rooms to retire to and kissing her hand.

Emmie supposed that was the sort of world she lived in now. She sighed. Why on earth had he not married someone who would take all this in her stride? Then she remembered. He had tried that, and it had not worked out. No doubt that had put him off titled brides. Rolling onto her back, she strove to remember just what it was he had wanted from her.

A respectable marriage had featured heavily in his requirements, in order to expunge the scandal of his divorce. Well, tucked away here in the country, so far from London, it was unlikely that she would commit any solecisms bad enough to reach the ears of high society.

Emmie had never been one to make tongues wag anyway. Except for that one unfortunate period of her life, she thought, her face reddening in the dark. How ironic that should be the only time she had previously spent in Jeremy Vance's company!

Hastily abandoning this unprofitable line of thought, she returned to the original. Now, what else had he asked of her? Slowly it came back to her. To be the sort of wife who would foster good relations with his neighbors and the local community, that was what he had said. He wanted the sort of wife who would sit on charitable committees. Emmie's heart quailed slightly at the prospect but after all, how hard could it be? Doubtless this was the biggest house hereabouts and most organizations would welcome its mistress with open arms.

What else? To be a good stepmother, that went without saying. At least, she hoped she could uphold that part of the bargain without too many problems. It was true, she had precious little experience of maternal relations herself, with her own mother having died so long ago, but she hoped she would find her way with an open heart. She was already fond of the child, and Teddy seemed to welcome a new stepmother in his life.

After all, if the boy was to be believed, it was he who had put her forward as a likely candidate for the role. She flushed again, thinking of Lily Skellern regaling her stepson with embarrassing tales of her debut. For a moment, she almost took pleasure in remembering Lily's mortified face at the wedding. Almost. Then she thrust the woman resolutely from her mind.

It showed a kind nature that Teddy had wanted his father to make reparation to her, even if the notion had been somewhat misguided. His apple truly seemed to have fallen far from the proverbial tree. His parents, when young, had been selfish and hedonistic with seemingly little regard for others. At least, that was how they had appeared to her at the time. Teddy, she thought warmly, was cut from a different sort of cloth.

A normal parent would not have indulged his son in the matter of his remarriage, of course. Who ever heard of a father allowing his child to pick out his wife? But then, Jeremy Vance was not conventional, nor never had been. He did as he pleased, and to hell with the consequences!

Then again, maybe she did him an injustice and the passage of time *had* altered him somewhat. Perhaps he truly believed he had had wrongs to right. She stirred uneasily; in some ways he *did* seem to have mellowed. On their journey here, he had been politeness itself and most assiduous in his dealings with Pinky. She could not imagine the Jeremy Vance of old being so kind.

Perhaps, now matured and wiser, he *did* feel some pangs of guilt about his former conduct. That might have been what swayed him into accepting Teddy's demands. Feeling suddenly rather cold, she hitched up her bedsheets and took a deep, steadying breath. Would she feel better this morning if she had spent last night in her new husband's arms?

Color crept into her cheeks as her mind wandered back to their wedding night. His presence in her bed had been far from familiar *or* comforting and yet, if she was honest, it had not been as jarring as she might have expected either. Recalling now her own behavior she felt a slight pang but at the time it had not felt awkward. Or at least not as awkward as it might have been.

In truth, Jeremy had seemed to revel in her embrace, and he had not tried to hide that fact from her. He was usually so easy and offhand in his manner that to see him so focused on her and so driven…it had been quite the revelation. It had been a heady feeling indeed to know that she could affect him so, but perhaps she had given herself too much credit. She had a vague idea that men were not so discerning as women when it came to such matters.

Still… He could not have faked such a strong response to her, surely? He had been so extraordinarily passionate, but it was not just that, she thought slowly. He had seemed, well, *thrilled* to finally *be* with her like that. And in the aftermath, he had seemed so happy and relaxed that it had quite disconcerted her. She had not expected the easy affection and the avowal that he had missed her all this time. Now that part *had* been jarring to her. To claim such a thing… It could not possibly be true. Could it?

She breathed out and tried to consider the matter impartially. To be fair, he always made it plain that he took pleasure in her company. Even in the old days, he had sought her out in plain view of everyone. Still, back then, they had all thought he was singling her out to make an object of fun out of her. Even she had thought so. She had just been too dazzled to resent it too much.

Now, suddenly she was not so sure. Could it be that all along Jeremy Vance had wanted her fiercely? She found herself breathing hard. Her instinct was to recoil from such an astonishing notion, to upbraid herself for an idiot. Even as a green girl of eighteen she had not been stupid enough to believe her personal attractions were equal to even half of her fellow debutantes.

But if so… If so, then why *had* he made such a target of her? He had been bored, she acknowledged. He had been ripe for mischief. And yet…why her? Suddenly, she recalled Lord Atherton's astonishing words on her wedding day. What was it he had said? Something about her embodying Jeremy's every physical ideal.

She still could not quite grasp that as a concept. It seemed so very unlikely. And yet, when she had asked him if the Venuses of his collection were very fleshy, what was it he had said? *That is the way I like them.* Emmie bit her lip. If he had spoken the truth, then that meant the reason he had singled her out all those years ago was simply because he had been attracted to her.

Again, she thought of Lord Atherton's words to her on the dance floor. *He was attracted to you, like a moth to the flame, and I believe you were in much the same condition. Well, in any case, things have worked out for the best, much the same as if the natural conclusion had been drawn all those years ago.*

The natural conclusion. For some reason the phrase resonated with her and made her think of their wedding night once again. Something nagged at her, as though she had overlooked some vital clue to her new husband's nature. Once more she recalled his almost ecstatic relief at the consummation of their union.

It had *not* been mere pretense. Jeremy had reacted as though they had finally reached the culmination of something they had set in motion long ago. A conclusion both desirable and long awaited, something he had devoutly wished for. Remembering his fervent, intense reaction to her, she felt a dawning realization. Lord Atherton had spoken nothing but the truth. Jeremy Vance was extremely attracted to her, and probably always had been.

Slowly, Emmie sat up and hugged her knees. He had wanted her then, and he wanted her now. The realization left her almost dizzy. If that were true, then she need not feel so hopelessly inadequate in her new position. Her wretched situation had simply enabled Jeremy to get something he had wanted all along, nothing more, nothing less. The idea was an oddly liberating one.

Oh, no doubt Teddy's feelings had played a part in his decision, along with the necessity for a respectable wife who would smooth things over for him. But after all, if she possessed *something* at least that he wanted, something that she already possessed, then hopefully he would grant her some grace in the other areas where she did *not* match up to his ideal.

And Emmie could surely throw herself wholeheartedly into these new roles of wife and mother. It was the least she could do after he had rescued her from penury and disgrace. If she showed willing, surely Jeremy would show patience with her numerous shortcomings. The notion cheered her immensely. He had certainly been courteous toward her in their recent dealings. Perhaps he would continue to do so.

She felt her spirits perk up hopefully before a cold little voice whispered in her ear. *If he finds you so irresistible, then why has he not slept with you once since your wedding night?* That brought her up short. Emmie gave her head a little shake. She needed to have more confidence in herself. Letting her share a room with Pinky on the road had doubtless been due to courtesy. Last night was harder to explain away but after all, could that not also be due to consideration?

A knock on the door startled her. She lurched upright and fixed her eyes on it. A familiar golden head peered around the door.

"Good morning, Emmeline," her husband said. "Can I come in?"

"Oh yes, of course," she answered, feeling quite flustered.

He came into the room at once, resplendent in a long smoking robe of quilted black and gold. He was clearly *en dishabille*, for his curling hair was not in its usual immaculate style but looked tousled, tumbling around his brow. Predictably, it did not detract from his good looks.

He sat down first on the bed, and then swung his legs up and lay down flat beside her, crossing his ankles and placing his hands behind his head. He turned his head to look at her, asking politely, "How did you sleep?"

"Very well, thank you," she answered.

"You found the bed comfortable?"

"Yes. Have you, er, been awake long?" she asked, determined to hold her own in the conversation. He nodded, but did not elaborate, his eyes running over her, making her skin prickle. Noticing the direction of his gaze, Emmie glanced quickly down at the neckline of her nightgown but found all was decent.

"Did Madame de Flores make you any new nightgowns, Ballentine?" he asked casually, and Emmie flushed. "What?" he asked, noticing her embarrassment. "You're surely not so bashful, wife, that the mere mention of nightgowns can put you to blush!"

"Certainly not!" she responded, feeling stung. "I just thought, well, that you were—"

"Admiring your magnificent bosom?" he suggested lazily.

She turned quite bright red. "Well, yes," she admitted, "but now I find it was merely the tattiness of my nightgown that caught your attention, which is not at all flattering."

He gave a sudden laugh. "If I could see your bosom to admire it, then I would," he assured her. "But alas, I cannot through that horror of a nightdress."

"Madame promised to send on the rest of my trousseau. I lost track of what she was making but it's possible there may be a nightgown included."

"Let us devoutly hope so."

"I am sorry you find it so repellent," she retorted with more than a hint of sarcasm.

"I don't find it remotely repellent," he countered swiftly. "I am merely trying to be accommodating. Let me know if my efforts are not appreciated and I will drop the semblance at once."

Emmie pounced on his words gratefully. So, he *had* been trying to be thoughtful! She sagged against the pillows with relief.

He slid his slippered foot across the mattress to nudge her own concealed beneath the covers. "I wish you would tell me what you are thinking, Ballentine," he said slyly.

After all, why not? "Is that why you did not sleep in the same bed as me last night?" she asked frankly.

For a moment he looked quite stunned, and Emmie could not hold his gaze. "Do you see that door over there, Ballentine?" he asked, nodding toward the opposite side of the room.

Emmie glanced in that direction and saw a discreet door, papered over like the wall. "Just about," she answered.

"It connects my bedroom to yours," he explained.

"Oh?"

He nodded. "The key is on your side," he said significantly. When Emmie continued to gaze at him blankly, he elaborated. "If you are agreeable to a conjugal visit, then you must unlock the door to let me know that fact."

"Oh," Emmie repeated, "well, no one explained that to me."

The expression on his face wavered. "I have a suspicion I am going to regret asking this," he said, "but *would* you have unlocked it last night?"

"Yes," she admitted simply.

He groaned and covered his face with his hand. "Emmeline, how could you do this to me?"

"You know I am not yet familiar with the finer points of marital etiquette," she said defensively.

"Yes, I suppose that is true," he admitted, peering through his fingers at her. "But even so…"

"Why do you not have a key for your side?" she puzzled aloud. "What if I am agreeable and you are not?"

He gave a choked laugh. "Then, I suppose I simply would not try the door."

"Yes, but—*oh!*" she said, feeling suddenly foolish. "Oh, I see."

"I am almost afraid to ask at this point," he admitted, "but what is it that you see?"

"Well, that you may come through the door to *my* side, but I may not pass through it to intrude on yours," she said awkwardly, plucking at the coverlet.

He hesitated. "That is certainly the convention," he agreed, "but I cannot imagine I would bar your way if you did venture my side of the door."

Emmie opened her mouth to ask if Lady Amanda had never walked through. Thankfully, she suppressed the impulse in time. She felt faintly horrified with herself. She might not know much about married relations, but she knew such a question would have been highly indelicate.

"I thought I would give you a tour of your rooms," Jeremy said casually.

"Rooms?"

He nodded. "All the ones on this corridor are your own private quarters."

"Oh." *Good grief.* "Are they all like this one?" Emmie asked, casting her eyes around the opulence of the bedroom. It reminded her of *One Thousand and One Nights* with its walls in a pattern of cobalt blue leaves and orange flowers. Hanging from the ceilings were many brightly colored glass lamps in the Turkish style and in the middle of the room was a low table surrounded by plump tasseled cushions.

He shook his head. "Heaven forbid. Amanda had them all done out in different themes. Whatever took her current fancy." He gave her a smile. "You look rather out of place amid all this, Ballentine. Like you wandered in here looking for your maiden aunt."

She threw him a startled look. "No doubt the excessive modesty of my nightgown is at fault."

"Oh, undoubtedly," he agreed.

"It's a very lovely room," she ventured. "Won't you be sorry if it is all changed on my account?"

"No," he said. "I would be disappointed if you did not put your own stamp on the place."

"Because the setting does not suit me?"

"Because currently it has no good associations for me," he corrected her gravely. "Have you your robe?" he asked abruptly.

Scooting over to the edge of the bed, she glanced about for her trunk. "Um…"

"Your bags will have been unpacked already. He nodded toward a door painted with orange and blue flowers. "In there."

Emmeline stood up and made for the door, her bare feet sinking into the luxurious rug. Instead of finding a closet, she found the door led into a huge dressing room, complete with several large wardrobes, empty shelves, and chests of drawers. A triptych of three large vanity mirrors lined the far wall, throwing back her reflection at her. He was right, she did look rather lost.

"Do we share this room?" she called back over her shoulder as she peered into one wardrobe and found her few dresses already hung up and neatly pressed.

"No, I have my own," he answered from the adjoining room.

Catching sight of her dressing gown, Emmie hurried to retrieve it, wrapping it around her and fastening the belt. Out of the corner of her eye she spotted her humble carpet slippers on a fancy shoe rack and hoped the maid who unpacked them had not noticed their threadbare state.

She hurried back into the bedroom, almost bumping her head on a low-hanging lamp. "I'm ready."

Jeremy was over by the window now, drawing back the orange velvet curtains to reveal tall windows. "What do you think of your view?"

Emmie moved to join him as it had been too dark to appreciate it the night before. Her room looked out onto a green vista dominated by what looked to be a miniature temple, surrounded by a grove of trees. "Goodness, what is that? A summer house? It's very grand."

"The folly," Jeremy explained. "My father had it built on the occasion of his marriage. As a gift for his bride."

"Oh! Did your mother like it?"

"I have no idea. They were divorced by the time I was two."

Emmie strove to hide how taken aback she was. She had not known that his own parents were also divorced. On impulse, she slipped her hand into his, squeezing his fingers. He looked surprised, lifting their grasped hands to regard them with a strange expression on his face before shooting her a quick smile.

"Come along," he said, leading her out of her bedroom, still clasping her hand in his. "All the rooms down this corridor are yours," he reiterated, opening first a door which was another entrance to her dressing room. Wordlessly, he closed it again and opened another which revealed a large bathroom decorated in elaborate mosaic style tiling and dominated by a large claw-footed tub.

"I took a bath in here last night. Is it just for my use?" she asked, quite startled. He nodded. "Well, it's a far cry from the communal bathroom in Winkworth Street," she remarked, making him smile.

The next door led to a large private sitting room lavishly populated with black lacquered furniture, Oriental in style. "This is where you write your letters, receive your own personal guests etcetera," Jeremy said, leading her into the middle of the room.

Emmie gazed around in wonderment. She had never seen a room quite like it. There were elaborately painted cabinets filled with little jade curios, a large ormolu bureau, a six-paneled screen decorated with samurai warriors and many gilt chairs inlaid with mother-of-pearl which looked impressive, if not exactly comfortable to sit in.

On the walls hung oil paintings of exotic birds, flaunting highly colored plumage, and two deep purple chaise longues were set on either side of the fireplace. Overall, the effect was so intimidating she could never imagine relaxing in such a room.

"It's, well, all very beautiful, but rather imposing somehow." She was tempted to lower her voice. It almost felt like she was intruding into someone else's space.

Jeremy flashed her a wry smile. "Wait till you see the state rooms downstairs."

This was far from reassuring, but she attempted to rally. "What a pretty little table," she said, glancing down. It had a charming chinoiserie effect, though now she looked closer at it she fancied it was a decorated tray set on a stand.

"Apparently, it's an opium table," Jeremy said dismissively.

"Oh!"

"Disregard the furniture," he said. "You can have it all done out as you like."

Emmie paused. "But what would you do with it all?"

"Stuff it in the attics I expect. I think Teddy has a fondness for the cabinet of curios. He might have that."

"I see," she said doubtfully, though all she really saw was that money was no object to Jeremy Vance. Suddenly, she remembered the furniture she already owned. "I have that furniture on its way from Bath," she reminded him. "Do you suppose it will have arrived already?"

"I'll ask."

She glanced about the room, trying to imagine it emptied of all its treasures and filled instead with the leftovers she had preserved from her days in Porchester Square. She felt a terrible conviction it would not be an improvement.

"I'm not even sure that my father's old things would look well in here," she admitted in a rush of confidences. "He liked solid respectability when it came to furniture. It's all terribly cumbersome and rather ugly."

Jeremy laughed. "If that's how you feel about it then why, pray, did you bring it with us?" he asked, quite reasonably.

Emmie bit her lip. "I suppose it was sentiment really. Some of it has been with me since I was a child. My father must have paid a good deal of money for it at one time."

"So, you are sentimental, are you, Ballentine?" A strange smile played about his mouth, and he sounded more curious than censorious.

"I suppose I must be." She thought briefly of the rosewood box she owned and its shaming contents from the past and swallowed. "About some things at least."

"What sort of things?" he asked, looking intrigued. "Apart from ugly furniture."

"Actually, I do not think I am particularly sentimental," she said decisively. "Pinky collects clutter like you would not believe, dried flowers, tickets, painted cards, all sorts of ephemera. I have been a good deal more disciplined over the years to prevent such accumulation. Really, I have only ever preserved the odd letter here and there."

"Whose letters?" he asked casually. "Stockton's?"

Emmie gave a dismayed gasp. The wound was still fresh, and it felt like he had unexpectedly poked it. "I used to preserve Humphrey's letters, yes," she admitted with careful dignity. "However, when I learned of his perfidy, I consigned them to the fire. I felt I had no right to keep letters from a married man."

"Very right and proper," Jeremy responded at once. "I now have yours to him in my possession by the way."

"In *your* possession?" she repeated blankly.

He lifted an eyebrow at her. "Naturally, I demanded them when I returned your ring. It is customary, I believe, in such events as a broken engagement."

Emmie's thoughts whirled. A hundred questions sprang to her lips. *What did he say? How did he look?* She did not dare utter any of them aloud. As it turned out, she did not need to.

"As a matter of fact, he was not home when I called. Instead, I spoke to his able partner in crime. To *dear Clara*, the wife of his bosom."

Emmie gave a faint gasp. "You met her?"

"I did. I gave her a false name, of course, I thought it best to keep things discreet." His gaze seemed to dare Emmie to question him further. When she lowered her eyes, he carried on thoughtfully. "Clara had quite an eye to the main chance, if I am not mistaken. I suspect she might be the brains of their union. She would not hand over your letters until I flashed the ring. Then she forked them over alright. Slipped your ring right onto her finger."

Emmie flinched slightly and Jeremy stopped talking. In truth, it had not even occurred to her to demand the return of her letters. The idea of Humphrey doing anything dastardly with them still seemed ludicrous, despite everything she now knew.

Would Clara have perused her letters too? she wondered with faint horror. Would she and Humphrey have laughed at them together, thinking her their dupe? She felt slightly queasy at the idea. She suspected they would have been a dull read, filled as they were with her daily worries and money-saving schemes.

In the novel she and Pinky had recently sat up till midnight reading, the heroine had written her letters to her lover in either storms of ecstasy or of despair. The hero had kissed the pages on receiving them and clutched them to his breast. Humphrey's and her letters had been quite a different sort of correspondence.

"You haven't read them, have you?" she heard herself ask with sudden misgiving.

"Why, Ballentine! I have been raised a gentleman," he reproached her. "How could you dream of asking me such a thing?"

She eyed him suspiciously while he pretended not to notice. "Where are they?" she asked awkwardly. "You have put them somewhere safe?"

"Of course, I packed them in my trunk, but they're in a locked drawer in my room now. I will return them to you whenever you want." He hesitated, then asked, "If I had written you letters, Ballentine, would you have preserved them?"

She gave him an incredulous look. "My lord, we both know you never so much as scrawled me a note." Good grief, how *could* she allow her voice to sound so stupidly wistful? If she was not careful, he would guess everything, including that she still had all those old dance cards bearing his bold signature. "I think you are romanticizing our past somewhat," she said with an awkward laugh.

He did not say anything for a minute, just released her hand. "Would you prefer that I did not?" he asked in an offhand voice. "If you're finding it tiresome, I could always dispense with the fond reminiscences."

Emmie could not speak for a moment. She felt suddenly out of her depth, as though she had strayed into dangerous waters. "I could hardly ask that of you," she said hesitantly, "not when the very reason you married me was to reassure your son on that score."

"But you would, if you could?" he asked in a tense voice.

Was he annoyed? She knew he enjoyed alluding to their ridiculous past together. It was all a great joke to him. She lifted her chin. "Nothing so dramatic." She hesitated. "Though, to tell the truth, I would consider it a great favor if you no longer alluded to the Hawfords' ball." *The worse night of my life*, she thought but did not voice.

He went very still and for one horrible moment, she thought he would refuse. Then he shrugged. "Nothing could be simpler, Emmeline," he said succinctly. "Consider it forgotten. I won't raise it again." He smiled but somehow it was not remotely reassuring. She looked at him, trying to gauge his mood. He quirked a brow at her. "Come, we have much to do this morning, and you have not yet breakfasted."

"Have you breakfasted?" she asked in surprise. He surely had not ventured downstairs in that elaborate dressing gown, had he? She had a lurking suspicion he was naked beneath it. She could see not the smallest hint of a nightshirt poking out of it.

"I never eat breakfast," he said dismissively, leading the way out of the fancy sitting room. He did not offer her his hand and she did not quite have the nerve to reach for it this time. Instead, she followed him back to her bedroom, devoutly hoping this was the last time any mention of that wretched night would sour things between them.

On reaching her room, they found Teddy loitering outside the door. "There you are," he exclaimed, sounding aggrieved. "I knocked and knocked but could not make myself heard."

"That is because we were not in there," his father explained, placing a hand on his curly head. "I was just showing your stepmother her rooms."

Hearing a step in the corridor, all three of them turned to see a neat maid approaching, carrying a loaded tray. "Ah, here is Lottie with your breakfast," Jeremy said.

Teddy turned to Emmie immediately. "Can I take breakfast with you, Mama?" he asked, plucking at her sleeve.

"Of course," she answered, once she had recovered from the surprise of being addressed thus. She opened the door to let him dart inside.

"You may regret that," Jeremy said dryly. "He'll talk your ear off and make lots of crumbs."

"I don't mind, I have previously breakfasted with Master Teddy and remain undaunted," she said, throwing the door open wider for the maid Lottie to pass through.

"Will you take your breakfast in bed or at that funny floor table, milady?" the maid asked hesitating on the threshold.

"On the table!" Teddy clamored, and peering into the doorway, Emmie saw he had already seated himself there upon one of the cushions.

"The low table will be fine," Emmie answered. "Thank you, Lottie." She turned to Jeremy. "Are you not coming in?" she asked, a faint challenge in her voice.

"I don't eat breakfast," he repeated, though she noticed he loitered still outside her door.

"For the company, then," she suggested. He shook his head but did not walk away. "Have it your own way," she said lightly, then turned and walked into her new bedroom, swallowing down her disappointment.

Really, if he meant to deprive her of Pinky's company, the least he could do was provide his own by way of exchange! Making for the table, Emmie lowered herself onto the cushions opposite her stepson. "I wonder, Lottie, if you have heard anything of my friend Miss Pinson this morning?" she enquired.

The maid, who was kneeling now, was busy transferring items from her tray onto the table. "Oh yes, milady," she said comfortably. "She's taking breakfast with Mrs. Cheviot in her private parlor. Getting along famously, Annie said they were."

"Mrs. Cheviot is the housekeeper here, I believe? I think I met her last night."

"That's right, milady, for thirty years all told."

"What's this? Bacon and eggs?" Teddy asked hopefully, peering under one of the silver cloches. "Kippers!" he pronounced with disgust. He lifted another lid and pulled a face. "This must be meant for the nursery, Lottie," he said grandly. "Take it away."

Emmie peered across the table to see what had caused his displeasure. It appeared to be a bowl of porridge. Lottie ignored his high-handedness. "*This* one's bacon, eggs, and devilled kidneys," she said, placing the dish next to Emmie. Teddy's aspect brightened at once. Setting down the final few items, a pot of tea, a pot of coffee, a jug of cream, and a sugar bowl, the maid straightened up. "Is there anything else I can fetch you, your ladyship?" she asked politely.

"I think you must have thought of everything," Emmie responded, looking down at the crowded tabletop.

"Another coffee cup, please, Lottie," Jeremy said, sliding onto a cushion next to Teddy. Emmie's spirits rose precipitously.

"Right away, my lord." She curtsied and hurried out of the room.

Teddy sent his father a sidelong look. "You're eating with us, Papa?"

"Simply enjoying the company, my son," he replied, his eyes on Emmie as she took possession of the teapot.

"Tea, Edward?" she asked politely.

He nodded. "With milk and sugar. Mama—I mean, my other mama, would never let me eat in here," he commented, peering into the little jars of jam, curd, and marmalade. He dropped one of the lids and sent it careering into the sugar bowl.

"I wonder why," Jeremy said dryly, moving the milk jug away from him to safety.

"She said I always gave her a headache before noon," Teddy replied, quite unabashed. "Do you get headaches, Mama?" This was directed at Emmie.

"Very rarely," she assured him. "It is a good thing you have both joined me, for I could not possibly eat even half of this spread."

"They are simply trying to ascertain your likes," Jeremy replied. "What *do* you like, Emmeline?" he asked, fixing her with a very blue gaze.

"Tea and toast, and maybe an egg," she answered, ignoring his pointed tone and reaching for the sugar bowl.

Jeremy smirked, pulled a plate toward him, and doled out half of the bacon and eggs for Teddy.

"Not that spicy sauce, Papa!" his son protested with a grimace.

"*I* know," his father replied, carefully avoiding the devilled kidneys. He pushed the plate toward Teddy and then lifted another lid to reveal sliced toasted bread. He lifted this and set it down next to Emmie as she stirred her tea. Then he flopped down onto his side propped up by cushions, seemingly content to watch them eat.

It was such a strange setting, Emmie thought, watching Jeremy loll on velvet cushions in his golden robe. He looked like a character out of a picture book. A spoiled princeling in a magical kingdom. "This is rather fun, like having a picnic," she commented aloud, buttering her toast.

Teddy grinned at her, his mouth full of egg. "Let's have all our meals here," he suggested hopefully.

"Certainly not!" Jeremy retorted. "How would you like it if we took over your nursery for every meal?"

"I should not care." His son shrugged. "Besides, I rarely eat my meals there these days. I'm too big," he boasted.

Jeremy rolled his eyes. "Do not listen to him, Ballentine," he cautioned. "This is mere flummery. Teddy frequently takes his meals in the nursery though perhaps not as often as he ought. He is growing sadly spoiled."

"You should not call Mama that," Teddy said disapprovingly.

"Call her what?" Jeremy looked startled.

"By her surname," Teddy elucidated, reaching for a slice of toast.

"Why should I not?" Jeremy enquired. "Do you not address your closest friend as Arbuthnot?"

Teddy paused as though flummoxed, then he seemed to identify the issue. "She is not your *friend*, Papa," he responded sternly. "She is your wife."

"Why can she not be both?" Jeremy asked, but when Emmie's gaze flew to his face, he was not looking in her direction.

"She just can't," Teddy insisted, still frowning. "It stands to reason."

"Nonsense. Aunt Mina calls your uncle by his surname," he pointed out.

Teddy opened his mouth as if to argue and then closed it again. "Ye-es," he agreed uncertainly after a moment's reflection. "I suppose she does." He looked thoughtful. "You mean, she calls him that because Uncle Nye is Aunt Mina's best friend?" he asked.

"Do you know, I rather think he is," Jeremy concurred.

"Are you speaking of your sister and her husband?" Emmie asked as Lottie reappeared to set down another cup and saucer before disappearing again.

"Uncle Nye is Papa's brother too," Teddy put in as Jeremy murmured the affirmative, helping himself to coffee.

Emmie had just decided he must mean brother-in-law when Jeremy cleared his throat. "Half," he said hurriedly. "Different halves," he added with a dismissive gesture. "I'll explain later."

At this point Teddy sat up with an exclamation. "The key!" he said, pointing at the door which led to Jeremy's suite. "It's this side now!" He looked around the table with wondering eyes. "Papa always keeps it locked and on his side of the door!"

Emmie looked toward Jeremy, who had briefly closed his eyes. He opened them again, looking rather pained. "Teddy," he said. "Do be quiet and eat your breakfast."

12

After they had breakfasted, everyone drifted off to their own quarters to dress, with plans to reconvene for a tour of the formal rooms downstairs. Emmie had just selected an apple green reception dress, which had seen better days, when Lottie peeked in at the doorway of her dressing room.

"I wondered if you might be in need of a helping hand, milady," she said hopefully.

"That would be very kind," Emmie said at once, for she usually had Pinky's help with out-of-reach fastenings.

Lottie bustled in at once and made unerringly for the few drawers that contained Emmie's stockings and undergarments, making the selection for the day.

"Was it you that packed all my things away for me?" Emmie guessed. "Thank you so much. You must have been busy while I was fast asleep."

Lottie beamed at her. "I always wanted to be a lady's maid," she confessed, "but, well, I never got a fair chance with—" She broke off her words in confusion and turned red.

"With my predecessor?" Emmie asked lightly. "You must not think I will be offended by your referring to such things. I am well aware that Lord Faris was married before."

Lottie's shoulders relaxed. "Well, yes. She took against me on account of I sometimes hum a tune under my breath when I'm not thinking. She said it was 'an intolerable dirge' and she would not stand for it, so I had to fall back on a chambermaid's duties."

"I see, what a pity."

"But 'praps you won't be so particular, milady. In which case I could have another shot at it." She looked so eager that Emmie did not have the heart to refuse her.

"Do you have such a thing as a combing jacket, milady?" Lottie asked as Emmie seated herself before the dressing table.

"A what?"

"It is a garment specifically designed to be worn over your nightgown while I brush your hair," Lottie explained. "That way, any shedding will not get on your clothes."

"Oh, I see. No, I'm afraid I don't," Emmie admitted. "I don't think I've ever owned such a thing, not even during my London season."

Lottie looked rather crestfallen at this news but when Emmie informed her that she was expecting the imminent arrival of new clothes from a fashionable modiste, she perked up a little. "Doubtless, she will have made you one, milady, if she knows what's what," she opined with confidence. "And a nice sacque gown for you to wear during your morning toilette."

The neat maid cast a somewhat disparaging look over Emmie's nightgown. *Oh dear*, Emmie thought. No one was impressed with her nighttime attire but after all, it had never been intended for such scrutiny! She hoped Madame de Flores had included a sacque gown with her trousseau or Lottie would be most disappointed. "Possibly," Emmie responded cautiously. "I sort of, well, gave her free rein over the contents."

"And if she has not, you can always write to her and order one, now she's got your measurements," Lottie said blithely.

"You seem very knowledgeable about a lady's toilette, Lottie," Emmie commented as the young woman started sectioning out her abundant hair in a businesslike fashion.

"Yes, milady. I was properly trained by her ladyship's—I mean the *former* Lady Faris's original French maid, Eloise. She always intended returning to Paris but when both replacements from France did not suit, she trained me and Eliza from scratch in the hopes that one of us might do in her stead."

"What happened to Eliza?"

Lottie's expression soured. "She's still with our old mistress now, so far as I know. Took her with her, her ladyship did. She preferred the way Eliza executed an Apollo's knot." Lottie sniffed. "I expect she's living godlessly on the Continent now," she continued disapprovingly. "Always had a flighty streak did Eliza Simpkin."

"Oh, I see," Emmie said, vaguely aware that an Apollo's knot was a popular hairstyle. "Well, it turned out fortunately for me in any case," she said placatingly.

Lottie's expression brightened. "Yes, milady, thank you, milady," she said, her quick, clever hands braiding a section of hair which she then wound about Emmie's head like a riband, coaxing a series of drop curls to frame Emmie's face, spraying them finely with water. "You could do with a pot of nice waxy hair pomade, milady," she commented.

It was true that while Lottie worked, her mouth full of hairpins, she did hum rather tunelessly under her breath, however Emmie found she did not really mind it. Once the front of her hair was arranged nicely, Lottie did up the back in a professional-looking chignon.

"That looks very well indeed," Emmie exclaimed as Lottie angled a mirror to show her the full effect.

"Some flowers might be nice for decoration, milady," Lottie suggested tactfully, and Emmie realized her hair accessories were not up to the expected standard. "If you were agreeable to my doing your hair again, I could always bring some with me," she offered.

"That would be lovely, Lottie, thank you."

Once fully dressed, Emmie hurried down the corridor to find the sweeping staircase leading down to the hall. She had been tired the night before and the dim lighting had not shown just how high the painted ceilings were or how detailed the marble friezes that decorated the walls.

Without thinking, she found herself slowing to a more reverent pace, as though in church, and trying to make as little noise as possible as she crept down the steps. Rounding the final bend, she spotted Teddy, dressed quaintly in a frilly shirt and knee breeches, sitting on the third step from the bottom.

"There you are!" he exclaimed, jumping to his feet. "You took an age. Are you ready for your tour?"

"Yes indeed," Emmie responded at once. She glanced about at the quantity of marble statues thronging the hall. "Where is your father?"

"He's not down yet. Why are you whispering?" Teddy asked.

"Oh, sorry, I did not realize I was." Emmie cleared her throat. "Why is your Cupid playing with snakes?" she asked, pointing to a nearby statue, hoping to distract him from her awkwardness.

"That's not Cupid, that's Baby Heracles," Teddy answered promptly.

"I have heard of him," Emmie admitted, "but the picture I have in my mind is of some bearded brute bulging with muscle, not an infant."

"Yes, we have one of him like that in the long gallery, wrestling with the Nemean Lion."

"He was much prettier as a baby. No wonder the snakes like him."

"Well, I don't know about that," Teddy said doubtfully. "His stepmother sent them, you know, to destroy him in his crib."

"Good gracious! Did she really?" Emmie peered closer at the statue's serene expression. "I take it her wicked plan went awry. The child does not look remotely distressed."

"No, because it was too late," Teddy explained. "He had already gained godlike strength from drinking his stepmother's milk. She was a great goddess and was tricked into nursing him at her breast when he was a newborn."

Emmie blinked. "So, his stepmother…?"

"Was Hera, queen of the gods. Heracles was named in her honor. His name means 'Glory of Hera.'"

"That's rather sad," Emmie remarked, looking at the chubby alabaster baby. "I suppose they named him that in order to placate her. Were they ever reconciled?"

"Oh yes, after he died." Emmie's confusion must have plainly shown for Teddy continued, "Only his mortal side died. His immortal side ascended to Olympus where he and Hera were reunited. In the end she let him marry one of her daughters, I forget her name," he said airily.

"Hebe," Jeremy supplied, arriving at the step above them.

"Oh yes, that was it," Teddy said vaguely as Emmie's eyes widened, taking in Jeremy's appearance.

This must be what he wore when relaxing in the country. How silly, that she had somehow expected him always to wear elegant frock coats and trousers of the palest, most delicate shades. Today, he was dressed simply in a burgundy waistcoat and shirt with nankeen trousers.

Noticing her abstraction, he glanced down at his ensemble. "You approve I hope, Ballentine?" he asked with a lift of his brows.

Emmie flushed. "Of course! You are always impeccably turned out, my lord," she said, embarrassed she had been caught staring.

Teddy tugged at Emmie's sleeve. "Don't you think, Mama, that it would have been better if Baby Heracles had tamed the snakes his stepmother sent instead of strangling them?"

"I do," Emmie agreed at once, glad of the distraction. "Then he would have had pet snakes. Only think how impressive a baby with pet snakes would have been. I daresay his nurse would have fainted on the spot."

Teddy nodded enthusiastically. "I've always thought so. I've named these two Fang and Fitz," he said, stroking the stone snake heads. "Heracles could have given Fitz to his twin brother, Iphicles. Then they would have had a snake apiece."

"Heracles had a twin brother?" Emmie asked with interest. "Why am I only just hearing of this, and why, pray, do you not have a statue of Baby Iphicles?"

"Because," Jeremy interrupted, sounding amused, "Iphicles was a mere mortal child and not the son of a god. He cried when the snakes appeared and was entirely useless in subduing them."

"But wouldn't that have given the statue a pleasing asymmetry?" Emmie protested. "One baby laughing and playing with the serpents, the other crying and cringing away from them."

"The baby did not play with the snakes until they were dead," Jeremy pointed out dryly. "The two of you are creating a wholly new fiction around snake-taming babies."

"A jolly fine fiction," Teddy put in. "I'm going to pretend that's what really happened from now on."

"So am I," Emmie decided. "It's a far superior story. Perhaps the stepmother really sent the snakes to be their pets all along, and the gesture was simply misunderstood. Stepmothers are always doing rotten things in stories. I suspect they are much maligned."

"Hera was not precisely Heracles's stepmother, and she was nothing at all to Iphicles," Jeremy objected, frowning faintly. "You two seem to be deliberately confusing the issue."

"What do you mean, she was nothing to them?" Emmie asked. "Did she not nurse them at her breast? Did she not give Heracles his fantastic strength?"

"She did not nurse Iphicles," Jeremy responded firmly. "And why are we loitering on these steps instead of proceeding into the hall?"

Hastily, Emmie descended the last few steps and Teddy slipped his hand into hers. "Let's us two pretend that was so, Mama," he whispered, giving her hand a squeeze. Emmie nodded in perfect agreement.

"You should not indulge him in these flights of fancy," Jeremy groaned. "His knowledge of the classics is already sadly patchy."

"I'm afraid it is too late," Emmie said, lifting her chin. "For I have already decided to be a very encouraging sort of stepmother. Besides, I think his imaginings quite charming."

"You just wait," Jeremy warned but there was a smile playing about his mouth while Teddy looked smug.

Emmie turned about to cast her eye over the grandeur of the magnificent hall. The floor was of black and white marble and the ceiling, which she had noticed the previous night, illustrated with the pantheon of Mount Olympus. All about were strewn various treasures displayed on ormolu decorated tables with elaborately carved legs.

Feeling rather overwhelmed, Emmie turned instead to the nearest portrait. "And who is this imposing gentleman?" she asked.

"That," said Jeremy, "is my father, the fourth viscount."

Emmie's interest increased. "He looks rather formidable," she said, noticing the sitter's dark good looks and sardonic expression.

"Papa looks nothing like him, does he?" Teddy chimed in.

"No," she agreed, sneaking a look at Jeremy's blond perfection. "Not at all."

"You shall see who does when you meet my uncle Nye," Teddy promised.

Emmie briefly wondered what this relationship was that Jeremy had promised to explain at some later point.

"Let me draw your attention to the first and third Lords of Faris," Jeremy said, moving on and gesturing toward a couple of busts sat atop two Roman-style plinths. Emmie joined him and studied their profiles in thoughtful silence.

"That's not what their hair was really like," Teddy hastily explained. "They wore wigs in those days," he added disapprovingly.

Emmie turned back to Jeremy. "I think you have inherited the third viscount's nose, my lord."

"Do you think so?" He stepped up to the plinth and turned his head obligingly so they could compare.

"The very nose!" Emmie pronounced and even Teddy looked impressed.

"No one has ever noticed that before," he remarked, "have they, Papa?"

Emmie looked around. "But where is the second viscount?" she asked, for she could not see another.

"Not here. You will see him shortly," Jeremy explained. "He elected for a family portrait rather than a sculpture. He's in the dining room."

"Ah, a family man, was he?" Emmie mused. "I see you must also resemble the second viscount, at least in outlook if not in appearance."

A fleeting look of surprise crossed Jeremy's face, but he bowed slightly as though in acquiescence, and they proceeded from the hallway into the state dining room, which again, was a very grand affair.

Its red damask walls were covered in heavy gold framed portraits. "We have several pictures of Queen Anne here at Vance," Jeremy said gesturing to one of the last Stuart monarch which dominated one wall of the room.

"Because she raised your family to the peerage," Emmie recalled.

"Exactly so." He looked pleased she had remembered this detail.

"This is the second viscount," Teddy announced, halting beneath a large painting showing a bewigged nobleman sat on a chair and surrounded by daughters playing various musical instruments. To his right, the viscountess sat proudly displaying the long-awaited heir in her lap.

"The baby looks rather like a girl," Teddy said critically, "but that's actually the third viscount, Charles Augustus. The one you said has Papa's nose."

"And he had four older sisters," Emmie counted. "What a lucky boy!"

"By all accounts they were most devoted parents," Jeremy said.

"What happened to all of the children?"

Jeremy grimaced. "Maria died of smallpox at age sixteen, Elizabeth married a second cousin and died in childbirth, Lydia remained at home to look after her aged parents and we're not entirely sure what happened to Anna. She was struck out of the family bible, so it seems there was some scandal that was hushed up. Possibly she went overseas."

"She ran away to become a pirate," Teddy supplied. "That's what I would have done if I was her."

"Which one was Anna?" Emmie wanted to know. Jeremy indicated the youngest daughter, an impish-faced child dressed in primrose yellow. "Yes, I feel sure you're right," she said to Teddy. "Something about the way she handles that lyre tells me she could brandish a cutlass with equal aplomb."

Teddy giggled. They had moved on to the fireplace at this point and Emmie admired the large stone nymphs that stood either side, holding up garlands which hung down from the mantel. "Why, they are as tall as you are, Teddy," she remarked.

"The ceiling in here is considered particularly fine," Jeremy said, drawing her attention to the detailed plasterwork all gilded in gold.

"You cannot take all of your meals in here," Emmie marveled. "It is far too grand for everyday dining."

"Yes," Jeremy agreed, "there is a breakfast room on the second floor, which can be used for informal dining." The vague way he said it, though, sounded as though he had never personally done such a thing.

"When it is just the family, you mean?" Emmie enquired.

Jeremy and Teddy exchanged conspiratorial glances. "Papa often takes afternoon tea in the nursery with me," Teddy volunteered. Once again Emmie was forced to reconcile these new impressions of Jeremy with her own preconceptions. She would never have expected him to take nursery tea with his son most days.

"I know you do not take breakfast, for you told me the fact," she said slowly, "but where do you usually take your evening meal, my lord?"

He shrugged. "Whichever part of the house I happen to be in," he supplied.

"He has a tray," Teddy put in helpfully. Jeremy sent a quelling glance at his son and Teddy retreated to fiddle with the drawer on a large sideboard.

Emmie's attention wandered back to the fireplace. "I always thought nymphs would be a good deal svelter than those two," Emmie admitted, her eyes dwelling on the substantial forms of the stone figures.

"Why?" Jeremy enquired.

"To escape all those lusty gods," she answered immediately. "They look too hefty to be fleet of foot. I can't imagine that Apollo, or whoever it was, would have much trouble chasing them down."

A smile tugged at his lips. "I daresay my ancestor had similar tastes to my own." His gaze transferred from the marble nymphs to rest on her appreciatively. Emmie cleared her throat, and he glanced toward Teddy, who was headed back toward them.

"Let us proceed," he said, and they passed next into the music room, which was decorated in pale green, housed several instruments, and looked out onto the south lawn.

Emmie's favorite thing, though, was a series of charming miniatures in display cases, which depicted various daughters of the house dating from Tudor times right through to the second viscount's daughters.

"Oh!" exclaimed Emmie, leaning forward to examine them closer. "Please tell me you have a miniature of at least one of your resident ghosts!"

Jeremy laughed. "But of course! We have both," he said, taking her by the arm and leading her toward a second case of miniatures. "Allow me to draw your attention to Mistress Mary Vance, and next to her, Mistress Frances."

"They look the same to me," Teddy said disparagingly. He drifted over to the pianoforte and started plunking on the keys.

"Which was the spinster sister?" Emmie asked, looking from one to the other. Both had white oval faces, light brown hair, and rather hooded eyes.

"By all accounts that would be Frances."

Both sisters wore matching French hoods, though Frances's dress was green, and Mary's a rather murky red. There was not much else to differentiate between the two, other than their jewelry. Lady Frances wore a gold chain around her neck and Lady Mary a pearl brooch upon her bodice.

"I suppose I will only ever have the option of seeing Lady Frances, for I am already married, am I not?" she concluded at last. "And she betokens ill fortune, I think you said? Or was that the other?"

Jeremy looked thoughtful. "I'm afraid my experience was highly unusual, for I saw them both, walking side by side. Popular opinion has it that Mary heralds marriage, and Frances misfortune, but like I said, it can be hard to realize which of the two you saw unless you have a keen eye."

"I see," Emmie said thoughtfully.

Jeremy excused himself and, turning abruptly, told Teddy to stop creating such an infernal racket. "Is it too much to hope that Miss Pinson could resume his music lessons anytime soon?" he sighed in a swift change of subject.

"Oh yes, she is quite competent on the pianoforte."

"Well, thank heaven for small mercies. Did you hear that, Teddy?"

Emmie thought Teddy looked far from pleased by this news. Carefully shutting the fall board, he made his way over to them and leaned against his father's legs.

"Library next, Papa," he prompted.

"Yes, library," Jeremy agreed, resting a hand fleetingly on his son's curly head.

13

Jeremy thought Emmeline liked the library best, and he could not blame her, for it was certainly the most relaxing of the rooms they had shown her, with its muted golds and greens and mellowed oak bookcases. He watched her surreptitiously as she moved through the room, admiring its contents.

Not for the first time her words from this morning drifted through his head. *Is that why you did not sleep in the same bed as me last night?* They caused him a pang now, as they had then, along with a strong impulse to kick himself.

For the first time in his life, he was striving to be a considerate husband. The devil of it was that the more he tried, the less he seemed to succeed. He had considered leaving her alone last night, a supreme sacrifice on his behalf. He had congratulated himself on his thoughtfulness, even as he puzzled over the strange prompting to put her feelings first.

Far from being grateful, he had a lurking suspicion that Emmeline had viewed his self-restraint as indifference or even worse, neglect. What he should have done, he realized now, was sleep beside her without attempting further congress.

Likely, she had been ill at ease and nervous to sleep by herself in strange surroundings. It had not occurred to him, in truth, because he was used to being selfish in his dealings with women. The realization was not a comfortable one.

He looked up to find Teddy was showing her the false bookcase which hid the door to a concealed stone stairway. "The servants use it mostly," his son was explaining. "And this is Papa's desk, where he keeps the ledgers for his stables and the estate."

Emmie duly admired the huge oak desk, then the painting hanging above it caught her eye.

"My father commissioned that portrait," he said, crossing the room to join them. "On the occasion of my nineteenth birthday."

"The likeness is very good," she murmured. "Did your father also request you were painted on horseback?"

"Yes. My equestrianism was one thing about me that my father truly admired."

"Papa still has that horse. His name is Cadmus," Teddy said. "Did you go and see him when we got home last night, Papa? That is Papa's custom."

"Yes," he admitted, his eyes still on Emmeline. "Briefly." He wondered what she was thinking as she gazed up at the portrait.

"Nineteen…" Emmeline said quietly, and suddenly he knew what she was thinking. She was thinking that she knew him at that age. He hissed out a breath as he remembered her words that morning. They had been strangely painful. *I would consider it a great favor if you no longer alluded to the Hawfords' ball.*

Their eyes met and she turned hastily about, halting before a sixteenth-century Venetian rendition of Venus reclining naked on a red velvet sofa, while next to her a fully clothed musician played the harp for her entertainment.

Noticing her startled expression, Teddy said with faint disapproval, "There's lots of Venuses here at Vance. Papa collects them."

Jeremy cleared his throat. "There is an antechamber through there," he said, indicating an archway which led through to a room currently used as an overspill area. "I thought we could dedicate it to a collection of novels."

Emmeline's face lit up. "Novels? Really?"

He nodded, glancing around his impressive library. "The books in here are worthy tomes and the result of many years of collecting. I've scarcely read any of them though, and I suspect the same was true of my father. He just liked buying rare books and showing them off."

She nodded slowly. "Yes, when my father bought his London house, he purchased a good many books all tooled in red leather to display in his new library. I don't think the pages were even cut. They were all sold with the house and doubtless sit in other gentlemen's libraries now."

The three of them moved into the antechamber and he could see she was impressed by the space available. "I don't actually own that many novels," she said apologetically. "We used to borrow them mostly from the lending library."

"I ordered you some when I was in London," he said offhandedly.

"Did you?" She flushed, this time he hoped with pleasure.

"I wanted to buy you a wedding gift you would appreciate."

She looked a little awkward over this, then her expression brightened. "Are there any spare bookcases in the attic?" she asked.

He shrugged. "We can always commission some new ones made."

"I bet there are!" Teddy enthused. "There's all sorts of things in the attics. Shall we take a look up there after lunch?"

"No," Jeremy answered firmly. "We still have lots of rooms to show your stepmama. Teddy loves prying and poking up there," he said by way of explanation. "He would spend hours up there if we let him."

They proceeded with the tour. He fancied Emmeline's least favorite room was the formal drawing room, which admittedly was not the most welcoming room, decorated as it was in shades of white and gold. Seeing how she gaped at the recessed apse with its supporting Corinthian columns and full-size portrait of Queen Anne in her golden robes, Jeremy felt obliged to speak.

"In his defense, the first Lord Faris was hoping the queen would come and stay here at Vance for a state visit. Sadly, it never came off."

"I see," she responded, turning away from the portrait to gaze at the walls which were covered in good copies of various masterpieces.

"Queen Anne had an attack of gout at the last minute and couldn't come," Teddy explained as Emmeline halted before a copy of Titian's *Venus Rising from the Sea.*

Jeremy coughed. "Come and look at this," he said, gesturing to a huge foot wearing a sandal carved in gray stone. "The third viscount brought it back from his travels on the grand tour. He always maintained it was the only surviving part of the Colossus of Rhodes."

"It must certainly have come from a very large statue," Emmeline observed, joining him in front of the stone foot. "Was not the Colossus of Rhodes very famous?"

"It was one of the seven wonders of the ancient world," Teddy cut in excitedly. "It stood over one hundred feet tall!"

"Goodness," Emmeline murmured. "Fancy having part of an ancient wonder in your very own drawing room!"

"Yes," Teddy agreed before his face clouded over. "Only *some* people say it cannot be the Colossus's foot because according to *some*, it was made of brass not stone."

"Bronze," Jeremy corrected him.

"What nonsense! I feel sure there must be as many accounts saying it was made of stone as there are saying it was made of bronze," Emmeline said stoutly. "That is *always* the way, I find, when it comes to antiquities. You read one article and it firmly asserts one thing, then another refutes this and offers an entirely different theory. Accounts differ wildly. Who dared slander the Vance family honor in such a fashion?"

"The vicar, for one," Jeremy said mildly.

"And Lord Atherton for another," Teddy added indignantly. "He said my great-great-grandfather was probably *conned*."

"I don't believe that for one minute," Emmeline said, pursing her lips. "I am sure that is a monstrous slander and so I shall tell Lord Atherton next time I see him." Teddy looked gratified. "Probably the Colossus had some bronze embellishment or else held a torch made of bronze aloft or some such thing. I feel sure I have seen an image of him somewhere holding a torch."

"Stood astride the harbor?" Teddy asked excitedly. "We have a book in the library that shows a picture like that. Shall I go and fetch it now?"

"Not right now," Jeremy said firmly. "I think it must be time for lunch. Shall we head for the blue salon? I told them we would take it in there today."

Luncheon was duly taken in the blue salon. The blue silk wall panels were admired, as was the portrait of Jeremy's mother in her frothy pink ballgown and pearls.

"Now I see just where you inherited *your* looks," Emmeline commented.

"Except for his nose," Teddy reminded her.

Mrs. Cheviot herself appeared accompanied by two of the housemaids to lay out an impressive spread of finger sandwiches and a variety of little iced cakes. Emmeline asked after her friend and the housekeeper responded that she and Miss Pinson had enjoyed a nice cozy chat over breakfast. "I was sorry to see her go, milady," she said with a smile. "She was such good company."

"Go?" Emmeline asked, sounding alarmed. She shot an interrogatory glance at Jeremy.

He set down his coffee cup. "I had Colfax escort Miss Pinson over to Somerton's old cottage this morning to take a look at it. She will need to decide what needs to be done with the place to make it habitable. I felt sure she would want to see it as soon as possible."

A thousand questions seemed to tremble on Emmeline's lips. Finally, she settled for, "I would have liked to accompany her there. She may feel quite overwhelmed and need my support."

"I think you underestimate her," Jeremy responded coolly. "Don't you think she would rather show *you* around her new home once she feels mistress of it?" She opened her mouth to deny this, then seemed to reconsider, shutting it again. "Just as you can show her around this place now you have the lay of it," he added with satisfaction.

"Where is Somerton Cottage?" Teddy asked with a frown. "I don't know that one."

"Somerton was the gamekeeper who last resided there. I forget its actual name." He turned to Mrs. Cheviot, who turned to one of the maids.

"Gladys, your uncle lives in one of those gamekeeper's cottages, doesn't he?"

Jeremy helped himself to another sandwich, ignoring the suspicious glint in Emmeline's eye on hearing they were considered cottages for gamekeepers not governesses.

"Oh yes, Mrs. Cheviot," Gladys replied, "in the little house at the end. Oak Tree Cottage, uncle's is called, they're all named after trees in that lane. Now let me see, was it Elm Tree Cottage? Or Fir Tree?" She shook her head. "I couldn't rightly say. Beg pardon, milord." She bobbed an apologetic curtsey.

"It's of no matter, Gladys," he said. "I'm sure Miss Pinson will give us all the details on her return. She can fill us in over dinner." He turned to Mrs. Cheviot. "We will dine formally this evening, Mrs. Cheviot."

"Oh yes, milord, of course," she said, having clearly anticipated as much. "Will her ladyship wish to look over the menu with me this afternoon?" she asked hopefully.

Jeremy hesitated. He had intended to show Emmeline the rest of the rooms on the second floor but clearly the housekeeper was bursting to show her new mistress the more practical side of the house. Perhaps that would be better, he reflected, before deciding just to ask.

"Emmeline, now that you have seen all the reception rooms here at Vance, how would you like Mrs. Cheviot to give you an overview of the kitchens and servants' quarters this afternoon?"

She smiled at Mrs. Cheviot. "That would be most agreeable," she acquiesced, and Jeremy fancied the servants would have a much easier time of it with his second wife than they had with his first.

"Excellent."

"But Papa, I wished to show Mama my nursery!" Teddy objected.

"There may still be time for that after, my son."

"If there is, then I shall certainly ask Mrs. Cheviot to bring me to the nursery as soon as we are done," Emmeline promised.

Seemingly satisfied with this, Teddy returned to his jam tart.

Jeremy spent the afternoon writing notes to various people he needed to see after his Bath sojourn, primarily his estate manager and his man of business. Then there was his sister, Mina, of course, he thought, hesitating, pen in hand.

He would need to break the news of his marriage to her and Nye before much longer. It would not do for them to learn he was married from anyone else. He should really tell them in person. Could he invite them to dine with him tonight?

Though Mina had now visited him at Vance a few dozen times, he had never succeeded in getting Nye to set foot in the place. Despite the unlikelihood of their accepting, he ended up dashing off an invitation anyway.

Dearest Mina and Nye,

Teddy and I have returned to Vance. Momentous news to impart. Come to dinner tonight at seven if you can. Family only. Feel free to bring my nephew with you. I can send a carriage if required. Let Colfax have your response.

Your affectionate brother,

J.V.

Remembering Colfax was at the cottage with Miss Pinson, he scored out *Colfax* and wrote *Higgins*, the name of the second footman, then pulled the sash to summon him.

He did not even for one minute think that they would come, even less so when Higgins returned an hour later explaining he had been forced to leave the note for he had failed to locate either Mr. or Mrs. Nye about the place. Their young maid Corin, her hands full looking after Baby James, seemingly had no idea where they were to be found.

"What about Edna?" Jeremy asked, naming their most senior member of staff.

"It's her day off," Higgins responded. "She'd gone to visit with an aunt of hers."

"Curious," said Jeremy with a shrug. "Ah, well, I did not have high hopes to begin with. Thank you, Higgins."

14

Emmie spent an instructive afternoon with Mrs. Cheviot. Not only did she get shown around the extensive kitchen but also the still room, the larder, and the cellars. After word was sent to Mr. Garraway, he appeared to decorously escort her around the butler's pantry.

Both he and the housekeeper were most vexed that they could not locate a footman to show her the footman's waiting room. "That Colfax," Mrs. Cheviot tutted. "I might have known he was nowhere to be found. A law unto himself he is, but where's Higgins? That's what I want to know!"

In the end a maid called Bridget did the honors, and then accompanied Emmie and Mrs. Cheviot up to the third floor, where the servants were housed.

"It all looks very neat and tidy," Emmeline commented at the close of the last door.

"And now, I thought we could finish up in my rooms," Mrs. Cheviot said grandly. "Which are on the floor below. If you are agreeable, my lady, we could have a nice cup of tea and look over this evening's menu together."

"Of course, that would be lovely. I also wanted to have a word with you about Lottie, if I may."

Mrs. Cheviot and Bridget exchanged glances. "Of course, milady. Bridget, do run down and fetch us hot water for the teapot. Milady, if you will just watch your step here, we'll make our way to the second floor."

Mrs. Cheviot's rooms, a bedroom and her own private sitting room, were very comfortably furnished. The genteel style was very reminiscent of Emmie's old rooms at Winkworth Street. She did not wonder that Pinky would have enjoyed a nice cozy chat there this morning.

"Master Teddy told me you had a mantel scarf," she commented once she was settled in what the housekeeper assured her was "the most comfortable seat."

Mrs. Cheviot looked surprised. "There now, fancy the child singling that out for comment!" she exclaimed.

"I think it is because our own rooms in Bath reminded him of your tastes."

The housekeeper looked gratified. "Your dear friend, Miss Pinson, intimated as much. Now, why was it that you wanted to talk to me about Lottie? She has not done anything amiss, has she?"

Emmie explained that Lottie had ably helped her with her toilette that morning. "She seemed most competent, and I understand she is already fully trained for the position. I hope it would not inconvenience you too much to have her switch her duties?"

Mrs. Cheviot sucked in her cheeks. "It's not that, milady. Indeed if you were happy to settle for Lottie's services then that's all well and good. The girl will be thrilled. It's just Mr. Garraway and I imagined his lordship would want to engage one of those Parisien maids for you that's wise to all the latest frills and folderols."

Emmie had to hide her answering smile. "To be perfectly honest with you, Mrs. Cheviot, I do not think I will ever be 'bang up' to all the latest trends. I had a London season ten years ago and I did not enjoy it. I have no interest in being a leader or even a follower of fashion."

Mrs. Cheviot looked skeptical but did not argue the point. It occurred to Emmie that she was used to an entirely different kind of mistress. Still, she was kindly and patient as she poured Emmie a hot cup of tea and passed her a menu written in a neat though rather spidery hand. It comprised of six courses and looked vastly elegant.

"I really do not know that I could improve on this, Mrs. Cheviot, so I hope you are not expecting me to refine it. It all looks delicious. I can hardly wait."

The housekeeper sat up straighter and turned very pink. "Well, milady, I hope I am not being immodest when I say that I am used to running things pretty well on my own initiative. There was no lady in the house in the old lord's day, once his stepsister was married with a house of her own and his own marriage was so short-lived…well. I'll say no more about *that*," she said, pursing her lips.

"I was just admiring Jeremy's mother's portrait in the blue salon," Emmie said. "She was *very* pretty; I think he must take after her in appearance. Jeremy told me that his father had the folly built for her as a wedding present."

"Yes," Mrs. Cheviot sighed. "He was good at grand gestures, the old master, but he was not an easy man to live with. Sullen he was, and moody. Why, he could nurse a grievance for days! He fell out with everyone hereabouts at one time or another. The squire, the vicar, no one was safe from his temper. Now, I never agreed with what Lady Faris did, the current lord's mother, I mean. Up and running away like she did, but I daresay he drove her to it.

"She was a gentle and pretty spoken creature. Only child she was, of a widower who spoiled her. Ill prepared, she was, for married life with the likes of him! Used to cry she did, all the time. Fair broke my heart it did to see her pining away day after day, so pale and miserable. *I never should have married*, that's what she used to say, though afterward, we found out she married again and not so long after neither! But there, folks are funny."

Mrs. Cheviot checked the teapot and, finding ample remaining, poured them both another cup.

"I had not realized until recently that Jeremy's parents were also divorced," Emmie admitted, lifting her cup to her lips.

Mrs. Cheviot tutted and shook her head. "A sad business it was, very sad and the old master, wicked the way it was he took her leaving. Fair tickled about it, he was! Never thought she had it in her, that's what he used to say, and laugh. Laughed! Granted her a divorce he did, the only handsome thing he ever did by her, but she had to leave her child behind. His heir, you know, and Master Jeremy only a babe in arms. Must have broken her heart that must have done.

"Not but what, we found out afterward she had another baby, a girl that time, so hopefully that consoled her a little. That's his lordship's sister, Mrs. Nye." She cleared her throat. "She lives locally now but was raised in Wiltshire. She's married to an innkeeper." Mrs. Cheviot paused awkwardly for a moment before continuing.

"Very fond of her, his lordship is, and Master Teddy, though your predecessor, she did not think the connection a good one." Mrs. Cheviot sniffed. "Very high in the instep *she* was, on account of her father being Earl Tipton."

Emmie cleared her throat. "I was a little acquainted with Lady Amanda years ago," she admitted, "when I lived in London."

Mrs. Cheviot's eyes widened. "There now, I did not realize that!" She leaned forward. "You were debutantes together, then, going to all those fancy parties and being presented."

"She came out a few years before me, so I really only knew her by sight alone."

"And his lordship? Did you know him in those days?"

Emmie felt the betraying color creep into her cheeks. "Oh yes," she agreed lightly. "I knew him then."

"*Such* a handsome young man he was," Mrs. Cheviot sighed. "And so different from his father. I don't just mean in looks, though his father was good-looking in another way. I mean by temperament. Very sunny-natured as a child Master Jeremy was, and always fair spoken, even when he was sent down from school and in disgrace.

"'Mrs. C,' he used to say, 'you must not be cross with me for I could not bear it,' and indeed I never could be, not for long. No matter what tricks he played! He could charm the birds from the trees, that one," she chuckled. "And he *always* had a way of coaxing folk. Even his father could not resist him when he really put his mind to charming him.

"The times he threatened to cut him off without a penny, but he never did. Master Jeremy would always bring him around in the end. At the last, when he was on his deathbed, it was only Master Jeremy that would do. He could not abide the vicar or anyone else to sit with him. That says a lot, now, doesn't it?"

"Yes, I rather think it does." Emmie thought of her own father, whose passing had been swift and unexpected. Would he have wanted her to hold his hand at the end, if he had a choice? She did not know.

"Right sorry we were when we realized his lordship, his current lordship I mean, was headed down the same path as his father, and getting a *divorce*." Mrs. Cheviot lowered her voice over the offending word. "Not that we were precisely shocked," she said slowly. "The marriage was, well, far from *harmonious*. An estrangement, now, none of us would have batted an eyelid at that, but divorce…" She shot a look at Emmie's carefully blank face. "But the least said about that, perhaps, the better."

It was so tricky, Emmie thought. Strictly speaking, she knew she should not encourage gossip, but it was all so fascinating to hear about. "I have been very glad and thankful to hear everything you have told me, Mrs. Cheviot," she said honestly. "It has all been most enlightening." Mrs. Cheviot settled back in her chair looking gratified.

"Indeed, I have never been involved in the running of such a large house," she continued, "so I know I shall be so grateful for any guidance you can give me."

"Why, certainly, milady," the older woman assured her. "I will be most happy to oblige in any way I can."

By the time their conference was done, it was past four o'clock already. A passing maid escorted her to the nursery, where she found Teddy lining up tin soldiers in long drills.

"Here you are at last!" he exclaimed, springing to his feet. "I almost thought you had forgotten me."

"As if I could," Emmie said, gazing about the large room filled to the brim with books and toys and all the trappings of childhood. "Goodness, what a lucky boy you are to have so many lovely things!"

"Yes," he agreed sanguinely. "Come and see my new fort. It's much bigger than my old one and has a drawbridge that really lifts."

"Do the little cannons shoot marbles?" Emmie asked, examining the mechanism.

"Yes, I'll show you how. Papa bought it for me in Bath and had it sent back ahead of us as a surprise."

"Who is this?" Emmie enquired, peering into one of the rooms and finding one of the soldiers lying in a makeshift bed made from an ink-spotted handkerchief. "Oh, he's missing a leg!"

"That's Carruthers," Teddy said shortly. "He was grievously injured in battle."

"Poor fellow!"

"He's going to pull through," Teddy assured her. "For a while, though, it was a close-run thing. He had a fever and mistook the captain for his old, widowed mother."

"That is quite understandable. I do hope none of his fellow soldiers joke about it afterward. That would be too bad."

Teddy nodded. "If anyone does, it will be this fellow," he said darkly, picking up a soldier whose sloppily painted uniform gave him a somewhat slovenly appearance.

"Who is that?"

"This is Pomfrey. He's a bad hat." He leaned closer to her. "Even his old schoolmaster said he would go to the devil one day."

Emmie gave an obliging gasp. Teddy nodded solemnly. "Does no one think well of him?" she asked sadly.

Teddy seemed to consider this. "We-ell, perhaps his sister," he conceded at last. "But she's rather a simpleton," he said scornfully, "and believes the best of everyone."

"I expect he writes her long letters, telling her all his woes," Emmie said whimsically as she peered at Pomfrey's beady little eyes.

"Papa says he may come right in the end," Teddy admitted doubtfully. "He says his own schoolmaster said something very similar about him once."

Emmie gave a strangled cough. "You, however, do not have high hopes for Pomfrey's military career?"

He shook his head. "Even now, he is shirking guard duty," he said gravely. "He should be up here," he said, gesturing to one of the towers, "with Corporal Winthrop, but instead he is playing cards down here in the courtyard with Bayliss, who is a subaltern."

"Very shocking."

"I know."

They spent a very pleasant hour playing with the fort. Emmie had Pomfrey up before a disciplinary where it was pronounced he would get sent to bed without any rations that night. She told Teddy she believed this would make him think twice about his wicked ways. Teddy told her that he doubted it, and that Pomfrey had a stash of hidden rum that he would fortify himself with before bedtime.

"Goodness me. He's quite a resourceful fellow, isn't he?" she marveled.

"Who is?" Jeremy asked, sauntering into the room, and leaning down to kiss her cheek. Emmie gave a guilty start.

"Pomfrey," Teddy answered at once.

"Pomfrey?" Jeremy echoed in lively disgust. "I never thought I would hear anyone praising that scoundrel! What, pray, has Pomfrey been up to to earn your admiration, Ballentine?"

"Smuggling rum," Teddy expanded.

Jeremy threw a startled glance her way.

"That is not what I was admiring!" Emmie protested hotly. "I simply think he has some qualities which might recommend themselves, if they could simply be channeled into a more worthy direction."

"No one thinks Pomfrey has any redeeming features," Jeremy said damningly, sitting down opposite them on the rug.

"His sister does," Teddy objected.

Jeremy lowered the flag he had picked up to add to the tower. "I never knew he had one!"

"Oh yes," Emmie said knowledgeably. "He writes to her once a month, great long epistles all about his troubles."

"He would!"

She shook her head. "I am convinced Pomfrey is simply misunderstood."

"That's what his sister says," Teddy said eagerly. "She even wrote to the captain of the guard saying as much."

Jeremy narrowed his eyes. "I see that young Pomfrey has the knack of cozening womenfolk." He picked up the toy soldier to regard him in a new light. "I never knew that about him before."

Emmie tossed her head. "You are far too hard on him. I shall add my voice to his sister's and appeal to the captain on his behalf."

"I shall grow very jealous if you start writing to other men so soon into our marriage, Ballentine," Jeremy warned her, making her gasp. "In fact, I forbid it."

Emmie fought down her blush. "The captain, I am persuaded, is a most proper person," she said primly. "And would never dream of imposing on me through our correspondence."

"Yes," agreed Teddy, "and besides, I do not know if Mama could write letters small enough for him to read."

The next hour flew by, as it was discovered that the captain, whose name was Gerrard, had fallen madly in love with Miss Pomfrey by the power of her beautiful penmanship and kept her letter hidden in his breast pocket next to his heart.

"Poor Captain Gerrard!" Emmie exclaimed. "He must be a great romantic, I think."

"I may demote him," Teddy confided with disgust. "I can paint over his stripes and promote Stavers instead."

"I don't think we need to go that far," Jeremy disagreed. "Unrequited love is surely punishment enough."

"But what if he starts giving Pomfrey light punishments," Teddy objected, "so that his sister won't be angry? That would not be fair on the other men."

"No, no, he will go the opposite way," Jeremy assured him. "He will punish Pomfrey all the more, in the hopes he features heavily in his next letter to his sister."

"That is a truly *terrible* strategy!" Emmie pronounced.

"Yes, but poor Gerrard is a fool when it comes to love," Jeremy sighed. "His instincts are all wrong and he does not understand women at all."

"Yes, but I can't have a fool leading my campaign against the enemy," Teddy objected. "It stands to reason!"

"You misunderstand," his father said. "In military matters, Gerrard is *brilliant*, quite inspired. It is only in matters of the heart that he is sadly incompetent."

"Oh, very well," Teddy relented, lying flat on his stomach so he was eye level with the tin soldier. "But I will be keeping a close eye on you, Gerrard," he warned. "There will be no dilly-dallying."

He jostled the soldier and answered, "Yes, General Vance," in a squeaky voice.

At last Jeremy glanced at his pocket watch. "We had all better go and change for dinner," he said regretfully. "You too, Teddy. It's getting late."

15

Emmie was distracted as she dressed for dinner. Thankfully Lottie, reveling in her new position as lady's maid, made up for this. "Ooh, aren't they lovely!" Lottie gasped when Emmie retrieved the diamond hairpins she had worn for her wedding and passed them to Lottie to dress her hair.

"Yes, they were a bride-gift from his lordship," she said a little self-consciously.

Lottie's eyes were very wide. "Fancy! And did you have a very grand ceremony, milady?" Lottie had brought fresh flowers along to dress Emmie's hair for dinner and she was placing them now very artfully in her hair arrangement.

"Oh yes," Emmie answered absently, drawing on her evening gloves. She supposed she ought to wear them even though they were dining at home. She thought of the state dining room and realized embellishment was needed of her orange silk evening gown, which was about a decade out of style.

Noticing Lottie's expectant look in the mirror, she realized her maid was hoping for more details about the wedding. "It was at St. Matthew in the Avon in Bath," she added. "A very old church, twelfth century I believe, but it has recently undergone restoration and looks very smart."

"And did you have much family there, milady?" It crossed Emmie's mind that Lottie was fishing for information to take back to the servants' hall. But after all, why should she not? Her new position should ensure she had some exclusive tidbits about her mistresses to impart.

"Not on my side. I am an orphan, but Jeremy's stepaunt was in attendance," she recalled, though she could not bring her name to mind. "And Lord Atherton was groomsman. I understand he comes often to Vance."

"Oh yes, milady. He has been a frequent visitor over the years."

"And afterward, the wedding breakfast was held at the civic hall. It was quite a banquet. His lordship had invited, well, some society people from the time when we were first acquainted," she said in perfect truth. "A thoughtful attention I had not expected," she continued with an attempt at breeziness she was not entirely sure she pulled off. "Some of them I had not seen for years."

Lottie nodded, her eyes shining. "Would that be from when you were a debutante, milady?" she asked. Seeing Emmie's startled look, she added, "You mentioned that this morning, milady."

"Oh, of course I did. Yes, from that time," she agreed quietly. "That was when I first met Lord Faris. Only, he had not acceded to his title in those days and was just an honorable." She hoped this was enough information for Lottie to dazzle the other servants with, for she could not bring herself to embellish further.

Lottie beamed. "Your hair is dressed, milady. Shall I fetch your jewel case?" Emmie had just opened her mouth to decline the offer when she recalled it was no longer empty. Lottie was just clasping the string of lustrous pearls about her neck when a discreet knock was heard on her bedroom door.

Inexplicably, her heart leaped into her throat. "Come in!" she called, turning in her seat toward the connecting door, which she had already unlocked that evening. It did not move. Instead, it was the door into the corridor which swung open, and Pinky's head peered around it.

"I trust I do not intrude, Emmie dear," she said, her astonished gaze darting about the luxurious bedroom.

"Of course not, Pinky dear, come in. Lottie, this is my dearest friend in all the world, Miss Hannah Pinson. Pinky, this is my new lady's maid, Lottie."

"Oh, how prettily you have done her hair!" Pinky exclaimed, instantly winning favor with Lottie. "I am sure it is just as beautifully done as it was on your wedding day, Emmie!"

"Have you passed a pleasant day?" Emmie enquired, noticing that her friend was already dressed in her best bombazine gown for dinner.

"Oh yes," Pinky answered at once, coming into the room with her skirts rustling. "Oh, Emmie, the cottage is going to be wonderful, quite wonderful. Only fancy, there are two good-sized bedrooms, besides a little box room, a front parlor, and the *garden*," she said rapturously. "It is true that at the moment it is quite unkempt, but I mean to change all that and tend it *most* assiduously. And you will never guess what it is called!" she concluded, holding her breath.

Emmie considered this, remembering Gladys's words from earlier. "Elm Tree Cottage?" she hazarded.

"*Plumtree* Cottage!" Pinky declared triumphantly. "Is that not providential? Is that not a sign?" At Emmie's blank look, she added, "Do you not recall my saying that a cottage is not complete without larkspurs and a plum tree?"

"Oh yes, of course," Emmie hastened to assure her as Lottie clasped her diamond bracelet about her gloved wrist. She stood up. "Thank you, Lottie." She turned to Pinky. "Shall we?"

Pinky kept up her excited chatter about the cottage as they descended the stairs together. "The current furniture such as it is, is *not*, well, not in good condition but I am sure that I can make do, and bit by bit I can—"

"Well, the furniture from Winkworth Street will be here any day now," Emmie reminded her. "You must have whatever you want from that for your cottage."

Pinky halted on her step, turning toward her. "Oh, Emmie!" she gasped, her hands flying to her cheeks. "You must not think—I could not possibly—!"

"Nonsense, Pinky dear," Emmie said firmly. "I am sure you noticed how stuffed to the gills this place is with priceless treasures. Jeremy has already called in goodness only knows how many decorators and designers. I have nowhere to put our old furniture! Certainly, you must have it. I'll brook no argument on the matter."

She tugged on her friend's arm, dragging her down to the next step. "Now, by my reckoning, that means you have bedroom furniture enough for your two bedrooms and—"

Pinky turned to her and caught her in a spontaneous embrace. "You are far, far too good to me!" she said fiercely.

"Now, Pinky, don't you dare cry!"

By the time they reached the hallway, both of them were a little misty-eyed. Jeremy was in full evening dress and looking very elegant as he lounged in the huge hall, awaiting them. His smile as he crossed the floor to greet them gave her the oddest sensation of butterflies in her stomach.

He was just kissing her hand and asking Pinky about her day when the knocker sounded loudly at the main entrance. He straightened up with a look of surprise.

"Did you invite anyone, Papa?" Teddy asked as he descended the last few steps in a blue velvet suit with a decorated collar.

"No," Jeremy frowned. "Only—" He broke off as Garraway ceremoniously opened the door to reveal two visitors stood on the threshold. Three, if you included the baby the woman held in her arms. "Well, I'll be damned!" Jeremy said loudly, in obvious astonishment.

The man coming through the door laughed, a rather harsh sound. He looked an intimidating sort, tall and broad and with a brash air which his red silk waistcoat and black suit somehow enhanced. "Well, it's good to know I needn't mind my tongue too much among such company," he said dryly as they advanced into the hall.

"Come in, you're very welcome!" Jeremy said, recovering fast. "I'm glad you came." He shot an oddly agonized look at Emmie which she could not account for. "This is my sister, Mina, that I told you of," he said in a low urgent voice. "And her husband, William Nye. He—"

"Uncle Nye!" Teddy yelled, flying across the marble floor. The man caught him up in his arms and swung him around once before setting him back down again. "Mind your manners, you ruffian," he scolded, ruffling his hair. "Now greet your aunt in a civilized fashion."

His wife, by contrast, was good-looking in a rather understated manner. She was tall and wore her brown hair in a demure roll at her nape and wore very little decoration save for a mother-of-pearl hair comb and a cameo brooch depicting the profile of an old woman with a determined chin. She bent down and offered her cheek to Teddy, who obligingly kissed it.

"I am glad to see you looking well," she said calmly to Teddy. Then sent a challenging look toward Jeremy, which seemed to spur him into action. Offering Emmie his arm, they advanced to greet the newcomers.

"This is Baby James, Mama!" Teddy cried. "Come and see."

Was it Emmie's imagination, or had the lady paused at hearing him address her as Mama? She felt a sudden misgiving. Perhaps Jeremy's sister had been close with his former wife. Garraway was helping her to remove her cape and bonnet as Nye took the baby from her with a practiced move. Emmie noticed he wore no hat atop his black hair.

Suddenly, his likeness struck her, and she drew in a swift, sharp breath. She could not help the glance she darted toward the portrait of Jeremy's father. If nothing else, she had to check the fourth viscount had not stepped down out of the canvas to join them. But no, he was still there, gazing coldly out of his gold frame.

Jeremy's fingers briefly clasped hers in a warning squeeze, and she knew he must have noticed her stealing a look. Plastering a smile to her face, Emmie braced herself as the various introductions were made. Neither Mrs. nor Mr. Nye appeared shocked when she was introduced as Jeremy's wife, though they both subjected her to rather hard stares and she was informed that he answered to "just Nye, forget the mister."

Instantly, Emmie wished she was not currently flaunting every piece of jewelry she owned. It was a funny thing, but she had left her bedroom, anxious that her finery drew attention away from her faded silk gown. Now she wished for the opposite effect. Mina's understated gown of lavender silk and her cool politeness made Emmie feel ostentatious and showy.

Jeremy's sister was so different to him! She tried to remember what Mrs. Cheviot had told her earlier that day. Mrs. Nye had been raised somewhere other than Cornwall and had been the result of his mother's second marriage. That meant they had different fathers, of course, which made sense considering who Mr. Nye's father must blatantly have been.

No, she should not presume, she told herself as the first course was served, a cream of asparagus soup. He could perhaps be a cousin or some such thing. Then she remembered Mrs. Cheviot saying Mina's husband was an innkeeper. That seemed to suggest that the connection to the Vance family was not such a close one. Emmie's head reeled as she tried to puzzle it out. She hardly knew what to think.

A steady trickle of conversation was held throughout as Mina asked after Teddy's health and where they had stayed in Bath, and which spots they had visited. Jeremy's sister was very familiar with the town, having lived there for a good many years since childhood.

Jeremy drew Emmie into the conversation by explaining she, too, had lived in Bath and she and Pinky happily shared their favorite spots, mostly tea shops and bakeries. Mina spoke encouragingly of the Natural History Museum and the Botanical Gardens and some mutual ground was found in that they all admired the Royal Victoria Park.

Only one section of the huge dining table was in use, so at least they were sat close enough that none of them needed to shout. Then again, Emmie could see that Pinky was suffering acutely, sat as she was opposite Mr. Nye, who possessed that type of alarming masculinity that her friend shrank from the most.

It was curious, for though he spoke the least, he managed somehow to make his presence felt through a series of grimaces, snorts, or eloquent shrugs. Funnily enough, Emmie did not think that Mr. Nye was terribly at ease either. The next course was the fish course, filet de soles and lobster rissoles. Nye did not bother with the fish knife and fork though he tucked in heartily to the baked salmon in a hollandaise sauce.

He frequently tugged at his collar and shrugged his big shoulders as though he found his coat constricting. After the main course was served, a braised beef with roasted vegetables, he finally asked his wife if he could remove "the damned thing" and no sooner had she assented than he shrugged it off, dragged off his necktie, popped open the top collar of his shirt, and started rolling up his sleeves.

"I did not mean for you to make yourself *that* comfortable, Nye," his wife commented ruefully. He turned toward her and winked, slinging his arm over the back of his chair.

Jeremy laughed. "You must not scold him, Mina. If he can be made comfortable, perhaps he will grace us with his presence here again. Who knows?" Nye looked skeptical but made no reply.

"May I take my collar off, Mama?" Teddy asked, turning at once to Emmie.

"Your collar is not tight, Teddy," she pointed out. "Why should you wish to remove it?"

He frowned. "I am too old to wear lace collars now I am nine."

"Oh, but it's such a pretty collar, dear!" Pinky could not forbear objecting. "With such intricate lacework."

"That's why," Teddy glowered, glancing at his uncle for support. Nye affected not to notice. "Cousin James can have all my lace collars," Teddy said with sudden inspiration. "I daresay they are suitable for a baby."

"They would be far too big for him," Emmie said, glancing over at Baby James, who, in the absence of any nursery staff, was being passed between the two footmen. Currently Colfax had a firm hold of him and was rocking him with an easy grace, shifting from one foot to the other.

"Aunt Mina could alter them for him," Teddy said irrepressibly. "She has a big sewing box, I've seen it."

Mina pressed her lips together and Emmie threw a glance of appeal at Jeremy. "When you are eleven and sent off to school, you can relinquish your lace collars," Jeremy said firmly. "And not until then."

Teddy thrust out his bottom lip but fortunately, dessert appeared at this point to sweeten his mood. Today it was a selection of cream layered cakes and a chocolate mousse, all of which met with his approval.

Pinky tentatively asked Mrs. Nye if, while in Bath, she had a subscription to the lending library. Much to their surprise, she had not. "My father, being a schoolmaster, did not approve of novels," she admitted awkwardly. "In fact, he quite forbade them at the school, fearing they would cause moral degradation among his female pupils."

Emmie felt herself turn red and poor Pinky looked quite mortified. Jeremy spoke up at this point to tell Mina that she did not know what she was missing out on. He told her of their plans to dedicate an area of the library to a collection of novels and told her that she must feel free to browse them and borrow one when it had been set up.

"I don't know about that," Nye rumbled. "I like to be the one who degrades my wife's morals." Now it was Mina's turn to redden. Emmie noticed she flashed a look at her husband that seemed to promise retribution later. Not that he seemed perturbed. If anything, the brief smile playing about his lips would seem to indicate he looked forward to it.

After dinner, Emmie, Pinky, and Mina withdrew to the white and gold drawing room with Teddy and Baby James while Nye and Jeremy remained to smoke cigars and drink port. At least, Emmie supposed Jeremy would eschew the port and limit himself to an after-dinner smoke if past habits were to be relied upon.

Pinky visibly relaxed as they moved away from the menfolk. Emmie could tell that last remark about degraded morals had completely overset her. Higgins passed the baby to his mother and then left to fetch them a tray of drinks.

Teddy took Pinky by the hand and led her at once to the large stone foot to regale her with its dubious history. She and Mina sat side by side on one of the white sofas.

"I hope you did not think I share my father's views on novels," Mina said apologetically. "I did not mean to imply judgment earlier, merely to explain why I have never indulged. I always used to seek out the more thrilling reads myself in the periodicals we subscribed to. I daresay I should enjoy a novel very much."

Feeling relieved at this olive branch, Emmie smiled at her. "Then I hope you will borrow one from us when they arrive, though it is possible you do not have much time to yourself at present, with young James." They both looked at the baby. "He is a very bonny child, how old is he?"

"He will be a year old in August," Mina said fondly, turning the child in her lap.

"Teddy is very proud to have a cousin, he told us of him on our journey here from Bath."

Mina looked interested. "Did you live in Bath long, Lady Faris?"

"I wish you would call me Emmie. I lived there some eight years all told."

"As you will have gathered, I am from Bath myself. My father used to run a school there, The Hill School for young ladies. I used to teach there myself as a matter of fact." When Emmie nodded but showed no knowledge of that establishment, she looked a little disappointed. "I assume you were educated in London."

"Yes, though I did not attend school. I had a governess at home."

"Did I hear Jeremy say that Miss Pinson was your governess before she was your companion?" Mina asked.

"That is so," Emmie agreed.

"I understand she is taking over my nephew's lessons until he goes away to school." Mina hesitated. "I am glad Jeremy is thinking of his schooling again. Teddy has been without structure for too long. His previous tutor did not suit." She paused. "A pity, but there it is. And then there was his illness… His education has consequently suffered."

"He is improving by the day," Emmie said, glancing over to see her stepson disappearing out of the door with Pinky in tow.

"He certainly looks a good deal better," Mina agreed.

Higgins sailed in carrying in a tray of coffee. He placed it on a low gold table in front of Emmie. "Thank you, Higgins."

"Now where do you suppose that boy has dragged Miss Pinson off to?" Mina asked with a smile. "As far as his nursery?"

Emmie echoed her smile. "My own suspicion is that he has taken her to the library to show her an illustration of the Colossus of Rhodes. He wanted to show it to me earlier, but his father prevented him."

Mina gave her a curious look. "You are on excellent terms with my nephew I see," she said. "I am glad. I notice he calls you Mama already."

"That was at his own initiative, I assure you," Emmie explained hurriedly. "I am sure he will tell you all about it, but it was actually Teddy that picked me out for his new mama in the first place." She used the surprised silence that greeted these words to pour out three cups of coffee. "Cream?" she asked. "Sugar?"

Fortunately at this point, Teddy and Miss Pinson reappeared. Teddy was carrying a large leather-bound tome which he brought straight over to Emmie. As she had expected, it was open at the page showing the Colossus standing astride the harbor at Rhodes.

"What an impressive sight it must have been," she said. "Truly a wonder. Only see how the ships sailed between his legs!" She pointed to the picture. "Imagine being in that boat and looking up at the statue towering above you."

Teddy nodded. "It's a lucky thing he was wearing a loincloth," he said, dumbfounding all three ladies. Emmie felt her cheeks turn hot, while Mina went off in a coughing fit. As for Pinky, she was quite frozen in horror. "It says here," Teddy continued, quite oblivious to their reaction, "that an earthquake caused the Colossus to snap off at the knees, whereupon it fell into the sea. Don't you think that's rather too bad?"

"I wonder why they did not rebuild it," Emmie said loudly, hoping to distract him while poor Pinky recovered. Her friend was still standing aghast, a hand pressed to her slight bosom. Emmie hoped she was not having palpitations.

"I'll find out," Teddy said, seizing Miss Pinson's wrist. They retreated to the opposite sofa but not before Pinky grabbed her coffee to fortify herself with. She was still looking sadly shaken.

Emmie turned back to Mina, who was watching her. "You are good with him," she said, "but he is already far too much for your friend to deal with. I fear she is not up to the task of handling my nephew."

Despite the fact her words echoed Emmie's own fears, she had to make an effort not to bristle. "Hannah is not used to dealing with boys, that is all," she said defensively. "And it is only an interim measure after all."

Mina made no comment, and Emmie looked across to where Pinky and Teddy were now sat poring over the open book together. "He is such a sweet, imaginative child," she said.

"He is that. He is also a rare handful," Mina said, lifting her coffee cup. Before taking a sip, she plunked it back down again into her saucer. "Did Teddy really pick you out for my brother's bride?" she asked forthrightly.

"Yes, he did," Emmie replied and took a sip of hot coffee. "I think, you know, that it must have been that same imagination of his at work, and that same sweetness." At Mina's querying look, she said, "He heard from a third party, you see, of my unsuccessful London season ten years ago."

She took a deep breath. "Your brother was the only gentleman to sign my dance card without inducement," she shared, deciding to skate over the rest of it. "And Lily, the third party I mean, did not hesitate to paint me in a somewhat pathetic light. Instead of seeing me as a comical figure, the story engaged Teddy's sympathies and thirst for justice. He felt for my plight, and he wanted to see the balance redressed."

"Justice?" Mina repeated quietly. A glimmer of comprehension showed in her eyes which quite disconcerted Emmie. *Botheration!* She had not meant to betray Jeremy's role. She gripped her cup tightly. "My, er, finances had sadly dwindled since my London days. I was living in Bath pretty much in genteel poverty," she admitted, her throat closing over the words.

"Found it!" Teddy announced excitedly. "It says here, the citizens of Rhodes were afraid they had angered the god Helios, and *that* was why the Colossus fell. They did not dare to raise it again, in case they further caused his displeasure."

"What does the god Helios have to do with it?" Emmie asked, happy for a change of subject.

"That was who the Colossus was supposed to be, Mama," Teddy answered. "The sun god, Helios."

"Oh, I had not realized," Emmie murmured, feeling foolish and probably giving an even worse impression of Pinky's skills as an educator. "I thought the Colossus was quite a separate figure in his own right."

"Oh dear," said Pinky. "I always find these pagan gods so very confusing! I was quite under the impression that the god associated with the sun was Apollo."

Fortunately, at this point Baby James started to cry, and the subject was dropped altogether.

16

The rest of the visit passed without further event and as they took their leave, Mina pressed her hand and cordially invited Emmie to drop in and visit them at their inn, The Prizefighter, whenever she was in the locality, assuring her there was no need to stand on formality now they were family. Still, Emmie did not think she had made the greatest of first impressions on her in-laws.

Lottie took down her hair, helped her out of her gown, and put her jewelry away as Emmie tried not to dwell too much on this latest failure. Her social skills were bound to be rusty, she told herself. She had long been out of circulation. Not that she had ever been the most socially effervescent creature, even when she lived in Porchester Square.

Still, she had frequently acted as hostess for her father's business dinners without falling flat on her face, she thought. Or had his guests merely tolerated her as her rich father's lump of a daughter? She was starting to wonder.

Pinky, for instance, had friends she had corresponded with for years. The fact she had not seen them in an age did not impair her friendships in any way. There was Mrs. Stephenson and Miss West and old Canon Perryman and his sister and a great many more besides. Pinky was *always* writing to someone or else receiving long letters about beef tea and summer colds and tutting sympathetically or knitting them headscarves for Christmas.

Emmie still received the odd Christmas card from old acquaintances but even those had dwindled after so many moves in the past few years. Of course, she knew there were lots of reasons for this. Any friends who had *not* abruptly dropped her, she had herself created distance from. She had not wanted to embarrass them with her change in circumstance, any more than she had wanted to mortify herself.

Then, too, there had been the move away from London. Once set up in Bath, she had only ever corresponded with Humphrey, duplicitous wretch that he was, with the odd businesslike letter from Mr. Hardiman. Otherwise, she and Pinky had lived very quietly on their limited means. She had been fortunate indeed to have a friend like Hannah Pinson, she thought. Otherwise, she would have been quite alone in the world.

The sound of a door handle startled her, and she turned in her seat to see Jeremy peering through the connecting door. "It was open," he said, looking startled. "I was just…checking it."

"Yes," she agreed, "I unlocked it."

He seemed unsure how to proceed for a moment, then came through the door, shutting it carefully after him. "I'm sure you have lots of questions," he said, walking over to her and placing a hand on her shoulder. The look in his eyes, as they met hers in the mirror, was strangely wary.

Questions? Emmie eyed him in some surprise. "You're not dressed for bed," she commented. He had removed his jacket but was otherwise still fully dressed.

He looked down as though surprised. "No," he agreed, his fingers absently trailing along her shoulder to her neck. "I meant to, but then I just thought I would check the door."

Had he been expecting it to be locked? She opened her mouth to ask, but in that same instant he said suddenly, "Nye is my illegitimate brother, you know. His mother was a barmaid."

"Oh. Yes, I did think that was perhaps the case," she admitted, wondering why his expression was so guarded. "Is that who Teddy meant when he said I should soon see who resembled the fourth viscount?" He nodded. "I suppose it is just one of those funny circumstances of life that he ended up married to your half sister," she continued aloud. "There is no relation between them, of course, but all the same, it must have been a little awkward for you."

For a moment he looked conflicted. Then he sighed and scrubbed his eyes with his hand. "Not really. I arranged the match, you see."

"You arranged it?" Now she *was* startled.

Jeremy attacked his cravat, pulling it loose and casting it on the floor. "I thought, well, it's hard to explain my particular line of thought at that time." He met her eyes in the mirror again and winced, his gaze dropping away as he turned and walked over to her bed, sitting down on the edge.

Emmie said nothing; indeed, she was not sure what to say. Instead, she picked up a bottle of lotion and poured some into her hand.

"I was not thinking straight," he said after a heavy pause. "I was also drinking heavily at the time," he admitted, shrugging out of his waistcoat.

Their eyes met again in the mirror. "I noticed you no longer do that," she said lightly. "Drink, I mean. You did not at our wedding or at any meal we have taken since."

"No," he agreed shortly. "Not for two years now."

Emmie smoothed the lotion into her neck. "Is that why you stopped?" she asked.

He looked surprised. "Their marriage?" She nodded. "As a matter of fact, they're very happy together," he said at last, "though no thanks to me." When she said nothing, he sighed again before continuing in a flat voice. "In truth, there were a lot of reasons. Sometimes I was not very nice to be around, but you already knew that, didn't you, Ballentine?"

Emmie replaced the top on her lotion bottle and reached for the cold cream jar. They were on shaky ground again. *Their past.* She took a deep breath. "I'm not sure I made the best impression on your sister," she admitted. "She seems to have some decided views on matters of education."

He gave a short laugh. "Yes, that sounds like Mina," he said.

"I think she has concerns about Pinky becoming Teddy's governess."

He shrugged. "On about sending Teddy back to school again, was she?" he asked mildly. "She used to teach in a school herself and is a great proponent for them."

"Yes, she told me. The Hill School in Bath."

"Did you know it?" he asked with a flicker of interest.

She shook her head. "As you know, I had a governess. By the time I moved to Bath I was long past such things."

"Well," Jeremy said decidedly, "I am not sending him away just now. He deserves to have this summer at least to fully recover his health and adjust to"—he pointed his finger to his chest and then toward her— "the new status quo."

She nodded. "Yes, that sounds perfectly reasonable. And after all, it will be the first of May tomorrow." She bit her lip, hoping devoutly that Pinky could manage to hold things together for a few months at least.

"Are you finished with your toilette?" Replacing the lid on the jar, she nodded. "Come and lie on the bed with me," he said, patting the mattress beside him.

Emmie stood up and crossed to the bed. She hesitated before climbing under the covers, for he was lying on top of them, but he reached over and drew the sheets back for her. She climbed in and he started unbuttoning his shirt.

"So…what did you think of them?" he asked. "My family."

Emmie folded her hands over her stomach and contemplated the high ceiling above.

"Your sister seems a woman of character," she said slowly. "She's handsome, dignified, and well-educated. Her husband—"

"My brother," he interjected. "I do acknowledge the connection. I acknowledge it more than Nye, to tell the truth."

"So, it is widely known that you are half brothers?"

"It's known hereabouts, though little talked of these days. At least, not to our faces."

"I don't know that I should dare raise the subject myself," she reflected frankly. "Your brother is rather alarming." He laughed. "Did your father have a presence like Nye's or was it only in appearance that he takes after him?" she asked curiously.

Jeremy thought about this as he unbuttoned his shirt. "He had presence certainly, but Nye's owes a good deal to the man that raised him. Jacob Nye was a formidable sort. You would not trifle with old Jacob." He shrugged off his shirt.

"And your father?"

There was a slight pause before he answered. "You would not trifle with him either," he acknowledged wryly. "Though my father was more of a shouter whereas Jacob Nye could freeze a man at ten paces with his glare. That always seemed more impressive somehow. You may be sure that everyone paid their bar tab in a timely fashion."

He climbed under the sheets and closed his arms about her with a deep sigh of satisfaction.

"Do you think your sister and her hus—your brother I mean—" *That would take some getting used to.* "Are, well, pleased to find you are remarried?" Emmie asked haltingly.

"I don't know about pleased, but they certainly already knew the fact. It must be all over Penarth by now. Nye told me as much. That was why they came to dinner, you know, to get a good look at you. Nye has never set foot in the place before tonight." He paused before continuing. "I'm sorry I did not prepare you, Ballentine." His tone was apologetic. "I am fortunate that you are gracious and take things in your stride."

Gracious? Did he really think so? She could not ask, for he was kissing her, first her lips and then along her jaw. "You looked so pretty at dinner, Emmeline," he whispered. "I could barely take my eyes off you. I'm sure they noticed my preoccupation with my new wife."

As he had seemed a perfect host, Emmie found this hard to believe, however she was just glad he had not thought his hostess lacking. Thankfully, she slipped her arms about him, enjoying the feel of his bunched muscles. He was not a large man but even so, his body felt so very different to her own. He was lean and muscular where she was... He pinched her waist, interrupting her thoughts. "*Jeremy!*"

"I like how soft you are here, Ballentine," he said, his mouth very near her ear. "It affects me strangely." His hands slid down to caress her hips and buttocks as his breath rasped against her neck. He was not lying. She could tell because he was entirely naked and aroused. She had lately learned this was not something you could really mistake.

"Like your paintings?" she asked breathlessly as he kissed the point that met her shoulder.

"Yes," he agreed huskily. "You would make a *magnificent* Venus. I have always thought so."

Always? "I don't know about that," she responded doubtfully, thinking of the Venus hanging in the drawing room, emerging from the sea naked and wringing out her wet hair. "I think the Romans favored small, high bosoms and, well, mine are…not like that."

He gave a choking laugh. "Your breasts are perfection, Ballentine," he said. "They are sublime. If I was artistically inclined, I would dedicate poems to them. I'm almost desperate to see them again. May I?"

"Yes," she said in a muffled voice, but this time he did not reach for her buttons. Instead, his hands remained where they were, squeezing and fondling the fleshy parts of her that she had always been most self-conscious about. For a moment, she hesitated, unsure of her cue. Then she noticed his expectant air.

Oh. He was waiting for her to do it. To…to *bare* her bosom to him. Emmie's face flushed even brighter. Could she do this? She remembered their wedding night, how inflamed he had been by the sight of breasts.

Reaching for her buttons with trembling fingers, she undid them one at a time, until she reached the very last one. Then, taking a deep breath, she peeled back one side of the placket and then the other. His breathing grew harsher, but still, he watched and waited.

Emmie glanced down at her exposed cleavage. Her breasts were not as revealed as they had been last time, when they had been so scandalously freed out of the confines of her bodice. Taking a deep breath, she nerved herself to scoop out first one breast and then the other.

Jeremy's grip of her hips tightened convulsively. "Oh, fuck, Emmeline," he said in a raspy voice, and closed his eyes for an instant. When he reopened them, they seemed a little calmer. "I almost wish I did write poetry," he said thickly, lowering his face to kiss down first one breast before sucking the nipple into his mouth, and then repeating the process with the other.

Emmie whimpered. Before she knew it, her hand was at the back of his head, urging him closer still. He ran the tip of his tongue down the undersides of her breasts, before retracing the path to swirl his tongue around her hard nipples. She wanted his hands on them, like last time, kneading and cupping her aching breasts, but they were otherwise occupied, squeezing her backside in a firm grip.

Instead of paying more attention to her tender breasts, Jeremy shifted down, reaching for her hem and bunching up her nightgown to her waist. Once it was out of the way, he started dropping ardent kisses along her stomach, another part of her body which she had always been convinced was far from the ideal. Emmie breathed through her nose and did her best not to tense, even when he gently kissed around her belly button.

When he started enthusiastically mouthing the swell of her belly beneath it, Emmie could not hold back a murmur of protest. "You don't like that?" he asked, lifting his head again. His eyes were a little unfocussed. Did she imagine it, or did he sound a little disappointed?

"It's not that," she said quickly. "It's just…" She floundered, a strange suspicion forming. "Do *you* like it?" she asked impulsively.

"Your belly?" She nodded and his eyes dropped immediately to roam over it. "I bloody love it," he answered with a groan.

"You—?" Emmie stared at him in astonishment. "You are not serious!"

"It's beautiful," he said so matter-of-factly that she found she could not doubt his sincerity. "I want to feel the cool, soft skin against my face. May I?"

Slowly, Emmie nodded, and he pressed his face against her there, his hands at her waist, breathing in noisily. They remained like that for several minutes, until Emmie felt herself start to relax again. Then he kissed her there again, this time gently and reverently instead of ravenously.

"You have the most gorgeous belly in all the world," he sighed with what she could only deduce was pleasure.

"I've always thought that it was my worst feature," she admitted. "It's strange, hearing it so praised."

He looked incredulous. "Your worst?" He stared at her for a moment before shaking his head. "I'm guessing no one has really seen it before," he pointed out. "So, I'm not sure where you got such an idea."

"Well, no, but it sticks out to a distressing degree when I do not wear a corset to correct it."

"It has no need of correction," he said firmly. "It is perfect the way it is. When your room is redone, I want you to have a chaise longue in here," he said seemingly changing the subject.

"A chaise longue?" she repeated.

"Yes. I want you to recline on it for me, naked," he said, shifting down her body. Emmie's eyes widened. His hand was sliding up her leg now until it lodged between her plump thighs. Emmie shivered with anticipation.

For a moment, words appeared to hover on his lips, but then he seemed to catch himself. For a horrible instant it occurred to her that he had been about to reference the Hawfords' ball again. But that was absurd, she told herself uneasily. In what possible context could that come up in this moment?

"Why do you suddenly look nervous, Emmeline?" he asked, stilling his hand at once. "Do you want me to stop?"

"No!" she blurted, "I don't want you to stop. I was just…just wondering why you felt the need for a chaise longue," she lied weakly.

"Ah." He smiled. "That's because I want to worship you on it, like the goddess you are," he said, his fingers slipping inside her cleft to lightly trace her wet folds. "To pay homage to this divine body."

Emmie shifted against his fingers, she could not help it, or the little cry that burst out when his fingers slid right against that spot that was so sensitive. "Like…like that lute player in your painting. The one in the library," she asked breathily.

A sudden wicked grin lit up his face. "I'm not going sit at your feet and play you a tune, Ballentine, if that's what you're asking."

"Well, what are you going to do, then?" she huffed when his fingers refused to play the tune he had plucked so well before. Instead, this time they performed a dance that frustrated as much as it stimulated. She could only conclude it was on purpose, from how carefully he watched her face for her every reaction.

"This," he said, lowering himself onto the bed until she could feel his breath against her patch of intimate hair. "Could you open your legs a little wider, perhaps raise your knees?" he suggested politely.

Emmie gazed down at him in mingled surprise and astonishment. *What on earth…?* Wordlessly, she lowered her legs, and he resettled a little closer still, gently brushing the reddish-gold curls as his thumb parted her nether lips with a familiarity that made her gasp.

"Do you know, some people call this the mound of Venus?" he asked conversationally. Before she could even think of a reply, his mouth was pressed against her so scandalously that Emmie forgot to even draw breath. It was only when his tongue started to give a slow exploratory lick that she remembered the necessity to breathe.

"My lord!" she squeaked, all dignity flying out of the window. "*Oh!*"

Before long she was panting and squirming against his mouth, so much so that he had to adjust his hold of her, gripping her firmly around her thighs to pin her in place. Lifting his head, he said "Hold still, Ballentine" in an amused voice. "You wriggle like an eel."

Seeing his lips shiny from her wetness, she felt something inside her coil even tighter. With a faint moan, Emmie collapsed back onto her pillow, struggling to catch her breath.

"Look at me, Emmeline," he requested silkily. Emmie struggled up onto her elbows. "Are enjoying this?" he asked solicitously, only the faintest gleam in his eye suggesting he must already know the answer to this question.

Emmie struggled with words. "Y-yes!" she managed to splutter out. *Oh my God, were ladies supposed to admit to such a thing?* She was not sure. It seemed her education was woefully inadequate in lots of areas, not just mythology.

His smile flashed out. "That's alright, then," he murmured. "I wouldn't want to think I was the only one enjoying myself here." He sucked on his bottom lip. "You taste delicious, by the way," he told her softly. "Any requests?" Emmie regarded him speechlessly. *Requests?* "No? I'll just have to improvise, then."

Was he still joking about playing her a tune? she wondered incredulously. Then he doubled his efforts, plying his cunning tongue in such ways that Emmie had no time for thinking. He supped and sucked and *licked* at her as though she was the most delicious treat, and soon she was mindless and aching with need, while he feasted so unhurriedly on her. Her legs shook, she was so *wet*, and then the pleasure finally took her, and she cried out as it spread throughout her limbs, leaving her limp and breathless.

As she recovered, breathing shakily, he crawled back up the bed and took her in his arms, stroking her hair and kissing her cheek. "My God, you're the loveliest thing I've ever beheld," he said thickly. "And I'm such an undeserving wretch too." He sighed gustily and then kissed her lips lingeringly, as though it did not matter where they had just been.

"The loveliest thing?" Emmie repeated uncertainly when he drew back. "Even more than your paintings?"

"So much more," he assured her. "Instead of canvas, you are made of flesh and blood, and such *lovely* flesh too." His hands wandered downward to skim over her hips and buttocks, and he let out a groan. "I can't really delay much longer, or I will spend against your lovely belly, Ballentine."

"If you like it so much, I am surprised you think that would be a bad thing."

He gave a breathless laugh. "It would not be a bad thing at all," he admitted, "but I would rather be inside you right now, if you have no objection, of course." He quirked an eyebrow at her.

Instead of answering, she let her legs fall open and his eyes lit up as he stared at her. "Fuck, you look *so…*"

"Would you like to own a painting of Venus like this?" she asked daringly.

He gazed at her, breathing heavily as though incapable of speech. "Truthfully?" he croaked. "No painting could compare to the reality of having you in my bed like this, Ballentine." His eyes traveled over her greedily, devouring every detail. "Though, I would pay a good deal to own even a pale copy."

"Who would you be in the painting, I wonder?" she mused, still feeling boneless and satiated.

Jeremy gave a choked laugh as he clambered over her, settling between her legs. "A lustful satyr perhaps," he said with a grunt as the head of his manhood brushed against her tender, swollen parts. To her surprise, she felt a twinge of interest in proceedings, despite her languor.

"Are those the ones with the horns and the tails?" she asked breathlessly as he started to push into her.

"Nnnhhhhh." He made a sound of vague agreement. "Yessss," he hissed, though whether this was still in answer to her question she was not sure. He was far too beautiful to be a satyr, she thought, watching his expression turn blissful. He would have to be Apollo. "That feels *so* good, sweetheart," he said, closing his eyes. "You're so wet," he whispered as he sank into her. "Taking me so well."

When he opened them again, his blue eyes looked unfocused. "*Fuck*, Ballentine," he wheezed, concentrating on her face. "Are you ready for this?" She nodded and he shuddered, slamming his hips against hers, making her yell out as he plunged deep.

"Too hard?" he panted, trying to pull back, but Emmie wound her arms about him, dragging him closer.

"No," she moaned. "Don't go."

Jeremy's eyes flashed. "More?" he asked carefully. She nodded. "You have to say it, Ballentine." A smile tugged at the corner of his mouth.

"More," she whimpered. "Please."

"Please, Jeremy," he corrected her but gave a hard buck of his hips all the same, as though he could not hold back.

"Jeremy," she whispered, digging her nails into his shoulder before she could stop herself. He did not even seem to notice it, as he adjusted his position and drove into her again and again with increasing urgency.

"Tell me you want me, Ballentine," he insisted, his hands sliding around to her backside and dragging her closer still. "Tell me you al—" He bit off his words. "Tell me you still want me," he gritted out instead.

"I do," she gasped, wanting to please him. Wanting to say the right thing. "Still," she blurted. "I—I always did."

His eyes flew wide, staring into her own. "Yes," he breathed, "so did I. Always." And just like that Jeremy Vance came apart, his eyes boring into her, his hands gripping her buttocks tight. "God, you always make me feel so good," he groaned, and collapsed heavily on top of her.

Moments later, he rolled off her, still struggling for breath. "Want some water?" he asked, and grinned. "Your face looks a little red."

"Yes, please."

He sat up and sloshed some water from her etched water carafe into a glass. "I wonder why around you it is easier for me to breathe, Ballentine, and"—he paused—"I find I hate myself less."

"Hate yourself?" she repeated, alarmed.

He waved a hand. "I'm exaggerating, of course, but you know what I mean."

Actually, she didn't, but he did not press the issue, merely passed her a glass of water. As she gulped it down, he traced a finger down her cheek. "How do you do it?" he asked curiously.

"I don't know," she mumbled, handing him back the empty glass.

He took it, refilled it, and drank a glass himself. "You're even prettier post-coitally," he sighed. "I always knew you would be, of course. From the dancing."

"Dancing?" she repeated, feeling confused.

"Eyes bright, cheeks pink, lips parted…" he teased.

Suddenly, Emmie realized he was talking about all the dancing they had done years ago. She felt panicked that he would see fit to bring up those times at a moment like this, when her defenses were so completely down. If she was not careful, he would be bringing up that wretched conservatory business again!

Instead of receding further into the past, that fateful season seemed to draw ever closer, looming up at the oddest times to remind her of how things had once stood between them. Perhaps forbidding him to speak of it had somehow fixed those events even more firmly in their minds?

"What is it?" he asked tenderly. "Cold?" He slipped an arm about her.

"It's nothing," she said quickly, flashing him a smile. "Nothing at all."

"Let me take care of you, Ballentine," he said, his eyes so warm and full of tender concern. "We need to get cleaned up before you can sleep. Is that agreeable to you?"

She nodded, and he looked so sleepily happy she could not regret it. Jeremy spent the next twenty minutes assiduously tending to her as they washed and settled back into the bed together. With each passing minute she felt herself relax a little more in his company, until finally she was calm once again. He would not hurt her. She was being foolish.

Emmie was just dropping off to sleep when she suddenly remembered something. "You know, there are two purple chaise longues already in the viscountess's sitting room," she said drowsily.

"In your sitting room, you mean?" he replied, a frown in his voice.

"Yes."

"Are there?" He sounded genuinely surprised by this news.

"Yes, purple ones." He shrugged, and she reflected once again that he could not have spent much time in his wife's rooms. "We could always move one of them into here," she suggested.

A smile curved his lips as though he knew full well she was reflecting on his earlier words. "This room is currently blue and orange," he reminded her. "Do you not think the color might be ill-suited?"

It was Emmie's turn to shrug. "I am not really accustomed to whole rooms being so uniform in color and theme," she admitted.

He turned his head to look at her. "Even in your father's smart London townhouse?"

"Even there," she agreed. "We had a yellow saloon but even that had chairs that were upholstered in green velvet and over time more colors crept in."

"I see," he yawned, and his eyes closed. "Is it alright if I fall asleep in here?" he asked without opening them. "If you would rather I cleared out and left you, I will, of course."

"Why would I want that?" she asked in surprise, but Jeremy was already asleep. He said such strange things sometimes, she reflected, reaching out to touch his cheek. She wondered if she would ever really understand what was going on in that pretty head of his.

17

Jeremy woke early, and after kissing Emmeline's bare shoulder, he made his way stealthily back to his own rooms via the connecting door. Here, he wrapped himself in his dressing robe and rang the bell for his wash and shave.

It was only after Simons, his valet, started hunting around for his evening clothes that he realized he must have left them in a heap on his wife's bedroom floor. So much for conjugal discretion. "One moment," he told Simons and slipped back through the door to collect them.

Emmeline was still sleeping soundly, and he could not resist dropping another kiss on her delightfully rounded shoulder. He was half regretful for having left her so early, but it was his habit when in the country to rise at seven and then spend his morning at the stables. As it was, Masterson, his stable manager, would have looked for him in vain the previous day.

Simons took the proffered clothing with his eyes tactfully averted, and Jeremy dressed in riding clothes before heading out of the house. It was overcast at present, and if he was not mistaken, there would be rain later in the day. He headed down toward the racing stables at a brisk pace, for it was a good twenty-minute walk to reach the block where he kept his racehorses.

As he walked, Jeremy's mind dwelled pleasurably on the previous day. There was much to be happy about and not just the highly satisfactory ending to it. For one, there was the easy camaraderie she had already established with his son.

She had fitted in so well, seamlessly in fact, into their game of soldiers in the nursery. She had been charming with Teddy all day, chattering away with him in a natural and easy fashion. That side of things was already progressing far better than he could have hoped, even in his wildest dreams.

Emmeline might not think she made the greatest impression on Mina and Nye, but he was sure they thought her a vast improvement on his first wife. Amanda had wanted to cut the connection with his siblings altogether. Not that he had ever allowed it, but all the same, before Mina had come along, his relationship with his brother had been rocky, almost nonexistent at times.

Nye was both stubborn and proud, and moreover he had not needed Jeremy. Most likely he had resented his golden brother who had always lived in luxury at Vance Park while he carved out a living in a busy inn and among the boxing rings of Exeter.

Mina had been the key to cracking that particular nut, and though Jeremy might regret how he had gone about it, for his treatment of her at the time had been undeniably poor, luckily his sister had forgiven him, and things had worked out for the best. Now, even Nye had thawed enough to visit Vance and accept his hospitality.

All was going swimmingly. The only fly in the ointment had been Emmeline's request the previous morning that they never again mention the night of the Hawfords' ball. That had stung. Of course, even for him, the memory was bittersweet. Still, he would have thought that moment in the conservatory between them was worth preserving. It hurt somehow that she did not agree.

Overall, though, she had forgiven him a great deal, so he knew he did not have the grounds to resent her request. She had married him, despite his past behavior and he was extremely grateful for that fact. She wanted to look to the future, that was what she had said before and she was right. It was only, he did rather treasure their shared history and it felt confining somehow to know he could never allude to it again.

To give her her due, he had not been through the same repercussions she had. After that fateful season, he had not gone into a social and financial decline as it appeared Emmeline had. His steps slowed as he suddenly wondered if she had suffered more rather more reverberations from that night than he had ever realized.

Was it possible that someone had seen their clinch in the conservatory? Someone other than that fool chaperone woman, Smith or whatever her name was. Could it be that *she* had told Emmeline's father about their embrace, and then Emmeline had been forced to shoulder sole blame for it? Had her punishment been the abrupt end of her only season?

Before now, he had teased Emmeline by saying she had let him "practically ruin her" but had those teasing words struck uncomfortably close to the truth? He turned cold at the thought. *Had* he in fact truly ruined her prospects? Had *that* been the reason she had ended up withdrawing from fashionable society and become engaged to that idiot Stockton?

He racked his brains to try to think if he had ever seen her after that fateful night. It had all been such a miserable blur. He had not *wanted* to see her when he knew he no longer had the smallest hope of approaching her. Instead, he had used his engagement as an excuse to stop attending all those gatherings altogether. Why would he attend now, when there was nothing to be gained from them?

Amanda and her mama had been furious that he had not wanted to be paraded about like a caught fish, but he had been selfish enough not to care. She had the diamond on her finger, and he would say the vows in church. Other than the odd morning promenade, a few rides in the park, and a family ball at the Tiptons' townhouse, he could not remember much else from that period in his life.

The wedding had been next, a rainy day in June, then had been the honeymoon in Italy. What a wretched business that had been. It did not bear thinking about. No, he was pretty sure that the last time he had seen Emmeline, until that fateful morning in Bath, had been the Hawfords' ball. An event he had now promised never to mention again.

It seemed they were not to clear the air or even get things straight about what had happened between them during that strange period of his life when Jeremy had genuinely fallen in love for the first and only time. Of course, he had not realized that was what had happened, not until later. Not until Italy, in fact, when he had wandered into Saint Peter's Basilica and felt an almost crushing sense of loss.

That night he had got disgustingly drunk and said rather a few things to his new bride that should have been left unspoken. Ah well, Amanda had come right back at him with a few unpalatable truths of her own. They had more than likely deserved one another by that point.

"Milord!" It was Masterman, hailing him and dragging him from his thoughts. "You're just in time. We're about to start exercising them now in the long paddock."

Jeremy spent a productive morning at the stables, catching up on the progress of his current prospects. At midday he headed back up to the house to wash and brush up for luncheon. Colfax and Higgins were carrying a large box between them into the blue salon.

"If that's books," Jeremy said, one foot on the bottom step of the staircase, "carry them straight through to the library."

"This one's cake, milord," Higgins said, looking around.

"Cake?" Jeremy repeated blankly, glancing at the large box.

"Wedding cake, milord."

"Ah. Really?" He somehow had not realized it would follow them home.

"There were several packing cases of books, milord," Colfax added as they paused in the doorway. "We haven't brought them through yet. Also, a load of dresses have arrived from that fancy modiste in Bath."

Jeremy's expression brightened. "Excellent. Everything seems to have turned up at once."

"Yes, including those two wagonfuls of furniture from Winkworth Street."

Jeremy's face fell. "Oh, *that*. Is there some kind of outhouse we could store it in?" he asked. "Until she decides where she's going to put it."

Colfax cleared his throat. "Miss Pinson did mention that Lady Faris intends to make a present of some of it to her. For her cottage."

"Ah, capital idea!" Jeremy approved. "Can we have it directed straight there? Anything that does not fit can always come back here for storage."

Colfax gave a small bow and he and Higgins shuffled off with the huge box of cake. Jeremy ran up the stairs, washed and changed and descended again, wondering where he would find everyone for lunch.

After glancing in a couple of likely rooms, he found his wife, Miss Pinson, and Teddy sat in the blue salon, surrounded by piles of small white boxes decorated with silver writing and ribbon. He made straight for Emmeline, kissing her cheek and asking, "What is all this?"

"Cake," she answered promptly. "Only look at these cunning little boxes. They cut up our wedding cake and sectioned it into perfect squares to be mailed out to well-wishers. Isn't it clever?"

He felt instantly relieved the monstrous fruit cake was already portioned and packaged up. "Just how many pieces are there?" he asked with some misgiving.

She consulted an invoice that lay in her lap. "Three hundred and fifty."

"Good lord."

"Three hundred and forty-nine," Teddy corrected her through a mouthful of plum cake.

"We are about to have lunch, Teddy," Jeremy reproved him.

"Pinky is helping me to compile a list of people to receive cake," Emmeline said bravely, "but we only have eight people so far."

"Let's hear it," Jeremy said, dropping down onto the sofa opposite them.

"Mr. Thomas Hardiman and Mrs. Hardiman, you may remember, he was my father's most senior clerk. I have their home address for they always send me a card at Christmas." Jeremy nodded. "Then we thought, perhaps we would send Florrie, our landlady's maid from Winkworth Street, a piece. Miss Florence Pye."

"That makes three," Jeremy said, ticking them off on his fingers.

"None for the neighbors upstairs though," Teddy said darkly. "The soap stealers."

"Soap stealers?" Jeremy repeated.

"He means the Startrites," Emmie said hastily. "And no, we certainly shall not send any to that rascally family."

"And then there is my particular friend Miss West," Miss Pinson interjected. "Emmie was kind enough to say she would send her some cake as she sent a very pretty tray cloth which she had embroidered for you both as a wedding present."

"Most generous of her," Jeremy agreed. "I think she should have two pieces."

"Oh, really?" Miss Pinson perked up at once. "Oh, she would be most grateful, my lord, for then she could give the second piece to her old mother, who would be thrilled. She's an invalid, you see, and does not have much excitement in her life."

Emmie amended her list. "Two pieces for Miss West," she murmured.

"And I wanted to send a piece to Arbuthnot," Teddy said. "His parents did not bring him to the wedding, so he missed out. I think he should have cake and they should get none, for being so mean."

"Oh, I quite agree," Jeremy concurred at once.

"Would that not look rather particular?" Emmie asked with a frown. "Besides…" She cleared her throat.

Jeremy caught on at once. "Oh, you think it would annoy Mrs. Arbuthnot more if she received a piece of our commemorative cake? You are probably right. Besides, Arbuthnot seemed an agreeable fellow. Put them down for three slices," he decided generously.

"What about your godfather?" Emmeline asked Teddy. "Lord Atherton."

"Oh, Lord Atherton, yes," Pinky agreed. "He must certainly have cake. Such an agreeable gentleman."

"That one's a little tricky," Jeremy said. "Atherton currently has no fixed abode. Instead, he is an eternal houseguest, bouncing from one host to another. As he has fallen out of favor with his uncle, I am not sure at which address we would find him. Perhaps we should save his piece for when he visits with us this summer."

Emmeline scribbled a note. "Your sister, Mina, and—and your brother, William Nye," she said, moving down the list.

"And Baby James," Teddy reminded her.

"He cannot eat cake yet," Jeremy cut in, "but we must certainly send some to Edna, Corin, and Herney, their staff at the inn. And, er—" He turned to Teddy. "What is the name of their new ostler?"

"Bert," Teddy supplied promptly. "He takes snuff and has brown stains on his handkerchief." Miss Pinson suppressed a shudder.

"They must certainly all receive cake. Now, how many is that?"

"Fourteen," said Emmeline, totting them up.

"A perfect start," said Jeremy.

"Perfect?" Emmeline looked doubtful.

"Well, once we have added all our servants and tenants to the list and a few others besides, I am sure we will have our quota."

"Great Aunt Louisa?" Teddy suggested. "She is your godmother, Papa."

"Yes," Jeremy agreed. "She will certainly expect cake. Write down Lord and Lady Wickford," Jeremy directed Emmeline. "The address is Grosvenor Square, London."

"What about Grandpapa and Grandmama Tipton?"

Jeremy coughed. "That might seem a *little* tactless, my son."

"Oh. And Mama—my *other* mama, I mean," he said hastily, "did not send us any cake when she married that French man, did she, Papa?"

"He's Italian," Jeremy corrected him absently. Emmeline and Miss Pinson both turned to look at him in surprise. "He's Italian but lives in France," he explained.

"He lives in a den. Like a fox," said Teddy, adding to their confusion.

Jeremy frowned. "He lives in Paris," he said firmly. "And runs a rather exclusive establishment that caters to wealthy gamesters."

Looks of comprehension dawned on Emmeline's and Miss Pinson's faces. "I did not realize that Lady Amanda had remarried," Emmeline said quickly. "That must be an exciting life she now leads."

"Yes, and she always did enjoy an extravagant wager," Jeremy agreed.

Teddy turned to Emmie. "Can I keep this box, Mama?" he asked. "It's a useful sort of size. I might make it into a bed for Carruthers. It would fit into the turret room of my fort, just about."

"Of course. How is Carruthers today? I hope his leg is not paining him too much."

"It's still missing," Teddy answered sadly.

Miss Pinson looked startled. "Poor man! Is it a wooden one? My friends the Oxtons had a neighbor with a wooden leg. He suffered an injury from a piece of factory machinery and lost the limb from the knee down."

Predictably, Teddy immediately wanted to know all about the wooden leg. Miss Pinson reeled off some pertinent facts and then Teddy excitedly gave his own theory that the Oxtons' neighbor was in fact a pirate fleeing from justice.

Miss Pinson made feeble protests about Mr. Instow being of "the utmost respectability" but Teddy would not be swayed in his conviction. Neither would he believe that Mr. Instow's leg had been mangled by machinery. Instead, he was sure it had been bitten off by a sea monster during a raging storm.

Emmeline cleared her throat and left them to their discussion as she returned to her list. Jeremy helpfully threw her a few more names her way, Reverend Ryland and his wife at the vicarage, their two sons whose names he still could not recall, Squire Pebmarsh, and his two daughters at the Grange, the Needhams at Benham Hall, and the Tavistocks at Vance House.

"In fact," he concluded, "the sending of cake will no doubt initiate visits from them all. You will soon be inundated, Ballentine. I predict the vicar's wife will be first to call."

At this point lunch, a cold collation of savory pies, salads, and cold meats, was brought into the room and all talk of cake, neighbors and pirates abruptly ceased for at least half an hour.

No sooner had the remains of lunch been cleared away than Teddy informed Miss Pinson he was taking her to the dining room to show her the painting of his ancestress who had run away to sea.

"I hate to disappoint you, Teddy," Jeremy cut in smoothly, "but Miss Pinson must see it another day, for she has important business of her own to attend this afternoon." He explained about the arrival of their furniture from Bath. Miss Pinson was instantly out of her chair, all excitement. "You may take Colfax with you again and one of the grooms. You will need at least two men to unload the wagon."

Miss Pinson thanked him profusely as Emmeline sat looking unsure of herself. Jeremy turned to her. "Would you like to see the wagon first," he offered, "to decide what is to stay and what is to go to…" He glanced back around to her friend.

"Plumtree Cottage," Miss Pinson supplied happily.

"Plumtree Cottage," Jeremy repeated.

"Oh no." Emmeline shook her head. "Hannah is to have whatever she wants. The only thing I would like to keep for myself is—"

"The small papier-mâché tea table that was your mother's," Pinky finished for her, beaming.

Emmeline returned her smile. "Precisely."

"Well, in that case, Higgins can accompany Miss Pinson out to the wagon and fetch that particular item back," Jeremy decided, pulling the bell cord to summon the footmen.

"Can I come with you, please, Pinky?" Teddy butted in, plucking at Miss Pinson's sleeve. "I should like to see Plumtree Cottage, and I don't believe I have ever been inside that one."

Jeremy opened his mouth to reprove his son, but Miss Pinson had already replied in the affirmative, seemingly unaware of Teddy's appropriation of her sobriquet. "If that is alright with his lordship," she added anxiously, noticing his expression. "I would not dream of depriving him of—"

"That is quite alright, Miss Pinson. As long as you are sure he will not be in the way," Jeremy assured her swiftly, suspecting Colfax would be less than enthusiastic about Teddy's being underfoot during the fetching and carrying.

"And, would it be—I mean, could I possibly take a piece of wedding cake for myself?" Miss Pinson asked rather shyly, twisting her hands together.

"Of course, Miss Pinson," Jeremy assured her, reaching for the top box on the nearest pile and passing it to her. "You may have as many pieces as you like."

"Oh, just the one will suffice. Thank you *so* much," she said, clasping it to her chest. Once Colfax appeared, she and Teddy trailed away in his wake, hand in hand, chattering brightly about bedsteads and footstools and whether they thought the walnut cabinet would fit in the front parlor.

Jeremy turned to Emmeline, who was gazing after them rather wistfully. "Your friend must be very fond of cake," he commented, for he had seen Miss Pinson eat at least two pieces at lunch. "I really don't know where she puts it all. A puff of wind would knock her over."

"Oh, it won't be for eating," Emmeline answered absently. "Pinky isn't fond of fruit cake." At his quizzical look she explained. "She always puts wedding cake under her pillow."

He tipped his head, wondering if he had misheard her. "Under her pillow?" he echoed.

"Yes. It's meant to, well, induce dreams of your future husband," she explained, looking a little embarrassed. "Have you never heard of that tradition?"

"No," he said thoughtfully. "No, I had not."

"Oh, well…" She made a dismissive gesture with her hands. "It's silly, really."

Suddenly, he wanted to ask if she had ever indulged in such a superstitious tradition but felt strangely hesitant to question her about anything from her past. He felt he needed to tread carefully there. The last thing he wanted to do was suffer a setback with her. "Did I tell you, your trousseau has finally arrived?" he asked instead.

"Oh, has it?" She stood up. "I shall have to go up and look at unpacking it." She gave him a brave smile. "At least I shall now have nice outfits to receive the vicar's wife," she joked.

"Is that how you want to spend your afternoon?" he asked.

"Well, first I shall have to speak to Mrs. Cheviot about distributing all this cake," she said with a quick glance around the cluttered room.

"*Or*," he suggested, "we could *both* instruct Mrs. Cheviot as to the cake, you could send Lottie to unpack your new gowns, and I could bring the curricle around to meet you out front for a tour of the grounds."

Her expression brightened at once. "That *would* be lovely," she agreed. "Yes, let us do that."

Impulsively, he stepped forward and kissed her, and not her hand either, which would have been the correct thing to do. Emmeline looked so surprised, he did it again and was still kissing her when Mrs. Cheviot appeared in answer to her summons and what was more, he was not remotely abashed about it.

18

The sun continued to shine, and Jeremy derived a good deal of pleasure from bowling around the grounds, pointing out Vance's most notable features. He showed her first the regular stables, where he introduced her to his old favorite, Cadmus, and to Teddy's pony, Balius.

Next, he took her down to his racing stables, where she shook Masterman's hand and met their champion Bucephalus, who would have retired last year, except for the fact none of his offspring were shaping up to match either his speed or strength. Emmie asked to meet them both and watched Amyas and Atalanta exercising in the paddock.

"What do you think?" Jeremy asked as she rested her arms along the top bar of the fence.

"They are very beautiful," she said dreamily. "Though there is not much resemblance between them, is there?"

"They have the same sire but different dams," Jeremy explained.

"I feel sure they will blossom, given the chance to escape their famous father's shadow. Tell me, does Bucephalus have no daughters?"

"He does," Jeremy agreed. "Atalanta is a girl, named after the famous Greek heroine who was so fleet of foot."

"Which one of the two is Atalanta?" He pointed her out. "And will you enter her in races?"

He nodded. "She is currently the better prospect, for she is faster than her brother."

It was not until they had left the stables far behind them that Emmeline confessed she was an indifferent horsewoman. He noticed she looked relieved when he was not particularly bothered by this news.

"Shall I buy you a horse?" he asked as they strolled arm in arm beside the lake. "Or do you, Lady Faris, prefer to sit at your leisure in a carriage?"

"I prefer a carriage, but if you think I should try and improve, then—"

"A carriage it is," he assured her. "We have several at our disposal so I cannot see that it will inconvenience me in the slightest."

"Will your neighbors not think me very odd if I do not career about the countryside on horseback?" she asked.

"Some perhaps," he admitted. "Squire Pebmarsh's daughters are both enthusiastic horsewomen, but let me assure you, they did not like Amanda any better because she had an excellent seat."

He realized his mistake at once and readied himself for a barrage of questions about the Misses Pebmarsh or even Amanda's proficiency in the saddle but instead, Emmeline simply asked, "And do you attend many race meetings throughout the year?"

Jeremy felt wrong-footed. A flare-up of feminine jealousy would not have been unnatural or even unwelcome to him at this point. Why was Emmeline so determined to avoid such an opportunity? He frowned, then noticed she was still waiting for him to reply. Rapidly he reviewed her last question. "Historically, yes," he answered cautiously. "At least a couple of times a month." She nodded. "You do not object?"

"Object?" She sounded startled. "Why should I? Does not the Queen herself attend the races on special occasions?"

"She does," he agreed. "However, my aunt Louisa reads me a lecture at least twice a year on horse racing and its attendant vices."

Her lips formed a silent *oh*. "Because of the betting, I expect."

"Undoubtedly."

"Well, I do not mean to interfere with your pleasures," she assured him, though oddly enough, he found he was not particularly pleased to hear it. He could not think why, and he pondered this as she stood appreciating the view. Finally, it hit him. She was not acting remotely wife-like and strangely, this displeased him. Displeased him a good deal. How to address it though?

"I don't know about interfering with my pleasures, Emmeline," he said at last. "You are my wife. I think I would rather have you join me in them. What do you think?" He earned a surprised look in return. "Do you think you might ever like to try accompanying me, perhaps to one of the larger meets," he suggested. "Ascot maybe, on Gold Cup Day, when there will be lots of ladies present. You don't need to be a good rider yourself to appreciate the spectacle."

Emmeline's face flushed. "I would love to," she said, squeezing his arm. "Thank you." *Well now, that was rather more like it.* "When is it held?"

"June."

"Something to look forward to, then," she said cheerfully.

"Yes, something to look forward to," he agreed, pointing into the distance. "If we carry on walking this way, we will reach the folly and if you walk even further on, then you will reach a path that leads to our own private beach."

They had left the curricle and horses under the cover of some large oak trees, so they made now for the folly which stood atop a grassy slope. As they headed up the bank approaching it, rain started to fall.

Seizing her hand, Jeremy dragged her the last few feet, and they ducked inside the miniature temple. Inside, it was rather dark and a good deal dingier than he remembered. "This place needs sweeping out," he observed, noticing the accumulation of old leaves.

"Here's a bench," Emmeline said, plying her handkerchief over its surface before lowering herself gingerly onto it. "I hope it's not covered in cobwebs."

"There are candles somewhere hereabouts," he said, feeling along a ledge until he found matches and a box of candles. "Here we are." He lit one after the other and set them onto the spikes set up for that purpose before joining her on the stone bench.

Emmeline looked about her with much interest, but in truth there was not much to see other than gray stone walls. "Which god or hero of antiquity is this place sacred to?" she asked with a slight shiver as the rain fell steadily beyond the columns. He passed an arm about her shoulders.

"My father was not the fanciful type," he answered, "so it was never dedicated to anyone. When I played here as a child, I used to pretend it was a gladiatorial training school. I was both chief trainer and star pupil. I used to run up and down the bank as part of my training one hundred times, and I had a wooden sword, a gladius that I used to attack the columns with. I wanted my father to add a miniature amphitheater to the back where I could fight the minotaur, but he never would."

"Surely the minotaur would have resided in your maze, poor thing," Emmie pointed out. "Not here in the folly."

He laughed. "The maze was not here when I was a boy. I had it planted...later." As though noticing his hesitation, she turned her head to look at him. Luckily it was dark in the folly. "When I got married," he admitted with some reluctance. "It's a sort of tradition here at Vance to add something new to the house when someone marries in." Silently, he prepared himself to answer the inevitable question, but Emmeline did not ask it.

"Of course." She nodded. "This folly was built when your father married your mother, was it not?"

"That's right." Once again, he felt that strangely thwarted sensation. He had been apprehensive to tell her his plans to build a conservatory in her honor, for obvious reasons, but for her to not even ask made him feel deeply uneasy. Why was she sidestepping such issues?

"I want to build something new to commemorate our marriage too," he pressed on, realizing she was not going to rise to the bait. "There's an architect coming down for that express purpose."

"Goodness," she said lightly. "We will soon be inundated with architects and decorators! Will we have to dine formally every night when they are here?"

"Aren't you going to ask?" he said abruptly but at the exact same moment, Emmeline asked brightly, "What is in the center of your maze?"

He recovered first. "The center of the maze?"

"Yes. I'm curious."

You're curious about the wrong thing, he thought wryly but after all, perhaps the subject of conservatories was also prohibited. He focused instead on her query about the maze. "It's not a minotaur," he admitted half-regretfully. "Just a small fountain featuring a hippocampus."

"You will think me terribly ignorant, but what is a hippocampus?"

"It's a mythical beast, half horse, half fish."

"Oh, because of your shared love of horses?"

Shared? Oh, she meant him and Amanda. "I confess I thought only of myself," he said quite truthfully. "I'd always wanted a maze here at Vance and horses have always been close to my heart. I rather wish I'd had a minotaur now. Teddy would no doubt approve."

She smiled. "I am sure a hippocampus is just as good."

A silence that was not altogether comfortable stole over them as they both gazed out of the doorway at the falling rain.

"Shall we dine informally tonight?" he suggested. "Just the three of us."

"In the breakfast room on the second floor?" He nodded. "I'd love to. I haven't seen that room yet."

"Haven't you?" He frowned. "We must have missed that on your tour. It lies between your suite of rooms and mine."

"Ah." She paused. "It's funny, isn't it? How we all have our own rooms, even Teddy. And now Pinky will have her own house too."

Funny? He cast her a sidelong glance. "In what way?"

Emmeline did not answer at once, then she simply shrugged. "I suppose I am just not accustomed to so much space." Before he could answer, she said, "I think the rain has abated, my lord. Shall we return to the curricle?"

He stood up and blew out the candles and they made their way down the wet grass bank. "Mind your step," he cautioned. "The grass is wet."

Emmeline accepted his offered hand. "Where to next?" she asked.

He pulled a face. "Well, the hedges of the maze will be dripping with rainwater, so I think we should forgo that experience for another day."

"Agreed."

"We could walk around the formal gardens," he suggested. "And then the informal ones."

"What are the informal gardens?" she enquired.

"Nothing too exciting," he responded. "The ones located around the back of the house. Namely the kitchen gardens, orchard, and hothouse," he replied. "Or…"

"Or?" she repeated curiously.

"We could take a drive about the wider estate," he suggested. "I could show you more of the grounds outside the gates, the lodge, and the tenant cottages, including Miss Pinson's new abode."

She caught her breath. "Plumtree Cottage?"

"The very same."

Suddenly, the enthusiasm seemed to fade from her eyes, and she seemed to reconsider. "I don't know," she said slowly, surprising him. "I think you know that there was something in what you said before."

"What did I say?"

"That Hannah might enjoy showing me around her home once she has it all set up how she wants it. I should hate to…to take anything away from this experience for her. Now that I know how very much it means to her to have her own home."

She gave him a fleeting look. "I have you to thank for that, my lord," she said, coloring faintly. "I would not have realized her feelings on the matter if you had not said…what you said. Despite our closeness, I was quite blind on that subject."

Jeremy cleared his throat, feeling suddenly a little guilty. His motive in setting Miss Pinson up in a separate abode had been far from altruistic. "Sometimes it is like that with those we are closest to," he said rather tritely. "You have been a good friend to her over the years, I am sure."

"I hope so," she said quietly. "She has certainly been the very best of friends to me."

They had reached the curricle by this point and Jeremy helped her up into it before untying the horses. "So then…the gardens?" he asked, swinging himself up and sitting beside her in the seat.

Emmeline smiled and nodded. "The gardens," she agreed, and they headed back to the stables, to return the carriage.

They spent the next couple of hours wandering around garden paths and narrowly avoiding rainclouds by ducking under arches and arbors and whatever else afforded shelter. Jeremy introduced Emmeline to the head gardener, Hudgins, and two undergardeners, Smith and Iverson, who promised her as many flowers and fresh fruits and vegetables as she could possibly hope for.

Jeremy was not ready to part with her when they returned to the house, so instead he escorted her to the room she had mentioned she still hadn't seen, the private dining room. She tried to hide the fact, but he could see she was clearly disappointed as she surveyed the room.

"What were you expecting?" he asked curiously.

She looked evasive. "Well, it's just, you said it was for informal dining and this still looks, well, like a wholly respectable dining room," she admitted, making him laugh.

"Now, Ballentine, did you expect us to lie on low couches eating grapes in togas?" he teased.

"Perhaps," she admitted with a laugh. "Do you know, I think that table in my bedroom with the cushions elevated my expectations. I was expecting something rather more along those lines." She looked rather wistful.

"We could always move that table in here," Jeremy suggested. "Teddy would probably like that."

"Yes, I think I would like that too," she responded solemnly, surprising him. Jeremy blinked. Who was it who said she was a conventional creature? He could not recall at this precise moment.

Impulsively, he walked back out into the corridor and looked left then right for a passing maid. Bridget was just disappearing around a corner, so he called to her. "Hie Bridget! Send Higgins up here, will you, there's a good girl. I need some furniture moved about. Oh, and have Smith and Iverson sent in from the gardens. I want some items fetched down from the attic."

Emmeline looked torn between excitement and guilt when he reentered the room. She bit her lip and eyed the table and chairs. "Will it fit in the attic?" she asked.

He shrugged, then heard approaching voices. It was Miss Pinson, Teddy, and Colfax. "Maybe Miss Pinson could take it," he suggested. "Was there a dining set among the Winkworth furniture?"

"No, well, there was a small table and chairs for two, though they did not match—"

"Perfect, she can take this one." He exited the room again, catching the attention of the newcomers. "We're in here!" he hailed them. "Come and join us."

Teddy was on him in an instant. "Plumtree Cottage has three bedrooms, Papa, but the third is very small and a full-size bed will not fit in there, only a trundle or a bunk."

"Is that so? Miss Pinson," he said, turning to her. "What do you think of this dining set?" She hurried over to join him, looking very pink and breathless.

"Oh, it's vastly handsome, my lord. It looks to be Sheraton, if I am not mistaken. My dear papa always thought that Sheraton made such a refined style of furniture."

"Would it fit in Plumtree Cottage?" His words instantly threw her into confusion.

"Oh dear, I did not mean—I could not possibly—"

"It would fit, milord, just about," Colfax said with quiet authority. "Though she might have to line the chairs against the wall when they're not in use."

"Excellent." He turned back to the protesting lady. "I assure you, Miss Pinson, it is not in the least an imposition, on the contrary, you are doing us a favor. Now, tell me, are there any other items you need? We're about to brave the attics. Perhaps we should make a list."

Teddy whooped with excitement. "Pinky needs a piano, Papa, for her parlor. She has not had one since their London days."

Miss Pinson gave a faint squawk. "Dear child!" She faltered. "You must not—!"

Out of the corner of his eye, he saw Emmeline cross the room to take her friend's hand and give it a reassuring pat.

"You keep an eye out for a piano," Jeremy instructed Teddy. He cast a quick glance around the room. "Now, what else do we need in here? Low couches you said, Emmeline—"

"*You* said low couches!" she responded but he was not attending, as he noticed his second footman had sidled into the room. "Ah Higgins, there you are. You and Colfax need to load this furniture onto the wagon that has just returned and send it straight to Plumtree Cottage."

"Very good, milord."

"And when Smith and Iversen appear, have them sent straight up to join us in the attics."

"Yes, milord."

"To the attics!" yelled Teddy, leading the charge. Emmeline and Miss Pinson took after him, leaving Jeremy to bring up the rear.

19

The accounts she had heard of the attics had not been exaggerated. They were indeed stuffed to the gills with past treasures. Tables and chairs and goodness only knew what were stacked and piled on top of each other. Emmie spotted a green malachite table almost at once that caught her eye. "I expect this is terribly heavy," she murmured, even as she crouched down to inspect the clawed pedestal it stood upon.

"Well, some poor devil must have dragged it up here," Jeremy observed. "If it takes your fancy then someone else can drag it back down again."

"What about these, Papa?" Teddy panted, his head popping up from behind a rococo-style settee.

"No, really, Teddy, that is hideous," Jeremy pronounced with disgust. "In any case, it looks as though all the stuffing is leaking out of the side."

"Not the sofa, Papa. *These!*" Teddy stressed, pointing excitedly to a pair of tall standing world globes.

"I believe those are Georgian," Jeremy observed. "Your grandpapa used to have them in the library. By all means, we will take them *if* you think them suitable for our family dining room…" he said in somewhat doubtful tones.

"Mama?" Teddy deferred judgment.

"Oh yes, the very thing," Emmie agreed at once. Jeremy narrowed his eyes at her but nodded toward the undergardeners, who started making their way gingerly over piles of furniture to collect them.

Emmie looked around for Pinky and found her gazing about with her mouth wide open. It *was* rather like a museum storage room. "Have you spotted a pianoforte?" she asked, stepping carefully over a crate of assorted china.

"Oh, er, I hardly like to, um—"

"Here's one!" sang out Teddy.

Emmie and Pinky moved toward him. "I think that's a spinet," Emmie said, looking at the neat little instrument painted all over with flowers. "Am I right?" she asked, turning to her friend.

"I think so," Pinky agreed. "But I am sure it is *far* too valuable a piece to be allowed to leave the house."

"If you will have use of it, my dear Miss Pinson, then by all means you must take it," Jeremy interrupted them. "Instruments are meant to make music and if I am not mistaken, that particular spinet has not been played in many a year. It was my mother's."

"Oh!" Pinky looked aghast. "I would not dream of such a thing, my lord! Emmie, *you* must play for his lordship on his mother's instrument."

"No, Pinky dear," Emmie said firmly. "You must not allow your fondness for me to color your memories of my musical ability or lack thereof." She looked at Jeremy and pulled a face. "I cannot carry a tune to save my life."

Jeremy merely laughed, directing the undergardeners to retrieve the spinet, brushing aside Pinky's feeble protests.

"Now, what else?" he pondered. "I think we must have some kind of seating to retire to if we are to dine on cushions."

Eventually a wide pair of spoon-backed mahogany chairs upholstered in mustard velvet were settled upon, along with a large "conversation settee" in green damask.

"Why is it called a conversation settee, Papa?" Teddy wanted to know.

"You see those extra sections at each end?" Jeremy asked. "Separated by arms and a winged back? They are for the chaperones to sit in, to make sure that everyone behaves themselves."

"Is that really what they are for, Miss Pinson?" Teddy asked Pinky, slipping his hand into hers.

"Oh yes indeed," she agreed vehemently. "We used to have one in our front parlor at the vicarage. A very fine French one with fringing and carved legs. Now, do be careful and watch your step here, Master Teddy."

"Anything else tickle your fancy, Emmeline?" Jeremy asked. "No? Just the malachite table?"

She nodded. "We could take those colored glass lamps out of my bedroom to put in there too. That might look effective. Oh, and how about a painting or two for the walls?"

"What sort of thing do you think would match our eclectic theme?" he asked, making for the nearest crate of picture frames.

"Do you have any exotic seascapes?" Emmie asked. "Or perhaps a scene depicting the bustle of a Venetian marketplace?"

Jeremy looked doubtful. "I think there is a rendition of the Spanish Armada here somewhere," he said, rifling through the canvases. "What about this one of a nobleman lounging under a tree?" He turned it around to show her. "It looks Jacobean."

Emmie wrinkled her nose. "Ancestor of yours?"

"Oh, undoubtedly. Look at those turquoise tights. Only a Vance would think that appropriate tree-lounging wear."

"I don't like his beard," Emmie objected, "and that collar makes it look like he has no neck."

"It's the angle he's lying at," he protested. "Besides, the fashion of the time was to look entirely neckless." Emmie ignored him, making for the stack of paintings leaning against the nearest wall.

"What about this one of Judith removing Holofernes's head?" he called after her.

"Sounds horrible," she said over her shoulder without looking at it.

"My great aunt painted it. Judith is apparently a self-portrait, and the character of Holofernes was based on her first husband. Apparently—"

His voice faded as Emmie peered over the edge of the first canvas. *Oh!*

Suddenly he was at her side. "I forgot that was there," he said ruefully, his hand coming to rest on the small of her back.

"It's very…beautiful," she said, catching her breath and gazing down at the portrait of Amanda Liversedge resplendent in a dazzling white gown, her blond hair piled up on her head in a large chignon. She had almost forgotten just what a lovely creature she was. Amanda was depicted with one arm draped gracefully over a large stone urn, while the other held a white rose to her decolletage. *"Ode on a Grecian Urn?"* she asked lightly.

"More like *Isabella*," he said, naming another poem by Keats. "I suspect she has Lorenzo's head in that urn."

Emmie frowned. "You are confusing Isabella with Judith," she said firmly.

"I suppose I am," he said dismissively. "But as a matter of fact, I never cared for that portrait. It used to hang in the blue salon opposite my mother's portrait, but I relegated it to the attic after the divorce."

"Is that what your father did with your mother's portrait?" she guessed.

"Yes, actually. It's quite the family tradition." There was a faint edge to his voice. "Did you never give Stockton a miniature of yourself?"

"A miniature?" Emmie shook her head. "No, but if I had, I feel sure he would have returned it with my letters rather than sticking it in an attic somewhere." A sudden thought occurred to her. "You know, you never did give me back my letters to him."

"I know. They're in my room. You can retrieve them whenever you decide to beard me in my den."

Emmie looked at him with surprise. *Now, what did he mean by that?* "You want me to—?"

"Oh, Emmie!" Pinky called. "Do look at what we've found! Such a pretty inlaid chest of drawers. I think it's Louis XV."

Emmie cleared her throat. "Just a minute, Pinky. We're trying to find a picture." She returned her gaze to Lady Amanda's portrait, but she could feel Jeremy's eyes were still fixed on her face. Swallowing, she reached for the next canvas which turned out to be a drawing of an industrial building with a huge wheel next to it and a great big chimney. "What is this?"

He glanced at it. "The design for a mine," he said shortly.

"A mine?" Emmie was glad of the distraction. "One of your family was interested in industry?"

"That's where most of the family wealth originates."

"From industry?"

"From mines, specifically copper and slate. China clay, too, for a while, the stuff they use to make porcelain."

"I never knew that!"

"Well, my family never precisely broadcasted the fact we were involved in trade." He pulled a face. "Perish the thought! My father sold all the mines before his death. That, my dear, is why we are so very wealthy."

"And you prefer racehorses."

"I do."

Emmie pondered this. "Are they considered more genteel than mines?"

He looked amused. "Possibly but that is not why I like them. Did I tell you that Nye is a prizefighter? Sporting blood apparently runs in our veins."

"Papa! I like this one!" Teddy interrupted them from across the attic. With some difficulty, he hoisted up a colorful painting of a boy with a large green parrot sitting on his shoulder. The boy was wearing a large blue velvet hat with a high brim and holding a bowl of fruit from which he was plucking grapes to handfeed his bird.

"Yes, I like that one too," Emmie agreed.

"Then it's settled," Jeremy said decisively. "Let's get out of here before we are quite covered in dust. Iversen, can you help me with this table? Smith, grab that painting."

In no time at all they had the room set up with its new trappings. They set the green damask sofa by the window and the spoon-back chairs, malachite table, and two globes against the opposite wall. The focus of the room was the low round table surrounded by large, plump cushions as it was set in the middle of the room. The tall Turkish glass lamps now sat on the mantelpiece and all around the hearth. When lit, they would cast colorful reflections all around the room.

"Look at that," Emmie said, placing her hands on her hips and surveying their work. "Who needs room designers?"

Jeremy eyed the boy and his parrot painting critically. "Are we sure that picture is quite straight?"

Emmie considered it. "I think so, yes."

Teddy was lolling on the green damask sofa next to Miss Pinson. "Helloooo? No one is chaperoning us," he sang out, pointing to the extra seat on the end which was empty.

"Ignore him," Jeremy advised.

"I think the Turkish lamps look particularly well in here, don't you agree?"

"They do, though your bedroom may lack decoration now."

"A colorful rug might be nice in here," Emmie murmured, tapping her chin. "And perhaps a statue or two. This must be the only room in the house without any marble in it."

"I think we need to replace the curtains," Jeremy observed. "The green ones in here should be more emerald shade than sage."

"Yes, I think you're right."

Emmie lowered her voice. "When we agreed to dine privately in here tonight, I quite forgot about Pinky."

"Did you not tell me she was family also?" he replied with a raised brow.

Emmie flashed him a grateful smile. "Yes, that's true."

They ate their first dinner in the new setup that evening and did not even bother changing for dinner as it was "only family." It proved a novel experience, sitting cross-legged while eating a five-course meal, and they were a merry party throughout.

The only person who seemed a little affronted by the lack of ceremony was Garraway, the butler, who certainly looked askance as he set down the tureen of vermicelli soup but that might have been because he had to bend down lower and had a stiff back. Emmie did notice that it was Colfax who brought in the next four courses ably assisted by one of the housemaids.

"I hope the cottage is coming along, Miss Pinson," Jeremy said politely once the last course, a selection of Neapolitan cakes and a coffeepot, had been set down in the center of the table. "You must let me know if there is anything else we can help you with."

Colfax, who was lighting the colored glass lamps, gave a significant cough, interrupting Pinky's automatic denial. She colored hotly. "Oh! Er, that is, well, possibly the kitchen area could use a fresh coat of paint, my lord," she said guiltily. Colfax turned around and fixed his gaze on her, his expression carefully blank. "And, er, possibly the front parlor," she added nervously. "I think Mr. Somerton must have been a heavy smoker and, well…" She trailed off in embarrassment.

"In that case, I daresay the whole house could do with a lick of paint," Jeremy said calmly. Colfax gave a slight bow of assent at these words. "I shall ask Wallis to see to the matter at once."

"Oh dear, so kind, I do hope it is not too much of a bother—" Pinky dithered, dropping her napkin and becoming quite flustered.

"There's a good deal of brambles and rubbish in the back garden too, Papa," Teddy chimed in. "And a broken old cart is rotting to pieces in there. Mrs. Ennis, who lives in the cottage next door, told me that Somerton was a villain and up to no good half the time like as not."

Pinky's eyes widened. "Dear child—" she started in appalled tones. "My lord, I hope you do not think I encouraged—"

"Do not trouble yourself, Miss Pinson," Jeremy interrupted her laughingly. "If there is any scandal, Teddy is sure to root it out. He has a nose for such things. I will have Wallis send some men around to sort out the garden for you too."

"Oh, but I assure you, I mean to work on the garden myself!"

"And so you shall, but clearing the way is heavy work and must be done before you can make a start with your planting and so forth."

"He's right, Pinky," Emmie said gently, and her friend became very emotional. Teddy passed her his handkerchief, and she dabbed her eyes with it and thanked them all again for their "great kindnesses" toward her.

"Let's play an after-dinner game," Teddy suggested. "I vote forfeits."

Jeremy groaned. "This game gets very involved, and the rules change every time."

"First I have to leave the room for two minutes," Teddy said, clambering eagerly to his feet. "And you all have to put something small into the box…"

"What box?" asked Emmeline.

"Oh yes, we need a box," Teddy said, casting about. "Wait, let me go and fetch one." He ran from the room, whooping.

"What kind of small thing?" Pinky asked timidly.

Jeremy sighed. "A ring, a shoelace, a thimble, something of that kind." He was already removing a signet ring from his little finger.

"Would this suffice?" Pinky asked, unpinning her cameo brooch.

"Amply."

"What is the object of the game?" Emmie asked. "For him to guess who put what in the box?"

"Exactly."

"Then you two have chosen extremely obvious items. He will identify you in a trice."

"Some of us just want to get this over with," Jeremy answered cynically.

"Not me. I intend to be very devious." She rose from her cushion.

"Where are you running off to?" Jeremy asked, catching hold of her hand.

"To fetch my father's pipe tamper; I kept it as a memento. I think he will like it. It is a brass one, in the shape of a booted leg." He released her and she made for the door. "I won't be a minute."

"Well," Pinky said, re-pinning her brooch, "if Emmie is going to enter into the spirit of things so wholeheartedly, my lord, then I think we must also rise to the occasion."

Emmie did not hear Jeremy's reply because she had already left the room, but when she returned moments later, he, too, was absent. He was back by the time Teddy had located a box fit for the purpose and great hilarity ensued for the next hour as an increasingly bewildering assortment of knickknacks were produced for each round of the game.

These included a tiny bottle of sal volatile, a stick of sealing wax, an egg-shaped trinket box, a brass button bearing the image of an anchor, and a piece of jet carved into the shape of a piglet. Teddy was quite giddy by the close of the game and begged to keep the pipe tamper in the hopes it could replace Carruthers's missing leg.

Emmie doubted it would be a perfect match for the toy soldier but relinquished it in any case and Teddy bore it off with him when he went to bed.

"I hope that is not the only keepsake you have left to you of your father, Ballentine," Jeremy said regretfully.

Pinky had retired to her guest bedchamber not long after Teddy, so it was just the two of them now sitting next to one another in the yellow spoon-back seats.

"Well, I sold anything of value," she admitted. "His pocket watch and chain, his tortoiseshell cigar case, his cuff link collection."

He was silent for a moment. "Do you want me to try and track down any of his former possessions for you?" he asked at last. "There's a chance we could—"

"Oh no!" she interrupted him with a dismissive gesture. "Thank you for the kind thought, but that's really not necessary."

"I suppose you have letters of his, things like that," he ventured.

Emmie shook her head. "No. I never kept anything of that sort."

"No, I suppose you would not. You are not remotely sentimental, are you?" he said, and his voice sounded strange. "You did tell me that once before. Clearly, I was not paying enough attention."

When had she said that? For some reason, his words discomforted her. He sounded almost…disappointed with her.

"How would you like to have a picnic lunch on our private beach tomorrow?" he asked in a sudden change of subject. "Just the four of us. It was a pink sky tonight, so, with luck, we may have sunshine tomorrow."

Despite her sudden misgivings, her heart warmed that he thought to include Pinky in the treat.

"I should like that very much, my lord," she said. "Will you be going down to the racing stables first thing? I only ask as Teddy wanted to show Pinky and me the maze in the morning, weather permitting."

"Yes, that is my habit when in the country. I could meet you on the beach at midday if you like and arrange for Higgins to bring along the picnic hamper. Teddy can show you and Miss Pinson the way."

"That would be lovely."

"Well, then it's a plan," he replied smoothly. "Are you ready for bed? You've had a long day."

Emmie told herself that she must have imagined that strange note of discord.

20

Emmie could not say why precisely, but she felt a lingering uneasiness on returning to her bedchamber. Jeremy accompanied her as far as the door, kissed her hand, and then retreated to his own rooms. This surprised her a little. For some reason she had thought he might want to join her.

Lottie appeared to let her know her bath was ready and to help her undress for it. After that was done, Emmie drew on her robe and settled at her dressing table as Lottie dried her hair with a cloth and untangled it with a comb. As she brushed it out, her maid chattered away excitedly about the trousseau that had arrived from the Bath modiste.

"Ever so lovely everything is, milady. Three day dresses of such pretty colors and two evening gowns that are as fine as any I've seen. There's a quantity of undergarments as well, milady, all so pretty and delicate. I've pressed and put everything away in your dressing room."

Emmie roused herself from her thoughts. "Thank you, Lottie, that was most thoughtful of you. Any combing jackets?"

"No, milady," her maid said regretfully. "But there was a note that said a second parcel would arrive within the month, so there's still a chance."

"What about nightgowns?" Emmie asked, thinking of Jeremy.

"Oh yes, milady, and ever so pretty they are, trimmed with ribbon and lace and the most beautiful embroidery. I've set one on the bed for you."

Emmie glanced over at the bed and saw a long white nightgown with capped sleeves and a low square neckline decorated in pink ribbon. It was certainly a good deal more revealing than her old one.

"There's a new dressing gown, too, in a lovely pink brocade," Lottie added, nodding to a peg on the doorway, "so you need not worry you will catch your death of cold."

Emmie cleared her throat. "That's a relief."

"Shall I plait your hair into a braid for bed, milady?" Lottie asked.

Emmie considered this for a moment, her eyes straying to the connecting door. "No, thank you," she decided. "I'll leave it loose tonight." She had already washed and brushed her teeth, so after removing her old dressing gown and the last of her underwear, she donned her new nightgown and returned Lottie's good night as the maid departed with a neat curtsey.

Once alone, Emmie glanced at herself in the dressing table mirror. Maybe it was the candlelight flattering her, but she fancied the new nightgown was rather becoming. It was more tailored to her figure than the old one, which had been rather shapeless as well as buttoned up to her throat.

Fetching her new dressing gown off its peg, she admired the gold stitched flowers on the silky pink fabric before putting it on and walking to the door which led to Jeremy's room. Was she really going to do this? She cast her mind back to their previous conversation on the subject.

I cannot imagine I would bar your way if you did venture my side of the door. That was what he had said. In truth, it had not exactly been an invitation. Then again, he had seemed rather surprised when she had even suggested the possibility of her venturing into his domain.

For the first time, it occurred to her that perhaps Jeremy was *not* much of an authority when it came to marital relations. After all, by his own admission, his first marriage had been rather a disaster and his own parents had been divorced before he was two. How would he know much about how they worked?

According to Teddy's artless disclosures, his father had kept his side of the door permanently locked when married to Lady Amanda. Perhaps it was locked now, she thought, biting her thumbnail. There was only one way to find out. Extending her hand, she turned the handle. The door opened, and taking a deep breath, Emmie walked through.

Her first impression of the room was a lot of dark wood and green walls. Then she spotted him standing next to a large bed. Jeremy turned to look at her in surprise, frozen in the act of tying the belt to his black and gold dressing gown.

"Oh!" Emmie said, for she had been expecting him to be abed. "Are you going for a bath?"

"No, I've just had one actually," he said, and she noticed his hair did look slightly damp.

"So, did I," she confided rather awkwardly. After all the attics had been dusty. "Is your valet—?"

"Simons has retired for the evening. "That's a very fetching dressing robe."

"It's new," she said, turning in a circle for him. "From Madame de Flores."

"It's worth every penny," he said admiringly. "Very pretty. Are you going to come in? Or just hover there by the door." He walked over to the bed and sat on it, reclining against the pillows.

Emmie ventured further into the room, glancing about her with interest. "I like your room," she said, noticing several bronze horses scattered around the room on small pedestal tables. Another voluptuous Venus hung on the wall opposite his bed. This one was partially swathed in red velvet, though still flaunting her naked upper body, gazing at herself complacently in a mirror held up by cupids. Yes, this was definitely Jeremy's room.

"I hope there's a new nightgown under that robe, Ballentine," he commented.

"There is."

"Care to show it to me?"

"Not yet," she said, lowering herself onto a plush velvet seat.

He frowned. "Why are you sitting over there?"

"Well, I don't like to encroach."

His confused expression cleared. "Ah, so that's it. You've come for Stockton's letters," he said, rolling onto his side and reaching for one of the drawers. "Here." He tossed them onto the bed at his feet. "I should have given you them sooner, but it slipped my mind. I suppose they hold more sentimental value for you than your father's letters did." His tone was faintly barbed, though his expression remained aloof.

Emmie stared stupidly at the pile of letters tied up with string. She had forgotten all about her letters to Humphrey. Now that she came to think of it, she had asked about them earlier that day, and he had said something about her having to "beard him in his den."

That must be what he thought she was doing now. *How humiliating.* When she had come looking for him for an altogether different reason. *You stupid fool, Emmeline,* she told herself. *How can you still be chasing after him, eager for his attention, after all these years? Have you learned* nothing?

"Of course," she said slowly, "the letters." She stood up moved to the bed to retrieve them. "Thank you." She glanced about and made for the open fireplace, dropping the packet of letters into the flames before turning around. "Well, good night," she said awkwardly and started back toward the door.

"Emmeline—" he called after her, but she pretended not to hear him, hurrying her steps, slipping back through the door, and turning the key in the lock. She felt a sudden and dizzying anger sweep over her. She was practically shaking with it. Leaning forward, she rested her forehead against the door a moment to steady herself.

How *dare* he? The way he had just *flung* them at her like that. That *bastard.* That inconsiderate, unfeeling swine. Without giving herself further time to reflect or calm down, she walked over to her bed and retrieved the rosewood box she had concealed underneath it.

Straightening up, she walked out into the corridor and around the corner until she reached the door to Jeremy's bedroom. She was damned if she would ever use that connecting door again. It could remain locked forever as far as she was concerned.

Knocking on the door loudly three times, she threw it open and marched inside. Jeremy was off the bed now, stood in the center of the room. He had a stunned, slightly panicked expression on his face. "Why are you—?"

She flung the heavy rosewood box on the bed, where it bounced and landed upside down.

He transferred his gaze from her to the box, then back again.

"Open it," she said abruptly.

"What is it?"

"Open it," she repeated woodenly.

After looking at her rather searchingly, he walked over to the bed and sat down on it, drawing the box toward him, setting it right-side up, and locating the latch.

"Take a look," she said bitterly. "And you shall see whether I am *sentimental* or not."

"Emmeline," he said gently. "Won't you sit down beside me."

"No! I don't want to!" she said in a choked voice. When he made as though to set the box aside, she backed away from the bed and lowered herself into the same chair she had sat upon earlier.

Jeremy watched her warily, and only once she was settled did he return to the box, unfastening it and lifting the lid. He gazed down at the contents a moment blankly before drawing out a pair of monogrammed gloves. "Your father's?" he asked in some confusion, after inspecting the initials. "I thought you said you did not keep anything of his."

"No, I did *not* say that," she replied tightly. "I said I sold anything of value, and that I did not keep any of his letters. For your information, my lord," she began in a low, shaking voice, "my father only ever wrote to me when he wished to upbraid me. It is hardly likely that I should wish to preserve such communications. My father was a very driven man, some might even say ruthless. He was certainly very business-oriented. Ballentine's Trading Company was his true focus in life, *not* family and certainly not me."

Jeremy swallowed and set the gloves carefully aside before reaching back inside the box. He drew out an empty scent bottle with a few congealed drops remaining in the bottom. "And whose was this?" he asked quietly. "Your mother's?"

She jerked her head in affirmation. "Yes, I do not remember her but as a child I drew some comfort from knowing what she liked to smell like."

Next, he drew a pair of long white evening gloves from the box. "And were these your mother's too?"

She pressed her lips together and shook her head. "No. Mine," she said briefly.

He frowned slightly but returned to the box and drew out next an ivory silk fan trimmed in silver. "And this?"

Averting her face, she crossed her arms. "Mine also," she said, swallowing.

With growing bewilderment, he drew forth another fan, this one of white satin with broken sticks. "Will you explain?" he asked quietly. "Emmeline?"

"Explain?" she asked in a wobbly voice. "Well, might you ask. It's an odd collection, is it not? Very well." She stood up from her chair and approached the bed, snatching up the evening gloves and dangling them before his nose. "These gloves I wore to the Foxtons'," she said matter-of-factly. "You won't remember, but after we danced there, you escorted me off the dance floor and did not relinquish my hand.

"Instead, you walked me over to the potted plants and stayed beside me for oh, I don't know, probably five minutes of your idle life, whiling away the time by talking a lot of spite about the company at large. I don't remember what you said, in truth I could barely hear you.

"You see, the whole time, my heart was beating so loudly it drowned out your words and all I could focus on was the fact we still had our fingers interlaced and your palm pressing against mine." She threw down the gloves on the bed. "Stupid, isn't it? I could not bear to use them again and instead kept them as though they had once touched a holy relic."

Instead of looking for his reaction, she snatched up the silver ivory fan. "This, you took from my hand at the Wavertons' picnic party and used it to fan my hot face as you sat beside me and amused yourself for half an hour by paying court to me. I was *so* happy that I could not eat a thing, even though they had exotic fruits there that I had been looking forward to sampling."

She paused, caught up in the moment. "They were serving peaches in fancy napkins, I remember," she said in a faraway voice, "but they called them Persian apples." She gave herself a quick shake. "Silly how you remember such details."

Next was the broken fan. Still avoiding his eye, she picked it up between finger and thumb, holding it in the air and contemplating it in a detached sort of manner. "This is the fan I was holding that night at the foot of Lord Hawford's staircase, when your announcement was made," she said in a brittle voice. "It was very expensive, and I did not even notice that I had snapped all the sticks until I was sat in the carriage on the way home. As you can see, it was broken quite beyond repair."

The silence between them stretched out, until Emmie released the fan and it fell in a twirling sort of motion, like an injured bird falling from the sky. Jeremy reached out and caught it before it hit the ground. His swift movement broke her trance, and she stepped back, almost startled by it.

Jeremy straightened up very slowly and added the fan to his pile.

"Pray continue," she said politely, looking back expectantly at the box.

"Emmeline—" he started hoarsely but she made a sharp gesture with her hand.

"There's not much left now. It won't take long."

Almost reluctantly, he drew out the first of several dance cards. She waited until she saw it, the dawning realization in his eyes. She could not bear to watch as he opened each one in turn. It would not take him long to find his signature in every one. Barely anyone else had ever taken the trouble to dance with her after all.

Before she knew it, he was off the bed, and was trying to take her in his arms. "Ballentine," he murmured huskily. She did not make it easy for him, struggling and trying to push him away. She shoved a hand against his chest, and he caught it there.

"*Don't*," he said brokenly, "Don't push me away, Emmie-mine, I can't bear it."

Emmie stopped trying to free herself. Instead, she looked at her hand where it lay against his chest, resisting, yet touching his bare skin at the same time. His chest heaved beneath her fingers. "I'm sorry," he said softly. "I'm so fucking sorry. You're far too good for me. You always were. I hope you know that."

She would not speak, could not. The anger, both toward him and worse, toward *herself*, pressed down too heavily on her heart. She wanted to cry but not soft, healing tears. No, the tears she wanted to cry were angry, furious sobs of resentment and bitterness.

His expression seemed to show he understood at least some measure of her feeling, for he dragged her hand until it rested over his heart. "I don't have a rosewood box, Emmeline, but I kept you here always." His words were low and urgent.

His throat seemed to close over the words, and for a moment he struggled to speak. "I know, God knows I know that I"—he paused, choosing his words carefully—"that I was too destructive in the past." She could not help but stiffen slightly even at this vague allusion to it.

He continued in a ragged voice, "I worry that any vestiges we have left of that time are damaged and I cannot repair them, try as I might. I know you said we should build something new and forget the past, but I don't want to forget it!" His words were passionate now. "Because—"

"Stop," she begged raggedly, clapping her hands over her ears and screwing her eyes shut. He ceased talking at once. Slowly, Emmie lowered her hands, her breathing shallow and uneven. She felt herself sway slightly on her feet.

Pointing to the wooden box with a trembling finger, she asked in a low, shaky voice, "Does that not prove to you that I am not made of stone? Why must you poke and pry at the wound? It had practically healed until you came back into my life! I cannot—!"

"I'm sorry, Emmeline," he said quickly as her voice broke and she closed her eyes, a single tear running down her cheek. "I'm sorry. Forgive me. You're right. I was wrong. I won't—" He swallowed convulsively. "I won't ever bring it up again. I'll never, never bring it up again, my darling, I promise."

His hands hovered awkwardly at her elbows. "Can I—? Let me—?" When she did not move, just stood there like a wooden stock, he folded her carefully into his arms and Emmie let him comfort her, rocking her slightly. "God, I'm sorry, so sorry," he said against her hair, gently kissing her brow. "I'm so, so sorry, sweetheart. For everything. For…just *everything*."

When she remained still, he said quietly, "Will you stay? Will you lie in my bed with me? Just to sleep, I swear. I would like to try it, just once."

"Try it?" Emmie echoed. She had no idea what he was talking about right now.

"Having you in my bed with me, I mean. Will you?" She hesitated, knowing only too well that there would be sobbing before she slept. Ugly, jagged sobbing and ladies did not show such overset emotion. He released her at once, lifting her hand to his lips. "No? Then let me escort you back to your room, then, sweetheart. Just let me tuck you in."

"I'll stay," she said dully, though she was not really sure why.

He peered into her face. "You're sure?" he asked softly.

Emmie nodded and gave him a tired smile. "You likely won't thank me for it though," she predicted wanly.

"Why do you say that?" he asked, leading her over to the bed, and drawing back the covers for her.

"Because I'm going to cry myself to sleep," she said frankly. "Do you still want me to stay?"

"Yes," he said at once and she climbed into his bed. He walked around to the other side, extinguishing the candles and joining her under the covers, huddling against her back and passing an arm about her to hold her close.

Under the covers, in the forgiving darkness, Emmie pressed her face into the pillow and wept as though her heart would surely break. She wept for that stupid girl who had looked so eagerly for him with so much hope in her heart. That idiot girl who had been so excited to attend all those pretentious parties.

The girl who had hurried to his side as soon as he so much as beckoned. The girl who had worn her heart on her sleeve while everyone else laughed at her. The girl she had once been. She soaked his pillow with tears and racked her body with shattering sobs that left her feeling weak and calm at last.

The whole time, Jeremy Vance held her tightly to him. How odd, she thought, being comforted by the person who had reopened her wounds. Wounds he had inflicted in the first place.

21

Jeremy welcomed the early morning light as it came streaking through the cracks in his curtains. He had barely slept, and when he had, his dreams had been fragmented and disturbing, affording him glimpses of a past which had always been a source of shame for him but now… God. They *haunted* him.

He had always known he had behaved badly but…Christ almighty. He had not had the faintest idea. Not the smallest notion of how devastated Emmeline had been left in the wake of his disgraceful behavior. Somehow, all these years, he had twisted everything to believe himself the injured party.

Selfishly, he had thought only of his own pain, being forced to marry Amanda. When he did allow himself to think fleetingly of her, he had imagined pretty Ballentine married to some far nicer and worthier man than he. A thought that had twisted his guts and made his gorge rise.

He had always been wildly jealous of that man. A man who would pamper her and give her a multitude of children, and the life that she deserved, while he, Jeremy, was stuck in a loveless marriage feeling sorry for himself. Was it any wonder he had never looked into what had become of Emmeline Ballentine?

Without thinking, he tightened his arms about her. She murmured something in her sleep, and he forced himself to slacken his hold. And all the while, that man had never existed. Instead, by some cruel twist of fate, her father had introduced her to an even worse suitor than himself.

Jeremy's shoddy treatment had left her prey to that unprincipled swine who had then ruined her father's business, destroyed her good faith, and wasted ten years of her life while he kept his wife and child on the sidelines. Jeremy wanted to kill him.

Worst of all, he knew he had treated her just as poorly. His reckless, indulgent conduct had broken her heart, as well as his own. He had always known he was unworthy of that starry gaze she used to bestow on him. He'd been so greedy for it though.

He'd always fooled himself that, once out of her sight, the scales would fall from Emmeline's eyes and she would realize what a tawdry, worthless piece of shit he really was. The most he had ever hoped for was that on a cold night, she might secretly compare her dull, worthy husband's kisses to his, and he might not come off the worst for it.

Now he knew why there was no fond reminiscing on her behalf. There was no mistaking the damage he had wrought upon her. Not after the storm of weeping she had endured the previous night. He had ruined *everything* between them. There could be no doubt why even her memories were destroyed.

No wonder she hated when he brought up their mutual history. It had been like sticking a knife into her every time. And he had done it so fucking thoughtlessly too. Repeatedly. He hated himself. *Hated* himself. He could barely stand to be inside his own skin this morning. What the fuck had he done?

She had not even come into his room to get those fucking letters, he realized now, too late. She had come to seek him out. The first time she had ever ventured his side of the door, and how had he reacted? By being a nasty, jealous prick, that was how.

He had seen fit to judge her feelings for her father, and had jibed at her, despite hearing at least a couple of things previously that had made him suspect her father was a nasty bastard too. Remembering how pretty and nervous she had looked in her new nightgown, her toes peeping out beneath the hem, he felt a fresh wave of scalding shame wash over him.

Well, she would never trust him like that again. She had locked the connecting door, and if there was any justice in this world, it would remain locked against him forevermore. He, Jeremy, had hugely fucked things up and not for the first time. Not by a long shot. He could almost cry, he realized, dragging a forearm over his tired eyes.

Great. Now he was sniveling, like the craven worm he was. How could he have spoken to her like that, and ruined everything with a few careless, unguarded words? So fucking stupid, he would never forgive himself. Everything had been perfect all day, and then like a fucking idiot, he had wantonly destroyed the progress he had made with her.

She had warned him, and he had not listened. He had not left the past alone and now he must face the consequences, he thought bleakly. As soon as he judged the hour advanced enough, he carefully set about disentangling himself from her.

He managed to get out of the bed by very careful maneuvering but no matter how carefully he moved about the room, her sleep was broken, and Emmeline awoke, lifting her head to regard him blearily.

"There's no need for you to rise this early just because I am," he reassured her, but she was having none of it, already sitting up and rubbing her red-looking eyes.

"I don't want to scare your valet," she said, reaching for her dressing robe.

"Simons would survive the shock," he replied but she was already out of bed. "Promise me you won't do too much this morning." The strength of her passionate weeping the night before had almost scared him. Even though she had let him console her and hold her in his arms, he had been horribly conscious of his uselessness.

Suddenly, Emmeline lifted up the covers, looking from the mattress to him in consternation, her color draining away.

"What is it?" he asked quickly.

She covered her eyes with her hand. "I'm so sorry," she said stiltedly. "To cap it all, it seems my monthly has arrived."

"Monthly?" he repeated foolishly before comprehension dawned. "Oh…"

"Let me just… I'll strip the bed," she said quickly. "Don't come any closer!" The last words sounded panicked.

"Emmeline," he said gently. "All is well…"

She started to turn, then swung back around awkwardly. "Can you turn your back to me, please?" she asked with fragile dignity.

Jeremy hesitated, unsure what to do for the best. "Can't I help?" he asked. "I'm not afraid of a little blood."

"No!" Her answer was immediate and explosive. "I—I don't want you to." She stared down at her feet, her expression mortified. *"Please?"* she added in a desperate whisper.

Jeremy turned around, showing her his back. Immediately he heard her scrabbling about with the sheets. His chest hurt that she could not even trust him with this.

"I'm walking to the door," she said, and he heard by her voice the direction she was moving in.

"The connecting door's locked on your side," he reminded her hoarsely.

"Oh! Oh yes…" Her footsteps faltered.

"No one will be in the corridor at this hour," he assured her. "Not that it would matter, if they were," he added quietly.

Emmeline took a ragged breath, and he heard her feet turn toward the other door. It swung open and he guessed she was peering out. Then he heard her footsteps hurrying down the corridor to her own room. *Jesus*. Just when he had thought he could not feel any worse.

He did not head to the racing stables once he was washed and dressed, but instead saddled up Cadmus and headed for Mina and Nye's inn, which lay just outside Penarth. It did not feel right to continue with his usual routine. Not on a day like this, when his life lay around him in ruins.

On arrival, he stabled his horse and walked straight through the inn to the back rooms where he found his half siblings at breakfast in their private parlor. They greeted him cordially and Nye bade him "pull up a chair."

They did not offer him tea, as he never could abide the stuff, instead Mina slipped out to request a pot of coffee for him. Jeremy asked after his nephew, who, according to Nye, had screamed like a banshee till the early hours and was now giving them a moment's respite.

"You look as though you slept worse than us, by the dark circles under your eyes," Mina observed, sitting back at the table. "Edna will bring your coffee shortly." Jeremy maintained a stony silence.

"Well, he is a newlywed," Nye pointed out. When Jeremy could not return his smirk, he sat up a little straighter in his seat, and shot a look at his wife.

"Is all well up at Vance Park?" Mina asked, lowering her teacup.

Jeremy shook his head and Nye whistled. "You can't have made a mess of things already!"

"I would not be so sure about that," Jeremy responded gravely.

Mina opened her mouth but closed it again when the door opened, and their sour-faced maid Edna sailed in with a pot of coffee which she thumped down in front of Jeremy. "Thanking you kindly for my bit of wedding cake, milord," she said, and Jeremy realized he was in her good graces for once.

"You're most welcome, Edna," Jeremy responded, and she bobbed him a curtsey.

"Will there be anything else, Mrs. Nye?"

Mina thanked her maid and assured her they had everything needed.

"Do you suppose she put it under her pillow?" Jeremy asked as soon as Edna retreated.

Mina shook her head. "Edna dreams of Crown Derby tea sets, not husbands. Corin told me she was going to put her piece under her pillow though."

"What the devil are you two talking about?" Nye asked, helping himself to another piece of toast. Mina explained the superstition to him. "Well, why does Corin need dream about her future husband when she's been engaged to Ed Herney for nigh on twelve months? She knows his face well enough."

Mina rolled her eyes. "It's just a bit of girlish fun." She turned resolutely to Jeremy. "Now, tell us what is troubling you. It is to do with Emmeline, I take it," she said forthrightly. "What has gone wrong precisely?"

"Nothing's *gone* wrong, exactly," Jeremy began. "I'm beginning to think I started things on entirely the wrong footing with her." The worst of it was, he did not know where to even start with the retelling. Should he begin with his most recent disaster or that fateful season ten years ago?

It slowly dawned on him that despite seeking out his siblings, he was hardly in a position to lay his soul bare to them. He did not know if either of them would be prepared for how just how rotten it really was.

"I've backed myself into a corner where she is concerned," he said instead. "And we're, well, not *at liberty* to discuss things frankly."

"Why not?" Mina asked with a frown.

What could he answer to that? Jeremy struggled for a moment. "We once had a conversation where we agreed to be frank in that moment, but then be nothing but polite to one another forever afterward." That was true in any event.

"What the hell did you want to make a bloody stupid promise like that for?" Nye asked bluntly.

Mina gave him a speaking look and his brother folded his arms with an expression of long-suffering but otherwise held his tongue. "And the moment of frankness?" Mina asked encouragingly. "How did you spend that?"

"Errr…" Jeremy cast his mind back to that conversation in Hutton's tea shop where he had outlined what he wanted from a wife.

"By telling her a load of lies," Nye said damningly. "What?" he said in answer to his wife's unspoken exasperation. "It's written all over his face!"

Jeremy colored. "I told her I intended to marry her," he began defensively, "and I meant that part alright." Nye scoffed.

"Nye! This is hardly helpful," Mina said sternly, then turned back to Jeremy. "Is that when you told Emmeline your true motive in marrying her?" she asked gently. "I must say, even though I believe in perfect truth between husband and wife, I think that was a misstep."

Jeremy frowned at her. "What are you talking about?"

"Do you mean to tell me," Nye interrupted them, "that with all your fancy schooling, Faris, you told a woman you were marrying her purely because you wanted her in your bed?"

Mina spluttered. "Nye!" she protested.

"I mean, he made it pretty damned obvious! Did you not see the way he was watching her that night? Like a bloody hawk."

"Of course I never told her that!" Jeremy said hotly before turning back to his sister. "What exactly do you mean by 'my true motive.' Mina?" he asked.

"There is no need for reticence on the subject," Mina answered in level tones. "Emmeline told me of it herself."

"Told you what?"

"That you married her at Teddy's request."

"At Teddy's...?" Jeremy regarded his sister speechlessly.

Nye gave an explosive snort. "Is that what you told her? What a load of bollocks!"

"Nye, I really will not tolerate that kind of language in my private parlor," his wife told him firmly.

His brother leaned back in his chair, casting an indulgent look at his wife. "I've said my piece, I'm content."

Mina turned back to Jeremy. "Clearly, your wife took what you said too much to heart," she continued, "and doubtless she now thinks your affections are not at all engaged. Really, I cannot say that I blame her one bit, you have handled this very poorly, Jeremy."

"That's not why I married her! I never said it was for Teddy's sake..." His words trailed off as he thought about it. It was true he had never used that justification that morning in Hutton's but that *was* why he had renewed their acquaintance in the first place.

Could he really blame her if she had taken that as his primary motivation in marrying her? Now that he considered it, he *did* think she had said something along those lines just before she asked him to never mention the Hawfords' ball again.

What was it she had said? He went over the moment in his mind. He had asked her if she would rather he never spoke of their shared past together and she had replied, *I could hardly ask that of you, not when the very reason you married me was to reassure your son on that score.* He cursed aloud, making his sister wince.

God, last night was far from his only blunder, he realized belatedly. He had been hurt, annoyed that Emmeline did not want to hear him reminiscing, so he had not addressed it as he should have at the time. "I've been such a blind *fool*," he groaned.

"What *did* you tell her, then? About wanting to marry her," Nye asked narrowly. "That's what I want to know."

"A lot of things I thought she would find more palatable than the truth," he admitted.

"Such as?" Mina probed.

"That I wanted a wife who would be content living quietly in the country," he said vaguely.

"Well, that's not so bad," Nye said bracingly. "You probably *do* want that, don't you? It's about time you settled down."

Jeremy shrugged a shoulder. "Not really. I should not mind the odd jaunt to town still, if only she would deign to join me."

"Listen," his brother said, leaning forward, "what you need to do is forget all this 'politeness ever after' stuff and have it out with her, lay your cards on the table and clear the air."

"It's not that simple," Jeremy admitted. "As I said, there are reasons...certain episodes in our past that I have promised never to revisit with her. When I've tried, it has not gone well." He almost shuddered. "I've made things palpably worse between us."

"Jeremy has wronged Emmeline in the past," Mina explained patiently to Nye. "He needs to tread very carefully, not blunder about like a bull in a china shop."

Jeremy looked up quickly. "What did she tell you?"

"Very little. I picked up an inference, that was all. I'm right though, aren't I?"

"Who *hasn't* he wronged in the past?" Nye asked dryly. "That just makes her one of the family as far as I'm concerned. What did you do? Ruin her?" Mina gasped.

"No! Not that... Well, maybe socially," Jeremy admitted wretchedly. "I spoiled her marriage prospects and made a disaster of her London season. I courted her, quite openly, then turned around and married Amanda. I exposed her to public ridicule and private condemnation. I was incredibly selfish. I hurt her. Beyond forgiveness. Beyond repair."

They all three sat quietly for a moment, until Nye spoke. "Well, that was probably your biggest mistake," he said heavily. "That first marriage of yours."

"That was not my mistake, as it happens," Jeremy retorted. "I had no say in the matter. I was informed on my twelfth birthday of the betrothal."

Nye shrugged. "The lords of Faris have always been high-handed," he said pointedly. "I don't remember getting much choice either. Luckily, you picked better for me than your father did for you." He exchanged a look with his wife, reaching over to take her hand in his.

Jeremy was taken aback. "I'm nothing like him," he said in surprised accents.

"Never said you were."

"Well, he was your father too."

Nye shook his head. "No, he wasn't. Not in any way that counted. It was Jacob Nye raised me. Shame he didn't have a hand in raising you as well."

"Maybe if he had, I would have turned out a sight better than I did," Jeremy agreed.

Nye gave a grim smile. "He'd have taken a stick to you. He always said you were wild."

"Did he?" Jeremy wasn't really surprised by this. "I always rather liked old Jacob. He never complained about my bar tab."

"He always said you were good for it." Nye gave him a level look. "And you always were."

"Eventually," Jeremy agreed. "Do you know one time, he said I was too drunk to ride my horse home and had that old groom of his dunk my head in the water trough. The old devil damn near drowned me."

Nye chuckled. "Old Sam Teague? Bet he would have enjoyed that."

Jeremy pulled a face. "No doubt. He never had much time for me, did Samuel. Thought me quite the spoiled young lordling."

"It was him taught me to box."

"I know. I was always far more interested in your life than you were in mine."

Nye regarded Jeremy steadily for a moment. "You are worth knowing as it happens," he said abruptly.

Jeremy was surprised. "What makes you say that?"

"The boy." Nye paused. "*Your* boy. The way you are with him. If I ever compared our lives in the past, I soon realized I got the better bargain. You're ten times the father to your son than the old lord was to you."

Jeremy swallowed. "Thanks," he said hoarsely.

"But I'm a much better husband," Nye said cheerfully.

Mina leaned forward at this point. "What was the unpalatable truth you spoke of before, Jeremy?" she asked quietly. "The *real* reason you proposed marriage to Emmeline."

"That I love her," he admitted. "That I have always loved her, even when I was cruel and thoughtless and made her life a misery. That she's the only person I ever truly wanted at my side."

"Then you need to *show* her that's how you feel," Mina said earnestly. "If you can't speak of it, then you need to demonstrate this to her, in ways other than words. Be considerate of her fears, of her dreams, of her likes and dislikes. Be patient, and she will learn that she can put her trust in you. These things take time, and in the meantime, instead of spoiling her with material things, think of ways you can make her new life easier."

"Such as?"

"Oh, a hundred ways, I daresay. Be kind to that little friend of hers, Miss Pinson," she suggested. "It's plain she values her highly."

Jeremy nodded, but he had already been kind to Hannah Pinson, hadn't he? A little voice whispered in his ear that all he had really done was try to isolate Emmeline from her one true friend. He shifted uncomfortably in his seat.

"I don't just mean to take her shopping, or on excursions or day trips, Jeremy," his sister stressed. "You need to make her feel an important part of your everyday life. That's what Nye did for me."

For a moment, Nye looked as though he would speak, only to change his mind and lapse back into brooding silence.

"And how would you suggest I do that exactly?" Jeremy asked, a pucker between his brows.

"Introduce her to your friends and neighbors," Mina said promptly. "Help her establish her own life here in Penarth. Real life is not all picnics and walks in the park, Jeremy. She needs to feel that your connection is genuine, so that she can learn to trust in you."

Trust, Jeremy thought, thinking she would not even trust him to see her bloodied nightgown. Suddenly, he remembered Emmeline had said something else that morning in Hutton's tea shop. *It makes me fear that once again, this is all just a grand jest to you, and that I am once more the butt of the joke. That you, my lord, are not remotely in earnest.*

He swallowed and nodded slowly. "That makes sense," he said, his throat rather dry. He reached for the coffeepot. "Thank you."

He stayed for a while drinking coffee, and hearing about Nye's next boxing event at the inn, a topic that none of them had thought fit to raise previously at Vance. Jeremy was thoughtful on his ride home, reflecting on mending fences. It did not matter how long it took, forever if necessary.

He turned up at the stables two hours late and Masterson looked at him rather askance as he had missed a good deal that morning. Amyas had already had his hour and a half's exercise, for he worked better first thing, having an inclination to turn lazy as the day wore on.

"They neither of them have Bucephalus's work ethic," Masterman grumbled.

Jeremy agreed, but he watched Atalanta being put through her paces all the same, calling out encouragement to her handlers. After this, he watched the last two horses, only recently acquired and both showing distinct promise. "The dark bay's shaping up well," he observed, and Masterman's face visibly brightened.

"We could have a future champion yet," he said cheerfully. "Wait and see."

With an eye on the time, Jeremy returned to the house at twelve, uncertain if the plans he had previously made with Emmeline would still stand. Would she be at the beach, or would she have forgotten all about it after everything that happened?

He washed and changed, and after looking in at the dining room, which he found empty, Jeremy headed to the stable and collected Cadmus, making this time for the private beach.

Jeremy's spirits soared when he spotted the groom leaning against the empty landau with a bored look on his face. He straightened up on seeing his master approach.

"Can you take Cadmus?" Jeremy asked, dismounting and passing his reins to the man.

"Of course, milord."

He heard the laughter even as he clambered over the dunes and beheld the little party sitting on the brightly checked blanket. The sun was shining, Emmeline was wearing a new dress of primrose yellow, and he hoped to God it would be easy to pretend for a couple of hours that all was well with the world.

"Here you are," she said, looking up with a valiant attempt at a smile. "We brought the picnic hamper with us. Mrs. Oxley has prepared us an outstanding lunch."

"Ah, excellent." Jeremy dropped down beside her, briefly touching her ankle by way of greeting. He was too scared she might flinch if he tried to kiss to her cheek. "Hello, Miss Pinson," he greeted her friend, who was sitting shielding her eyes from the sun. "I hope you have spent a pleasant morning."

"Oh yes, my lord," she answered happily, and he realized Emmeline could not have confided in her what a swine he had been.

"I've brought along my cricket set, Papa," Teddy volunteered.

"Have you? Then we must certainly have an innings."

They ate sandwiches and drank lemonade under the blue sky, and after eating, he and Teddy introduced Emmeline and Miss Pinson to beach cricket.

Miss Pinson could not catch a ball to save her life and Emmeline could not hit one. Still, by the time they all flopped back down on the blanket an hour later, they were panting and smiling, even if a shadow lurked in Emmeline's eyes whenever they rested on him.

"Papa?" Teddy said suddenly. "Are you sad today?"

"Sad? Not at all!" he said heartily, sitting up and reaching for a bottle of water. "How could I possibly be sad on a day such as this? Just look at this glorious sunshine. Why, it's as warm as a day in July!"

He had a horrible feeling his words lacked conviction but luckily for him at this moment a thunderclap sounded, and they all scrambled to their feet.

"Rainclouds!" Teddy shouted, pointing to the sky as Jeremy and Emmeline started gathering up their things.

"Oh dear, oh dear," Miss Pinson muttered, making a grab for the cricket stumps. "And the hood is down on the landau too! We shall all get wet through! I'm sure there is going to be a storm."

Glancing sideways at Emmeline as he took her elbow, Jeremy hoped for the contrary. It would be nice to think that the worst of the storms was already over with.

22

The next morning the first of the designers arrived, a Mr. Penrose along with his team of three workmen, and that same afternoon, an architect called Mr. Wimble. Mrs. Cheviot discussed with Emmie the plans for putting them up. This consisted of providing guest rooms for Mr. Penrose and Mr. Wimble in the east wing and finding lodgings in various cottages on the grounds for their workmen.

Emmie assured their housekeeper that this all sounded highly suitable and agreed with her suggestion that formal dining should be reinstated to accommodate these new members of the household. She felt a little sad to lose the intimacy of their private dining room, but after all, one had to accommodate one's houseguests, and it might be easier considering how things had taken a decidedly awkward turn of late between herself and her husband.

As a consequence, breakfast, luncheon, and dinner were now formal affairs and felt decidedly stuffy after their family supper and the picnic lunch on the beach. She fancied Pinky, who had been slowly opening up to Jeremy's presence, shrank from two new gentlemen on the premises and retreated once more into her shell.

Teddy took a lively interest in Mr. Wimble, who was a shy and retiring young man, and ignored the somewhat pompous Mr. Penrose, who he had met before and was somewhat contemptuous of.

"He decorated Mama's rooms before. My other mama, I mean," Teddy elucidated. "He's very fussy," he added in a whisper. "But apparently, quite famous in London."

Emmie had to admit she did not care much for Mr. Penrose herself, for the man clearly had a high opinion of his own taste, and she had not enjoyed the brief consultation they had shared thus far about the decoration of her rooms. Neither of the two sketches he had produced had appealed to her in the slightest.

As for Mr. Wimble, she was not entirely sure what the architect's role was. When she asked him three nights later at dinner, he had paled, then flushed bright red and started stammering. Jeremy had interrupted at this point to explain he wanted to add a new annex to the folly.

"Oh, is it the amphitheater you always wanted as a child?" Emmie guessed.

Teddy's ears had pricked up. "Really, Papa?" he asked excitedly. "Are we to have an amphitheater?"

Jeremy had looked a little embarrassed. "No," he said heavily, shooting this down at once. "Decidedly not. I was thinking of adding a new 'ruined' section to the side of it, with fallen columns and skeletal arches, to appear as though the folly were once part of something far larger. We could have roses planted, climbing ones which would be trained to grow over the 'ruins' and form a pergola of sorts. Don't you think that sounds picturesque?"

Emmie tried to imagine it but failed. It sounded more gothic than classical to her but what did she know? "I look forward to seeing the sketches," she said encouragingly, and could not help but notice Mr. Wimble looked even more alarmed by the idea, casting a look of mute appeal at his employer.

When she mentioned his reaction to Jeremy later as they climbed the stairs together, he shrugged it off. "Wimble does not like to show anyone his sketches until he is entirely satisfied with them," he explained.

They reached her rooms first and Emmie hesitated at the door, unsure if Jeremy would accompany her inside. He had not approached her quarters in the past three days, not since their falling out. She was not even sure if he had checked the door to find she had unlocked it.

Of course, that might not have anything to do with their row. It might be because she was on her monthly right now and he had no interest in spending evenings with her while that was the case. She placed her hand on the door handle, and he cleared his throat. She turned to him at once, eagerly.

"Would you mind if I join you this evening?" he asked with scrupulous politeness. "Only if it is agreeable to you, of course. I do not mean to intrude."

"No, I would like you to," she assured him with a smile. She felt hugely relieved all of a sudden. The past few days of distance had rather chilled her. She hesitated. "Is the bedroom convenient, or would you rather we went into my sitting room?"

She thought he looked a little aback. "I only ask," she said in a hurry, "because I am not altogether sure when I am supposed to use it. I've barely spent any time in there thus far."

"I would rather sit on your bed and watch you at your toilette," he admitted frankly. "But if that would make you uncomfortable then, of course, I am happy to settle for whatever intimacy you will afford me."

Emmie blinked. "I am happy for you to sit on my bed," she said quickly, suddenly afraid he would retreat altogether. Now it was his turn to look relieved.

He smiled at her and made as though to follow her into her room, but she forestalled him with a hand on his arm. Jeremy halted at once. "Won't you—won't you go and put on your dressing robe, my lord?" she asked hesitantly. "Lottie will be waiting to ready me for bed. Once we have washed and undressed, then we can be at our leisure together and take our ease."

He relaxed visibly. "You would like that?" he asked, looking hopeful.

"Yes, of course."

"Then"—he paused—"will you wait for me to…to put on your face cream and brush your hair?" He spoke the words lightly but the way he avoided her eyes and colored faintly clued her in to the fact he was earnest in his request.

"Yes, of course, if you wish it," she answered with surprise.

He nodded and looked down to where her hand still rested on his arm. Quickly, Emmie released him and hurried inside to greet Lottie, who had her washing things and her nightclothes ready. Half an hour later, a knock on the door announced Jeremy's arrival.

He did not come via the connecting door between their rooms but used the door from the corridor. Emmie saw Lottie's raised eyebrows and hoped it would not lead to too much speculation in the servants' hall.

"I'll leave you now, milady, if that's everything?" Lottie asked.

"Yes, that is all. Good night, Lottie, thank you."

Emmie lingered at her dressing table as Jeremy flopped down onto her bed, dressed in his gaudy black and gold robe. He was watching her in the mirror, she noticed, as she picked up a jar of "otto of roses" and started dabbing it onto her face and neck. He seemed wholly riveted by the proceedings and Emmie reflected on the odd thing he had said about "settling for whatever intimacy she would afford him."

Was this one such intimacy? she wondered, rubbing in the lotion in sweeping circular motions. She had noticed from the first that Jeremy liked to watch her performing such attentions. It was so strange how entranced he was by it all.

Could it be because he had never known this kind of intimacy with a woman before? After all, he could not remember his own mother and it sounded as though relations with his first wife had broken down almost immediately.

"Mr. Wimble seems a nervous sort of man," she commented, reaching for a comb and making a show of smoothing her hair with it. Lottie had already given her hair a thorough brushing after her bath, so this was mere pretense, but she could not resist, seeing how he leaned forward to watch her efforts.

Tonight, she wore a nightgown trimmed with pale blue ribbon, and a frothy sort of over-robe with a good deal of lace.

"He's a sensitive sort of chap, Wimble," Jeremy mused aloud. "Highly strung, rather like a racehorse."

The slight frown on Emmie's brow cleared. "Oh, I see. Artistic temperament, I suppose." She had almost run out of things to do. Casting her eye over her dressing table, she picked up the glass stopper of her lavender water and ran it lightly over her wrists. Jeremy sat up on the bed to watch with interest this new step in proceedings.

"Precisely. Think of him as a second Fernando," Jeremy suggested. "Speaking of which, shall we crack open your crate of novels tomorrow afternoon? I have not so much as peeked at them yet, and it is certainly high time we choose the next for our book club."

Emmie's smile faded. "Pinky is moving out to her cottage tomorrow," she said quietly.

"So soon?" He frowned. "Surely the smell of paint must still linger throughout."

Emmie shook her head. "Teddy drove her over there yesterday in his little horse and trap and they said all the windows had been left open, so the remaining fumes were only very faint."

"All the more reason for us to choose a book before she departs, so she can take a copy with her. Did I tell you I bought them in sets of three?"

Emmie's eyes widened. "You bought three copies of every book?"

"Certainly, I did. I told you, did I not, that I wanted to start our own book club just for the three of us."

She was touched. Looking at him in the mirror, she said warmly, "That was a very generous thought, my lord."

He looked faintly embarrassed by such praise, waving it aside. "We will still have her often here, I am sure. We can send a carriage to collect her and drop her off at any time. You can visit her there whenever you like. There are Teddy's lessons too."

Emmie rose from her chair and walked over to the bed, removing her robe and settling herself under the covers. She did not know if he would stay with her tonight or not. She felt unaccustomedly nervous about it. "Did you fix on a schedule for Teddy's lessons?" she asked.

Jeremy nodded. "Three mornings and two afternoons a week," he said promptly. "He can have them here or at her cottage, whatever they decide upon."

"She mentioned inviting us around for tea and cake one afternoon this week."

Jeremy nodded, then yawned. "Do you mind if I take a nap in here with you?" he asked politely. "I will be sure not to wake you when I take off afterward."

"Of course not." She paused, before adding deliberately, "You are most welcome to sleep in here for as long as you like."

When she woke at midnight to go and change her menstrual cloth, she found him still sleeping soundly beside her. On returning from the bathroom, she half expected to find him gone, but to her surprise he was still there and remained there until seven o'clock the next morning when he went off to his stables.

It proved a wet and rainy day, and after breakfast in the state dining room, Emmie and Pinky retired to her private sitting room to meet with Mr. Penrose for an hour to discuss prospective ideas. This time instead of his sketchbook he brought along a notebook and pencil.

"And have we had any new ideas, Lady Faris?" he asked with a patronizing smile, trying to settle in one of the uncomfortable-looking chairs and wincing over the tight fit. Both Pinky and Emmie had already rejected those, before settling side by side on one of the purple chaise longues. Pinky kept glancing nervously over her shoulder as though afraid she might tumble off without the back support.

"Well, I have been thinking and I like flower gardens," Emmie said bravely. "Could we possibly use that as inspiration?" Even as she said it, she knew it was the wrong thing to say.

Mr. Penrose drew in a sharp breath, then cast her a pitying look. He tapped his pencil against the pages of his notebook. "Could you elaborate on what precisely you would like me to achieve through such a theme?" he asked with faint contempt.

"Some semblances of a flourishing garden," Emmie replied, quite at a loss.

"I fear, my lady, that you lack sufficient vision for this task," he said with a good deal of condescension.

Emmie felt a twinge of annoyance, but as she had shot down both of his proposals so far, she felt she could hardly ask him for a third suggestion.

At this point, Teddy drifted into the room. "Ah, here you both are," he said with some indignation. "I've been looking everywhere. What are you doing, Mama?" he asked, walking over and leaning against her chair.

"Mr. Penrose and I are trying to decide on the new decoration for this room," she said brightly.

"Why don't you just do what my first mama did?" he asked.

Mr. Penrose stiffened in his seat. "I hardly think—" he began but Emmie spoke over him.

"And what did she do?" she asked, turning to Teddy.

"She would just give him an object and tell him to furnish the room around it."

Emmie blinked. "An object?"

He nodded. "In this room, it was this," he said, skipping over to the six-paneled screen decorated with samurai. "She bought it in London."

"Well, that would certainly make things a lot simpler," Emmie said. "So, I simply find one piece of furniture that I like and then Mr. Penrose uses that as inspiration for decorating the whole room?" Teddy nodded.

"I do not think such a method would work in this instance. The first Lady Faris was a very *unique* woman of taste—" Mr. Penrose began in a patronizing tone.

"Well, she said *you* were a colossal bore who likely wore a corset," Teddy interrupted him in his high, clear voice. "She said you creak whenever you sit down."

Pinky made a muffled sound of distress.

Emmie murmured, "Teddy!" and held her hand out to him. He walked back from the samurai screen to stand dutifully beside her chair. Mr. Penrose turned an unbecoming shade of puce. "I have the very thing," Emmie said, holding up a finger. "One moment!" Rising from her chair, she walked out and retrieved the papier-mâché tilt top table that had belonged to her own mother, carrying it back into the room.

She set it down before Mr. Penrose, who made a great show of recovering his dignity by whipping out some pince-nez from his waistcoat pocket and placing them delicately on his nose. He inspected the small table with a look of distaste on his face.

"It already looks like it belongs in here to me," Teddy observed with a shrug. "It is black and gold and painted with flowers."

Emmie was struck by the truth of his observation. "It does, doesn't it?" she marveled, gazing around the room. "Do you know, I think with a few adjustments, this room could be made very comfortable. Do you not agree, Pinky?"

"Adjustments?" Mr. Penrose said frigidly. "*Comfortable?*" He spoke the word as though it was an insult.

"Yes," Emmie continued calmly. "I do not like any of those chairs," she said, taking in the inlaid seats with the sweep of her arm. "And these chaises are not plump enough. Instead, I want some nice comfortable seats that you can sink into, and some matching sofas. I will be joining some ladies' committees at some point," she remembered aloud, "so I need adequate seating in here. Also, a desk. I am supposed to write letters in here, so I have need of one." Not that she knew who she would be writing to, but that was beside the point.

"Oh, that all sounds most appropriate," Pinky chimed in loyally. "Why, I am certainly looking forward to sitting in our old chairs in Plumtree Cottage. Nothing so comforting as a good serviceable armchair." She turned eagerly to Emmie. "I wonder, shall I go and request a nice pot of tea for us all?"

"You could ring the bell, dear," Emmie suggested. "No need to walk all the way downstairs."

"Oh, er—" Pinky turned a little flustered. "I am certain I saw Colfax's livery flash past the doorway just a moment ago. I feel sure I can catch him before he descends."

"Very well," Emmie said with surprise, but perhaps after all, her friend wished to discuss some detail concerning Plumtree Cottage. Colfax had been helping her with the preparations a good deal. Pinky hurried out and Emmie turned back to Mr. Penrose. "Now what were we—?"

"Do not forget you need a statue, Mama," Teddy interposed.

Emmie turned toward him blankly. "A statue?"

He nodded, lowering his voice. "You remember, Mama? The twin babies."

"Ah, yes, the twin babies." She turned back to Mr. Penrose, who was sitting stiffly upright in his uncomfortable seat. "If you could possibly source a sculpture of twin baby boys from antiquity, holding a pair of snakes, I would be most grateful." Mr. Penrose stared at her, open-mouthed. "If that is not possible," she continued calmly, "could we perhaps commission one? After all," she said, glancing around the room, "now that we will not be replacing all this other furniture, we could use the budget on the sculpture, could we not?"

Mr. Penrose made a spluttering sound, but it was clear he was defeated by this point. He inclined his head and scribbled some notes in his book. "A statue. Antiquity. Two male infants. Two snakes."

"And they must look as though they are all getting along famously," she stressed. "The babies and the snakes must be on the very best of terms."

It seemed he could think of no rejoinder for this. Instead, he asked in shaken tones, "And for your bedchamber, Lady Faris?"

Emmie was momentarily surprised, for she had gained the distinct impression that Mr. Penrose liked to draw out his consultations as much as possible. Now it seemed he could not get their business over with soon enough. They had not even *mentioned* her bedroom up until this point.

"Ah, now that I do want completely changed," she admitted. Although she liked the blue of the wallpaper, she was not the greatest admirer of orange, and since the table, cushions, and lamps had been removed, the room was looking a little bare.

Teddy sat up in his seat. "I bet I can guess," he said. "One moment!" He darted from the room, and Emmie and Mr. Penrose sat in awkward silence. If his suggestion was something dreadful, Emmie wondered if she dared suggest a rose garden as theme. Was Mr. Penrose sufficiently crushed to accept such a suggestion now?

Teddy reentered, brandishing a small statuette of Venus. "Am I right, Mama?" he asked eagerly.

"Oh well done, Teddy!" she said, seizing hold of the suggestion at once. "You are quite right!" She gave him a little round of applause and Mr. Penrose wiped his brow with a silk handkerchief.

"Plaster, columns," he murmured feverishly, his pencil moving across his page. "A votive niche perhaps?"

As he did not seem to require their input, Emmie exchanged a glance with Teddy, and he started chattering about how soon they could set off to the maze. "I mean to show you three different routes," he said proudly. "And I have a ball of wool I borrowed from Mrs. Cheviot for Miss Pinson to unravel, so she feels safe she will not get lost."

"That was a very kind thought," Emmie told him, hoping Pinky would not get too hopelessly tangled up in the process. Ten minutes later, after taking a few measurements, Mr. Penrose left them to work on his designs in the library. He took his departure coldly, though Emmie was not sure if this was due to his crushing defeat or his corset. Either way, she fancied she would not have any more problems with Mr. Penrose.

The next couple of hours were spent pleasantly, if damply, walking first down to the folly and then to the maze. Emmie and Pinky strolled arm in arm with Teddy leading the way with authority, carrying the still-furled umbrella as though it were a scepter.

"Mama," he began tentatively when they reached the folly, "what did you mean at dinner last night when you asked if Mr. Wimble was building an amphitheater?"

"Well, that was just a joke, really. I thought it would entertain your papa," Emmie told him. "You see he told me how he used to pretend the folly was a gladiator training school when he was a child."

"A ludus," Teddy agreed. "He used to practice with a wooden sword and strike the columns with it. Like this!" He swung the umbrella with purpose, demonstrating the exact technique one should employ.

"Careful, dear," Pinky entreated mildly.

"Well, I wish he *would* build one," Teddy said glumly. "It would be a jolly sight more impressive than a fake ruin with roses growing over them. Can you not persuade him, Mama? It need only be a small one."

They ducked inside the folly and Emmie struck a match and lit a candle, revealing the dark interior to Pinky and the half-moon bench.

"What would we use an amphitheater for?" she asked, noticing Teddy was still hovering expectantly for her answer. "If we were to persuade him, then I imagine we would need to convince him it would serve some purpose."

Teddy's expression brightened. "Well, we could reopen the ludus," he suggested. "And I could start training there. Uncle Nye promised that when I'm ten he will give me some boxing lessons, so I could practice in the amphitheater."

Emmie nodded. "And I suppose we could also put on other performances in there, of a less combative nature."

Pinky's ears pricked up. "You mean like poetry recitation and plays?" she asked.

"Why not? We could even display some of your artwork in the folly. Would that not be nice, Teddy? I know you two have plans to do some sketches on the grounds."

"We could have a show!" Pinky said, clapping her hands. "Maybe even a musical concert in here! If it was cleaned up a little," she added, glancing around at the dusty chamber. "That domed roof might produce a nice sound."

Teddy looked a little less enthusiastic about these suggestions. "Ye-es," he agreed cautiously. "We *could* do that, when it is not in use for fighting," he conceded generously.

After inspecting the folly and walking the circumference of the area Teddy was convinced would work best for an amphitheater, they proceeded to the maze, which was not as disorientating as Emmie had expected. Really, it would be quite hard to get lost in it, despite all the tall hedges.

"Oh, what a lovely fountain!" Miss Pinson exclaimed when they reached the fountain at the center. "It would make such a pretty sketch. Is it a seahorse?"

"A hippocampus," Teddy informed her. "The horse half is supposed to look like my father's favorite horse, Cadmus."

"Was his likeness used?" Emmie asked with interest.

Teddy nodded. "Shall you try to find your own way out now? And then you can attempt it on your own with the ball of wool." Pinky looked alarmed. "Don't worry," Teddy assured her. "You won't see me, but I will make sure you do not get too lost."

"Take heart," Emmie said bravely. "I feel sure I have a good sense of direction."

They did get lost but as Teddy kept popping out from behind hedges and silently pointing the way to them before disappearing again, they managed to find their way back out again without too much fruitless wandering.

The second attempt to find the center with the ball of wool was a lot more chaotic and at one point, Emmie even suspected that Teddy was leading them astray.

"Oh dear, this wool keeps snagging and it feels like this has taken twice as long to reach the middle as the first time," Pinky lamented.

"Teddy did say there were different routes," Emmie reminded her. "This one must be the long way round."

"If only the hedges were pruned a little shorter," Pinky fretted. "Then we could see direction we should be headed toward."

"That's not how it works." Teddy's voice spoke out from somewhere nearby, making Pinky give a startled yelp. He rolled out from underneath a hedge. "At one point you have to feel like you're heading *away* from the center," he said earnestly.

"Pinky, you must never come in here alone," Emmie advised her friend. "If you wish to sketch the fountain you must have a footman accompany you." For some reason Pinky turned rather red at this suggestion.

"Higgins won't mind," Teddy said, dusting himself off. "But Colfax is sometimes rather grumpy."

"You simply mean he won't dance to your tune, Teddy," Emmie replied firmly. "I have always found him most obliging." The last thing she wanted was for Pinky to turn tongue-tied and nervous around Colfax, who had been so helpful with all the arrangements for Plumtree Cottage.

Luckily, her friend did not seem to be listening, for she was bent over the ball of wool, trying to dislodge it from a tree root. "Oh dear," she mumbled. "I hope Mrs. Cheviot will not mind her wool being covered in leaves and bits of twig."

They were in high spirits when they returned to wash and brush up before lunch, which was perhaps just as well, for Mr. Wimble was as quiet as ever and Mr. Penrose somewhat withdrawn. Jeremy was a little late and Emmie breathed a sigh of relief when he came through the door with a warm smile for her and a cheerful greeting for everyone else.

As soon as the food was served—cold chicken and ham, curried eggs, salad potatoes, bread and butter and cutlets—he turned to Pinky and asked to join them in the library after luncheon, explaining about the unboxing of the new novels.

"What a treat!" she said, eyes shining. "I will own, I am very excited to see what books you have purchased for dear Emmie."

"Not just for me," Emmie replied. "For Jeremy has purchased three of every one, so that we three may read them together and gather together to discuss them once you have moved out."

Pinky leaned forward. "Three copies of every novel?" she queried.

"I know," Emmie said, "the extravagance! But you see, he was entirely in earnest about us starting a book club."

"Of course I was in earnest," Jeremy broke in as Pinky started to blink back sudden tears. "I found our conversation around *Love's Innocence Fled* most illuminating. I look forward to many more such discussions."

"That is so kind," Pinky sniffed. "And almost like having our very own lending library here in Vance Park."

"Why, so it is!" Emmie said, lowering her fork. "What a lovely way to think of it. I don't suppose," she said, turning to Jeremy, "that there are any committees formed hereabouts to start one?"

"A lending library?" he said slowly. "I have no idea. I rather doubt it in such a small place as Penarth. Perhaps you could start one?"

"A committee?" she responded, quite startled.

"Why not?" he asked coolly.

"Well, it might be a little ambitious to leap right into starting one as chair, when I have never actually sat on one as a rank and file member," she pointed out.

"Well, you could join the one to repair the church roof first and use that for practice."

As they had attended Penarth's local church, St. Werburgh's, the previous Sunday and sat in the family pew, Emmie knew for a fact its roof was intact. "I shall wait for Reverend Ryland's wife to visit and tell me all about the local worthy causes," she decided.

"Very sensible," Jeremy agreed. "Has Teddy offended Penrose?" he asked in undertones as lemon pudding and a large jam tart were deposited on the table.

"No," Emmie answered in a bold-faced lie. She could not bring herself to allow her stepson to be punished for his part in defeating the designer. He was her staunch ally after all.

"The man seems unaccustomedly subdued," Jeremy murmured.

"I can't think why. We have agreed very nicely on how to furnish my rooms."

"Excellent. I want to speak to him next about painting a mural in the folly."

"A mural?"

"I was thinking the judgment of Paris."

Emmie's face fell. She glanced quickly at Teddy, but he was currently badgering Mr. Wimble with questions. "You are *not* dedicating the folly to Venus, are you?" she asked with a sudden misgiving.

Jeremy lifted his eyebrows. "Why not?"

"It is possible to have too much of a good thing, my lord!" she reminded him. "I believe Aesop said as much."

"Nonsense!"

"Well, it was someone like Aesop in any case, and Teddy thinks there are too many representations of Venus here at Vance already!" she hissed. Should she tell him that her own bedroom was to be decked out in such a fashion? For some reason, she had decided she wanted that to be a surprise.

"When Teddy is master here, he can rededicate it to whoever he thinks fit!" he retorted. "I happen to like Venuses. They remind me of you. They always have."

Emmie spluttered faintly. "How about ancient heroes and heroines?" she suggested. "We could have..." Her mind turned blank.

"Atalanta?" Jeremy suggested.

"Yes! After your horse, and the famous heroine," she said vaguely, having forgotten the story. "She had a golden apple too, didn't she?"

"Three of them," Jeremy agreed, "but none of them said 'To the Fairest,'"

"And, um, Theseus and the minotaur!" Emmie dredged up from memory. *Who was the one with the golden fleece?* "Only think how pleased Teddy would be!" she continued when recollection failed.

Jeremy glanced across at his son, who was chattering away to the unresponsive architect. "It would puff up his consequence even more! He would expect his own personal amphitheater next."

"I'm afraid he already does," Emmie admitted. "But I have thought of several uses we could have for one," she continued earnestly, "and it really would be a useful thing to have here at Vance."

Jeremy's outraged expression instantly softened into one of diversion. "You think a Roman amphitheater would be a useful thing to have about the place, do you, Ballentine?" Clearly, he derived much amusement from this, a smile playing about his lips.

"Well," she said weakly, "you did say that it is customary for the lords of Faris to build something new at Vance when they marry."

"I did," he agreed. "But an amphitheater was not precisely what I had in mind."

"Well, I wish you would reconsider."

"For you? Of course." He reached across and picked up her hand, carrying it to his lips and kissing it. "Wimble, are you listening?" He glanced across at the architect. "My viscountess wants an amphitheater. You must start on that as soon as the current plans are drawn up."

Teddy whooped and jumped out of his chair to run around the table to join them. He embraced first Emmie and then his father.

"Just a small one!" Emmie added, suddenly feeling guilty she had pressed her advantage. It occurred to her that she could ask him for anything at this point and he would likely indulge her. Was it purely affection or that and a mixture of guilt that prompted his generosity?

Drat the man. Why did he have to be so distractingly attractive? she wondered as he ruffled Teddy's hair. And why was she so relieved to finally see a smile that was reflected in his eyes? Recently, she had started wondering if underneath his sunny charm, Jeremy was not as happy as he appeared. That perhaps he never had been. Had that been why he had always drunk to excess?

On the beach that day when Teddy had asked that question, *Papa, are you sad?* she had seen him for a moment without his surface glamor. The expression on his face had been strangely wistful. Just for a moment, he had looked so crushed to be left out and excluded from their happy party.

She had felt the strongest impulse to reach out to him and draw him in. Absurd really, as Teddy was *his* son and he had facilitated Pinky leaving her! Stupid to feel he might want to be included in their schemes. After all, they were married, and he had told her at the outset what kind of wife he wanted. He had made no mention of friendship, or even companionship, that she recalled. He wanted a quiet sort of wife who would not give him headaches. The kind of wife who did not make scenes.

She winced slightly, remembering her emotional outburst a few evenings ago. *That* most definitely had been a scene. She had broken their agreement and he had been exceedingly kind about it. Was it her imagination, or had he been treating her with an extra pair of kidskin gloves ever since? It made her uncomfortable to think it could be hanging over them still, like a cloud obscuring the sun.

She knew that part of the reason for her breakdown was the onset of her women's monthly. That was often precipitated by heightened emotion and Jeremy had certainly suffered the brunt of it. For several nights now, she had lain awake, vowing to make up for her slip.

She hoped he was not disappointed in her. The thought gave her a cold feeling in the pit of her stomach. It had been unfair of her to fling their past in his face like that. She *never* should have shown him that shameful box. Her cheeks burned even now at the thought of it as she and Pinky followed Jeremy into the library.

Then it suddenly struck her. She had not seen that rosewood box since that night. Had she left it in his room? She froze where she stood in the middle of the room, halfway across the Aubusson rug. Luckily, Jeremy was lifting the lid from the crate and Pinky was peering inside it, so they did not notice her sudden consternation.

She ought to remove her mother's perfume bottle and her father's gloves and hurl the rest of it into the fire, she resolved, just like Humphrey's letters. Holding on to painful memories was *stupid*, futile even. She needed to let them go, along with any lingering resentment. It was hardly fair now she had agreed to build a life beside him.

Joining them at the crate, she slipped one arm through Pinky's and one through Jeremy's, so the three of them stood linked together. "Let's make this the first official meeting of our book club," she suggested. "The second meeting we can hold at Pinky's house in a month's time."

Jeremy's smile, once again, was warm and genuine and Pinky positively glowed. Finally, Emmie felt like she was on the right track. She vowed not to deviate from it again.

23

Jeremy trod very carefully over the next few days. He felt that things were starting to mend, slowly but surely, after his horrendous blunder earlier in the week. He had not dared to check if the connecting door between their bedrooms was still locked but other than that, he spent every night sleeping beside his wife in her bed.

Emmeline had seemingly picked up on his fascination with her nighttime routine and did not appear to object to his observing them. Indeed, she seemed most willing to gratify him in this, something he was wildly grateful for, though he did not really understand it himself.

They established a new routine, where he joined her every evening after dinner and Teddy was put to bed. She would wait for his arrival, and he would watch her brush her hair and then they would sit in bed together, side by side, reading the latest novel they had settled upon.

He enjoyed it, he really did, though he felt strongly compelled to treat his wife as though she were made of glass and he frequently had to reread a page or two when his attention wandered to dwell on her profile.

His attentiveness was amply rewarded, for day by day he could see Emmeline growing more relaxed in this arrangement until she scarcely paused before joining him under the covers and he could take her hand in his or even kiss her cheek without startling her.

He had not taken it further than that though. He felt he had no right to. Not after…everything he'd put her through in the past and present. He kept her rosewood box, stashing it in his wardrobe next to his dressing case. When he was feeling particularly masochistic, he would lift the lid and even handle those tragic remnants of their past.

They never failed to overwhelm him, so he could only imagine what effect they must have had on Emmeline over the years. He was both touched and appalled she had kept them all this time. She could not have treasured such items, so why had she kept them? As objects to reproach herself with? As a lesson to herself, never to care for anyone so undeserving again?

Presumably, she would want it back at some point, if only for the mementoes of her parents, but in the meantime, he felt he had a right to custodianship. He deserved that they should bring him pain.

He was still struggling quite a bit with his own feelings when it came to his wife. He wanted simultaneously to worship her, to share his life with her, and, ultimately, to lay his head in her lap and ask her to please love him. It hurt to know they might *never* be on such terms.

It was all his own fault, he knew, and he had no right to focus on the little ball of self-loathing that felt like a hard stone inside his chest, not when she had conceded him so much already. It was just that, without her forgiveness, he felt like it would grow bigger every year until it eventually consumed him and choked him to death.

But that was all nonsense, of course. He was just being selfish again, expecting her to make everything right with his world. Emmeline had been more than honest with him about her own feelings. She did not want to hear his confession. She wanted the past to remain where it was, dead and buried.

She did not trust him with her heart, and he could not say as he blamed her. He was a man, frankly unworthy and undeserving of her in every way. The only thing he could do at this point was watch his step and look to improve significantly in the future. Building an amphitheater really seemed the least he could do to make up for his shortcomings.

Should he cancel the conservatory he had hired Wimble to build? A couple of days previously he had the idea to make it an orangery instead. Would that be sufficiently removed from Emmeline's painful memory to make it acceptable to her?

Emmeline cleared her throat. "I've been thinking about my duties," she said one evening as they sat side by side in Emmeline's bed, propped up with pillows and reading their latest novel, *The Haunting of Jennings Hall.*

Jeremy lowered his book and considered her blankly. "Oh yes," he said, as his brain scrambled to catch up with her words.

"The things you require from a wife," she prompted. "You remember?"

"Committees," he murmured. "Something about getting along with my neighbors?" The details were rather foggy now in truth.

"Yes. Well, you remember I told you I met with the vicar's wife?"

"Yes," he agreed cautiously. "You said she seemed nice."

"She did. She said she would put my name forward to someone called Lady Sharpe, in connection with her Good Works committee."

Jeremy shuddered. "Lady Sharpe!" he repeated. "Lord preserve us!"

"Who is she?"

"A regular old tartar!" Jeremy replied roundly. "If you'll take my advice, you'll avoid her like the plague!"

She sat up in surprise. "I thought you would be pleased with my progress!"

"Oh yes," he said hastily. "I am, of course."

"Well…good," she said uncertainly before returning to her book.

Jeremy read half a page but found he had retained none of it. He lowered his book again. "Emmeline?" She looked at him enquiringly. "That discussion we had. Remind me, did it even occur to me to enquire what it was *you* required from a husband?"

"Well, yes, I mean you asked my terms. Don't you remember? I told you about severance pay for my father's clerks and—"

"Oh yes, your terms for marriage," he said, waving this aside. "I don't mean that. What I *should* have asked you was what you desired from a husband."

She eyed him thoughtfully. "Well, at the time I suppose my expectations were not at all high. You see, Humphrey and I"—Jeremy braced himself—"spent so little time together. The business appeared to have so many demands on him, and then I moved away from London, of course, but even when I lived there, we were rarely together. Once I knew his, well, his *situation*, the lack of courtship made perfect sense, but over the years I had become accustomed to feeling a fiancé was something quite distant from my everyday life. I suppose that will sound strange to you," She sounded almost apologetic.

"Yes and no," he admitted truthfully. "Amanda and I led almost completely separate lives under the same roof for many years."

"Did you—?" She hesitated, plucking at the coverlet.

"What?" He turned more fully toward her, adjusting his pillow. "Ask me. I promise I won't take offence."

"Were you ever…like this?" she asked, gesturing vaguely between the two of them. "With your first wife."

"Never," he admitted at once. "We shared very little intimacy even in the early years of our marriage. Certainly nothing remotely like this. Neither of us desired it, you see."

"Oh." He thought another question hovered on those pretty lips, so he waited. "But you *do* want this with me?"

"Very much so."

She smiled at him, and he had to catch his breath. "Good," she said. "If I had known anything about it, that morning at Hutton's, then I would have asked for a husband who would act as friend and companion to me."

A friend and companion? Jeremy swallowed, feeling horribly conflicted all of a sudden. He nodded, rolling onto his back so she would not see this reflected in his eyes. This was good, he told himself firmly. You trusted a friend and companion. Mina said his wife needed to learn to trust him.

Out of the corner of his eye, he could see she was still watching him, a faint look of concern on her face. He cleared his throat. "When I said that about joining committees, I did not appreciate quite how busy you would be. If you think it will be too much for you, then—"

"Oh no," she said quickly. "I think it will be a good thing. Since Pinky moved out, I have been missing female society a good deal."

Jeremy frowned. He had no idea how she could be missing Miss Pinson when she had seen her every day since her move. "You said she was settling well in her cottage?"

"Oh yes, she adores it. She has all her rooms laid out so nicely now, with all her things around her. I think that spinet of your mother's is her favorite piece, and that dining set you gave her is her pride and joy. All her new neighbors have visited to admire her front parlor. Only she thinks she might need a dog," she rattled on. "She has been offered first choice of a puppy from a litter two doors down. Not the Ennises but the family next to them, the Thomases."

"A dog, really?" he asked. "For some reason, I imagine Miss Pinson owning a cat rather than a dog."

"Well, in the day she is perfectly happy and content in her home, but at night, poor Pinky is rather nervous. She imagines tapping on the windowpane, or someone moving about in one of the rooms downstairs. If she had a dog, she thinks that would calm her nerves considerably."

Jeremy felt a strange pricking of his conscience at the idea of Miss Pinson's nameless nighttime dread. "Likely the noises are merely her neighbors," he said uneasily. "It will just be the Ennises moving about next door, or else a tree branch tapping at the window."

"Yes," Emmie agreed, "and Pinky knows that really."

"I hope this book we chose is not giving her bad dreams," he said, indicating *The Haunting of Jennings Hall*, although in truth he was finding it far from hair-raising so far. Alas, none of the characters were proving as dynamic as Count Stefano. "We could always swap it for another."

"She had not actually started it when I saw her today," Emmie admitted. "She has not had time, what with entertaining calls from all her neighbors. You know, she has been enjoying herself excessively. She even baked a seed cake from her great-aunt's recipe. She is most looking forward to our taking tea with her tomorrow. She asked me quite particularly what sort of sandwiches you prefer."

"What did you tell her?" Jeremy asked with interest.

"I told her egg and cress, or ham," she said a little self-consciously, "because I know she has a plentiful supply of both. The Ennises keep chickens and gave her a dozen eggs as a welcome gift, and Mrs. Cheviot gave Teddy and me a hamper of things to take along today to fill Pinky's cupboards. There was a large cured ham in there."

"I hope she has saved some of her seed cake for me," Jeremy said. "I've never tried it. Or should we take some of our wedding cake with us?"

"There's none left," she informed him promptly. "It has all been sent out. Mrs. Oxley is making us a small celebration cake to take with us tomorrow."

"You think of everything."

"Incidentally, what *is* your favorite sandwich? A wife should know these things."

"Can't you guess?"

"You're tricky," she said, tapping her chin. "You're a man, so I might guess salted beef, but you are very refined so you might prefer cucumber."

He laughed. "As a matter of fact, you almost had it right to begin with. Ham and tomato, but the tomatoes aren't ripe yet."

"Aren't you going to guess mine?"

"I already know yours, Ballentine. I've watched you nibbling daintily on them at least half a dozen times. Cheese and chive."

"You are very observant."

"Not really," he answered with a shrug. "Only when it comes to you." He allowed his eyes to roam over her a little too warmly and had to turn away, clearing his throat. "Now," he said briskly, "are we going to read this book, or aren't we? For all we know, Miss Pinson might sit up all night and read the whole thing cover to cover."

Emmeline's dimple flashed out and she picked her book back up, furrowing her brow. As soon as she was absorbed in the story, he let his thoughts wander back to his current predicament. This was all good progress, he assured himself.

She was growing comfortable and relaxed around him, even when he strayed into her personal rooms. She no longer seemed to resent him rehoming her friend. She wanted to know his favorite sandwich. That had to count for something, surely?

Inadvertently, he found himself wondering if her courses were over and done with by now. His eyes strayed from the page to wander over her shapely legs, currently obscured by the bedcovers.

Giving his head a quick shake, he returned to the plight of the tenants of Jennings Hall and suppressed his less noble thoughts. What was it his sister had urged him to employ? Patience and tact. Something along those lines anyway. Surely to God, he could maintain this equilibrium until Emmeline could learn to trust him a little.

The trouble was, he did not think she had ever trusted him much in the first place. How could she? He had never given her cause.

24

One Month Later

Emmie rolled over and contemplated the empty spot in the bed next to her. She sat up. It must be after eight. Jeremy would have gone down to the stables already. He was surprisingly disciplined when it came to spending his mornings there. She worried her bottom lip with her teeth. Things were still not quite right between them.

Ever since their falling out, her husband's polite consideration had increased to an almost alarming degree. He even brought it into the bedroom now, the one arena where previously he had been wholly unbridled in his passion for her.

Not anymore. Her monthlies had been over with for a good week before he had courteously asked her if she had reached the end of her current chapter. When she had answered him yes, he had inserted her bookmark for her and set her book aside, asking her if she would be agreeable to his "husbandly attentions."

She had answered the affirmative again, somewhat bewildered by his manner. Then he had rolled on top of her and, well, you could not describe what followed as *polite* precisely, but it had certainly been the most "hands off" approach to proceedings that he had ever employed with her.

He had not sworn once, and he did not even squeeze her posterior, or mouth her breasts as he normally did. From what she could tell, his eyes had been closed for most of it and his mouth tight shut. He had barely made a sound, and this had so constrained her that Emmie had stifled her own, an unnatural proceeding that had frustrated her and made her feel quite out of step with her own body.

Worst of all, after they were both breathless and spent, he had *apologized*, as though what they had done was something she might not have enjoyed. Then he had climbed out of the bed and disappeared to his own rooms, leaving her a mass of confusion.

Half an hour later, returning from the bathroom, she found him once again sat up in her bed, reading *The Haunting of Jennings Hall* as though the strange interlude had never occurred. Odder still, he was wearing a nightshirt, something she had not heretofore known he so much as possessed.

295

Before extinguishing the light on his side of the bed, he had kissed her cheek, wished her a good night, and turned his back to her. The next morning, she had put it down to a mere aberration, the result of some strange mood or him not feeling quite right, maybe something like indigestion.

Then the same thing had happened the following night, and two nights after that. And now it had been the pattern for a whole month. She did not know *what* to think. Was it simply that they were settled now into married life? Had he grown so accustomed to her person that he no longer wished to fondle and fuss over her as he had done before?

Did her charms no longer torment and please him as once they had? The thought was a lowering one, and besides, somehow, she could not *quite* believe it. There was still his vast Venus collection for one thing. Those hefty beauties did nothing more than hang on his walls all day and he had never tired of *them*. No, it could not be that, surely.

It was not even as though she could turn to anyone for advice. Dearest Pinky, in addition to be quite caught up in homemaking at present, would be flummoxed by such a predicament. Moreover, Emmie did not think she could embarrass her oldest friend by broaching such an indelicate subject.

There was no one else she could ask. Strangely, Lord Atherton flashed into her mind for an instant. He had imparted some very interesting information about Jeremy at their wedding. His words drifted back into her head, making her flush. *You embodied his every physical ideal.*

She found herself hoping he was still coming to Vance this summer. He had said a few things she could use further elucidation on. That throwaway line about Charlie Symonds for one, and something else... What had it been?

Suddenly, she sat up, remembering the other thing Atherton had told her about Jeremy. *I never suspected it as a callow youth, but I think he has always been...left out in the cold.* Emmie caught her breath. So, she was *not* the only person such a thing had occurred to. Had she been right that day on the beach, when she thought he looked like a little boy, looking in on a party he was not invited to?

If so…then Jeremy Vance was lonely. He must have been lonely all his life. *That* was why he had taken his supper in the nursery with his son. It had seemed so strange to her when Teddy first told her that about the sophisticated and urbane Jeremy but now it made perfect sense. So, he *did* want companionship from a wife, even though he had not asked for that.

She supposed that, really, his actions should have revealed that to her since they had come home to Vance Park. The book club, the sleeping in her bed, the unlocking of the connecting door, the private dining room, all of them should have been clues for her to solve the puzzle.

This excessive civility, though, what had brought that about? She couldn't even explain why it bothered her, for he had always been attentive and courteous in his manner toward her. *No*, she corrected herself firmly. That was not strictly true. That was more of a recent development. He had *not* always been polite.

He had not been polite when he led her into that conservatory and kissed her so hard he had bruised her lips. He had not been polite when he had made her the talk of the season by monopolizing her attention and cornering her at every ball. He had not even been polite when he had turned up at Winkworth Street that day and proposed to her with such casual assurance.

He had known she was over a barrel, and he had been almost gleeful of the fact. *Gleeful*, because he had her where he wanted her, cornered into a trap of her own making and desperate for escape. Escape that he could offer her on a golden platter if she became his wife.

Emmie gave her head a faint shake as she tried to make sense of it all. He still bewildered her. The man was so *confusing*. She had thought, after his engagement to Lady Amanda Liversedge, that his pursuit of her must have been a cruel sort of jest. That he had chosen to alleviate his boredom by making sport of her, only to drop her flat and leave her broken-hearted at the end of it.

But now… Suddenly, she was not so sure. She was not sure of *anything*. Taking a deep breath, she allowed herself to think of…*that* night. She touched her lips remembering the desperate way he had kissed her in that conservatory, how afterward he had buried his face in her neck, his grip on her, almost painful, when he had held her so tight, as though he never wanted to let her go.

Then she remembered his face at the top of the staircase as his engagement was announced. His eyes glittering and hard, that cold, brilliant smile. She had thought the contempt she could see blazing there was directed toward her, even though he had not so much as glanced her way. But what if—she caught her breath—what if his contempt had been directed toward himself?

It was true, he had kissed her since that night with urgency, with passion, and with need. Not recently, it was true, not now he was being all measured and civil with her, but on their wedding night, he had trembled when he touched her. He had been desperate for her, but it had still not approached that level of...of... Words failed her.

Anguish. Could it have been anguish? she wondered now, tears springing to her eyes. Just for a minute, she allowed herself to consider the possibility that Jeremy Vance had been in pain that night at the Hawfords' ball when he knew what was about to unfold. When he knew that after that night, they would never be together again.

Emmie sobbed. She could not help it. She snatched up her pillow to muffle the sound.

Surely not. Surely... Lowering the pillow, she tried to recall if she had ever heard the precise circumstances behind Jeremy's engagement. It was no good, it was all a pain-filled blank. She remembered the congratulatory applause, the excited whisperings of what a picture-perfect couple they made, and precious little else.

Someone had whispered that the man stood alongside Lady Amanda was her father, Earl Tipton. Someone else had mentioned their families were long acquainted but that was nothing unusual among the aristocracy. Emmie had nodded, a painful, forced smile on her face. In one gloved hand she crushed her dance card between her fingers, in the other, her fan sticks had given with a loud snap.

Emmie could not even remember the carriage ride home afterward, though she was sure Mrs. Laverdale must have had some choice words to impart. If she had, they had made little to no impression. All she really remembered was knocking on her father's study door the next morning and requesting an interview with him.

That was when Emmie had told him that she was not cut out for high society and that he would receive no lofty offers for her hand. Her father had been disappointed but not terribly surprised by this news. He was always a realist. The chance of her making some dazzling match had always been slim.

Mrs. Laverdale's services had been dispensed with. Emmie had attended no more balls, and it had been the following week that her father had started bringing a "promising young man" from his firm home to dine with them. That man had been Humphrey. The rest, as they say, was history.

A knock on the door startled her. Lottie bustled in. "Your bath is ready, milady."

"Oh, thank you, Lottie."

As Emmie lay in the tub, immersed in water up to her chin, she realized she could not allow things to carry on as they were in this unsatisfactory manner. Something would have to be done, moreover *she* would have to do it. But what? What could she *do* to shock Jeremy out of his boundless civility?

Their wedding night being much on her mind, it was perhaps not surprising that his words in the bathroom at Winkworth Street drifted suddenly into her mind. What was it he had said? Something about wanting to watch her take a sponge bath? *Crouched over it with your hair pinned high on your head. You would look just like a bathing Venus.* Those had been his words.

She sat up, remembering the kindling look in his eye when he had voiced this thought. He had been in deadly earnest; she was sure of that. He really had wanted to see her play out such a scene. Considering how much she now knew he enjoyed watching her at her dressing mirror, it made sense that he would desire such a thing.

Did she have the nerve to do it, that was the question. At this point, Lottie entered the bathroom, carrying fresh linens. "I've set out your pale blue dress for today, milady, the one with all the pretty lace, as you've got visitors today and then your tea party at Miss Pinson's."

"Lottie," Emmie began airily, in a complete change of subject. "Do we have such a thing in the house as a sponging bath?"

Her maid looked surprised. "Yes, milady. I believe there's one in the cupboard over there." She walked over to it and removed a large round tray. It looked much superior to the one at Winkworth Street, which had been a cheap affair. This one looked weightier and more substantial. "Here it is."

"Just the thing!" Emmie said brightly.

"I should have offered its use to you, milady, only I thought you might appreciate the luxury of a full bathtub."

"Oh, I do," Emmie assured her. "'Tis only in this hot weather, sometimes a quick wash between a change of clothes is useful."

Lottie nodded and replaced it where she found it. "If you ever want me to make it ready, just let me know, milady."

"Thank you, Lottie."

"And the pale blue dress?"

"Oh, that will be perfect. You always pick out my outfits beautifully."

Lottie looked pleased. "If the weather holds, you could take your parasol and new lace gloves to match."

"Do I own a parasol?" Emmie asked in surprise.

Lottie gave her a reproving look. "I set out all the lovely things from that most recent parcel, milady. Laid them all out for you to see in your dressing room. All sorts of accessories were included this time, lace caps, fichus, and bonnets. A quantity of fine things."

"I own so many lovely things now, I've quite lost track," Emmie admitted guiltily. "The dressing room shelves must be quite full."

"There's still plenty of room," Lottie said complacently. "And so, I told his lordship when he asked."

"You did?"

She nodded. "He always wants to know if there's anything you might be needing. I told Mrs. Cheviot, and she agrees he's quite the doting husband these days. She said we've never had such a picture of domesticity here at Vance, not in her lifetime, what with him squiring you to church on a Sunday, taking you to visit his tenants, and dining out with your neighbors once a week."

"Well, one must do one's duty," Emmie responded vaguely. Was this really what passed for the height of domesticity in these parts? Things were certainly done very differently in grand houses.

She and Jeremy had so far been to dine with their nearest neighbors, Nellie and Amos Tavistock, an elderly brother and sister who lived at an elegant residence called Vance House. It had once belonged to the estate but had passed to his half brother on the event of their father's death.

The Tavistocks, who rented the house from Nye, were a very good-humored pair and Emmie had liked them a good deal, though she had secretly been surprised to hear that such an old and respectable pair could be Jeremy's favorite neighbors. She supposed his smart set of friends were all London-based, but still she felt some confusion.

From the outset he had told her he wanted her to cultivate closer relations with his neighbors and accordingly she had accepted all invitations they had received in the vicinity. So far, they had dined once at the vicarage, and had received invites from The Grange and Benham Hall to sup with the squire and the Needhams respectively.

From what she could discern, this seemed to be the sum total of "county" families in the vicinity. To be honest, Emmie could not remotely see how entertaining these few straggling neighbors would take up a good deal of her time. Yet Jeremy had made it sound like such a large undertaking.

"I've asked Mrs. Cheviot to invite the Tavistocks and Reverend Ryland and his wife to dinner one night this week. They are pleasant company, and we must have some society for Mr. Wimble and Mr. Penrose while they are here after all."

Lottie looked unconvinced. "Miss Blanche Pebmarsh would probably put more of a smile on that dismal architect's face than that old Miss Tavistock," she opined.

Emmie laughed. "Jeremy said we should invite the Pebmarshes only *after* we have first dined with them next week." She had been introduced to the misses Pebmarsh outside church a couple of weeks previously and privately thought Mr. Wimble would be wildly intimidated by both of them. Miss Delia was hearty and eager with a loud laugh and Miss Blanche was self-assured and rather dismissive.

"Who is calling on you this morning, if I might make so bold?" Lottie asked curiously as she approached the bath with a drying cloth.

Emmie stood up and was promptly enveloped in the wide square of linen. "The Rylands," she responded, "and then later, Mrs. Needham and her daughter are coming over from Benham Hall."

Lottie nodded her head knowingly. "Ah yes, Mrs. Needham is an invalid, is she not, poor lady? And her daughter"—Lottie's face took on a disapproving expression—"a cold, uncaring sort of girl."

Emmie turned in surprise. "Is that what you've heard? Jeremy described Mrs. Needham as perfectly charming and her daughter as pleasant enough, though very reserved."

Lottie sucked in her cheeks. "It's not for me to say, but I've heard a tale or two from the servants over at the Hall," she said darkly. "That girl's got a spiteful streak, make no mistake."

Emmie's eyebrows rose. Well, these two sounded a good deal more controversial than the vicar and his wife and the elderly Tavistocks. "I shall certainly be interested to meet them."

Her visit with Mrs. Ryland should have been a comfortable affair, for this was their third or fourth meeting now, but as she had brought along her husband, things remained on a more formal footing.

Mrs. Ryland was a middle-aged woman of comfortable appearance whose keenest interests were her two sons, her husband, and the good of the parish, in exactly that order. Reverend Ryland was a stern man, tall and stooping. He had a remote, detached air, as though he was always thinking of something else which was far more important than the present. She found it hard to imagine him as a father of two boys.

Emmie elected to meet them in the music room, as the doors opened out onto the terrace, affording them a delightful view of the south lawn as well as letting in a nice breeze on a sunny day such as today. Higgins brought in the tea tray, and they sat and conversed for half an hour or so before the vicar asked if he might be permitted to walk outside and clear his head. He had written a sermon before setting out and his study had been rather stuffy.

"Of course, Reverend Ryland, please take as long as you like. It's so lovely out there today," Emmie responded kindly.

"Charles suffers so with his bad heads," Mrs. Ryland confided, leaning forward.

"What a shame! I expect he has an extensive correspondence to keep up with."

"Oh yes, he is always most assiduous to his duties."

Without the vicar's presence, both ladies relaxed somewhat. Emmie told Mrs. Ryland all about Pinky's new cottage, and the vicar's wife promised to go and call herself to welcome the lady into her new home. "We have seen her in church and look forward to having her as an active parishioner. Naturally, you will miss having your friend close at hand," Mrs. Ryland sympathized. "My unmarried sister moved in with us for six months after my oldest, Clarence, was born. How I missed her when she returned to our father's house! There is nothing like female companionship for a woman."

"Yes, it is true. Though I am fortunate in that I will still see a good deal of her."

"Of course," Mrs. Ryland mused, "your primary difficulty will be cultivating acquaintance in the vicinity that are not *wholly* beneath you. We live in a very quiet corner of the world, and I'm afraid there are no comparably grand families in the neighborhood to compare to the Vances. You've met the squire, of course, Squire Pebmarsh," she said thoughtfully. "He is a widower of some sixty years and lives at The Grange with his unmarried daughters, Miss Delia and Miss Blanche Pebmarsh."

"Oh yes, I have met them, but only briefly. We are going to dine with them next week."

Mrs. Ryland continued as though she had not spoken. "Now, Delia, the elder, never married and is past prayer for it now. She's quite hopelessly eccentric and never goes anywhere without a rabble of ill-behaved spaniels." Emmie nodded, thinking Delia might not be so bad.

"As for Blanche, *she's* quite her father's favorite but terribly unconventional. She's broken off at least two engagements to my knowledge and spends most of her time in the stables. *Not* what I would consider ideal company for you, Lady Faris. but there have been Pebmarshes at The Grange since the days of Edward VI. They are a very old and established family in the area."

"Oh, I am sure," Emmie murmured obligingly.

"No doubt you will be guest of honor at their dinner party. They've always been terribly keen to include Lord Faris in their social sphere, but over the years he has so seldom accepted any invitations to dine with us all." She shot a strangely speculative look at Emmie. "I believe at one time people did rather wonder if Miss Blanche might not be angling for a third proposal from that quarter…"

"Oh indeed?" Emmie replied politely. "I look forward to getting to know them all."

Mrs. Ryland looked a little disappointed by her tepid response. "Of course, things are different now, and that is why everyone is so terribly thrilled that you are mingling with us locals. It is such a shame our little circle is not wider for you. Now, let me think, who does that leave? Of course, there is Benham Hall and the Needhams…"

"Mrs. Needham is coming over to visit with me later," Emmie volunteered.

"Oh, now she will make you a *most* suitable acquaintance, Lady Faris," she exclaimed, sounding pleased. "Angela Needham is a truly lovely woman. Always so gracious and such refined manners, despite the hard life she has had, and the cross she has to bear," she concluded cryptically before taking a sip of tea. "She rarely ventures out from Benham Hall these days due to her ill health," she sighed. "*Such* a shame. She has always had a delicate constitution from what I understand."

"What a pity," Emmie replied dutifully. "Hopefully today is one of her good days."

At this point, the vicar drifted back in through the open doors and walked over to inspect the framed cameos on the wall.

"Now, you must not be offended if she does not stay long with you," Mrs. Ryland rattled on. "It will be purely due to her health. If her son, Edgar Needham, was at home, he would certainly have fulfilled the social obligation, but he is in London on business, which leaves only the daughter." Mrs. Ryland pursed her lips, her nostrils pinching. "It cannot be expected that Miss Halperston will put herself out on anyone's behalf," she said bitterly. "The daughter is from Mrs. Needham's *first* marriage, you know," she said with stress. "And quite different to her half brother, who is always so tender and solicitous to his mother."

"Mariah," her husband said reproachfully, turning about to face them. "That is not kind. Miss Halperston has many duties at home, looking after her sick mother and running the household. It can hardly be expected that she should have time for social calls."

"Now, Charles, you *know* how unfeeling and hard that girl is! Why, many is the time when we have discussed the matter in perfect accord!"

Reverend Ryland sucked in his cheeks. "Mariah," he said warningly, "you will give Lady Faris the impression we are sad gossips."

"No, no," Emmie protested. "You are among friends here."

The vicar relaxed and Mrs. Ryland looked appeased. She turned impulsively back to Emmie. "Oh, I almost forgot!" she exclaimed. "I wrote to Lady Sharpe, as I said I would, proposing your name as a nominee for our little committee and what do you think?"

"She agreed to look me over?" Emmie suggested, thinking of what Jeremy had said about Lady Sharpe. The vicar gave a small cough.

"She, well, she proposed that you invite the ladies to hold their next gathering here at Vance Park," Mrs. Ryland said, a little color creeping into her cheeks. "Then, as one of the points of business, we could hold a vote on your proposed membership."

The vicar looked a little embarrassed. "Please understand, Lady Faris, my wife is aware this is an unconventional request, but Lady Sharpe is"—he hesitated—"a somewhat *forceful* character."

"I am not offended," Emmie responded not entirely truthfully. In truth, Lady Sharpe's "request" sounded to her rather rude. It seemed more like a demand to use Vance Park as a venue. Still, Jeremy wanted her to join the ladies' committee, so she would have to swallow down her feelings on the matter. "Please let Lady Sharpe know that I would be delighted to host the next committee meeting here at Vance."

There were smiles all around. Still, Emmie did not feel altogether sorry to see the backs of the Rylands. She wondered, rather wistfully, how Teddy and Pinky were getting on that morning at their sketching lesson. Would they be roaming around the grounds or romping down on the beach by now? She doubted somehow that Teddy would be wholly focused on his lesson.

She knew where Jeremy would be, of course. He would be down at his racing stables until lunchtime. If it was not for the imminent arrival of Mrs. Needham and her daughter, Emmie would have considered walking down there to join him there.

In truth, as his wife, she ought to show more of an interest in his horse racing, she decided. From what Mrs. Ryland imparted, at least one of the squire's daughters spent all her time in the stables. She found herself wondering, if Teddy had not demanded to meet Miss Ballentine, would Jeremy have naturally gravitated toward Miss Blanche Pebmarsh in time?

The thought disturbed her so much, she got up out of her chair and wandered out onto the terrace. Standing there in the sunshine, she decided to take a turn around the garden to while away the time before her next visitors arrived.

It was already very warm, and she could hear the gentle buzz of bees as she walked along next to the flowerbeds. Shielding her eyes with her hand, she contemplated the blue sky. There was not a cloud in sight. She wished devoutly that the same could be said of her marriage.

25

Jeremy waved a final farewell to Miss Pinson, who was stood at her parlor window madly waving her handkerchief, and helped Emmeline into the carriage. Teddy, who had decided midway through pudding that he wanted to stay the night at Plumtree Cottage, was still scowling.

"But why can I not stay the night, Papa?" he pouted as he settled back onto the seat, his arms folded across his chest. "The smallest bedroom would be perfect for me. No one else could fit in there."

"In events such as these, my son, it is customary to wait until you are invited," Jeremy said, climbing in behind them.

"Miss Pinson would have let me!"

"Nevertheless, you cannot simply decide these things yourself," Jeremy retorted firmly, before glancing over his shoulder to tell Juggins to drive on. "It is the height of bad manners to invite yourself into someone's home."

They now took tea with Miss Pinson every Wednesday, and she came to dinner at Vance Park every Friday evening. They had quite settled into a routine. They were in the landau this evening, so the roof was down. With a huff, the boy turned his face away to stare out at the country lane as they bowled along it.

"Pinky likes to have plenty of notice before an event, Teddy," Emmeline said placatingly. "You haven't got your nightshirt with you, or any of your wash things. She would have worried about that. She likes to have everything planned out to the smallest detail."

"So, I will be allowed to stay the night at Plumtree Cottage sometime soon?" Teddy asked eagerly, whipping around.

"If Miss Pinson invites you," Jeremy said sternly. "And not before."

His frown relaxed. "Oh," he said, looking thoughtful. "I expect she will very soon."

Jeremy eyed him narrowly. "You are not to start hinting outrageously," he said with foreboding, but Teddy affected not to hear him, leaning his arms on the side of the carriage, and resting his head on his forearm.

"I think he's tired," Emmeline murmured. "He's had a long day. Apparently, they traipsed all around the grounds sketching trees this morning."

"Hmmm," Jeremy answered noncommittally, his eyes still on his son's curly head.

"How was your morning at the stables?" she asked. "Any improvement from Atalanta and Ajax?"

"Amyas," he corrected her absently. "Some progress perhaps," he said cautiously. "Though neither of them shines as brightly as Bucephalus did at their age."

"Not all of us show promise in the first flush of youth," she said lightly. "Bucephalus must have been a diamond of the first water."

"He was," he agreed, "but you are right. I shall not give up hope."

"Perhaps you can still buff them to a shine," she added. Then before he could answer, she said softly, "Pinky seemed very happy this evening, did she not?"

"She did, quite in her element."

"I'm glad for her," Emmeline said decisively. "I rather dreaded her leaving me, but I cannot regret it now. Not when everything has worked out so well for her."

He answered her smile with one of his own, fighting down the twinge of guilt. Even Emmeline admitted it was for the best. "How was your morning?" he asked to distract himself.

"Oh, it was…fine," she answered. "The vicar and his wife called on me and then Mrs. Needham and her daughter." *Dull and duller*, thought Jeremy. No wonder she could not meet his eye. "Oh, and some good news. You will be pleased to hear that the next meeting of the Good Works committee will be held here at Vance," she said continued with a valiant attempt at enthusiasm. "Lady Sharpe has been so kind as to confer the honor."

Jeremy hesitated. "This pleases you?"

"Of course," she said quickly. "I am achieving the goals you set me, am I not? It was very kind of Mrs. Ryland to propose my nomination."

"I expect she was more than happy to bring it about. How did you find the Needhams?"

Now it was Emmeline's turn to hesitate. "They were not really what I was led to expect," she said at last.

"And what was that?" He tried to remember whatever he had told her about Mrs. Needham with her faded prettiness and her stiff, proud daughter.

"Mrs. Needham talks a lot about herself, doesn't she?" she said vaguely, then added, "I know that is often the case with those who suffer ill health. By contrast, Miss Halperston barely said anything at all."

"Ah yes." Jeremy winced. "The daughter is not thought to have much by way of personality."

"Really?" Emmeline looked surprised. "That is not what I heard."

"What had you heard?"

Emmeline cast a quick warning look at Teddy, who was now listening with interest. "Oh, that she, well, that she is rather reserved but not without a certain force of character," she said awkwardly.

"Miss Halperston is only pretty when you get her alone," Teddy contributed suddenly.

"Pretty?" Jeremy repeated with surprise. "Miss Halperston?"

"Yes," Teddy said. "When anyone else is there, she just fades into nothing. It's because of her mother. I don't like her mother at all."

"*Teddy*..." Jeremy began remonstratively.

"I don't think I like Mrs. Needham much either," Emmeline chimed in, her cheeks turning pink. "There's, well, just something about her that I just can't warm to. Something not genuine. She, well, she said a couple of things that quite gave me pause..."

"What kind of things?" Jeremy asked, not liking the troubled pucker between her brows.

"Nothing definite," Emmeline said quickly. "It was more implied." She lifted her chin. "I don't think she can be an easy woman to live with. I feel sorry for that girl," she said defiantly.

"*That girl* cannot be much younger than you," he pointed out wryly.

"I know, but I suppose being a married woman I cannot help but think of her that way."

Jeremy smiled at her. He couldn't help himself, despite the odd turn the conversation had taken. "We could always cut the acquaintance," he answered with a thoughtless shrug.

"Cut the…?" Emmeline sat up straighter in her seat. "I thought you wanted me to repair relations with your neighbors, not reduce them even further!"

Oh yes. Silently he cursed himself. "I meant, you need not regard Mrs. Needham. She seldom leaves home in any case. I expect she only ventured out today out of curiosity to see the place. She's never been to Vance before to my knowledge."

"Mama, my other mama I mean, always said she was an invertebrate whiner," Teddy said helpfully.

"Inveterate," Jeremy explained hastily. "And your mama never had much patience with ill health." He turned back to his wife. "Perhaps you could try to draw Miss Halperston out of her shell," he suggested.

Emmie nodded. "Perhaps," she said, but still looked puzzled by his attitude. Thankfully, they had now swung up the avenue to the house, so Teddy began his usual game of pointing out the statues as they came into view.

"There's Hermes!" he exclaimed. "And Ares!"

By the time he had counted off the twelve major Olympians, they had reached the front steps of the house.

Teddy now seemed reconciled to the fact he was sleeping in his own bed that night, but Jeremy still accompanied him up to his room. Emmeline came along, too, as a matter of course.

"I need to put something in the nursery before I go to bed," Teddy said with an air of mysterious import, pausing at that door.

"What is it?" Jeremy asked.

His son hesitated before reaching into his pocket and drawing out a little peg doll wearing a purple crocheted dress and bonnet. "Miss Pinson made it for me," he admitted with some reluctance.

"Well, that was kind of her," Jeremy said calmly, wondering at his son's expression.

"It is Miss Pomfrey," Teddy admitted, sending his father a faintly embarrassed glance.

"Miss Pomfrey!" exclaimed Emmeline. "Has she journeyed to the fort to visit with her ne'er-do-well brother?"

Teddy nodded again, this time with more enthusiasm. "She has come to plead Captain Gerrard for clementines."

"Clementines?" Jeremy repeated. "Is she at risk of developing scurvy?"

"I thought that was limes," Emmeline said, taking the proffered doll and examining it. "Look at her brown wool hair and little painted face. I declare I am quite jealous! Pinky never made *me* any peg dolls." Teddy looked rather smug to hear this. "Yes, she looks just as I imagined her," she concluded and handed her back.

"Pomfrey is up for court martial again," Teddy explained patiently. "So, Miss Pomfrey wants the clementines for him."

He passed Miss Pomfrey to Jeremy, who agreed she was most cunningly wrought.

"You mean *clemency*," Jeremy cut in, handing her back to his son. "She has come to plead for clemency."

"Yes," said Teddy serenely. "That's what I meant."

"Well, I am sure she will succeed," Emmeline said confidently. "Captain Gerrard's heart is sure to melt the minute he catches sight of her."

Teddy darted inside the nursery. "You really do look remarkably pretty in that dress," Jeremy commented as they awaited him in the corridor.

"Ballentine," she prompted. At his querying look, she added, "You have not called me that so much lately."

"Haven't I?" She shook her head. "You like it when I call you that?" She nodded and he felt his heart turn over. At least he was permitted this one leftover from their past. Even as he opened his mouth to reframe the compliment, Teddy reemerged.

"How went the introduction?" Emmeline enquired.

"He melted alright," Teddy said, nodding in a satisfied manner.

Jeremy caught Emmeline's eye, and they shared a look of amusement. "Come along, General Vance," he said to his son, "let's put you to bed."

Once Teddy was settled in for the night, he escorted Emmeline back to her bedchamber. "I'm going to bathe and change," he said, halting at her door. "Then, if you're agreeable, I'll return with my book for the night." She nodded, looking strangely nervous. He paused. "Or would you prefer your own company tonight?"

"No!" she assured him swiftly. "I want you to come back!"

Thank God. He smiled at her and kissed her cheek. "I won't be long," he said and made for his own rooms. When he returned half an hour later clad in his dressing robe, Emmeline was not dressed for bed, but was sitting at her dressing table wearing a frilly wrapper he had not seen before.

It was very becoming, and he looked his fill as he walked over to the bed and lay down there to watch her apply her face lotion. Instead, she piled her hair on top of her head and skewered it there with a few pins, then rose from her stool and walked over to the bed, halting before him.

He looked up at her, eyebrows raised, but made no move. "I've had an idea of something I would like to try," she said abruptly. "Will you indulge me in this?"

"Of course," he answered at once, setting aside his book. "What is it?"

She held her hand out to him. Jeremy rose from the bed and stood before her.

She took his hand. "You are not allowed to say anything," she explained quickly, "but must just follow me." Somewhat bewildered, Jeremy did as he was told and was promptly led to her private bathroom.

Emmeline cleared her throat and squared her shoulders. "I have not yet taken my bath," she said airily and pointed to a chair which Jeremy recognized as belonging to her sitting room. "You sit there," she said imperiously.

For a moment, he did not move, so stunned was he. Then, obediently, he lowered himself into the chair. For one thrilling moment, Jeremy had imagined she was about to bathe in front of him, but to his crushing disappointment, the large tub was empty.

What was she doing? He watched, mystified, as Emmeline walked over to the cupboard and lifted out a large round object, setting it down in the middle of the floor. It took a moment for Jeremy to register what it was. *A sponge bath.* His heart gave a great leap, and he cast an incredulous look at his wife. She met his gaze squarely.

"Now you must sit there, and not stir, mind," she told him warningly. "If you do, then I shall be forced to take steps." When he sat forward in his seat, looking more intrigued than concerned, she added, "I will punish you in the fashion that goddesses always punish foolish mortals who overstep the mark. I shall transform you into a deer, or a star constellation, or a plant, something of that nature," she concluded sternly.

"I will not dare to move a muscle," he promised croakily.

Emmie nodded. "Then you may remain," she said loftily, as though conferring a great favor. Jeremy could not catch his breath. He could not believe she was *doing* this. For him. His eyes tracked her as she walked across the room to fetch two large ewers of water and set them down, one after the other onto the floor next to the bathing tray. Next, she collected her rose-scented soap and her washcloth before returning to the center of the room.

Then she started to unfasten her wrapper in a businesslike fashion. Jeremy cleared his throat, wanting to tell her to slow down, and she paused in the act of untying a ribbon. She glanced toward him reproachfully, and he held his tongue, sitting back in his chair. Still, her fingers slowed in their progress, though whether to punish him or because she had read his mind, he was not sure.

Once her fastenings were dealt with, Emmeline took a deep breath and flung the wrapper open before shrugging it from her shoulders and casting it aside. Underneath it, she wore only a filmy petticoat which offered a scanty sort of modesty at best, and not for long either, as she soon whipped that up and over her head.

Then she was gloriously naked. Jeremy sat back in his seat, rapt and drinking in the view. He had never seen her nudity in its entirety before, all at once. Usually, his view was hampered by bedsheets or his own body. Not this time. This time he could see her magnificence unimpeded. It was a heady experience, and he felt somewhat intoxicated.

To his relief, Emmeline's demeanor remained unhurried as she positioned herself over the deep, round tray and poured the first of the jugs of water all over herself, angling it to pour down her back, then her front, down her arms and legs, until her whole body was glistening wet. Then she turned around, affording him a lovely view of her backside, and crouched down to retrieve her bar of soap.

Jeremy caught his breath. Had she done that on purpose? Surely not. He scanned Emmeline's face as she nonchalantly turned again, displaying her front, and started rubbing the soap over her lovely full breasts. He made an involuntary noise in his throat which he abruptly stifled when she paused. He held his breath.

Only when she was assured of no further interruption did Emmeline commence soaping herself again, under her arms and down her sides. To his fascination, her expression was entirely serene now, as though she had settled into her role of confident bathing goddess and felt secure in her divine status.

She proved this when she turned again, twisting to look over her shoulder as she soaped the backs of her plump thighs and her round buttocks. No statue of a bathing Aphrodite had ever made his breath catch in his throat as she did, however much they had caught attention.

Her abundant hair, only loosely confined on the top of her head, was escaping to cluster about her head and neck in damp ringlets, which he longed to touch and thread his fingers through. Bending down again, she retrieved her washcloth and started dragging it over her rounded limbs in circular sweeps, until no inch of her had escaped its attention.

He watched the whole process, enthralled, until she discarded her cloth at last and crouched down to pour the second jug of water over her body and wash away the soap. Jeremy sat forward in his seat to watch the last of the water run down her ankles.

In truth, he was torn. Part of him was content to sit here and watch his wife wield a drying cloth about her person. If he was lucky she might even reveal some kind of lotion. She had to have some trick for keeping it so perfectly supple and dewy. On the other hand, he was almost trembling with the need to touch her.

Emmeline looked directly at him for the first time since she started her wash. There was a hint of uncertainty in her eyes, as though now she had finished, she was unsure of her next move. Jeremy took the initiative. "May I dry you, Emmeline?" he asked huskily.

She appeared to consider before glancing around the room. "I think the linen towels are in that cupboard over there," she said, pointing. Jeremy needed no further encouragement. He sprang up from his chair, and fetched a couple of towels, setting one down on the floor for her to step onto.

She accepted his proffered hand, and he helped her to step out of the sponge bath and then started carefully, almost reverently patting her neck and shoulders with the other.

"Your towel is rather small," Emmeline murmured. "Lottie usually fetches me a much larger one."

"Yes, but you see I want to keep you naked as long as possible," he responded with perfect truth. She gave a soft laugh which warmed his heart. "Have you any lotion in here?"

"No."

"No lotion?" He was surprised. How did she keep her skin so soft?

She shook her head. "There's some in my room," she volunteered. "But it's far too expensive to use on my whole body. I only use it on my neck and face."

"From now on, you use it on your whole body," he said firmly. "Hang the expense. Direct the bill my way, you need not pay it out of your allowance." It suddenly occurred to him that he had been somewhat remiss on that front. "Have we discussed the matter of your pin money, Emmeline?"

"No," she admitted. "But I have not yet spent all the money you left me in Bath. You ended up paying Madame de Flores instead of me, so I still have heaps left."

Jeremy gave a murmur of agreement. He was not sure he had left her enough to settle up that lady's extortionate bill. Still, it had been worth it. Emmeline's new wardrobe was a source of endless delight to him.

He knelt down to dry her stomach and hips and work his way down her legs. "I want to go and fetch your lotion, Emmeline, may I?"

"Yes, if you really want to."

He scarcely waited for her assent, leaping to his feet and hurrying to her bedroom. Having retrieved the bottle of lotion, it occurred to him that he really needed a much more comfortable chair for Emmeline to sit in for what he had in mind.

Hesitating, he peered into her sitting room. Yes, she had been right. There was a pair of chaise longues in there which looked luxurious enough. Making up his mind that instant, he propped the door open, and, setting the lotion down, dragged the nearest one toward the door.

Once he had got it out into the corridor, it was only a few feet to Emmeline's bathroom. Giving a soft tap on the door, he opened the door and wedged it open with the chair, dragging the purple and gold couch into the mosaic bathroom. It was a good thing the room was a large one.

"It actually doesn't look too bad in here," he commented with surprise as Emmeline watched him open-mouthed. He noticed with displeasure that she had helped herself to a bigger towel and was presently cowering behind it. "It all adds to the high Roman theme."

"I thought you went to fetch lotion!" she commented, looking in confusion from the chaise to him and then rather pointedly at his empty hands.

"One moment." He disappeared back into the corridor to fetch the bottle which he left in her sitting room. "I have it," he announced, returning, and turned the chair about to wedge it under the door handle. "Don't want anyone interrupting us, now, do we?"

Emmie agreed nervously and he approached her, holding out his hand. "Still willing for this undeserving wretch to service you?" he asked, unable to keep the heat out of his voice.

"Of c-course." She faltered, blushing warmly and placing her hand in his and dropping the towel. His heart swelled at her gesture of trust.

"How about reclining on that for me?" he said, glancing over his shoulder at the chaise. "While I lotion your limbs."

Her eyes grew very wide. "Like Venus?"

"Like my own personal Venus," he agreed, walking her over to it and seeing her seated upon it.

"We will have to be careful. The velvet will be quite ruined if we spill lotion on it." Emmie sounded nervous.

"It is *I* who has to be careful," he corrected her, "lest I incur your divine wrath."

"Oh yes, of course," she agreed, "that's what I meant."

Jeremy hid his smile as he removed the stopper and poured the milky fluid into his hand.

"Warm it between your palms first, shepherd. If it is cold, I will not be pleased," she prompted him, lowering herself onto the couch. "I've decided you're a shepherd, by the way."

"So I gathered."

She shifted around a bit, trying to arrange herself comfortably and yet not indecently. It turned out there was no way that she could recline without showing the patch of curls between her legs. Finally coming to that conclusion, she gave up the struggle and occupied herself by trying to drape one arm across her breasts in a pose that did not look wholly unnatural.

Jeremy watched her below his lowered lids as he massaged the lotion between his palms. "Anything else?" he asked huskily.

"Yes, you may remove your robe. Your beauty is pleasing to mine eye, and I do not see why I should be the only one naked here," she pronounced grandly.

This time Jeremy could not hide his grin, but as his hands were covered in lotion, he had first to wipe it over her calves and knees before he could shrug off his robe. It was a good thing today had been a warm day in June, otherwise they would both be covered in goose pimples by this point. As for Jeremy, he felt far too hot to suffer from that condition.

"Not cold, are you, beautiful?" he whispered as he smoothed the lotion in leisurely sweeps of his hands over her skin.

"No," she sighed, and he could see when she finally relaxed to his ministrations, for she let her arms fall and stopped worrying about affording him a view of her spectacular breasts.

"Won't you put one arm behind your head?" he suggested respectfully. "You might be more comfortable that way."

"Is it that way in the painting?" she asked.

"Do you know, at this precise moment, I can't even bring the painting to mind," he admitted. "It pales in comparison to the reality."

She held his gaze for a moment, then reached up to rest her head against her arm. "Like this?"

"Beautiful," he repeated as she settled into place. He took his time, until he had coated her all over, including her hands, her feet, her ankles, her wrists. No patch of skin was left untouched. Then he brushed kisses against the indentations at the insides of her elbows.

"Is this permissible?" he whispered, gently rearranging her legs so that he could kiss the dimples at the backs of her knees.

"Yes," she agreed in a murmur, her eyes half closed by this point. "Oh yes. Wherever you want."

"Wherever?"

She gave a sound of drowsy assent.

"Even if it wakes you up, oh great one?"

Her eyelids flickered. "Even then," she agreed.

Jeremy grinned and kissed up her thighs. "Don't dare take offence now, goddess, for I gained fair permission," he warned.

Emmeline gave a sleepy smile and then sucked in her breath. "*Ohhhh!*" she said, eyes opening wide. "Well, what a very impudent young shepherd you are!"

26

"Emmeline?" Jeremy whispered. She gave a sigh. "Will you eat breakfast with me?"

She opened her eyes. "You don't eat breakfast," she reminded him, turning her head to look at him. He was plastered to her back with his arms encircling her.

"I know," he admitted huskily, "but I'm not ready to part with you just yet."

"What time is it?" she prevaricated, squinting at the window. She felt utterly languorous and far too comfortable to climb out of bed.

"It must be sometime after eight."

"You did not go early to the stables," she exclaimed in surprise.

"No," he agreed mildly. "Masterman will be most put out."

"Hmmm." Suddenly, she remembered something and sat bolt upright. "I forgot about the bathroom!" she exclaimed, throwing back the covers.

"What about it?" Jeremy asked in surprise.

"I meant to get up early and clear away the evidence," she said, standing up. It was only then she remembered how Jeremy had dragged the chaise longue into her bedroom last night. It stood in the middle of the floor, looking very out of place. He had been right. The vivid purple looked most jarring among all her peachy-colored bedroom furniture.

Recalling with embarrassing vividness how thoroughly he had pleasured her on that same couch, she cast about for her dressing robe, pulling it on.

"Evidence?" Jeremy laughed, but Emmie was already halfway out of the door. The dressing room door was partway open, and she could hear Lottie singing to herself in her curiously off-key voice. *Bother!* Emmie crept past the door to her bathroom and found that, as she had expected, everything had already been tidied away.

Chagrined, she took a quick wash and brushed her teeth before hurrying back to her bedroom. "It's all your fault!" she grumbled as Jeremy regarded her with amusement from the bed. He did not seem remotely troubled by his nakedness this morning and was stretched out shamelessly beneath the covers.

"If you hadn't attended to me so assiduously with—" She broke off in horror. She had almost said *your tongue*! Instead, she gasped, "With, er, lotion, I would not have been so comfortable and overslept. And now Lottie will wonder why I took a bath at such an odd hour!"

"You look very put out," Jeremy commented, propping himself up on one elbow. "I did not know taking a sponge bath was such a scandalous thing."

"It's not that!" she said, quite flustered. She knew, of course, she was being ridiculous. "She will think me an inconsiderate and untidy mistress!"

He tutted. "Not at all, she will congratulate herself that she is much needed. Besides, surely Lottie was the one who filled the ewers with hot water for you in the first place?" he guessed reasonably.

"No," she corrected him absently. "For I asked Gladys."

He shrugged. "Most likely she will not wonder about it at all. It is summertime and you have a husband that frequently shares your bed. Either of which might necessitate you needing to wash in the middle of the night. Let's breakfast in the family dining room," he suggested in an abrupt change of subject. "We'll let Wimble and Penrose sit to the formal table without us."

"What about Teddy?" Emmie asked.

"We can send for Teddy to join us."

Emmie acquiesced, but when Lottie was tasked with passing on the message, she returned to inform them that Master Teddy had taken an early breakfast in the nursery and had already set off for his lessons at Miss Pinson's cottage in his pony and trap.

"They must have had plans for an early start," Emmie commented. "More sketching, do you suppose?"

"Most likely he's just fired up to start waging his latest campaign," Jeremy opined dryly. "He will be laying siege to Miss Pinson assiduously until he achieves that end."

"Which campaign would that be?" Emmie asked with interest.

"Inducing Miss Pinson to invite him to stay overnight at Plumtree Cottage," he replied with an upward quirk of his lips.

"He will not have to work so very hard for that." Emmie pulled a face. "Poor Pinky will deny him nothing."

"She no longer thinks boys are quite so terrifying?" Jeremy enquired.

"No, I don't think she does," Emmie mused. "Teddy has apparently cured her of that complaint."

Jeremy looked rather doubtful. "I only hope he has not lulled her into a false sense of security," he murmured.

"Which dress will you be wanting this morning, milady?" Lottie enquired. "The new jonquil crepe or the apple green muslin?"

"Your mistress will not require dressing until after breakfast, Lottie," Jeremy interjected. "We will be dining informally, just the two of us, in our dressing gowns." He glanced down at his own black and gold creation, and Emmie blushed, realizing they were both entirely naked under their robes.

"Yes, milord. Shall I run down to inform the kitchen?"

"Thank you, yes." Lottie obligingly disappeared and Jeremy dropped back onto the bed. "Come and lie down here with me awhile, wife."

"To what purpose, pray?" Emmie asked archly.

"To while away the time until our breakfast is ready."

"Certainly not. I am going to find my slippers," she said, crossing the floor to enter her dressing room. She smiled to herself, hearing his indignant splutter behind her. Things were definitely improving. There had been no apology the previous evening for one thing, and no nightshirt for another.

His reaction to her shallow bath had been all she could have hoped for and more. It was true that he had still handled her with the utmost care, almost reverently, she might even say, but she supposed she had rather imposed that role on him with all her talk of goddesses and mortals.

The only thing that troubled her slightly was that he had been fully intent on her pleasure at all times, as though his own hardly mattered. He had been so insistent that she was to be the focus, and she alone. This morning, though, he seemed relaxed enough.

Retrieving her slippers, she reentered the bedroom and sat at her dressing table to try to impose some order on her unruly head of ringlets. Jeremy watched contentedly until Lottie reappeared to take over the attempt. Then he stood up and headed toward the door.

Emmie quickly turned away from the mirror. "Where are you going?" she asked.

"To fetch *my* slippers," he explained. "And have a quick wash."

"You need not go the corridor way," she told him. "Use the connecting door." He halted at once, and she threw a quick look at Lottie, who was wholly absorbed in her task. Seeing her warning glance, Jeremy did not utter whatever reply he had been about to make, but he did give her a slow smile before changing his direction at once and heading for the other door.

He was not long. Lottie had just stepped back from dressing Emmie's hair when he reentered the room. "Shall we?" he asked and promptly escorted her to the private dining room on their own floor. By the time they sat on the cushions at the low table, both a teapot and a coffeepot were awaiting them.

Emmie poured, while Jeremy propped his elbows on the table and watched her with his head tipped to one side. Higgins brought in a tray of assorted dishes and set them down with a short bow. "Excellent," Jeremy murmured, though Emmie suspected he would eat none of it.

"I have not seen much of Colfax lately," she commented, passing him his coffee cup. "Higgins seems to be fulfilling all his duties at present."

"Colfax asked permission to take his two-week leave," Jeremy explained.

"Has he gone to visit relatives?"

"No." Jeremy cleared his throat. "He's, er, helping out at Plumtree Cottage."

Emmie set down her teacup. "Really?" It was the first she had heard of it.

"Well, my estate manager sent a team to clear away all the rubbish from the garden, but as I understand it a good deal of work still remains to be done. I did offer the services of one of the undergardeners, but Miss Pinson declined the offer." Jeremy paused, sending her a fleeting glance. "She said several kind friends had rallied around and offered to help."

"Several kind friends," Emmie repeated. "I suppose Colfax must be one of them. Pinky does have rather a knack of collecting friends. She could not visit the bakers without striking up conversation with someone or other." Usually, though, Emmie reflected privately, these would be genteel folk, much like Pinky herself, eminently respectable and often rather down on their luck. Altogether *nothing* like Colfax. Aloud she continued, "She's much better at it than I. She has at least a dozen people she regularly corresponds with. I expect they will all be coming to stay with her, now she has two spare rooms."

"Well, according to Teddy, one of the rooms is extremely small and only fit for a person his size."

Emmie disregarded her stepson's biased view. "Do you know, when I visited last week, I interrupted a singsong in her parlor. There were at least six people crowded in there, around her spinet singing 'Barbara Allen.' Colfax was one of their number now that I think of it," she remembered. "He has a surprisingly good singing voice."

"Did you join in?" Jeremy asked, buttering her a piece of toast.

"No, for they all stopped singing when I walked in and turned quiet and awkward."

"Ah," Jeremy said, placing the toast before her. "Well, you are lady of the manor now. No doubt some of them consider you outside of their social sphere."

"Yes, I suppose so," Emmie agreed, trying not to sound forlorn. "Pinky leaped up at once, but I told her I had just brought along some of Hudgins's flowers from his glass house and beat a hasty retreat. I did not like to break up her party," she explained, playing with her teaspoon. "I—I don't know why exactly, but the thought of Pinky and Colfax of all people is just so jarring to me."

Jeremy looked amused. "Well, it seems they are firm friends now, so you must try to disregard your own feeling about your footman being friends with her." Emmie started to protest it was not a matter of social status at all, but Jeremy cut through this, saying, "Do you suppose when they are alone, they are simply Hannah and Len?" He laughed. "If you could see your face. I know she acts as though she is a little old lady, but she cannot be much more than forty."

"She isn't," Emmie agreed quickly. "I know that. She has always acted older because her parents had her late in life. And then she lived with a great-aunt for several years, so she had always lived with old people. The truth is, she cannot have been more than eighteen when she turned up on my doorstep to take up her role as my governess."

"Yet to you, I suppose she always seemed an adult," Jeremy said, removing the covers to reveal eggs, bacon, and bread rolls.

"Well, yes," Emmie agreed lamely. She watched as his expression became thoughtful. "What are you thinking?" she asked impulsively.

"I was wondering," he said slowly. "Do you think Teddy might grow up to have a penchant for very proper and timid maidens, like Colfax?"

"Colfax?" She couldn't say why precisely but Emmie felt disquieted by his words.

"Yes, his tastes run decidedly in that direction when it comes to women. Surprising, isn't it?"

Suddenly, Emmie remembered that first day she met Colfax and how intently he had stared at poor Pinky. "But I don't think Hannah would like that at all!"

"Like what? Being the recipient of Colfax's admiration? Why not?"

"Well, simply because!" Emmie spluttered. "Hannah hates feeling embarrassed or discomforted. She's not, well, *shy* precisely, but she is never fully at ease with people until she knows them and trusts them and then they become part of her little trusted circle."

"Has a man ever featured within that circle?"

Emmie thought fleetingly of Pinky's friend circle, which had always been maintained largely through correspondence. "Never."

"So, because she has never been admired by a man heretofore, you presume she would never enjoy the experience?"

Emmie frowned. "Not exactly. It's just, Colfax seems a hundred miles away from any gentlemen Pinky has ever expressed admiration for."

"Oh. Has she ever expressed much by way of admiration for the opposite sex?" he asked casually, lifting his coffee cup to his lips.

Emmie thought about this for a moment. "Well, she admired very much Canon Littleworth's oration in church," she said lamely.

Jeremy smirked. "That is an altogether different thing."

"I suppose I imagined she never brought up such things because she had no interest in them," Emmie admitted slowly.

"Perhaps," he said lightly, "or perhaps it was because she never saw any likelihood of taking a suitor. You must admit that she enjoys the vicarious thrill of reading romantic novels."

"A harmless pursuit," Emmie countered. "Despite what some people imagine!"

"Oh, I quite agree."

"And *Colfax*? I just cannot see it. He must be younger than her for one thing."

"Only by about five years or so. What you really mean is that he is altogether too virile for someone like your staid Miss Pinson? Admit it." Emmie pressed her lips together and turned away, feeling annoyed. "You know, she might not even have felt at liberty to discuss such matters with you," he suggested gently.

The thought dismayed her. "Why should she not? Whatever do you mean?"

"Because of the difference between you in station," he suggested mildly. "There is a barrier of sorts between employer and employee. Or maybe because she started out as a figure of authority in your life and Miss Pinson is a stickler for preserving such distinctions."

"Nonsense! We have long since passed that stage. I told you, did I not, that I consider her to be family by this point."

"You did, but…" He let his words hang in the air.

"But what?" Emmie demanded, feeling thoroughly needled.

"You never told her about me, did you, Ballentine?" Emmie regarded him a moment speechlessly. "That morning at Winkworth Street was the first she had ever heard of me, was it not?"

Emmie felt herself turn very hot and red. "That was not due to…anything you suggest!" she answered crisply. "Rather I did not tell her because I was fully aware of how badly I had conducted myself, abandoning everything she had taught me about behaving with decorum. I knew she would be disappointed in me if she knew how I had left myself wide open to criticism and ridicule."

"In fact, because you still saw her as an arbiter of your behavior," he said simply. "If you still preserved that distinction, is it any wonder, then, that she did too?" His words felt like a slap to her face. "Don't look like that, Emmeline," he said quickly and reached across for her hand. "I did not mean—that is, I apologize. I have been insensitive again."

She attempted to rally, seeing the concerned look on his face. If she was not careful, he was going to start being overly solicitous again. "No, no," she said quickly. "It's not that. Not at all. I just never dreamed—" She broke off her words. She *hated* thinking she might have stifled Pinky somehow and now her friend could not confide in her.

Emmie took a deep breath. "I will have to—to make a concerted effort not to be so close-minded," she said firmly. "I must take a lesson from your book and be more open and outgoing. I will try to make more friends." A series of emotions flitted across Jeremy's face, panic and relief, before settling into one of mild perturbation. "You look puzzled," Emmie observed.

"It's just—" She waited patiently for him to continue. "I don't have many friends myself, Emmeline. Not really. I would say I only really have one that truly counts and that is Atherton."

"What about Squire Pebmarsh?"

"I'm *friendly* with Squire Pebmarsh," he emphasized. "That's a different thing. Being on friendly terms is easy, being a true friend is not. I know how to be charming," he said slowly, "but I can never be bothered to maintain the façade. It takes too much work."

She laughed at his plaintive tone. She could not help it. "Now you sound like Teddy."

"He is like me, isn't he?"

"In the best possible way," she agreed. At his quizzical look, she explained, "All the whimsy and none of the vice."

Jeremy's expression sobered. "Ah," he said comprehendingly. "Quite so."

"Personally, I don't mind your vices so much, these days."

He turned his head sharply to look at her. "Careful, Ballentine," he warned. "Or I'll start taking you at your word."

Emmie caught her breath but did not quite know how to answer. "So," she said weakly. "We have a friend apiece. Neither of us is exactly swimming in bosom friends, are we?"

"We have each other," he said roundly, lifting her hand to his lips. "And besides, you malign yourself. I can think of two more people that care very much about you." At her quizzical look, he said, "You have the Hardimans. Mr. Hardiman tried to take a firm line with me when I told him we were to be wed. If he could have brow-beaten me into offering him more information, he would have.

"As it was, he chased me down the street after I paid him his severance money to secure my address. He said he needed to be sure of your safety and that he knew his wife would want to write to you, so I had little choice but to give it to him. I am surprised she has not written already."

"Oh, but she has!" Emmie responded warmly. "I received their letter shortly after we sent out the wedding cake. Mr. Hardiman added a postscript in his own hand. They were very worried about me, but I replied and reassured them that everything had worked out for the best. It was only, well, a little awkward. Reading between the lines they were obviously very shocked about my broken engagement and subsequent marriage." She avoided Jeremy's eye. "I could not address it openly, so it felt like I was tiptoeing around the issue somewhat."

Jeremy's mouth tightened. "I do not know why you are so careful with Stockton's reputation. Why not expose him and be done with it? You owe him nothing." Noticing her shocked reaction, he paused, and fearful that he would apologize again, Emmie continued in a rush.

"You are quite right about the Hardimans. Mr. Hardiman has been a good friend to me over the years. He always looked out for my interests, and his wife, Harriet, is a gem. I would like to consider them friends, but I think I would need to build on the acquaintance to make that so."

"Then do it." Jeremy shrugged. "You could always invite them to stay with us at Vance for Christmas, or perhaps a couple of weeks next summer."

"Really?"

"Of course. Nothing could be easier."

The dangerous moment seemed to have passed and Emmie was glad. "I do not know how comfortable they would be staying at such a grand residence as Vance Park," she admitted, "but I think I *will* invite them. Thank you."

They smiled cautiously at one another and Emmie breathed a sigh of relief. Good lord, their conversation seemed fraught with pitfalls lately! She needed to watch her step. "Are you going to the stables this morning?" she asked, striving for a casual tone.

"Yes," he answered abruptly. "Would you do me a favor, Ballentine?"

She froze in the act of reaching for the bacon. Oh, he was going to ask her not to raise the subject of Humphrey between them again, she realized with sudden conviction. That had been stupid of her. Bracing herself to be reproved, she swallowed and nodded. "Of course."

"Would you sit in my lap while you eat your breakfast?" he asked.

Emmie, feeling quite astonished, set down the bacon with a thump. "Sit in your…?"

He sat up and gestured between his legs. "Right here," he said, as if it was the most reasonable request in the world.

"I don't believe I'm really built for lap-sitting," she said awkwardly.

"Why don't you let me be the judge of that?"

Oh, good grief, he was serious, she realized, staring at him. Somewhat flustered, she clambered her way over the plump floor cushions to reach him with as much dignity as she could muster. He uncrossed his legs to make room for her, and she sat between them, giving her dressing robe a self-conscious tug to make sure all was decent.

"That's better," he said with satisfaction, sliding his hand down her side to rest with great familiarity against her hip. "Now, what were you about to partake in?"

Emmie sat there drawing a blank. She could feel his warmth surrounding her, his thighs on the outside of hers, her bottom resting against his groin. It was very distracting.

"Bacon, wasn't it?" he prompted smoothly.

"Oh yes," she agreed, clearing her throat. "Bacon."

"You'll have to reach across." Emmie did so, stretching forward to reach for the dish and then settling back again between his legs. For some reason, her pulse was racing altogether too fast for something as mundane as taking breakfast.

Jeremy's hand was caressing her side now, stroking against the silky fabric of her robe. His other hand reached across to snag her teacup and saucer. "Won't you have another cup?" he suggested. "You'll have to reach for the teapot, as I can't from here."

She gave him a suspicious look out of the corner of her eye. She was suddenly struck with the oddest conviction he wanted her to keep reaching across the table in front of him. But why on earth would he? Setting her strange impression aside, she reached forward for the teapot and heard his faint hiss of breath behind her.

Emmie's cheeks heated at the idea he might be looking at her bottom. She set the teapot down and settled back against his front. Was it all in her imagination or was he getting oddly excited in this scenario? She felt flustered and rather hot. Hands not quite steady, she poured herself a cup of tea.

Jeremy tutted behind her. "Dear, dear, you forgot the milk and sugar, Ballentine. Whatever will you do?"

Emmie glanced across the table. Everything was situated on the other side, where she had originally been seated. "I'm starting to think you should have come and shared my cushion," she joked feebly.

"But where would have been the fun in that?"

Emmie tsked under her breath and surged forward once more to reach for the milk and sugar. This time, when she lifted her bottom to lean forward, Jeremy's one hand slid over her posterior to squeeze one cheek, as the other slid around to her front and popped open three of her buttons, his hand insinuating itself between her skin and the robe.

Emmie held her breath, and not just because it was her stomach he was idly caressing. "I can't tell which is softer," he mused. "Your skin or the silk of your robe."

"It's probably all that lotion," she answered, breathing back out. Really, she should have lost her inhibitions by now. She *knew* which parts of her he savored the most, however peculiar it might still seem to her.

"You still need sugar," he reminded her smoothly.

"I can take my tea without it," she prevaricated.

"There's no need anymore," he replied with a frown in his voice.

"That is true." A little slower this time, Emmie tipped forward, reaching for the sugar bowl. This time, he surged up behind her, shoving her forward onto the table. "Oh!" Emmie's hand shot out to steady herself and the sugar bowl rolled out of her hand to land perilously close to the edge of the table. "Jeremy, the sugar!" she breathed urgently. Half of it had already tipped out of the bowl.

"You had better reach for it," he advised.

She bit her lip. "But if I do…"

"What?" he asked curiously as his thumb slid repeatedly over her belly button.

"What will you do?" she asked breathlessly, turning her head to look at him.

"Well…" He seemed to consider this. "I was thinking about lifting up your robe and taking a good look at your backside."

Emmie gave a gasp. "You saw plenty of it last night!" she reminded him.

"Not enough though. I'll probably never get enough of that particular view." His voice roughened over the last few words, giving her a peculiar feeling.

Emmie remained frozen where she was, unsure of her next move. When he, too, remained immobile, as though waiting for her decision, she reached slowly for the sugar bowl. Then she felt it, the whisper of her hemline sliding up the backs of her legs. Pressing her lips together to prevent her whimper, Emmie closed her fingers about the sugar bowl and dragged it back toward her, leaving a telltale trail of granules across the tabletop before she could set it down upright.

"Some spilled," she murmured, and the next thing she knew, she could feel the cold air against her bottom, and Jeremy's hand slid down from her stomach to slip between her legs, cupping her there and providing a buffer between her and the table.

"Is this comfortable for you?" he asked casually.

Emmie was not sure how to reply. It was not *uncomfortable*, precisely, but it did feel rather odd lying across the table like this, half exposed. She also felt squirmy and strangely excited. "Ye-es?" she wavered.

"What about…if I do this?" he asked, pressing up against her from behind again.

"I—I don't mind it," she admitted with a hitch in her breath.

"What if I was to undo my robe?" he asked silkily, his fingers starting to rub between her legs.

"Your robe?" she panted, feeling herself grow embarrassingly wet from his ministrations.

"Yes, mine."

She considered this a moment. There could be only one reason for him to be undoing *his* robe. It was so hard to concentrate when his fingers were creating such havoc with her senses. "I—I would not mind." There was a rustling noise and the next thing she knew she felt the press of his hard flesh from behind. He was fully erect and demanding entrance.

"Oh!" she uttered, her eyes watering.

"I think we need to put your knee up on the table surface, Ballentine," he puffed. "Or I'm not going to fit inside."

"My knee?" she shrilled in panic, half twisting to look back at him.

He gave a breathless laugh. "Too undignified?"

She was glad he could not see how red her face was. "I—I'm not sure."

"How about if you take a sip of tea at the same time?" he teased. "Would that give it a more respectable air?" Emmie's tongue was too tied to answer that one. "Shall I stop?" he asked suddenly.

"N-no." Bracing her palms carefully between the dish of bread rolls and a plate of eggs, Emmie tentatively lifted one leg. Instantly, his hand was there at the back of her knee, guiding it carefully until he set it down on the table. Emmie breathed out with a rush.

"Comfortable?"

"Yes, I think so."

"Tell me if that changes at any point in proceedings." His voice sounded tense now. Less amused. It had a rougher edge to it. He started to push inside her. Emmie's eyes flew wide at the pressure, at the unaccustomed position, and, once he was fully seated, at the sensation of fullness.

His thighs pressed hard against the backs of her legs now, and it was only at this point that she realized he had not actually kissed her that morning. She blinked in shock that he could have skipped such a thing. Was it because he had lavished so many kisses on her last night, and this treatment was to redress the balance?

His fingers moved again against that small bud of flesh between her legs that radiated so much pleasure, and the jolt of it caused all such thoughts to fly from Emmie's head. "*Oh!*" she cried out, and Jeremy started to move behind her in brisk, vigorous movements that soon had the dishes rattling against the surface.

Oh dear, perhaps they ought to have tidied everything away first, she thought, trying to focus on the vibrating lid of the teapot. If she could just keep her eyes on that, and not lose concentration, then she could prevent herself from collapsing in a heap onto the breakfast things.

As it was Jeremy's vigorous thrusts were shoving her forward with a distinct lack of ceremony. She was a little shocked by such rough treatment, but it was hard to protest when all she could do was moan and sink by degrees onto her elbows, pushing the bacon and tomatoes further and further across the surface.

"What *would* the servants think, Ballentine, if they walked in on us now, I wonder?" Jeremy's words, a harsh rasp, penetrated her pleasurable haze, until she gasped with horror at the very idea, and, strangely, reached her crisis point in that same instant, shattering apart and collapsing with a soft wail into a tray of breakfast rolls.

Jeremy slammed into her hard one last time, and then planted deep, shuddering and groaning. He followed her down, breathing hard against the back of her neck. "Fuck, I'm sorry, Ballentine," he wheezed at last. "Just give me a minute and I'll set us to rights."

Emmie lay there feeling stupefied. At least she'd avoided the eggs.

27

Emmie still felt somewhat dazed as she met with Mr. Penrose in her sitting room an hour later. At first, in the aftermath of their vigorous coupling, she had been enveloped in a euphoric haze. Jeremy had helped her upright, grabbed a napkin to brush the flour from the bread rolls off her chest, and been very tender as he had examined her elbows and knees and helped her to her feet, straightening the table into some semblance of order.

Then, as the fog had receded, she realized he had *apologized* again. That had given her a nasty jolt. Looking shamefaced, he said something about his ardor no doubt being due to an excess of self-restraint the previous night and given an awkward laugh. Then he had kissed her hand but did not meet her eye as he had escorted her to her own bathroom, as though she was an invalid instead of a perfectly healthy woman and willing participant!

Admittedly, she had been a little sticky and in need of a wash, but he had acted like he had done her some grievous wrong! Emmie's crazy high spirits had plummeted back to earth as she shut the bathroom door on him and started unbuttoned her dressing robe.

As she went through her ablutions, she could not avoid concluding that she must have been at fault somehow for her bathing initiative. She must have put him under too much pressure with all that bossing around she had done, and now he felt guilty for what they had done this morning. She supposed it made some sort of sense.

That scenario she had created had been the problem. It had made him solely focused on her pleasure and not his own. That was why he had been so enthusiastic this morning, presumably. Was she not supposed to have enjoyed it? Suddenly, she felt horribly embarrassed by her own fervent response.

Presumably Viscountess Faris should have smacked his hands away and begged him to remember her sense of decorum instead of letting him paw and pet her like that at the breakfast table, let alone rut her over it afterward. Now she just felt horribly unsure of herself all over again.

Still thinking of it later that morning, she sighed, and Mr. Penrose looked up from his sketchbook in perturbation.

"It's not the sketches," she assured him hastily. "I just have a slight headache this morning."

"Perhaps we should postpone our meeting, Lady Faris?" he suggested politely.

"No, no, I will be fine presently." She forced herself to concentrate on the drawing in front of her, instead of Jeremy's confusing conduct. This time, it was a sketch of her transformed bedroom. "Will it not be a great undertaking to add all these fake columns to the room?" she asked slowly.

"Not at all," Mr. Penrose replied, looking sure of himself. "They will hardly present a challenge as they will not need to withstand the elements, being indoors."

"And this marble effect on the walls? How will it be achieved?"

"Mere paint and lacquer," he explained. "The technique is fiddly, but the final effect is well worth it, and I know a splendid tradesman I can book to achieve it."

"And this large scallop shell above the bed...?"

"A wall painting. I will paint that myself," he added with mock modesty.

"I do like it," Emmie said truthfully, for the room did look pretty in its tones of pink and cream. Mr. Penrose had added a good deal more detail since their last conversation. She could see that he had added the mirror with the frame decorated with cupids and a red velvet chaise longue.

A chaise longue. Emmie felt her heart thud painfully. Had this idea been a terrible mistake? Would having her room done out as Venus's grotto mean that Jeremy would feel compelled to be scrupulously gentle and assiduous to her forevermore? She gulped. "Yes, it is looking very fine," she said aloud.

Mr. Penrose preened. "Yes, I thought you would be pleased," he said with his customary self-satisfaction. "I did as you asked and took the Venuses of Vance for my inspiration." He frowned. "The only reference that I could not trace was the cupid mirror."

"Oh, of course," Emmie replied without thinking. "That painting is in Lord Faris's bedroom so you won't have seen that one, but I think it must be his favorite."

Embarrassed comprehension seemed to dawn on Mr. Penrose's face. "I *see*," he mused and instantly struck a line through a full-size statue of Aphrodite he had placed in the center of the room.

"Why are you removing the statue?" Emmie asked in surprise.

"She seems suddenly superfluous," he said shortly. "We will have attendant doves, and perhaps a statue of Eros instead. They are the companions of Venus, are they not?"

She watched him sketch in a pair of Grecian urns and fill them with roses. "The dressing table will still need to be a focus of the room," she reminded him, thinking of Jeremy's preoccupation with her being sat at it.

"This is your dressing table here," he said, gesturing to a vaguely penciled shape.

"I see." She nodded, unable to think of a reason to completely change their plans at this late stage. No doubt Mr. Penrose had found her a far more troublesome client than the previous viscountess, she thought glumly. She could not say she blamed him at this point.

Jeremy did not appear to lunch, which dismayed her, though she was not really surprised. He had gone to the stables very late that morning. Still, being forced to sit in the state dining room and make polite conversation with Mr. Wimble and Mr. Penrose depressed her spirits even further.

She was just reflecting that Teddy must have taken his lunch with Pinky when the lady burst into the room, puffing and panting, and looking fit to drop.

"Pinky!" Emmie cried, jumping up from her seat. Mr. Wimble let out a startled yell and almost fell off his seat. Ignoring her timid guest, Emmie hurried to her friend's side. "Whatever is it, my dear?"

Her poor friend clutched at her hand, her face quite white with fear and her own hands trembling. "Something terrible has happened, I'm sure of it!" she said tearfully, clutching her side. "The dear boy, Master Teddy! He never appeared for his lessons as we arranged. Oh, I'm so terribly worried that something has befallen him! I walked the entire way, scanning the hedgerows and ditches in case he'd met with an accident on the way, but I found nothing and no sign of his pony!" She collapsed into sobs as Emmie helped her into a chair.

"Pinky, you must be calm. We will send word to Lord Faris down at the stables." She looked about and found Higgins hovering. "Higgins, please can you send for Lord Faris at once and explain that it's urgent. Teddy did not show for his lessons with Miss Pinson this morning."

Higgins hurried from the room and Emmie turned back to her distraught friend. "You arranged to meet especially early this morning, did you not? I wonder...?"

"Early?" Pinky's red-rimmed eyes widened. "Oh no! Indeed, we had agreed to meet rather later than usual, for we spent so long over our sketching earlier in the week." Her anxious eyes scanned Emmie's face. "Lord Faris assured me that we could alter the daily hours accordingly."

"Oh, I am sure, Pinky, please do not distress yourself over that. At what time was Teddy due to join you?"

"Half past ten," she replied promptly. "I delayed until eleven, for sometimes..." Her voice faltered. "Well, sometimes the dear boy can be a *little* late." She dissolved into tears again. "But *never* later than half an hour! So, I knew, you see, that something *must* be very wrong."

"I quite see," Emmie said, biting her lip. For one thing, she saw that Teddy was a poor timekeeper. Why had he left the house so early that morning? He must have had some other plans. What on earth could have happened to him? Her mind careered wildly from one unlikely possibility to another. His maternal grandparents had kidnapped him! His mother had reappeared from the Continent and laid claim to him!

With a concerted effort she got a hold of herself and straightened up, Pinky's hand still held tightly in her own. Mr. Penrose was sat hungrily tucking into his lunch while Mr. Wimble eyed watched nervously over the table as though he found them wildly unpredictable creatures he did not quite like to take his eyes off.

"Do not trouble yourselves, gentlemen," Emmie said sarcastically. "Please continue eating your fill." She turned back to her friend. "Pinky, shall we remove ourselves into the music room? That is the most comfortable room in my opinion."

Pinky rose on unsteady legs and Emmie bolstered her up as they made their way through to the music room. Poor Pinky was practically limping by this point and Emmie suspected she had blistered her heel by hurrying the whole way on foot.

"Sit down here, dear, and I will have a nice cup of tea brought through," she urged, seeing her friend into a comfortable chair.

Emmie had just hurried back into the hallway when she saw Colfax advancing down the corridor with a surprisingly wrathful expression on his face. He checked his step at the sight of her, halting before her.

"She's here?" he asked eagerly. "Where is she?"

"The music room," Emmie stated, and he turned on his heel at once, leaving her standing. "Have you heard any news?" she called after him as he disappeared in the direction of the music room, affecting not to hear her.

Emmie hesitated, then decided discretion might be the better part of valor at this point, so she left Pinky to Colfax's tender mercies and went in search of Bridget to fetch them a fresh tray of tea. No sooner had she given the order than she hurried back. Before she had even reached the music room door, she was astonished to hear upraised voices.

"You know *nothing* about the bond that child and I share!" Pinky's voice said shrilly. "Let me tell you, if he is beaten as a consequence of your vile slander, I will never, *never* forgive you!" Emmie blinked to hear Pinky's unaccustomed vehemence. She had reached the doorway now and stood there in shock to see her friend in such a state. "He is my charge, my responsibility and such a sweet little boy!" Pinky burst out passionately, striking her scrawny chest with her fist.

Emmie hurried forward, dismayed to see her friend so distressed. Colfax was staring right at Pinky, his face pale and tight and his chest heaving. "Pinky dear, you must calm yourself. I am sure there is no need for such passion. Please tell me," she said, turning to Colfax. "Do you know of my stepson's whereabouts?"

"I do," he answered gruffly. "It was just as I suspected. He's hightailed it to the fair at Marston, along with the vicar's two young scamps. They planned the whole jaunt. There was no need for Miss Pinson to go haring off like she did, distressing herself and—"

"It's not true!" Pinky sobbed. "You malign him. He would not do such a wicked thing. I am sure something terrible has befallen him."

Emmie pressed her lips together. It seemed highly likely to her that Teddy would have absconded for such a tryst. She and Colfax exchanged a look. "Pinky dear," she said soothingly and knelt beside her friend's chair. "You will give yourself the most dreadful headache if you carry on this way." A footfall in the doorway had her quickly turning her head, but it was only Gladys with the tea tray. "Here is a nice pot of tea, now shall we—?"

"What's this all about?" Jeremy's voice cut through them all as he strode in the room in his riding clothes. He swung about, taking in the scene. Colfax took a step forward, but Jeremy's gaze rested on Emmie quizzically.

"Teddy did not turn up for his lessons," she explained quickly, "and Pinky has walked the entire route he would have taken and found no sign of him. Colfax has discovered a plot to attend a fair with the Ryland boys over at…" She turned back to Colfax.

"Marston," he supplied readily enough.

"Right," said Jeremy grimly. "Then, that is where I am headed now. Colfax, you will accompany me."

"Oh but—" Pinky started up from her seat in agitation. "My lord, you must not—"

Jeremy hesitated and for one horrible moment, Emmie thought he would be dismissive of her. Then he walked toward her, taking Pinky's hand in his. "You must not distress yourself, Miss Pinson. This is not the first time that boy of mine has decided to kick over the traces. Nor the last, I suspect. I hope you will let my wife make you comfortable in one of the guest rooms. You look like you need a lie down."

Pinky collapsed back into her seat, clearly not reassured at all. Jeremy turned to Emmie. "I'll bring him back," he said, taking her hand and squeezing it before striding from the room. Emmie looked at Colfax, who was still watching her friend with a bleak expression on his face. The Adam's apple in his throat bobbed, and for a moment Emmie thought he would speak, then he bowed his head and followed her husband out of the door.

It slammed shut after him, and Pinky sat with an aghast expression on her face. "Oh dear." Her eyes filled with tears. "Oh, he is such a *dear* little boy! Oh, I am convinced he did not mean anything naughty by it!"

There was much handwringing and weeping before Emmie could convince her to drink her cup of tea and nothing could induce poor Pinky to eat so much as a morsel. "Oh, if he should be whipped for it," poor Pinky lamented, "I will never, never, never forgive myself! If you had only heard the pitiless way that Leonard, I mean, Colfax spoke about it! He said—he said—"

"He said Teddy deserved a hiding most likely," Emmie interrupted calmly. "He must have been very indignant on your behalf. All the same, I do not think that Teddy would really hold it against him. You should hear the way he disciplines his toy soldiers."

Pinky lifted a hand to her brow, and Emmie set about convincing her to take a lie down upstairs with the curtains closed and a damp cloth on her brow. Eventually, Mrs. Cheviot, having heard about the commotion, slipped into the room and added her entreaties to Emmie's.

"Lawks, you must not think anyone blames you for the young master's wildness, Miss Pinson!" she said comfortably as they climbed the stairs together. "He's just showing his Vance blood, that's all. Why you should have seen the tricks he pulled on that old tutor of his. Scant ceremony he showed him, you may be sure!

"Right fond of you, Master Teddy is. I'm sure he'll have some nasty cheap bit of boiled sugar stored for you in his pocket and expect you to forgive him everything when he presents you with it!" She tutted fondly. "The wickedness of the boy! And now his lordship's had to ride all the way to Marston and back, it's too bad of him, really it is! And young Master Clarence and Master Freddie, the vicar's boys, will need bringing back, too, and they'll be in disgrace and the vicar *most* put out by it all!"

They saw Pinky settled comfortably in her old room and Emmie sat in a chair by her bed until her friend lay calm at last. She was on the verge of sleep when she said suddenly in a tired voice, "You'll never guess who I bumped into last night. Walking down my lane past the duck pond."

"Who was it, dear?"

"The Vance ghost," she answered simply, giving Emmie quite a start. "Or one of them at least. The one that foretells misfortune."

"Lady Frances!" Emmie said stunned accents.

Pinky nodded. "She walked right past me in her red dress. Seemed to be in quite a hurry."

"Did she, well, say anything to you?" Emmie asked curiously.

"No. Not a word. Just nodded her head at me. I couldn't quite take it in at the time. I was so surprised by her French hood. By the time I realized why she was dressed that way, she had already passed me, and when I turned about, there was no trace of her at all."

"That was why I was so alarmed when the dear child did not turn up this morning. Are you quite, quite sure that there is nothing to worry about?" she asked, turning fearful eyes on Emmie. "Only, well, the heir to Vance Park has disappeared, and *I saw one of the family ghosts.*"

"Quite sure," Emmie said firmly, reaching over to pat her hand. "You are thinking of our current novel, *The Haunting of Jennings Hall*, which features a lost heir. Don't you remember what Jeremy said? He saw both ghosts himself as a child and nothing too dreadful occurred." At least, she thought that was what he had said. Something about it happening on his twelfth birthday.

Pinky seemed comforted by this thought and closed her eyes again. "Yes, that is doubtless what I am thinking of," she echoed, drifting off into an exhausted sleep, and Emmie crept out of the room to await the others.

After returning to the music room, Emmie took up her novel to distract herself, but Pinky's strange encounter occupied her mind. She walked over to the display case of cameos and examined Lady Frances's and Lady Mary's miniature portraits again.

Now which one of them died young and which died a spinster? She could not remember for the moment. She felt a little jealous that both Pinky and Jeremy should have seen the family ghosts and she had not seen a trace of even one. She must ask Teddy if he ever had, though she felt sure he would have volunteered such information by now, young rascal that he was.

She hoped he did emerge from this scrape unscathed. Jeremy had looked so intractable, despite his words to her friend. Accompanied by his two companions, surely nothing too dire would have befallen the boy. She could not settle to her book, and hearing voices an hour or so later, she threw it down and jumped up as the door opened. It was Jeremy and beside him, a tearful, chastised-looking Teddy.

"Oh, Teddy!" Emmie cried, hurrying to his side. "You are not hurt? Nothing ails you?"

"No, Mama," he sniffed, glancing up at his father. She embraced him briefly and found he was very sticky and rather dusty.

"Then he *was* at the fair at Marston?"

Jeremy nodded. "He was indeed. What do you have to say to your stepmother?"

"I'm sorry, Mama." Teddy's expression was soulful and contrite. His bottom lip quivered.

"I'm very glad to hear it, Teddy," she responded gravely but not unkindly. "Because of your tricks, poor Pinky has blistered her heels and cried herself into a raging headache. She also fell out with a good friend of hers because she refused to believe you could be guilty of such naughtiness."

"I bet it was Colfax," Teddy said resentfully. "He told me I am not allowed to call her Pinky."

"If she did not give you express permission to do so, then he is quite right," Jeremy responded coldly.

"May I see her, Mama?" Teddy appealed.

Emmie hesitated. "She is sleeping now, Teddy," she prevaricated.

"Then no, you may not," Jeremy cut in sternly.

"But I do think it will be a fitful and disturbed sleep until she is assured of Teddy's safe return," Emmie said, seeing Teddy's palpable dismay.

Jeremy gave her a level look. "What do you suggest, then?"

"I think Teddy should be bathed and put in his nightclothes and then allowed to see her for ten minutes only," Emmie said with decision.

Teddy gasped, clutching at his father's sleeve hopefully. "Papa?"

"Very well, but consider yourself extremely fortunate, young man."

"I do. Thank you, Mama," he said politely.

"You will take your supper in the nursery this evening and have an *extremely* early night," Jeremy added.

Teddy lowered his eyes and wished Emmie a subdued "Good night."

Jeremy nodded to her and then escorted his son from the room. Emmie returned to her seat, judging her husband was best placed to deal with this situation without her trailing in their wake. Indeed, she was touched that he had deferred to her judgment at all.

Picking up her book, she tried once more to lose herself in *The Haunting of Jennings Hall*. It was not easy, and when Mrs. Cheviot tiptoed into the room to ask about Master Teddy, she was glad to cast it aside and explain that Colfax's deductions had been proved correct.

Mrs. Cheviot pursed her lips, but there was a decided gleam in her eyes as she retreated, no doubt intent on spreading the word in the servants' quarters. Emmie went up to change before dinner, donning a gown she had not worn before of cream satin decorated with rows of green silk leaves and extravagant pink roses.

She was perhaps a touch overdressed for dining at home, but they *were* expecting guests at dinner—Amos and Nellie Tavistock and the vicar and his wife. Considering what had happened, she supposed the Rylands might not show up, given both their sons were now in disgrace.

It turned out however that the Reverend Ryland and his wife were very keen to attend and assure their hosts that both Clarence and Frederick were receiving appropriate punishment for their part in the crime. Jeremy, when he finally appeared, listened very seriously to what the vicar had to say and then suggested that the boys had succumbed to the promptings of youthful folly rather than any terrible wickedness.

Mrs. Ryland looked visibly relieved, while the vicar squared his shoulders and suggested that his eldest, Clarence, more than likely deserved the lion's share of the blame, as he was the oldest of the three boys and "likely the ringleader." Jeremy refused the opportunity to apportion blame and said he was sure that all three boys must be equally at fault and held accountable, despite Amos Tavistock's determination to make light of the situation, asserting that "boys will be boys" and telling several tales of his own boyhood misdemeanors.

After smiling politely at the older gentleman's exploits, Jeremy explained to the Rylands that Teddy had been sent to bed early and would forfeit the privilege of riding over to his lessons for the foreseeable future. Starting tomorrow, one of the grooms would drop him off and pick him up each day in the trap. Mrs. Ryland opined that Master Teddy would feel this punishment "very keenly," and Jeremy agreed but pointed out that such privileges were earned, and Teddy had showed himself sadly undeserving of such trust.

Reverend Ryland looked much struck by this and sent a few thoughtful glances Emmie's way over the next two courses. When they took their leave at the end of the night, he shook her hand, and told her that he believed she was exerting a beneficial influence over Vance Park. Emmie was startled and wondered if he was referring primarily to the fact they now sat in the Vance family pew every Sunday.

When she voiced this suspicion later, while seated at her dressing table, Jeremy snorted. "More like he attributes my responsible parenting to your improving influence."

Emmie lowered her hairbrush. "Oh, but that's nonsense! You have always been a good father, I am sure."

He nodded. "Yes, I like to think so, but mind you, I never fostered such close contact with the vicarage before now. The vicar never dined here before, so he is probably wholly in ignorance of my excellent parenting."

"He's never dined here before?"

He shook his head. "Amanda was wholly contemptuous of 'provincial company.' It's probably just as well. The one time Edgar Needham dined with us, she drank too much, sat on his lap, and embarrassed the poor lad with her blatant overfamiliarity. The whole thing was an unmitigated disaster."

Emmie found herself remembering Lord Atherton saying Amanda had either issued tantrums or indecent proposals. "I'm sorry to hear that," she said awkwardly.

Jeremy shrugged. "I always knew Amanda was an errant flirt. I have been something of a flirt myself in the past. I've always believed it to be a harmless practice in the main, but then I knew that neither of us would remain remotely faithful in our marriage." Emmie tried to hide her reaction to these words but realized she had failed miserably when he added, "It's often the case in fashionable marriages, Ballentine."

"I wouldn't know anything about that," she answered primly before she could stop herself.

He shrugged. "How about yours?" he asked after a heavy pause.

"Mine?" she asked in confusion. "You mean Humphrey? He was not remotely flirtatious."

For a moment, Jeremy looked as though he had swallowed something rather unpleasant. "You were never married to Stockton, Emmeline," he said tensely. "Must I point that out to you?"

"No, of course not!" She turned in her seat to look at him. "What—then what did you mean?"

"I was harkening back to the subject of fathers," he explained rather tersely.

"Oh. Sorry." She considered the subject, trying to match Jeremy's impartial tone when he said he had been a flirt in the past. Had he flirted with Squire Pebmarsh's daughters? she suddenly wondered, remembering Mrs. Needham's subtle, *insinuating* comments on that subject. Horrid, sly words that were hard to pin down.

Goodness, how she had disliked her! The wretched woman had been smiling the whole time she had voiced her surprise, oh so gently, in Jeremy's choice of *second* bride. It had given Emmie a horrible sort of satisfaction afterward to learn that her predecessor had not cared for her either!

To be fair, it had not only been Mrs. Needham who had hinted at Jeremy's popularity with the opposite sex. Even the vicar's wife had implied that Blanche Pebmarsh had hoped to capture his interest.

With a jolt, Emmie realized that Jeremy was still looking at her expectantly. "Being my father's daughter was not so bad," she said quickly to cover her abstraction, "but I should not have wished to be his employee. In fact, to tell the truth, I could have wished he had done things differently in a fatherly capacity, though he could be entertaining and even pleasant company when he was in a convivial mood."

"What kinds of things would you have liked him to do differently?" he asked at once.

"Well, he could have given me some insight as to his business, for one. He left me in an entirely ridiculous position on his death." Jeremy was silent. "I consider it *his* fault that I made foolish decisions after he had passed," she said indignantly.

"You mean, appointing Stockton as head of Ballentine Trading?" he asked silkily, and Emmie had to force herself not to bristle.

"Yes," she agreed. "In fact, that was *entirely* my father's fault. He told me to do that. It was practically the last thing he said to me." She hesitated. "Though, perhaps I would have done that in any case," she added fairly.

Jeremy looked annoyed. "Did your father tell you to marry him?" he asked confrontationally.

Emmie nearly gasped. Refusing to meet his gaze in the mirror, she shook her head. "Not as such, though he told me I could do a lot worse. I think—I have always thought deep down that he encouraged Humphrey to propose to me."

Jeremy nodded. "I doubt he would have had the nerve to do so if your father had not sanctioned it, but I don't know how you could do much worse than wed a bigamist," he added dryly. "Even I did not manage quite those depths of depravity."

Emmie felt herself turn red. "Of course, Humphrey would never *actually* have married me," she said wretchedly. "That would have been a crime."

Jeremy shook his head. "Must you always rush to his defense?" he asked with disgust.

Emmie set her hairbrush down very carefully. Talking of Humphrey around him was definitely a mistake, she was learning. It had the unfortunate effect of making him antagonistic. "You never said how Teddy's interview with Pinky went," she said brightly, changing the subject. Her voice sounded high and unnatural. "Please tell me."

He did not answer at once, expelling his breath in an irritated hiss of air. "About as well as can be expected under the circumstances," he answered at last. "Teddy climbed on the bed beside her and was most contrite. Miss Pinson wept over him and likely thinks of him as more saintly than ever," he answered irritably. "I fear Mina was right. Your friend is no match for him."

Emmie felt a flash of annoyance and had to tamp it down. Had she not said so from the very first? And he had refused to listen to her! Pointing this out now would doubtless be a mistake, so instead she bit her tongue. "You will never guess who Pinky met last night," she carried on, her steely calmness sounding artificial even to her own ears.

He scrutinized her for a moment before responding. "Who?"

"Lady Frances Vance."

"Lady—?" Jeremy looked startled, sitting up.

"Yes, one of the family ghosts." She nodded. "She met her in the lane, and Lady Frances nodded to her."

Jeremy, who had looked as though he was about to dismiss this as so much nonsense, hesitated. "She nodded?" he asked slowly.

"Yes. Pinky said before she could register who it was, she had passed her by, and then you know, when she looked back over her shoulder, she was gone. Vanished into thin air."

"Extraordinary," Jeremy murmured. "But then, I suppose she *is* practically a Vance by this point."

"Is that what she did when you saw her? Nodded, I mean."

He opened his mouth and then shut it again. "That was all a very long time ago," he said dismissively. "I'm sure I can hardly remember it now." His answer, Emmie was convinced, was a barefaced lie.

"Why do you suppose Pinky saw her now?" she persisted, unable to hide her curiosity. "I am quite convinced she did, you know. She said she noticed her red dress and French hood and feared it was some terrible portent."

"Her *red* dress?" he repeated carefully, then gave a short laugh. "Well, there you have it. Miss Pinson did not receive a dire warning from Lady Frances at all. She saw her sister. She needs to put her wedding cake back under her pillow."

"You mean—?" Emmie gasped.

"Who knows? Maybe Lady Mary was simply feeling bored and mischievous." He climbed off the bed and sauntered over to the connecting door. "Do you know, I feel rather tired this evening. I believe I'll retire early."

Emmie shrugged her shoulder. "As you wish, my lord."

He narrowed his eyes at her, one hand on the door handle. "Doubtless you are tired after all the excitement of the day," he said with icy politeness.

"Doubtless *you* are, you mean," she corrected him. "The ride to Marston and back must have put you *quite* out of temper."

He huffed again. "It was not the ride that put me out of temper," he retorted, then seemed to bite back his next words. He stood there for a moment, seemingly waging some inward war with himself. Emmie watched him closely. He was trying to avoid saying anything else contentious, she decided.

"Will you make me a promise, Ballentine?" he asked casually, though she could tell from his bearing that he was not remotely at his ease. "Will you promise me that we will have no more talk of Stockton for at least, oh, I don't know, a calendar month, say?"

Emmie regarded him speechlessly. He spoke as though she was always raising the subject of her former fiancé! She had only mentioned him now because she had misunderstood his question. And in any case, had not Jeremy mentioned him first? Seeing her husband's raised brow, she roused herself to answer his request. "Very gladly!" she responded tartly.

He slammed the door after him and Emmie was strongly tempted to cross the room and lock it after him!

28

The next morning dawned, wet and rainy. By the time Emmie awoke, Jeremy had already departed for the stables. She checked with Lottie. The addition of Teddy and Pinky at the breakfast table did nothing to enliven proceedings for both were red-eyed and restrained this morning, speaking mostly to one another in low voices.

After breakfast, Emmie heard a knock on her sitting room door and the pair of them walked in. Teddy presented Emmeline with a picture he had drawn of Heracles and Iphicles with their snakes. No longer represented as infants, both bulged with muscle and wore brightly colored loincloths.

"Thank you, Teddy," she said, admiring the drawing. "They look a very able pair of heroes."

"Yes," he agreed, leaning over her chair. "This one is Iphicles. As you can see, his muscles are *slightly* smaller than his brother's, but to make up for it I have given him the bigger of the two snakes."

"Yes, and you have given Heracles a small beard I see."

Teddy nodded and looked pleased she had caught his attention to detail. Pinky cleared her throat, giving her charge a significant look. "May I drive Miss Pinson back to Plumtree Cottage this afternoon, Mama?" Teddy asked tentatively.

"No, Teddy," Emmie responded quietly. "I am afraid not." Both looked instantly crestfallen. "Pinky will give you your lesson this morning and then one of the grooms will drive her back after lunch. Now you run along to the nursery. I want to have a quick word with Miss Pinson before she joins you there."

Teddy looked disappointed but resigned as he heaved a heavy sigh and walked out of the room, casting a reproachful look back over his shoulder as he went.

Emmie motioned for Pinky to be seated. "How are you feeling this morning, Hannah?"

"Oh, absolutely recovered!" her friend assured her. "Thank you for letting the dear child see me last night, his lordship explained it was at your insistence."

"You are more than welcome, and I am very glad to hear you are feeling better."

"Yes." Hannah twisted her hands. "I only hope that Teddy's punishment will not be too severe. We all know he is a delicate child and—"

"Hannah, I must interrupt you there. I believe we must trust my husband's judgment when it comes to reprimanding Teddy for his misbehavior. After all, he knows him best and it seems this is not the first time his high spirits have led him astray. Although he has been ill, I think he must be practically recovered by now if recent events are to be taken into consideration."

Pinky pressed her lips together and Emmie continued calmly, "You cannot have forgotten that awful family in Yorkshire, where the children were so indulged and spoiled that you could do nothing with them. We would not want Teddy to end up like that, now, would we?"

Pinky sat wide-eyed for a moment, words clearly struggling to burst from her lips. Finally, she bowed her head. "Yes, perhaps you are right," she said in a choked voice. "It is just that, well, he has grown very dear to me."

"I know." Emmie smiled. "And I am glad for it. But we must not allow our partiality to blind us to the fact he needs firm guidance. You told me yourself that you believe Jeremy to be a good and fond father."

"Oh yes, I do," Pinky agreed at once.

"Well, then."

Her friend sighed. "He was very kind to set my mind at rest. I hope I did not offend him."

"You did not offend him in any way," Emmie assured her. "Colfax, however, is a different matter." Pinky turned rather pink. "I will not say any more on the subject for I know this new friendship is not one you yourself have raised with me."

Pinky looked alarmed. "Oh! Well…it is so lately sprung up and you have been so busy," she prevaricated.

"We both have," Emmie agreed.

Pinky's eyes met hers. "Do you think I have offended Colfax, then?"

"I think you have hurt his feelings, yes."

"Hurt his feelings?" She faltered.

"You were rather cutting, dear," Emmie said gently.

Pinky pressed her hands to her reddening cheeks and did not speak for a moment. "I was so upset, you see," she said jerkily. "I confess, I do not altogether recall precisely *what* I said in the heat of the moment." She lowered her hands. "I was so afraid for Teddy, and I had the greatest conviction that it hardly mattered what I said, for Colfax was not attending a single word.

"I could tell from the look on his face." She sent a fleeting look at Emmie. "Men have looked at me with that expression all my life," she said, startling her considerably. "Your father, Mr. Stockton, all of them. I knew Colfax was going to do what he thought was right, and devil take my opinion on the matter."

Emmie sat back in her seat, quite startled. She had never heard her former governess speak of the devil in anything but biblical settings. "Perhaps you are right," she heard herself say slowly. "He was certainly very sure of himself."

"They always are," Pinky replied with just a hint of bitterness, but it was clear her mind was elsewhere. They sat in silence for a moment. Then Pinky admitted fairly, "Though in this case, it turned out Colfax had good cause."

"You should have told me Humphrey was dismissive of you, Hannah," Emmie said, still shocked. She always knew, of course, that her father had thought Pinky a poor, insipid creature, but *Humphrey*! That was an altogether different matter.

"Oh, but that's nothing out of the ordinary." Pinky shrugged. "You and Teddy and, I think, Lord Faris are the only ones who have ever thought my opinion counts for anything."

Emmie's shoulders relaxed slightly. She remembered the flash of hurt in Colfax's eyes before he had rushed from the room. "I think perhaps that Colfax cares about your opinion too," she said carefully. "He has known Teddy far longer than us, and you have to admit his instincts were right in this instance. His reaction was likely so strong because he did not like seeing you so upset over it. He, well, my husband has mentioned to me previously that Colfax holds you in high regard."

"Lord Faris said that?" Pinky asked, looking flattered. "Well, in that case, I will have to think of some way of making amends. It is true he has given up his precious leave to help tame my garden," she added guiltily. "And I did berate and scold him as though he was one of my charges."

Emmie gave a weak laugh. "You have never scolded me in anything but the mildest of tones, Hannah dear, and I'll wager Teddy has never been berated by you in such a fashion either!"

Pinky blinked. "No, I suppose not," she conceded sheepishly. "I can't think what came over me."

"Your protective instincts maybe," Emmie suggested. "And perhaps you felt comfortable enough to give vent to your feelings with Colfax."

Hannah smoothed her skirts but made no comment. "I should probably go and find him," she said, "and get my apology out of the way before I start on Teddy's lessons."

"He's not here this week, remember?"

"Oh, but surely he won't have gone to work on the cottage after the way I treated him!" Pinky cried.

"I think you'll find he has."

"Oh! Oh dear…" her friend fretted.

"I am sure he will still be there this afternoon," Emmie said with a smile. "And by then, you may have decided how to make it up to him." For a moment she thought of the ghost in the red dress but pushed it from her mind. "Perhaps you could make him your famous seed cake?" she suggested. "Jeremy enjoyed it very much."

Pinky brightened. "Yes, I could certainly try that," she agreed. She cast a distracted eye over the painting Teddy had gifted to Emmie. "I must ask his lordship if he would lend me one of his books on ancient mythology," she muttered. "Really, I am terribly ignorant on the subject. Do you know, the other day, Teddy charged across my lawn, launched himself into a pile of grass cuttings and yelled 'I'm a snake-taming baby called Sophocles!' I hardly knew how to respond."

"Iphicles," Emmie corrected her automatically.

"I beg your pardon?"

"The snake-taming baby. Its name was Iphicles, not Sophocles. Well," she added conscientiously, "he didn't tame them precisely."

"What did he do, then?" Poor Pinky asked, looking quite bewildered.

"As I understand it, he cried."

"Well, I must say, that seems a good deal more typical behavior for a baby."

Emmie laughed; she couldn't help it. After a moment, a little uncertainly, Pinky joined in.

Her friend had not long left her for the nursery when the maid Bridget tapped on the sitting room door. Emmie had just started on her second letter to the Hardimans and set this aside as the maid approached with a folded letter.

"This was sent over from the inn, milady."

"The inn?"

"The Prizefighter," she elaborated, naming her in-law's coaching inn.

Emmie took it, wondering if it was a note from her sister-in-law encouraging her to stop by. She had never taken her up on her previous offer to call on them. Turning it over, she suffered a nasty shock, for the handwriting was horribly familiar. *Humphrey!* What on earth could he be doing at Mina and Nye's inn? And why would he be writing to her? Her heart thumping in her breast, she thanked Bridget, opened the envelope, and smoothed out the page.

Dear Emmeline,

I hope you will believe me when I write that in spite of everything, I devoutly hope this letter finds you well. I have found it incumbent upon me, for several reasons, to travel down to this part of the world and seek out assurance on this matter.

You cannot possibly know the agonies of remorse that I have suffered these past three months, how much I have reproached myself with, and how racked I have been by guilt for the role I played in the situation in which you now find yourself.

Needless to say, shame has dogged my every step since I last saw you. As you know, the sad demise of Ballentine Trading has left me without occupation, so you may picture how I have trudged the streets ever since looking for suitable employment.

You may imagine my surprise when bumping into one of the old clerks, Harold Hillman, I learned that he and the other employees had received a sizeable sum by way of reparation for the abrupt loss of their income. Not only this, but that some mysterious nobleman had involved himself in the affair.

I expressed my astonishment, but Harold would not, or could not, tell me anything more on the matter. Instead, I was forced to seek out one John Hardiman, who I knew you always held in some regard. You may think this a strange thing to do, but there was some other matter I had with the man, namely the need for a character reference.

However, once I had gone to the trouble to arrange this interview, instead of shedding light on the matter, Hardiman turned around and demanded a series of answers to such extraordinary questions that I hardly knew where to put myself!

From his discourse, I gathered that you had subsequently rushed into marriage with none other than a peer of the realm! However, I could find out nothing further, for when I could offer no explanation for the turn of events, he became outraged with me, refused to write me my reference, and ordered me from his presence!

I need hardly say how truly astounded I was to learn you had married so precipitately, without taking counsel from your friends. Much shocked and mortified by Hardiman's conduct, I was left with no other recourse but to travel to your former address in Bath to beg a forwarding address from your old landlady who I had met on one or two occasions. She coldly refused my request, doubting you would welcome further communication from me and moreover claiming she had no information to impart!

Her callous attitude quite shocked me, and sadly, I had no option but to encourage the confidences of that impertinent maid of hers, who, at considerable cost to my pocketbook, showed to me an extravagant wedding cake box embossed with a crest and the names of Lord and Lady Faris of Vance Park in Penarth, Cornwall.

Finally, I had your direction, however unlikely it sounded, and you may be sure that I deliberated a good deal on the proper way to proceed. Only after consulting my dear Clara did I feel emboldened to pursue a course of action which culminated in my traveling all the way to Cornwall to secure my peace of mind. The dear helpmeet of my life agreed that it was only right that I assured myself of your subsequent safety and well-being.

Will you meet with me, Emmeline? I have taken a room at a coaching inn which I understand to be a mere matter of miles from your new residence. I can stay three days. Despite some initial misgivings, the place seems to be moderately respectable, and I can hire a private parlor for our meeting.

I apologize for the suddenness of my request and hope you will not be too surprised by my appearance in the locality. I wronged you, I know, but is it too much to hope that you might absolve me of some of this grievous burden I bear and set my mind to rest?

I will wait with much anxiety of spirit to hear back from you.

Yours respectfully,

Humphrey Stockton

Emmie lowered the page, her mouth dry and her heart racing. She could not *believe* Humphrey was here in Penarth! That he had traveled all this way, and to what purpose! She could not make it out precisely from his long-winded letter. To secure her forgiveness? For her to absolve him of any wrongdoing? Either would be absurd, it could not be so.

She read it a second time and could not help but decide his purpose was twofold. He wanted for her to both appease his own conscience, and to assuage his vulgar curiosity. She shook her head with disbelief. On top of that, she had a sneaking suspicion that if he had heard she was still living on a pittance in Bath she would not have heard one word from the man!

She sat there a moment, deep in thought. What if Humphrey should ask one of the staff at The Prizefighter if they knew anyone from Vance Park? Would they tell him of the proprietor's connection to Jeremy? That could be awkward. She would not really want her in-laws to know she was formerly engaged for ten years to another man.

Her blood ran cold when she remembered how Jeremy flew off the handle when even the subject of Humphrey was raised. How awkward this all was! She could hardly dash off a clandestine note to Humphrey and arrange to meet him at her own sister-in-law's establishment. Even writing to refuse such a meeting seemed fraught with difficulty.

What if he should show up here, demanding an interview with her? After traveling such a distance, it seemed unlikely that he would meekly turn about and leave with his tail tucked between his legs. She started out of her chair, then sat back down again. Should she consult Pinky? She at least *knew* Humphrey and could perhaps offer some impartial advice.

Then she remembered what Pinky had told her that very morning. That Humphrey had treated her greatest friend dismissively and she felt even more indignant that he should show up now, demanding answers about her own conduct. The nerve of the man!

What to do though? That was the quandary. Only last night, Jeremy had asked her to promise there would be no more talk of Humphrey between them for at least a month. And here she was today, in receipt of a letter from him, no less. She bit her thumbnail, frozen with indecision. Drat the man!

She stood and walked to the connecting door, knocking on it tentatively. There was no answer. He must be at the stables as was his habit. After a pause, she opened the door and walked through into Jeremy's bedchamber. She was practically tiptoeing, which was ridiculous, but she could not help but think herself something of an intruder.

All was as she remembered it from that awful night. The bronze horse figurines, the painting of Venus, lots of dark wood. This time, she ventured further than his bedroom, into the adjoining room which contained a desk and several sitting chairs. Making for his desk, she picked up a pen and wrote him a note on his own headed paper.

Dear Jeremy,

Please see the enclosed letter from Mr. Stockton. I am setting out now for Mina's inn and will take Lottie with me to act as chaperone. I will meet with him as he suggests in one of the downstairs rooms. If you return at lunchtime perhaps you will come and join us? If it is not too late, that is.

Please be assured that as soon as I have dismissed ~~Humph~~ Mr. Stockton's concerns, and sent him on his way, I will return home. Please do not worry. I will see you soon.

Your ever-loving wife,

Emmeline

Folding Humphrey's letter inside her covering note, she stuffed both inside an envelope and addressed it simply "Jeremy." Then she stood for a moment, unsure where best to put it so that it would catch his attention. After all, he might not venture as far as his desk.

Wandering back through to his bedroom, she debated setting it on his pillow. Then again, when he returned for lunch, he never took a nap. His purpose, after all, was to change out of his riding clothes. Inspiration struck, and she tried a door which led to his dressing room and propped the envelope on his dresser.

Then she escaped back into her own room to track down Lottie and explain their errand.

29

Jeremy spent a discontented morning at the racing stables. He felt irritated with himself, let alone Masterman, who kept trying to discuss their prospects for an upcoming race. For some reason, Jeremy just could *not* focus this morning. He turned away from Atalanta's trainer with a curt nod. "Carry on," he said briskly, then turned to his stable manager. "I'll watch the rest from the office."

Masterman looked taken aback by this unusual decision, but before he could voice his surprise, Jeremy made his escape and headed for the office they shared, which overlooked the exercise yard. Once inside, he turned the key in the lock. He wasn't fit for company presently.

Throwing himself into the captain's style seat, he swiveled around to face the window, but though his eyes followed Amyas being put through his paces, his thoughts were a million miles away. He should have spent the night in Emmeline's arms, not pacing his own room like a caged tiger.

The trouble was, he had not felt in a worshipful mood, and he knew by now that he could not trust himself to keep things respectful or to keep a guard on what might come tumbling out of his unprincipled mouth. Not when he was feeling the way he did.

He had been a good deal too…rough with her the previous morning. One did not fuck one's viscountess over a table, even if it was in their private dining quarters. He groaned, dropping his head and massaging his temples as he tried not to remember how she had felt beneath him, how she had responded, how hard he had come. *My God.*

It was no use. He would *never* forget it. He never wanted to, even though he should. Even though he *must*. Emmeline deserved to feel cherished and adored, nothing less. Not after the appalling way he had treated her in the past. Anything less might make her doubt the sincerity of his feelings. And sadly, the events of the past couple of months had shown she *did* harbor doubts when it came to him.

And who could blame her? Certainly not him. Their history had shown only too well how little he was to be depended on. He would never, ever forget the way she had broken down that night. Clenching his fist, he vowed he must *never* allow himself free rein to upset her like that again. That meant leaving her presence whenever he felt dangerous words hovering on his tongue. It meant walking away when he wanted to give vent to the fiery jealousy that burned in his chest.

And yet, Ballentine looked so magnificent when her eyes were bright and flashing and her cheeks flushed pink with indignation. He loved it when she went toe-to-toe and pushed *back* at him. It had been so hard to walk away last night when she had accused him of being "out of temper" and had snapped back at him. His lips curved upward involuntarily when he remembered her cross delivery of her "very gladly!"

He wanted *so* badly to have a blazing row with her. An honest-to-God confrontation where the bitterness burned clean away. Then he could fall on her and slake his lust on her, and tell her, just *tell* once and for all how much he had always loved her. Deep down, he had this strange conviction that if he could only *confess* how things had always been with him, then all would be well.

Except, he knew full well that was not the case. He couldn't really understand *why* he had this lurking feeling that it would. Every flare-up with Emmeline had revealed how deeply the hurt he had caused her ran. He dared not jeopardize this second chance he'd secured with her by the skin of his teeth. He could *not* lose her again.

His instincts when it came to the love of his life were frankly undependable and all over the place. He supposed some men must just have better natures than the one he was blessed with. Perhaps their words, instead of turning cutting and sharp, were always mild and measured when they spoke to the ones they loved. They probably never longed to slam doors or shout or stoke fires when they should appease, conciliate, and apologize.

Presumably he inherited such impulses from his late father. The old man had been a bad-tempered bastard with an ungovernable temper. He supposed it was not surprising that beneath his mother's looks, the contentious Vance blood surged through his veins.

Really, he should embrace this new lifestyle of mannerly and good behavior, he thought bleakly. His rows with Amanda had been ugly and acrimonious. They had never brought about anything remotely resembling harmony. Neither had they inspired him with anything more than disgust for the both of them.

The only thing he had required of his first wife was she gave him a son before she saw fit to take the first of many lovers. At the time, Amanda had been furious; she had been insulted, beyond repair by his "vile insinuations" about her character. She had even moved out of his London townhouse to stay with her married sister in Kent for a couple of weeks in high dudgeon, sending him many hysterical letters on the subject.

When he had not responded, her mother, Lady Tipton, had sent Amanda's brother, the honorable Hugo, to pay Jeremy a visit. Jeremy had been frank with his brother-in-law, explaining how he had found her dishabille in a clinch with his friend George Lister. Her brother had been embarrassed; her mother furious.

Amanda had cried and blamed Lister, had blamed too much champagne, had blamed Jeremy's callous neglect. Jeremy had agreed, the champagne had been flowing freely, Lister was a personable chap, and it was true that he *was* more than just a little bored of his wife's company. By this point, they had been married two whole months.

In the end, he had spoken plainly, explained that he would voice no objection to Amanda's having affairs, provided she give him *first* his heir and a spare. He believed he was being entirely reasonable in the matter. Her brother, Hugo, had been forced to agree. A week later, Amanda had rejoined him back in London. The subject was glossed over and when it was later confirmed that she had fallen pregnant, they had both been pleased and relieved by the outcome.

Once the pregnancy was underway, it had not taken long for relations between himself and Amanda to devolve entirely. Lister had fled London, mortified, despite Jeremy's assurances on the matter. Despite Lister's defection, Amanda had found no shortness in admirers. Jeremy accepted it was unlikely he would receive a legitimate spare to accompany his heir, and had instead followed his own inclinations, which had included an opera singer or two. They had lived largely separate lives whilst residing under the same London roof.

They had carried on this way until six months later when, shortly after Teddy's birth, his father's unexpected death meant Jeremy had succeeded to the title. He had then made it plain that he would not tolerate her bringing "London ways" to Cornwall. At Vance Park, he expected them both to present a respectable front.

Amanda had laughed at his hypocrisy. Why should they care what his Cornish neighbors and tenants thought of how they lived their lives? She would not lower herself by making such a pretense for the benefit of a bunch of yokels.

Jeremy had then assured her that in that case she was welcome to stay in London. She had been furious at the implication that she, his viscountess, was not welcome at his family seat. Things had become poisonous for a while until her desire to play mistress of Vance had finally won out and she had agreed that any house parties would not include any of her cicisbeo.

Those had been the lines upon which his first marriage had operated. Was it surprising that he had a somewhat warped view of how these things worked? He supposed, thinking back, that he and Amanda had at least been mostly honest with one another, if nothing else.

It was odd how much he yearned to bare his black soul to Ballentine. He longed to discuss their misguided past. He wanted so badly to explain why that stupid, lonely, spoiled, and neglected nineteen-year-old had wrought such wanton havoc on her life. Then, maybe against all the odds, she could understand him, even forgive him and eventually come to like him again.

For she had liked him, once upon a time. It had *not* just been his money or connections or social standing. Emmeline had lit up for him when he entered a room. She had *glowed* when he approached her. She had eyes for no one but him when he was in her orbit, and he had bloody loved it.

But it had been wildly unrealistic of him to think he could ever get that back. Trying to tease her, as he had in the old days, trying so desperately to get back onto the same footing they had once shared had been both arrogant and miscalculated. Emmeline had been right. Those days were over and ought to be allowed to fade into the past.

That conservatory he had hired Wimble to build, God, yet another horrendous blunder. She would be *appalled* to learn that he had thought such a thing would be an appropriate bride-gift. His stupidity almost took his breath away. For him, that night was a treasured memory but for her...the polar opposite.

He would get Wimble to convert his plans into an orangery. Or would that still be offensive? Jeremy did not really know at this point. His poor character was doubtless to blame. He breathed out. The sad fact was, he needed to ignore the promptings of his heart when it came to his wife.

Instead, he should be grateful for what she *did* allow him. Living a life of stifled politeness was a small price to pay if it ensured Emmeline's continued presence in it. Standing up from the chair, he decided to make his way back to the house a little early today.

That way he could smooth things over with Emmeline before luncheon and show himself in his most amenable light. She would be relieved to see he could be reasonable and correct his behavior given time to reflect on his many failings. She would see that marrying him was not a huge lapse of judgment on her part.

Returning to the house, his heart still heavy, he found Teddy taking his leave of Miss Pinson on the front steps. He hailed the lady and asked about the morning's lessons, eyeing his son sternly all the while. She was quick to assure him that Teddy had been most assiduous to his books and Teddy stood looking chastened and meek.

Jeremy professed himself glad to hear it and they waved her off as the carriage swept down the drive bearing her back to Plumtree Cottage. Teddy, eyeing his father shrewdly as they reentered the house, expressed a desire to return to his nursery for a quiet afternoon, for he did not feel like joining the others for luncheon, especially if Mama was not here for it.

Jeremy paused on the bottom step. "Mama is not here for lunch?" he repeated. His mind raced. Had he forgotten some engagement?

"No," Teddy replied, bounding up the staircase before him. "She took Lottie with her but will be back before dinner."

Jeremy followed him up the stairs with a frown on his face and they parted ways at the top, as Teddy made for his nursery and Jeremy turned toward his own rooms. Where could she have gone? Into St. Ives? She had expressed a wish to explore that little town. Maybe she thought he would skip lunch again today and she could not face such dreary company without him?

That thought perked him up a little but then instantly he felt annoyed that he had not thought to invite her to lunch in St. Ives himself. He knew just the spot she would enjoy. Now, he would have to sit opposite Wimble and Penrose for his sins and reflect further on his own shortcomings.

Tugging at his cravat, he walked through to his dressing room and saw the envelope propped up on his chest of drawers.

30

Emmeline thanked the fresh-faced young maid, who bobbed a curtsey, nodded to Lottie, and then trotted out of the small parlor to let Humphrey know that Lady Faris awaited him below in one of the private parlors.

"Do you know her?" Emmie asked nervously as Lottie settled herself unobtrusively into a corner seat.

"Corin? Oh yes, her family's lived in these parts for years. Nice girl. She was in domestic service at Vance Park for a while, though it was before your time, mind you."

"Really? She looks very young." Emmie sat down, then stood up again. What *was* the etiquette for meeting with a former suitor who turned out to have been married the whole time? She did not think any manual on manners would cover quite such an eventuality.

Lottie was looking about the place with lively interest. "Have you ever visited this inn before?" Emmie asked her, nervously clasping her hands together. She was wearing a new pair of kid gloves embroidered with her initials E.V. Suddenly she remembered how the debutantes would whisper about "the hidden language of gloves."

All she could remember now was that flinging one over your shoulder meant "follow me" and wearing one hanging halfway off your left hand meant indifference. Or was it the right hand? She couldn't quite recall. Maybe she should drag one halfway off to let Humphrey know how little she cared for him these days?

"I've never been here before," Lottie replied cheerfully. "My old mum never quite liked the place, on account of its former associations. Course, it's gone quite respectable now. In spite of the prizefighting what's held here on the second Friday of every month. Quite nice, isn't it? I like the horse brasses. Polished up nice and bright, aren't they?"

Lottie's prattle soothed Emmie's spirits, and she agreed that yes, the room looked very clean and cheerful despite the dark wooden screen and elaborately etched glass. She felt a little guilty that this, her first visit, was being conducted on such surreptitious terms.

She had not seen her sister-in-law, but she had caught a glimpse of William Nye through an open door to the tap room. She did not think he had seen her though. She hoped he had not, in any case. Emmie felt furtive and underhand but really, it was much better this way.

If she could just send Humphrey on his way before Jeremy so much as heard he was in the neighborhood, then the whole business could be over and done with before it could cause them too much fuss and pother. A knock on the door had Emmie whipping around to face it.

"Come in," she called, her voice not quite steady, but to her surprise, it was not Humphrey, but William Nye who stood in the doorway, a tea towel flung over his shoulder and his shirt sleeves rolled up to his elbows.

"Lady Faris," he said, clearing his throat.

Emmie tried not to look as horrified by his appearance as she felt. "Mr. Nye!"

"Thought I recognized the carriage outside," he said.

"Really? But I did not bring the one with the crest," she said and then blushed guiltily.

One dark eyebrow shot up at this rejoinder, but he made no comment on this. "Thought you might want to know, we've got a private parlor for family use," he said, angling a thumb over his shoulder. "Want me to show it to you? I'm sure you'd be more comfortable in there."

"Oh." Emmie's face fell. "That's very kind of you, but you see, I am not here as family today but rather at one of your patron's requests." She flushed at her clumsy explanation. "I should not want our business to intrude on family quarters," she said earnestly. "It wouldn't be right."

"One of my patrons?" he repeated blankly. He looked from her to Lottie, and back, then came into the room, shutting the door carefully behind him. "Which one would that be?"

"You, er, you wouldn't know him!" Emmie gasped. "He's, well, he's come from London."

Nye's eyes narrowed and he seemed to come to some decision. "You," he said, pointing to Lottie. "Go and wait for your mistress outside in the public parlor. Tell Corin to fetch you a glass of port, on the house."

"Ooh lovely!" Lottie said, rising with alacrity and making for the door. "Thanks ever so!"

Emmie's heart sank. "Oh, er…"

Nye faced her with a shrewd gleam in his eye. "London?" he said pointedly. "Fussy-looking fellow, pudding faced? What business has he with you? Blackmail?"

Emmie sank onto the wooden bench, feeling quite drained. "No!" she protested. "No, of c-course not!"

"Don't think I'm judging," he said, shrugging a massive shoulder. "That brother of mine has plenty of dirty linen of his own. Only I can't let you meet with some shady customer under my own roof, now, can I? Not in good conscience."

"You won't let me meet with him?" Emmie cried in dismay. "But you must! He'll be down at any moment!"

"Not without me present," he clarified, folding his arms. "I'll just stand quietly by. I won't speak a word or get in your way. I'll just be here to make sure there's fair play. I'll be like one of those footmen of yours up at the Park," he said, looking pleased with his sudden inspiration. "You must be used to those cluttering up the place by now."

Emmie regarded him, aghast. His hulking presence looked *nothing* like a footman. "You don't understand! Humphrey, well, he…" A tap at the door made her jump. "This must be him now!" she hissed.

Nye turned pointedly aside, producing a glass from somewhere which he started polishing unhurriedly with his tea towel. "Er, come in," Emmie quavered, given very little choice in the matter. The door opened and Humphrey came in, wearing his best navy suit and red waistcoat.

"*Emmie!*" he exclaimed, his voice swelling with emotion. To her consternation he made straight for her.

Unnerved, she retreated until she had put the table between them again. "Good morning, Mr. Stockton," she said freezingly. "I'm afraid my husband could not accompany me this morning as he is occupied with business presently, but I have my brother-in-law here with me to, er, ensure all is decent."

Humphrey finally noticed Nye lurking in the corner of the room and visibly flinched. "But, this, er, is surely the landlord of this establishment, is it not?" He faltered, quickly looking away.

"That is also correct," Emmie conceded.

Humphrey looked extremely disconcerted. "I do not understand," he said flatly.

"Will you not sit down?" Emmie asked pointedly. If he sat down, then so could she. With a show of some reluctance, Humphrey lowered himself onto the wooden bench opposite her and Emmie did likewise.

"What are you *doing* here, Humphrey?" she asked forthrightly. "I confess, I am quite at a loss."

"Doing here?" Humphrey repeated incredulously. "Did I not explain, at great length, in my heartfelt letter to you on the subject?"

"I could scarcely make head nor tail of it," Emmie said, lifting her chin. "But I recall quite well our final meeting when you rushed from the room after confessing your prior *connection* to another." She sent a quick glance at William Nye, whose ankles were now crossed and whose gaze was fixed on the lamp fitting.

"You ordered me to leave!" Humphrey retorted indignantly. "You refused to let me explain myself further!"

"I did not wish to hear your excuses," Emmie said frigidly. "And what's more, I still don't!"

Humphrey gulped. Clearly, their interview was not going as he would have wished. He extracted a handkerchief from his pocket and mopped his brow. "Will you not try and see things from my viewpoint?" he appealed.

"You played me for a fool," Emmie said tightly. "For *ten* years. What more remains to be said?"

"I… Well, if you do not require explanations, perhaps I do!" he expostulated. "Who is this mysterious nobleman, for one! That's what I want to know!" At his vehement tone, Nye uncrossed his ankles and straightened up. Humphrey eyed him nervously. When he spoke again, his voice was more restrained. "Clara told me he claimed to be a Count Stevens when he showed up, demanding the return of your letters, but then I find out you are married to a Viscount Faris!"

"They are one and the same," Emmie said with dignity. "Count Stefano is my husband's alias when he wishes to employ discretion."

Humphrey spluttered. "And what about Hillman and the others receiving compensation?" he continued with an injured air. "Whereas I could not even get a letter of recommendation! What about—?"

Whatever he had been about to utter, they were never to know, for at that moment, the door burst open, and Jeremy came in with a face like thunder, seized a hold of Humphrey, hauled him from his chair, and punched him square in the face.

Emmie covered her mouth with her hand and sat transfixed with horror as Humphrey dropped like a stone and lay groaning on the floor with a bloodied nose. Seemingly unsatisfied with this, Jeremy immediately pounced on him and dragged him to his knees, apparently intent on punching him a second time.

"Mercy!" shrieked Humphrey.

"Jeremy!" Emmie cried, finally finding her voice. "Please stop!" When her words fell on apparently deaf ears, she turned to William Nye, who was watching proceedings with interest. "Oh, can't you stop him?" she appealed.

"Seems a shame to do that," Nye answered.

Finding her feet, Emmie rounded the table and tugged at Jeremy's shoulder. "Please stop, my lord," she sobbed. "For my sake."

With some reluctance, Jeremy released Humphrey's shirt and let the poor wretch drop back to the ground. Stepping over him, he turned to face the fireplace, gripping the mantelpiece and catching his breath.

"Give him a moment," Nye advised when Emmie took a step toward him. "His blood's still up." He walked over to Humphrey and, catching hold of his jacket, dragged him over to a chair in the corner and deposited him there, where he sat slumped, pale and shaken. "I'll fetch some brandy," Nye said and left the room.

Emmie approached Jeremy cautiously. For the first time, she noticed he still wore his riding garb. He must have come straight here after reading her letter. Maybe it had been a mistake to leave that for him. Throwing caution to the wind, she threw her arms around his waist. "Don't be angry with me," she begged. "I thought—"

A footfall sounded in the doorway, and Emmie took a step back as another maid, older than the first, swept into the room with a bowl of water and some cloths. This one had a pinched, disapproving face as her eyes travelled over the room. "Thought it was fight night next week!" she exclaimed with disfavor, crossing the room to administer to Humphrey. "What a mess! Bleeding all over my nice clean floor!"

Humphrey gave a muffled sound of pain as she tended to his face, and Jeremy turned from the fireplace at last. "My apologies, Edna," he said. "It won't happen again." Reaching into his jacket, he extracted his wallet and set a couple of notes on the table. "For recompense," he said. "Add it to your Crown Derby tea fund."

Edna looked somewhat mollified by this. "Handsome of you, milord," she acknowledged and left Humphrey's side to tuck the money into her apron. "I'll just go and fetch my mop. Not much more I can do for 'im. His nose is broke."

Humphrey gave another anguished moan and Nye stepped into the room with a bottle of brandy and three glasses. "Broken, is it?" he asked with a gleam of approval. "Thought it might be."

Emmie turned anxious eyes on Jeremy, but he still would not meet her gaze. Nye sloshed brandy into the glasses and handed one to her and Jeremy and then one to Humphrey, who tried to refuse it, but had it pressed into his hand anyway.

"Well, Stockton," Jeremy said, setting down his own glass untouched. "I think we had better reach some resolution here. I'll make it plain, if you ever show your face in this part of the country again, I'll see you prosecuted."

Emmie, who had been taking a cautious sip of brandy, lowered her glass. "And I will have charges brought for attempted marriage fraud and breach of contract!" she added with spirit.

"Me prosecuted?" Humphrey squawked. "Lord Faris here has just committed an offence against my person! In front of two witnesses no less!"

"I think you'll find that neither one of them will testify on your behalf," Jeremy said mildly, "though I do see your point. Very well, I will amend my position. If you show up again hereabouts, I'll see to it that you never bother my wife or anyone else ever again. It would not be too difficult for me to arrange," he added thoughtfully. "As is often the case in provincial places such as these, the word of the local liege lord is considered tantamount to law."

Humphrey's jaw dropped. "I—you—" he spluttered in nasal tones. "You are threatening me! This is outrageous!"

"No," Jeremy said patiently. "What is outrageous is you contacting another man's wife and writing her a *damnably* impertinent letter."

Humphrey shot a resentful look at Emmie. "That was not meant for your eyes, my lord!"

"I can well believe it," Jeremy responded dryly.

"I—I had some very real concerns that induced me to write that letter," Humphrey insisted, clasping the bloodied cloth to his nose. "I assure you, my motivation was pure!"

"Then let us deal with your *concerns*, once and for all," Jeremy said, producing the letter and unfolding it. His eyes scanned the first few lines contemptuously. "I am not a peer of the realm, by the way, as I have never been appointed to the House of Lords."

Humphrey sniffed, though whether that was due to his nosebleed or any other emotion, Emmie could not say. Jeremy returned to the letter, quoting aloud, "'I need hardly say how truly astounded I was to learn you had married so precipitately, without taking counsel from your friends.'" He lowered the letter. "To which friends do you refer?" he asked pointedly.

"I assure you that Hannah Pinson has been with us every step of the way, and I do not consider anyone else to be in any way relevant. As for *you*," he said jeeringly. "You stood no friend to Emmeline. In fact, you willfully deceived her for years purely to line your own pockets at her expense."

While Humphrey reeled from this charge, Jeremy resumed browsing the rest of the letter. "Your *dear helpmeet* no doubt encouraged this meeting in the hope you could induce my wife to part with even more money to furnish the comfort of your family," he concluded damningly. "It must be hard for you pair of leeches indeed, now that you do not have her to bleed dry."

Humphrey flailed out an arm in feeble protest, but words seemed beyond him at this point.

"Nothing more to say?" Jeremy asked. "In that case, we will take our leave of you." He held out his hand to Emmie, who took it at once. "Say goodbye to Mr. Stockton, Emmeline. You won't be seeing him again."

"Goodbye, Mr. Stockton," Emmeline said, her eyes still on Jeremy. She could not fail to notice that her husband had not looked at her directly since entering the room.

31

They took a hurried leave of Nye, who, to Jeremy's evident surprise, rounded the bar to shake his hand and clap him on the back. "Not bad, Faris," he said, looking him up and down. "Not bad at all. I have hopes of you yet. I'm glad to see you put an end to all that mannerly bollocks. Truth is, Mina steered you astray a bit there." He winced. "It's true we take walks on the beach and plan our future together and such, but before we got to that point, we had to have it out. Truth be told, I didn't take my blinkers off before she gave me the shock of my life and screamed in my face that she hated my guts."

Turning to a mystified Emmie, he said, "You'd better come along to dinner with us next week. Mina's been waiting for you to call here first. She's got some odd notion that springing an inn on you isn't quite right and proper, but I think we can dispense with such ceremony between family, don't you?"

"Oh y-yes, of course! Thank you for, well, for standing by and ensuring fair play," she said, borrowing from his own vocabulary.

A smile tugged at his lips. "Well, it wasn't exactly London Prize Ring Rules," he said, eyeing Jeremy's grazed knuckles. "But it did at a pinch."

Lottie was waiting for them in the public parlor and to Emmie's consternation was standing over the bloodied bowl of water whispering to Corin. As soon as she saw them, she hurried over, looking wide-eyed and excited. Emmie had a sinking suspicion that at least some garbled version of events would find their way to the servants' hall. She only hoped she would not feature too harshly in the retelling.

Once outside, Jeremy saw them both into the carriage and mounted Cadmus. "I'll see you back at the house," he said briefly, and Emmie's heart sank. *Oh dear, oh dear*, she thought and hoped he was not going to withdraw once more into icy politeness. Looking up, she saw Lottie watching her avidly.

"Reckon your old friend from London will be returning there pretty sharpish!" Lottie said with satisfaction.

"I expect so," Emmie agreed.

"His lordship saw to that. Never seen him so irate. Mark my words, I said to Corin, soon as I saw him barging in, things are turning ugly! And then we hear the scuffle and Master Nye appears calling for hot water and brandy for the guest from room three. 'What for at this time of the morning, it's not godly,' that old servant of his replies. 'He's already had his shave and the hour's not decent for liquor.' Then Master Nye he turns round and says, 'His lordship's knocked him down and bloodied his nose for him.'"

Emmie stirred in her seat, wishing her brother-in-law could have been a little more discreet.

"Funny, isn't it?" Lottie rattled on. "Cos everyone always agreed his lordship had nary a jealous bone in his body, what with the way her previous ladyship used to carry on, and him never batting an eye!"

Emmie cleared her throat, unsure of how to reply. "He…he never showed any jealousy before?"

"Not one bit!" Lottie responded with alacrity. "Not even when she provoked him ever so! That tutor of Master Teddy's, she used to embarrass everyone, the way she hung all over him! And then, there was that time she made a proper show of herself over Mr. Needham from Benham Hall. His lordship just looked bored. The poor gentleman took off like a scalded cat!"

Lottie settled back into her seat, getting comfortable. "Mrs. Cheviot used to say that mebbe that was what she wanted all along, for his lordship to defend her honor like, instead of simply looking the other way, but he never did. Not even once." She shot a speculative look at Emmie. "And then today, you go to say goodbye to your old London friend and what does he do but up and draws his cork! Clean broke his nose, too, that's what that old servant said. She reckoned he'd have two black eyes before long too!"

Emmie fanned her hot face with her glove. "It was all very unfortunate," she murmured, at a loss how else to respond.

"It's not as though he could have thought there was anything untoward going on, not when you took me with you as chaperone," Lottie pointed out. "Maddened with jealousy, that's what he was." She nodded contentedly. "You mark my words."

Arriving at the house, they found Jeremy already awaiting them. He opened the carriage door and helped her down. He had not changed, and she noticed his disordered neckcloth had flecks of blood on it. "I need to speak with you privately," he said grimly as soon as Lottie had disembarked.

"Of course."

"Upstairs."

She nodded her acquiescence, and he drew her straight into the house and up the stairs. To her surprise, he led her to his rooms, to the adjoining sitting room she had glimpsed that very morning. Once inside, with the door shut, he turned to her. "Before I start, is there anything you want to say?" His tone was perfectly controlled and calm.

Oh God, he *was* going to be all polite again, and she couldn't *bear* it. What should she do? Apologize? No, that would not suffice. If she went all polite as well, they would get nowhere. Right, it was clearly up to her. She squared her shoulders.

"Why did you do it?" she asked in a loud, clear voice. "Why did you kiss me like that, and then go and announce your engagement to Amanda Liversedge. That's what I want to know. I've always wanted to know. Why?"

He blinked. Whatever he had been expecting her to say, it wasn't that. For a moment, he did not speak. Then he simply said, "Wasn't it obvious, Ballentine?"

"Not to me."

He gave a short, mirthless laugh. "Then let me enlighten you. I announced my engagement to her because I was given strict instructions to. Our marriage was an understanding between our families for years. My father arranged the whole thing with Lord Tipton on my twelfth birthday, though I did not actually meet the lady until some years after that."

"So then, you knew all along?" she said quietly. "The whole time I knew you, that you were unofficially engaged to another?" There was a heavy pause and then he swallowed and nodded. Emmie's head swam. "Why was it such a big secret, then?"

"A secret?" He looked mildly surprised. "I don't know that it was ever a secret, precisely. I never really spoke of it because, well, I considered myself damned lucky to get something of a reprieve. Her parents were content to wait for it to be made official, but no later than her twenty-first birthday. Amanda wanted the chance to flaunt herself as a debutante and I was damned eager to experience some of the delights of town before I was forced to the altar. I was two years younger than her, so that meant—"

"It had to be formally announced at the Hawfords' ball," Emmie uttered.

He breathed out. "Yes," he agreed. "Lady Hawford was Amanda's godmother. Why did you think it was a secret?"

"Because everyone acted so surprised and excited when you announced it, of course!" she burst out. "Talking about what a beautiful couple you made and how it must have been love at first sight! Also, I think it's pretty obvious that an honorable man would not have *dallied* with me, and engaged my affections, when he knew all along that he was intended for another!"

"You're right," he agreed quite readily. "My actions were not those of an honorable man. Over the years they very rarely have been. But all the same, at that time the choice of bride was not mine to make. If I could have avoided it, I would *never* have announced it that night. I would never have married her at all. You must know that, Emmeline."

"How would I know that? You never told me anything. You just kissed me senseless, and then left me at the bottom of the stairs, while you stood at the top of them and announced you were to be wed. It was the most painful night of my life!" Tears sprang to her eyes. "So very, very painful, and you will *never* understand how I felt! Standing at the foot of those stairs while you—while you—"

"You think I do not understand a broken heart?" he interrupted her incredulously. "How do you think I felt having to make that *bloody* announcement? I had been dreading it since the day I met you. It had not bothered me particularly in the beginning. Marriage was just a duty, like many others that were incumbent on my position. And then I met you, at the Wallingfords' tea party in Cavendish Square."

She gave a start. "What? You didn't think I'd remember the occasion I first saw you?" he asked challengingly. "Well, I do. Even in that moment, when I first laid eyes on you, I knew that *nothing* would ever be the same again." He glanced across the room, at his side table as though looking for something. Then he seemed to recall himself, unclenching his fists and taking a steadying breath.

"If you imagine you were the only one who suffered then you are wrong," he said unsteadily. "Knowing the announcement was drawing closer and closer with each day, and that we would have to part... I had to drink like a demon even to get through it. If I had not..." His words trailed off angrily, and he shook his head.

"I never should have imposed on you like I did but I could never regret that time, how could I? It was the only time I have ever—" He could not continue for a minute. "Been truly happy," he concluded after a heavy pause. "It was wrong of me," he said again, his voice hoarse, "but, I have never, ever forgotten a single moment I spent in your company, and that kiss we shared is my most precious memory of all." His voice shook.

"I have never entered a garden room, or an orangery, or anything remotely resembling a conservatory that did not make me think of it. Amanda knew I did not love her and that my heart belonged to another from the start. I got disgustingly drunk on our honeymoon and told her so. Not that she cared, not really. She just thought it was her due that every man should adore her. She was a little put out to learn her new bridegroom did not care tuppence for her and never would though."

Emmie stared at him. "You surely did not tell her that I was the object of your affection?" she asked incredulously.

"I didn't have to tell her." He shot her an ironic look. "You and I had danced very near to the flame together that season. It had not escaped everyone's attention. Amanda lacked many things, but intelligence was not one of them."

Slowly, she shook her head. "You almost make me feel sorry for her! To be told *that* by your new bridegroom..."

"Your pity is quite wasted on her. We neither of us married for love."

"Still...there is such a thing as rubbing salt in the wound."

Jeremy laughed. "Well, she made sure to return the favor over the next nine years, let me assure you."

"Besides," Emmie said, ignoring this comment. "We did not marry for love either."

He was quiet for a moment. "*You* may not have done," he said at last, leaving Emmie open-mouthed. He turned and walked over to a side cabinet where a jug of water and some glasses stood. Pouring himself a glass, he tossed it down. Emmie wondered if he had looked around earlier because he had felt in need of a more fortifying drink than water. She remembered he had not drunk the brandy Nye had proffered.

Swallowing, she opened her mouth to speak, but he forestalled her. "I wish you would extend to me some of the forgiveness you see fit to lavish on Stockton," he said, still facing the wall. "But no, when it comes to your husband who adores you, you insist on believing that I married you as some sort of penance and whimsical indulgence of my son!"

"I—I never said that!" she stammered.

He turned about to face her. "I love you, Emmeline. You loved me too, once. I *know* you did. If you could only find it in your heart to forgive me, then you might be able to feel something for me again. Won't you at least try?" This last was an appeal that cut right to the heart of her. She stared at him bereft of speech.

When she did not speak, an obstinate look stole over his countenance. "I won't give up hoping for that, Emmeline. And I may as well tell you now that I am building a conservatory to commemorate our marriage. A conservatory that Wimble is designing for me. I mean to make it the grandest and most ostentatious conservatory in the country and then, I mean to seduce you in it, successfully this time, and to feed you grapes and do every other decadent thing with you that I've dreamed of doing with you and to you for years and years!"

His chest heaved. "I'm tired of trying to be the perfect, considerate husband to you, Emmeline, so you're just going to get the one you've got. Faulty, far from perfect, and frequently wrong."

"I'm perfectly happy with the one I've got," she protested, but clearly not loudly enough, for he carried on as though she had not spoken.

"If you think I am going to respectfully retire from the field, you are quite mistaken in my character. I'm going to build that bloody conservatory and that ridiculous amphitheater and whatever the hell else takes my fancy in my stupid, hopeless quest to try and win your heart.

"I don't care what it takes, but it might be kind of you to give me some pointers somewhere along the way, as I clearly am not hitting the right targets. Fair warning, though, I mean to go all out now, so you'd better prepare yourself for an onslaught."

He said the words so direly that Emmie did not know whether to laugh or cry. Instead, she hurried across the room and threw her arms about him. He caught her, a surprised look on his face, and they lurched over to a convenient sofa, which they both collapsed upon.

For the briefest of moments, he hesitated, then his lips were seeking hers with a desperate urgency she was only too happy to assuage. "Ballentine," he panted between kisses, "could you ever—?" She was too eager for his kisses to find out what he was asking her specifically. Instead, she tried to assure him with the enthusiasm of her embrace that she would deny him nothing.

Eventually, she drew back, reluctant to part, but eager to hear the words again. "You—you always loved me, then?" she said, half fearing she had misunderstood him. "Even ten years ago?"

"I loved you desperately. I was so *fucking* miserable that season, because I knew at the close of it, I would be married to Amanda. I only felt alive on a handful of occasions that entire twelve weeks. You want to know when? It was during every snatched moment I spent with you. The rest of it, I spent numbing myself with drink. How's that for a confession, Ballentine?" Her eyes filled with tears, but she could not speak. "Or how about the fact I was perilously close to making you an entirely disgraceful offer." His gaze fell away from hers.

Her heart skipped a beat. "What kind of offer?"

"Becoming my mistress," he said harshly. "I had nothing else to offer you. Only the fact I respected you and had a strong suspicion you would hate me afterward prevented me. I wrote you a letter in Italy that I had to burn. I behaved disgustingly around you. I can hardly stand remembering how I conducted myself that season. I have tried to forget it ever since." He looked so shamefaced that Emmie could not look away.

"I wouldn't have hated you," she admitted quietly. "I could not have accepted, of course, but actually, I think I would have been rather flattered in a foolish sort of way."

"Emmeline," he groaned. "Don't. Do not make me regret my past any more than I do already."

She gave a breathless laugh. Suddenly, she felt light as air. Jeremy Vance loved her. He had loved her all along. She laid her hands on either side of his face. "I love you too," she said simply. "I always have, and I always will. I used to think it was a terrible sort of curse, but now I know it is quite the opposite."

"Always?" he whispered with such a hopeful look dawning in his eyes that it somehow made her heart ache a little.

"Always," she responded warmly. "Even when I thought you were quite undeserving of the honor."

He kissed her again, wrapping his arms around her tightly. "Oh God, tell me again, Ballentine," he breathed into her neck. "Don't ever stop telling me."

"I still love you. I've always loved you. But I can't carry on kissing you like this," she added firmly.

"Why not?" he asked, peering down at her.

"Because of your cravat," she said apologetically. "It's covered in Humphrey's nose blood."

He grimaced, tearing it from his neck at once and casting it onto the floor. "I should go and wash," he sighed with frustration. "I haven't changed out of my riding things yet, but I don't want to let you out of my sight."

"I could wait for you in your bedroom," Emmie suggested tentatively, blushing slightly. "Under the covers."

"Really?" He hesitated. "You would not prefer your own? Last time we were in mine…" He pulled a face.

"Let's make some better memories there," she suggested brightly.

He disentangled himself at once and leaped off the sofa. "I'll send for hot water." His eyes roamed over her, as though he found it hard to tear himself away, and then he crossed the room, shouting for his valet and shedding his waistcoat.

Twenty minutes later, they were huddled under the covers together naked in his bed, reassuring one another of the strength of their continued love and affection. Their first joining was hurried and almost clumsy in their combined haste to consummate their renewed bond.

Emmie had a suspicion she was grasping him too tightly but every time she tried to ease up her hold of him, he made his dissatisfaction plain. In the end, she simply gave in to her promptings and squeezed the life out of him. It seemed he could not get enough of her in any case. Even when their bodies lay entwined, sated and replete, he did not stop kissing her and murmuring sweet words of love into her ear.

"This is what our wedding night should have been like," he sighed at last as they collapsed onto the mattress, side by side. "Though honestly, I can't regret the one we had. I felt so hopeful that we would reach this place eventually."

"And after all, we have," she agreed.

He smiled faintly, and as though he could not bear even such a short distance between them, he shifted onto his side toward her and slipped an arm about her waist. "Yes. Eventually."

"It didn't really take that long. We have not quite been married three months even!" she pointed out. "And we did have rather a few *misconceptions* to clear away."

"It took a lot of effort and a good deal of suffering," he said sternly, "if you take our ten-year separation into account."

"Oh, that."

"Yes, that. I wish I had simply told you everything from the start," he said regretfully, resting his brow against hers. "I should have just laid my soul bare to you and been done with it."

"Which start?" Emmie asked. "Do you mean ten years ago or...?"

"God no, not then!" he shuddered. "I was a vicious brat back then. You were far better off without me. No, I mean three months ago. When I found you again."

"You were not a vicious brat!"

"Yes, I was, Emmeline," he said sincerely. "It took me years to start to straighten out and get some basic decency. God, I shudder to think of myself at nineteen. I shouldn't have been allowed in polite company."

She tutted. "You make yourself sound worse than Count Stefano."

"Because I was," he said. "Stefano is a villain of the moustache-twirling variety, whereas I...I was the nasty everyday variety. Less glamorous and a good deal more detestable."

"I would not say less glamorous," Emmie objected, "you were both glamorous *and* detestable."

He did not smile. "Emmeline, do you think—?"

She waited. "You could ever forgive me," she supplied when he could not finish his words. He gave a short nod. "You have already asked me this question, Jeremy," she said gently.

"You made no reply," he pointed out. "You were too busy kissing me."

"Does that not give you clue as to my answer?" she teased.

He reached across to take her hand and place it on his chest. "Maybe," he admitted. "But I'd still like to hear you say the words."

"I forgive you, Jeremy Vance," she whispered. "With my whole heart."

He swallowed convulsively. "I'm ashamed to say it, but I was so fucking miserable at the time that I did not even fully consider *your* feelings. I thought you would find someone better than me within a twelvemonth. I could not believe that you could feel one tenth of what I did. I was such an arrogant prick."

He rolled onto his back and Emmie turned to face him, wrapping an arm about him for comfort. "God forgive me," he continued in a low voice, "I did not even realize what I felt for you was love, not at the time." He squeezed his eyes shut as though the memory pained him. "I just knew I wanted to be around you so badly, and that the thought of never seeing you again made me feel…empty inside."

He turned his head to meet her gaze, his hand clasping her thigh as though for comfort. "But you see, I'd always felt empty until I met you, so it wasn't an unfamiliar feeling. I just didn't know any better. Then once I did…I realized too late what it signified."

Seeing his bleak expression, Emmie rubbed her hand over his heart in a gentle circular motion. "It's a good thing you've finally explained yourself to me," she murmured. "Because now I understand why you kept bringing up that night and causing me so much offence."

"Offence!" he echoed. "I kept bringing it up, because to me, that kiss in the conservatory was my most treasured memory. I was trying to— to reconnect us to our past."

She nodded. "Whereas I associated it always with what happened directly after," she said slowly, realizing that he must always have wanted to unburden himself to her. *That* was why he kept raking it all up, and she had resisted so hard, unwilling to travel down such a painful path with him again.

"You tried to show me your rosewood box," she said softly, resting her chin on his chest, "and I told you lock it back up and throw away the key. Forgive me, my love. I clung to past resentment and did not think I had it in me to absolve you."

"The fault was not yours, but mine," he said swiftly. "But speaking of rosewood boxes, did you realize I still have yours?"

"Yes, I did realize," she said absently, her mind on other things.

"What are you thinking about so deeply?" Jeremy asked with a frown. He caught her hand in his and intertwined their fingers.

"Oh, I was just reasoning things through."

"What things?"

"Well, just how every time I disappointed you, you backed off and became so, well, polite and distant."

"You never disappointed me," he said quickly. "I turned polite because I feared I had upset you beyond all reason." He hesitated. "That last time we were in here together," he said, glancing about his room. "God, I'll never forget how much you cried. It haunts me still."

"Yes, I know. I shocked you badly. I thought you already knew."

"Knew what?"

"That you had broken my heart all those years ago."

A flash of pain showed in his eyes. "I knew I had disappointed you, but I had no idea," he admitted. "I thought— To be honest, over the years I thought you must have been far better off without me. I made such a failure of my life. The drinking, the terrible marriage…everything. I tried to think of you as a perfect memory, preserved forever in that time, because when I imagined you living a life of happy contentment without me…"

"Then what?" She lifted her head to look at him.

"Then I grew maudlin, bitter, and jealous," he admitted guiltily. "Over the years, I tried to push you out of my thoughts altogether. The last thing I wanted to know was that you were blissfully married to some solid man of business and a happy mother of five children." He gave her an uneasy glance. "I'm unspeakably selfish like that."

"I see," she murmured.

"And then I found out that life had treated you so unfairly, Ballentine. And instead of being appalled by the hand you had been dealt, I was *gleeful*." The arm about her waist tightened perceptibly. "Because that meant *I* still had a chance to get you up the aisle. If Stockton had not confessed all to you that morning, I still would have found some way of outing him from your affections."

"How precisely?" Emmie did not really know why she was encouraging him so, but perhaps it would be best for him to fully unburden himself. Also, it was strangely fascinating to hear the inner workings of his head.

"Well, I would have set a private investigator on him, for one thing, to uncover some dirt or other. There *had* to be an underlying reason for that ridiculously long engagement. The truth would have come out and I would have seen him disgraced and maneuvered you into marrying me."

"Hmmm."

"If not that, it would have been by some other means, fair or foul. I knew I had to make you mine. It felt like fate."

"And so, we were married," Emmie murmured. "But we still weren't being terribly honest with one another."

"Except in the bedroom," Jeremy interjected.

"Yes, in the beginning, the gloves always came off in the bedchamber. It was when you started being so apologetic there that you really worried me."

He looked alarmed. "I hope I was never aggressive with you!"

"Aggressive?" Emmie was startled. "That was not my meaning. I meant kid gloves, not boxing gloves."

"Oh." He looked relieved.

"Sorry, I did not mean—"

"No, no, I take your meaning now. At least… Are you saying, Emmeline, that you do not want me to be overly polite in the bedroom?"

"Yes," she agreed at once.

Jeremy looked stunned for a moment, then he laughed. "Ah, Ballentine," he said, pulling her into his arms. "I think I can safely promise never to be *too* polite in that arena again."

"Just promise me you won't apologize again afterward, that's all, as though you regretted anything we had done."

He sobered at once, tightening his arms about her. "I never regretted a thing. I was just scared you did not want me, as I wanted you. Besides, I have not apologized once since you played the bathing goddess for me, have I?"

"Yes, you did. After that time on the breakfast table," she reminded him.

He looked surprised. "That was different! I apologized because I went too far with you that morning. You could have burned your nose on the coffeepot, and I likely would not even have noticed!"

"Yes, you would, for I would soon have let you know," Emmie contradicted him. "It's nice when you're worshipful," she said, coloring hotly, "but it's also nice sometimes when you are not."

He drew back. "Really?" he asked cautiously, a faint gleam in his eye. She nodded. "And you promise you would tell me if I ever did anything you were not comfortable with?"

"Yes, I would. I told you quite plainly I did not like you talking of the Hawfords' ball, did I not? And that was long before we had cleared up any of our misunderstandings."

"You did, but I did not really listen," he said ruefully.

"Well, no, but that was not a matter of physical comfort, but emotional."

"I still need to improve drastically in such matters, and I will," he promised, pressing her hand to his lips. "I never want to let you down again."

She smiled at him. "I wish—" She broke off her words, shaking her head. "No, it's silly, really."

"What is?"

"It's just, I wish you could have come to me all those years ago and told me how you really felt. I spent so many years thinking what I felt for you wasn't reciprocated. That I had made a complete fool of myself over you. But if I had known that you—that you loved me back—"

"So we could *both* be desperately unhappy, instead of just me?"

"We *were* both unhappy, you stupid man! Besides, if you had only done that, then we could have faced it together."

"Emmeline," he groaned, shaking his head, "there was nothing we could have done, my love. I was promised to another and—"

"Yes, there was," she insisted.

"My father would never have permitted—"

"But *my* father was rich in those days," she interrupted him. "He would have given us money, and what would it have mattered if your father *had* cut you off. The estate and the title were entailed and would have come to you eventually. You could have lived with us at Porchester Square and been like Atherton."

"Like Atherton?"

"Titled and connected but possessing no fortune."

A smile tugged at Jeremy's lips. "Your father would have thought me a useless fop."

"He would have loved your title though," she pointed out practically.

Jeremy smiled. "I did not even possess that in those days."

"You had the promise of it, however. He would have loved to think he had bought a title."

He reached for her hand, drawing her closer. "Would you really have married me, if I was disowned and dispossessed?" he asked in a low voice.

"Yes," she answered promptly. "I've always been an absolute fool where you are concerned, Jeremy Vance. Though..."

"What?"

"You're right, of course," she said regretfully. "Practically speaking, my father's fortune could not have maintained this place for many years. If your father had left his money elsewhere, realistically you would have to have sold Vance Park as soon as you inherited it."

"Don't let's be realistic," he said swiftly. "Instead, tell me some more about how you would have supported your penniless young husband."

It was Emmeline's turn to smile. "I would have doted on you," she said, wrapping her arms around his neck. "I would have spoiled you and hung off your every word."

"You could still do that," he said quickly, "if the inclination took you."

"And of course, I never would have even considered Humphrey."

"How can you even think of mentioning him right now?" he said, sounding annoyed.

"It would have been a terrible scandal, wouldn't it?" she whispered, laying a hand against his cheek.

"If we had eloped?" he asked, his expression of irritation fading.

"Yes."

He nodded. "But then, we were already acquainted with scandal, you and I." His smile faded and he said suddenly with feeling, "I wish to God I'd had the guts to do it."

"To elope? So do I." Her eyes turned dreamy, and he rolled her onto her back, lowering his face to hers.

"Except," she said suddenly, putting a finger to his lips. He drew back to look at her. "We would not have Teddy. So, we can't really regret that we did not marry young, can we?"

He blinked. "Yes, I suppose that is true."

"What you probably should have done," Emmeline continued musingly, "was approach me with that indecent proposal of yours. I, well, I probably would have not been able to resist you," she admitted shamefacedly.

"Emmeline!" he said in a raspy voice.

"Well, you already know you had only to crook a finger at me, and I would follow you," she said guiltily. "I had no dignity at all where you were concerned, as evidenced by that conservatory incident."

"*Emmeline*," he groaned, tightening his grip about her. "Don't tell me that, for lord's sake. I'll be crooking my finger at you all hours of the day." She laughed.

"I thought about making you my mistress a disgusting amount," he confessed rawly. "I even told Atherton I wanted to approach your father about it at the time."

Her mouth fell open. "Did you really?"

"Yes, so you see, I really was an absolute bastard with no scruples and precious few morals left to me."

"But you did not approach him," she pointed out gently as she tried to imagine how her father would have reacted. He would have been flabbergasted, she thought and almost burst out laughing.

"Only because I knew he would never agree to it. I looked into his reputation and realized such a thing would not fly with him, more's the pity."

"You could likely have convinced me though," she pointed out, "and seduced me away from my father's protection."

He looked torn, propping his head on his hand. "I wanted to, believe me, but I wanted better for you always, Emmeline. You deserved better than being some man's kept woman, even if that man was me. Though, if I had known you would turn around and get engaged to a married man—" he started wrathfully.

"Yes, that was stupid of me."

"It was not remotely stupid," he said, abruptly changing his tune. "You were horribly deceived."

"And my heart was broken, so I did not really care who I married. I just did what my father asked of me."

"As did I," Jeremy concurred. "So, neither of us was really at fault for our first disastrous attempts toward the altar. Our second attempt, however, is a resounding success."

"Do you really think so?"

"I do."

She tipped her head to one side in consideration. "Do you know, if you had approached my father, he would have been quite dumbfounded. He thought me utterly lacking in appeal and frequently lamented the fact I took after his side of the family and not my mother's. His people were all very solid and stocky. It was a great disappointment to him that I was not a slender beauty."

"He must have been a fool," Jeremy said dismissively. "You are a beauty and not everyone favors the slender kind. No wonder he blundered so badly over Stockton. He had a huge blind spot where you were concerned."

Emmie forced a smile. She should not have raised her father as a subject. It always made her feel a little sad.

Jeremy slid an arm about her shoulders. "You know when I was young, my father would always tell me that his bastard was worth two of me. He blamed my mother, of course. It's in the breeding he would say. I favored my damme and not my sire. Then, when I grew older, he was forced to concede that my temperament was nothing like my mother's. As you know, I was very wild. I was expelled from Eton, got sent down from Oxford, and blotted my copy book in every way known to privileged youth."

"And that did not please him either?" she guessed, touched that he was sharing this with her.

He snorted. "I think it did in a way. He could do nothing with me, which infuriated him, but apparently, he would brag of my excesses among his cronies. Said I might take after my mother in looks but I was full to the brim with vices. A family trait apparently."

"Aren't fathers funny?" Emmie sighed. "Do you think we would have turned out differently if our mothers had been around?"

Jeremy considered this a moment before replying shamefacedly, "Truth to tell, I do not think mine would have wielded much influence over me. Everything I have since learned from Mina leads me to believe her entreaties would have fallen on deaf ears and I would not have heeded her one bit."

"I expect you would have been charming to her though," she responded loyally.

"Oh, I am sure. Mina says she would have doted on me and hung on my every word. I expect I would have been her darling boy who could do no wrong. If anything, she would likely have influenced me for the worst!" Emmie laughed. She could not help it. He grinned. "I expect she would have been an awful mother-in-law to you as well. Always aiding and abetting me and encouraging my worst excesses."

"Very likely! Rather like old Mrs. Rumstead," she said, thinking of a terrible old woman she had met in one of his farmers' cottages, wielding her malign influence over three daughters-in-law, and spoiling her youngest son.

Jeremy rolled over her. "Let us not discuss my tenants at this juncture."

"Oh? What would you rather discuss?"

"What kind of mistress you would have made me," he said, robbing Emmie of all breath.

"What do you think?" she asked breathlessly.

"A fantastic one," he said thickly, and she decided to prove his theory right.

32

They did not emerge for supper. Instead, Jeremy had their meal sent up to their private dining room. "We won't send for Teddy tonight," he decided. "He can take supper in his nursery and fully reflect on his sins."

"You know, the fact he's getting up to all sorts must be a good sign, as far as his recovering health is concerned," Emmie reflected, drawing on her frothy wrapper.

"True. He'll definitely be ready for school in September, I know that much."

"He still seems rather young to me, to send away to boarding school," Emmie said.

"To be honest, he was fine at Paverton Hall last time. It was me that missed him so much I jumped on the first excuse to recall him."

Emmie fastened the last button and turned around to face him. "Is my hair a mess?"

"It is a veritable riot of curls. I rather like it."

"I expect I look more Medusa than Aphrodite."

He laughed and they walked through, hand in hand, to find the first course already waiting for them, and Higgins disappearing discreetly back through the door.

"I hope no one noticed that I did not touch a morsel of that breakfast the other morning," Emmie said, sinking down onto a cushion.

"What do you mean?" Jeremy asked innocently. "You definitely touched the bread rolls. I had to wipe the crumbs off your front."

She pulled a face at him, and he laughed. "I think you should sit in my lap again this evening."

"No thank you," she responded briskly. "I want to actually eat something this time." He smirked. Removing the covers, she found Mrs. Oxley had prepared them a light consommé served with bread. Spooning herself some, and then passing it to Jeremy, she helped herself to some bread and glanced across at him. "Are you really building a conservatory here at Vance?"

"Yes," he confirmed, spooning some into his own bowl. "The most extravagant conservatory in all Cornwall."

"You kept that very quiet."

"Yes, for having commissioned it, it suddenly occurred to me that you might find it in somewhat poor taste."

She snorted. "It can't be in any worse taste than your own private amphitheater!"

"That's entirely your fault, Lady Faris," he said, pointing at her with his spoon. "You were the one who persuaded me to that particular piece of nonsense."

"True," she conceded, taking a bite of bread. As she chewed it, she wondered how things were going along downstairs. "Mr. Wimble, poor man, will be relieved that he doesn't have to dodge my conversation in future, now I know what he is truly working on. I wondered why he always looked so frightened of me."

"Beautiful women intimidate him," Jeremy responded at once.

"I fancy Lottie might be spreading the word below that you punched an ex-admirer of mine from London today."

"More than likely, I'd say. Let tongues wag. I never really cared about causing scenes." He shrugged. "Who knows, it might even improve my reputation. Nye certainly seemed to like me all the better for it."

"Do you think it will?" she mused. "Improve your reputation, I mean? All this work I am doing trying to get on the right committees and all that was really needed was for you to kick up a dust in an inn!" To her surprise, he did not laugh at this, but propped himself up on one elbow looking very serious.

"Which brings me to another confession," he said ruefully, reaching for her hand across the table. "The truth is, Ballentine, that everything I told you about my motivation for marrying you was a massive lie. Not like that!" he said swiftly, seeing the fear rise up in her expression. "I wanted to marry you very badly, you *know* I did," he said with conviction.

"What I mean is that I never cared a damn about you joining the local board of ladies for education or building bridges with my neighbors or any of that other stuff I spouted. I didn't care about you being a picture of respectability or even a good mother at the end of the day," he confessed. "Though it is a happy circumstance you turned out to be one, of course."

She looked completely at sea. "Then why did you say—?"

"You were quite right that day in Hutton's tea shop," he carried on. "It never made any sense that I should think you the ideal candidate to reform my image. Your own brush with society was hardly exemplary." He gave a wan smile. "You practically let me seduce you in full view of fashionable London, now, didn't you, my darling?"

Emmie drew in a sharp breath. Before she could object, he said, "You could spill drunkenly out of carriages twice a week, lose your diamonds, waltz with whomever you like, and gamble away my entire fortune and I still would not want to divorce you."

She stared at him. "Jeremy—"

"Do you want to know something truly shocking, Ballentine? You could do practically anything and I would let you get away with it."

She thought about this for a moment. "Practically?"

"No lovers," he said. "I could not stomach that."

"You would divorce me?"

"No," he said quickly. "But they would end up buried in shallow graves under the terrace."

"Jeremy!"

"I know. Very shocking, but it happens to be the truth."

She nodded thoughtfully. "I see."

"What do you see?"

"That you mean to be a very tolerant husband. You almost make me feel quite guilty that I cannot return the sentiment."

"What do you mean?"

"Well, just lately it has dawned on me that I have something of a jealous streak. It came as quite a shock to me."

"Jealous? Of me?" He sounded more pleased by the notion than anything.

Emmie nodded. "Yes, for all the ladies hereabouts keep dropping hints about your popularity with the fairer sex. It has become quite wearing."

"Who has?"

"Mrs. Ryland, for one," she said, "intimated that everyone was expecting you to become engaged to Blanche Pebmarsh as soon as your divorce became official."

"Blanche Pebmarsh?" he exclaimed incredulously. "What nonsense. Blanche Pebmarsh never talks about anything but riding to hounds. She's quite obsessed with hunting and fishing. I've never been remotely attracted to her or her to me. Her future husband is undoubtedly in the mold of a sporting parson. I'm quite shocked at the vicar's wife and I'm sure no one else can have said anything so ridiculous."

"Then you would be wrong," Emmie said sternly. "Mrs. Needham is another who made several such remarks."

"Well, you and Teddy between you have convinced me that Mrs. Needham is a ghastly woman masquerading as a persecuted mama. We will avoid her in future."

"And you must do your best to lay such rumors to rest," Emmie announced.

"Oh, I don't think I will have to make much of an effort in that respect," he said, turning to face her. "Anyone with eyes in their head will soon notice that I am entirely infatuated with my own wife."

"Even though every requirement you gave me was *completely* misleading?" She narrowed her eyes at him, pretending to be annoyed.

"Emmeline, I had to give you some motivation to marry me. And besides, you turned out to be so good at all those things."

"What about London?" she asked. "Did you mean what you said about that?"

"No, that was a lie too."

"What?" she squeaked in dismay.

"I mean, I don't care about London *society* particularly, but we do own a rather nice town house there, and the odd sojourn to the flesh pots might be rather enjoyable, with you by my side."

Emmie eyed him doubtfully. "You mean restaurants and theaters, and such things?"

"Precisely, and we could choose to socialize with people there that we like."

"Such as the Hardimans?"

"Such as the Hardimans," he agreed readily. "I'd like to squire you about a bit and flaunt you, why not?"

"That does sound rather nice," she agreed hesitantly. "And I suppose, when Teddy is older, we will need to throw a few parties, just to ensure he is introduced to some nice circles and is not ostracized."

"Neither he nor we will ever be ostracized, Ballentine. We would only have to show the faintest interest in reentering polite society, and we would be inundated with invitations. However, until you are ready, we will confine ourselves here to Cornwall. There are plenty of picnics and boat trips and days on the beach to be had."

Emmie's face suddenly fell as she remembered something. "What is it?" he asked, lowering his spoon.

"It's that meeting here at Vance tomorrow, of the Good Works committee, and I quite forgot!"

Jeremy laughed. "Cancel it," he advised callously.

"Oh, I couldn't do that. Poor Mrs. Ryland would be so embarrassed after she begged the favor on my behalf."

"Well, don't let them put you out. It doesn't matter a jot if you get voted onto their committee or whatever it is."

"It's a bit late in the day to tell me that!" she scolded him, but on the next morning, when Lady Sharpe was brought into her presence along with about fifteen other ladies all wearing very fussy outfits with lots of lace, she found she rather enjoyed playing the gracious hostess.

Lady Sharpe was a large woman, built on generous lines, she walked with a silver knobbed cane and wore a very large posy of flowers pinned to her breast. She looked Emmie up and down with shrewd eyes. "Lady Faris?" she said in some surprise, casting a withering look to the ladies standing on either side of her.

Emmeline extended her hand. "Welcome to Vance. I am most happy to make your acquaintance, Lady Sharpe."

"Well, well, pretty creature, aren't you?" she remarked in that blunt manner that only a very privileged few can get away with. "You quite put me in mind of someone I once knew a long time ago." Her eyes glazed over. "Now, who was it?" she murmured. "Adelaide...or was it Amabel Richlow. Any relation?" she asked in a rich, plummy accent.

"I'm afraid not. My parents originated from the Yorkshire region."

"Mm, I suppose not, then. Somerset!" she exclaimed suddenly, striking her walking stick against the floor for emphasis. "That was where her people hailed from. There now! I knew I would remember. Oh, she was a *great* beauty in the old style. All vying for her hand they were, my brothers and my Harry included!"

Lady Sharpe's eyes misted over. "Lord, what cakes they made of themselves over her! Had them eating out of the palm of her hand, she did! Not like these chits nowadays," she snorted. "Prancing around with their silly notions about twenty-inch waistlines and their ridiculous hats! A man likes to have something he can catch hold of, that's what my Harry used to say."

"Er, yes, of course," Emmie said blankly, casting a hurried look about the other ladies who all looked rather embarrassed and lost for words. "Shall we all proceed into the drawing room? I have had refreshments laid out there and all the chairs are arranged for us to be comfortable."

She had just finished shaking the hands of all the other ladies present and was asking them to be seated when she heard herself hailed from out in the hall.

"Emmeline!"

Emmie turned, recognizing her husband's voice. "If you will excuse me for just one moment, ladies," she said apologetically, hurrying out into the hallway. "What is it?"

He swept her up into his arms and started waltzing her across the floor. "Run away with me, Ballentine," he said whimsically.

"Where to?" She laughed, following his footwork instinctively.

"The beach?" he suggested. "We could build a hut out of driftwood and sleep under the stars."

"Sounds very sandy. Why aren't you at the stables with Mr. Masterman? He will think you're shirking your responsibilities again."

"Devil take him. I don't care if he does."

"Well, *I* care," Emmie insisted. "You promised me that you would take me to a race meet next month and I think it would be more enjoyable if one of our horses wins that gold cup." Jeremy threw back his head and laughed.

"What a lot of twaddle that Needham woman has been talking!" Lady Sharpe said in loud, carrying tones. "He's clearly infatuated with the gel! I'm glad I came to see how things stood for myself! I shall certainly ask Lady Faris if we can use their south lawn for the fete. I have no doubt she can twist that man about her little finger."

"I see she has my measure," Jeremy remarked, twirling her about. And it was clear he did not care one bit.

EPILOGUE

Six Months Later

The Christmas Ball at Vance Park

Jeremy dismissed his valet and examined his reflection critically in the mirror. He was wearing full evening dress tonight and checked the impeccable fit of his black tailcoat and white silk waistcoat before adjusting his cravat to his satisfaction.

His cufflinks gleamed in his reflection, complementing the burnished gold of his hair. He wanted to look the part of the perfect host tonight, beside his blooming wife. Absently, he fitted the hook of his watch chain into place and slipped his watch into his pocket. Now he just needed his gloves. Hearing a discreet cough behind him, he turned. "Ah, Colfax, here you are."

"You wanted to see me, milord."

"Yes, Emmeline tells me congratulations are due." If he did not know any better, he might have thought Colfax colored faintly.

"Yes, milord," he said woodenly after a moment's pause. "Miss Pinson has agreed to make me the happiest of men."

"I'm very glad to hear it. I was starting to think you were making slow work of your wooing."

Colfax's gaze softened. "Slow is the only way with a woman like my Hannah. She deserves my taking the time to court her right."

"Yes, I can well believe it. She's an excellent woman and I am fortunate to call her my friend. Who would have thought it, eh? Both of us respectably leg-shackled and living lives of blameless virtue. I never would have dreamed of such a thing back in our days in St. James's Square," he said, referring to his bachelor quarters.

Colfax cleared his throat, a twinkle lurking in his eye. "No indeed, milord."

"Which brings me to my next point. I want you to cast off your footman's livery and start training with Garraway in the New Year."

"Garraway, milord?" Colfax, for once, seemed quite taken aback.

"Yes, for the old man's looking to retire in a twelvemonth and move into the cottage I promised him. He's a widowed sister who's coming to keep house for him. They mean to deal quite comfortably together, so you see I have need of a new butler here at Vance."

"But—" He paused before resuming. "Milord, I'm not—"

"Not what?" Jeremy's eyebrows rose. "Butler material? I assure you that you are. The biggest snob I ever met was butler to a duke. He made his master look like an ant by way of comparison."

"But what would Mr. Garraway say?" Colfax wondered aloud. "I know he don't—doesn't—think that much of me and that's the truth."

"Well, that's where you're wrong. I discussed the eventuality with Garraway first over two years ago, so he'll be quite resigned to the fact by now. He said they go in fear of you in the servants' hall and that you're a hard man to know. Both are facts which will stand you in good stead as a butler. I think you'll find he has already been training you surreptitiously as his successor for a good while now."

"Well…" Colfax hesitated. "He does like to stick his oar into whatever I'm about, but I never dreamed *that's* what he was doing."

"He's quite the institution, is old Garraway. I shall miss him, but he won't be going far. His place will only be a stone's throw from Plumtree Cottage, so I'm sure he'll be turning up on your doorstep with homemade wine and demands to know what's to do up at Vance on a regular basis."

Colfax scratched the back of his neck. "Me? Butler, here?" he said in dazed tones. "Are you sure, milord?"

"I can think of no one else better for the role." He proffered his hand and Colfax shook it warmly.

"Thank you, milord. And if I might make so bold as to offer *you* my congratulations by way of return…"

Jeremy grinned. "Was it Hannah told you or Teddy? He's spilling over with the news. I'll be lucky if he does not tell every guest in the house."

Without waiting for Colfax's reply, he made for the connecting door and tapped lightly upon it, trying the doorknob.

"Are you ready for me within?"

Emmie jumped up excitedly from her seat. "Wait! I'll let you in." She felt a bundle of nerves to reveal her new quarters to him. Opening the door, she cleared her throat. "Prepare to be amazed," she announced, stepping back so Jeremy could see her sumptuous apartments in all their glory.

Instead of taking in the splendor of her newly decorated room, he followed in her footsteps, catching her hands and holding them out to her sides to take in the effect of her new evening gown. "Ravishing," he breathed, drawing her into his arms and sealing his lips to hers. "Madame de Flores has outdone herself."

"Do you like it? It is rather gorgeous, is it not?" Emmie smoothed her sumptuous skirts of richest red velvet. "And you don't think I'm showing too much?" She turned anxiously to the side, so he could see the full effect of her silhouette sideways on. "The gown had to be altered slightly to accommodate my growing waistline."

"You look truly magnificent." He reached out to touch her hair, which had been arranged into bunches of long ringlets, decorated with her diamond pins. "You look radiant, Ballentine. I can't wait to walk downstairs with you on my arm for everyone to see you."

She smiled back at him. "Well, you look splendid too," she said, shyly approving. "But then you always do. What do you think of my new rooms, by the way?" She made an extravagant arm gesture to indicate their surroundings.

Jeremy's gaze left her figure only with the greatest of reluctance. His eyes traveled over the Roman-style plaster columns, the pink marbled effect on the walls, the plump red and gold chaise longue, the large oval mirror, flanked by romping golden cupids.

A slow smile spread over his face as his eyes took in the mantelpiece covered in delicately jeweled and painted seashells and the large painting of the scalloped shell behind her bed. "It's incredible!" he said, turning in a circle to take it all in. "I love it."

"I'm not too sure about all of Mr. Penrose's details, but I do think he made a good job of it," she agreed.

"What aren't you sure about?"

"Well, this extraordinary chair for one thing," she said, walking over to stand before her dressing table. "Look at it." The accompanying stool had the appearance of a round stone plinth. "I'm not sure it's as comfortable as the old one was."

"You could always put one of these pink cushions from the bed on it," he suggested, "if it is not comfortable for your posterior."

"Perhaps it is not intended for me to sit upon?" Emmie said doubtfully.

"No, it certainly is."

"How do you know?"

"Read the inscription."

She bent down. It was labeled as though for a museum exhibit. "'The Fairest,'" she read before standing up with a red face. "I think Mr. Penrose must be having his little joke," she said, pursing her lips.

"Not at all, I think he understood his assignment admirably."

"What do you mean?"

"This bedchamber is clearly the bower of Aphrodite, goddess of love. Yet do you see the goddess represented herein?"

Emmie scanned the room fruitlessly. She could see doves, cupids, Grecian urns filled with hundreds of pink roses, an elegant statue of a winged Eros with long curling hair, a bow, and an arrow. She even spotted a golden apple labeled *The Apple of Discord*, set into a recessed niche, but she could not see a single solitary Venus.

"I thought he would paint one in the scallop shell," she said, glancing toward the huge pink shell painted so artistically above the head of the bed. "Like Botticelli's *Birth of Venus*, but he left it empty."

"He did not leave it empty, Emmeline. The shell frames my own personal goddess of love who will be sleeping beneath it. *You*."

Emmie's mouth fell open. "*Me*? But...but I assure you, I did not instruct him to depict *me* as Venus!" she huffed as soon as she got her breath back. "Such an idea would be absurd!"

"I think it is charming. It is precisely what I would have asked for, had I the nerve." He hesitated. "If you let it stand as it is, I will let that wretched boy have the folly decked out as he sees fit."

Emmie gasped. "Really?" Wimble's and Penrose's efforts had been concentrated thus far on finishing the new conservatory and the decoration of her rooms in time for Christmas. The renovation of the folly and building of the amphitheater were scheduled for the New Year, and remained a source of great contention between father and son.

While Jeremy had given up on the judgment of Paris, he had taken up the classical Muses, which he thought would work almost as well, while Teddy insisted that classical heroes would be a much superior theme.

"With a mural of heroes? And the twelve labors of Heracles?"

"Yes," he sighed. "Whatever he wants."

She returned to his side and wrapped her arms about his waist. "You truly are the most wonderful husband and father in the world, you know."

"Yes, I am aware." He grinned.

They kissed again. "Virtue is your reward," she told him demurely.

"*You* are my reward, Ballentine," he corrected her.

Smiling at him beatifically, she left the shelter of his arms to drift back over to her dressing table. Jeremy flung himself down on her new pink satin bedcovers.

"I wish we had a bit longer before our guests arrive," he grumbled. "I did not even get to watch you make ready. I don't know why you insisted we had to get dressed so early!"

"Because there is so much to *do*," she explained patiently. "Half the guests are already here, as our house guests! Poor Mrs. Cheviot is run quite ragged making everything perfect for them. She's been in quite a spin since your aunt Louisa and her husband, the Member of Parliament, got here. And then, when the *Tiptons* arrived…" She gave him a significant look.

"Well, that was all your idea. I take no responsibility for that decision." It had taken some persuading for Jeremy to agree to invite his former in-laws to Vance.

"They are Teddy's grandparents after all, and they have been perfect lambs so far. Ever since Lady Sharpe told me how much Lady Tipton regretted the rift, I knew we had to make some gesture, and they were so keen to accept. It would be such a shame if Teddy was to lose all contact with that side of his family, and it is not as though I have brought him any cousins," she said regretfully.

"You brought Hannah Pinson into his life," Jeremy pointed out.

"Yes, that is true." The thought cheered her, and she flashed him a grateful smile.

"And you will give him a little brother or sister next year. And if you think Mrs. Cheviot has not been enjoying herself immensely airing out all the guest rooms and ordering in a mountain of delicacies, then you are quite wrong. All the staff are reveling in it. I never dared hold a full-scale house party here at Vance before. Too much like hard work. They've loved having the best silver service and the best china back out after all this time."

"Well, you have been the perfect host so far," Emmie assured him. "Mr. and Mrs. Hardiman were singing your praises to me this morning after breakfast. They think the dissolute viscount they heard dark whispers about must have been some other man entirely."

"Oh, he was," Jeremy agreed affably. "He no longer exists. Just this paragon of rectitude who stands before you."

"I don't know about that…" she teased, reaching for her bottle of French perfume. Removing the glass stopper, she ran it over her wrists. "I was hoping for a glimpse of him before the evening's out."

"Really? To what end?" he asked with a flicker of interest.

She replaced the stopper. "I want us to sneak down together. Before our guests arrive. The ones who aren't staying here, I mean. The others will all still be in their rooms getting ready for at least another half an hour."

"And what will we be doing downstairs?" he persisted, a pucker between his brows.

"Well…" Emmie took a deep breath. "I want you to take my hand, like you did at the Hawfords' ball." His head shot up, but he did not speak, just stared at her. "And then," she continued steadily, only the faintest tremor to her voice, "I want you to say 'How about I give you something to remember me by, Ballentine?' and—and take me into the new conservatory."

He was up and off the bed in an instant. "Emmeline—" he began in a shocked voice.

"No, Jeremy," she said, holding up one hand to forestall him. "You said we would have this ball exactly how I wanted, and this is what I want."

He looked conflicted. "This is not *quite* how I envisaged us unveiling the new conservatory, my darling."

"Isn't it? But it's how I imagined it," she admitted.

"I was not nice to you that night, Ballentine," he said in a strangled voice.

"You were not nice to yourself either," she replied quietly.

He huffed. "You're saying you want me to take you into the conservatory, shove you against the wall, and kiss you so hard I bruise your lips?" he asked disbelievingly.

"Yes, please." Her answer seemed to confound him. "I think you would like it too," she added firmly. "I think it would, well, be like lancing a boil."

"Lancing a boil?" he repeated with horror.

"I think we should have done it months ago," she said earnestly. "Only we did not have a conservatory then. I suppose we could have used Hudgins's glasshouse but I did not want to upset the old dear. He was so wounded over the failure of that pineapple he tried to grow."

"Emmeline, are we doing this now? Because if so, time is of the essence," he said, consulting his pocket watch.

"I just need to put on my evening gloves and I'm ready."

"Well, then I just need to fetch something." He held up a finger. "One moment." To Emmie's surprise he headed back through the connecting door, into his own room. When he reappeared he held a slim cardboard box in his hand, tied up with ribbon. "Here," he said a trifle awkwardly, coming right up to her and handing it to her.

"It's not jewelry, is it?" Emmie asked with trepidation. "Because it's not Christmas yet and—"

"It's not jewelry." He was watching her with an oddly expectant air.

Emmie undid the ribbon and removed the lid to find an expensive-looking fan. "Oh, it's beautiful," she said, lifting it out of the box. "I love the detail—" Her words died on her lips. "But this…this is…"

"Your fan," he said simply. "The one you broke that night."

"At the Hawfords' ball," she whispered.

"Yes, I had it mended." When she could not speak, he started, almost awkwardly, "I hope you don't mind—"

She hugged him fiercely and after a moment, Jeremy's arms encircled her back. "You mended *everything*!" she sobbed.

"Emmeline…" They stayed as they were for a good long moment before Jeremy kissed her brow. "We'd better hurry if I'm to kiss the hell out of you in our conservatory."

She gave a watery laugh. "Yes, let's hurry. Now I have my fan, where's my gloves?"

"You're not using that fan tonight, are you?" he asked with surprise.

"How could I not?"

"White satin? With red velvet?"

"My gloves are white," she pointed out. "And I could not possibly use another fan, so do not ask me to."

He laughed. "If Lady Sharpe raises her eyebrows at you, so be it."

"Lady Sharpe would never. She's my staunchest supporter. Since that summer fund raiser I can do no wrong in her eyes."

"Come along, then, Lady Faris." He offered her his arm.

She took it. Together they swept out of the room.

The Christmas festivities were in full swing. Emmie cast a quick, assessing look about the drawing room, where everything seemed to be going swimmingly. The Nyes were talking with the Tavistocks, though by Mina's frequent glances toward the door, she guessed her sister-in-law was itching to slip away to select another novel from the library.

Mina had not only joined their book club but had outstripped them all when it came to burning through their collection of novels. It had brought the two of them a good deal closer, much to Jeremy's evident satisfaction.

The vicar and his wife were conversing with the Hardimans, who were starting to relax in their new surroundings. Teddy was helping Pinky to a glass of fruit punch, while Jeremy was speaking to the string quartet set up in the far corner and currently taking a break from their performance.

The evergreens were glistening with berries and chandeliers were glittering with lights. In short, everything looked pretty as a picture. Swiftly crossing through the hall, where she discovered Squire Pebmarsh and Mr. Penrose paying elaborate court to Lady Sharpe and the rest of the Good Works committee, she swept into the blue sitting room and found Mr. Wimble deep in conversation with Miss Delia Pebmarsh.

This was surprising, but even more so, was where Miss Blanche Pebmarsh had disappeared to with Edgar Needham. That gentleman had squired his much maligned sister, Miss Halperston, to the party this evening, but had then been whisked away by Blanche as the most eligible bachelor present, and Caroline now stood awkwardly alone, nursing a glass of lemonade.

"Who *is* that dyspeptic-looking young woman stood next to the potted fern?" asked Lord Atherton's voice at Emmie's ear. She turned, and he presented her with a glass of champagne.

"Thank you," she said, setting it down. "Good evening, Lord Atherton. I did not know you had arrived yet! That is Miss Caroline Halperston, and it is not dyspepsia that afflicts her, but rather a certain social awkwardness. It is too bad of her brother to abandon her like that! I suspect Blanche has dragged him into the music room, which I really meant to have remained out of bounds tonight."

"Then you ought to have locked it. Guests never have any respect for unlocked doors these days," he lamented. "Tell me, has she any money?"

"Money? Not that I am aware of."

He tutted. "A pity."

"Are you fortune hunting?" she asked him suspiciously. "If so, the Pebmarsh girls are a much better bet."

"They are *hardly* girls, my dear Lady Faris." Lord Atherton grimaced, taking a swig of champagne. "And they are both so disgustingly hearty. I can't stand hearty women." He shuddered eloquently.

"What time did you get here?" Emmie asked, "I did not hear you announced."

"Oh, I've only just arrived," he said comfortably. "Slipped up the backstairs and found my usual room awaiting me, bless Mrs. Cheviot's little heart. I changed my suit and had a little toddle around the dear old place, whilst having a smoke."

"And you've not seen Jeremy yet?" she asked, threading her arm through his. "I'd better take you to him at once."

"No hurry. I wanted to speak to you first in any case."

"Did you?" She was strangely flattered. "I was so sorry you did not come and stay with us in the summer. We expected you but you never came."

He smiled. "I thought I should leave it at least six months before I turned up here at Vance. That way I could skip those insufferable stages while you two were tying yourselves up in knots and suffering needless agonies on the altar of love. There is nothing quite so tedious as a pair of frustrated lovers." He gave her a sidelong look. "How long did it take you, by the way?"

"How long did what take me?"

"To winkle the truth out of him. I knew it wouldn't take you too long. Not after I gave you all those helpful hints at the wedding."

She narrowed her eyes at him. "And by that you mean, how long did it take for me to uncover his undying love for me?"

"Precisely," he said with satisfaction. "I always knew you had a decent head on your shoulders, despite that starry-eyed gaze of yours."

"It took me rather longer than it should have," she admitted honestly. He looked amused. "But it was more like three months in the end than six."

"Oh, bravo." He gave her a little round of applause.

"You are quite disgraceful, Lord Atherton," she scolded without heat. "Just as bad as you always were."

"Oh, I shall never change," he said smugly. "I'm a thoroughly bad lot and very comfortable in my wicked ways. By the way, why is your head footman glaring at me?"

"I have no idea. Have you greeted Pinky yet?"

"Effusively."

"That would be why, then," she answered. "He's very protective over her these days."

"Hmmm. Are you sure his designs in that direction are entirely respectable? He was quite the lad back in the day, was Colfax."

"Back in the day when he was preventing Jeremy from getting dunned on his doorstep and killed in duels every other week?" Emmie asked with an arched brow. "Yes, I have heard all about it. Jeremy has laid bare both his soul and his jaded past to me."

"Ugh," said Atherton. "You have my profound sympathies."

"And yes, I am quite sure about Pinky and Colfax. They're walking out together. Courting," she added in case he was unfamiliar with the term.

His stride checked slightly. "Really? Strapping Colfax and demure Miss Pinson?"

"Yes."

"Good lord."

"Jeremy means to make him butler here when Garraway retires so his prospects are quite good."

Atherton looked amused. "Well, Jeremy certainly could not get rid of Colfax. He knows where all the skeletons are buried."

"Yes. Probably because he helped bury them," Emmie agreed.

Atherton smirked. "I am surprised to see your husband's collection of Venuses has not increased since last I visited." Emmie thought fleetingly of her new bedroom decor but said nothing. "But perhaps, having secured the source of his fascination, his compulsion to amass such imitations has abated."

Her ears pricked up at this. "Do you mean to suggest his fondness for Venuses originated with me?" she asked with surprise.

"Didn't you know?"

"No!"

"He purchased his first in Italy, on his honeymoon. The one in your drawing room, where she emerges from the sea to wring out her wet hair."

Emmie was speechless. After a moment she rallied. "They do not look so very much like me, you know."

"My dear Lady Faris, I have two eyes in my head," he countered.

"Well, in any case..." She trailed off feebly as they came to a halt next to the portrait of Jeremy's mother.

Atherton looked over the portrait in silence. "I'm glad he did not fall for a similar type as his mother at any rate."

Emmie glanced up at the portrait. "She was very pretty."

"Always thought she looked a bit of a simperer myself," Atherton admitted, taking a swig of champagne.

They both contemplated the canvas. "Everyone agrees Jeremy is nothing like her in character. Mina, his sister, maintains that if their mother *had* been present during his childhood, she would likely have made Jeremy's character even worse by spoiling and fawning on him."

Atherton laughed. "For my part, I imagine Jeremy would have been very like Teddy as a child. You will have to keep a close eye on that boy," he said darkly.

"Nonsense! Teddy is a delightful and well-adjusted child. As soon as he heard of our history together, he knew exactly where to apportion blame, showing an unerring sense of right and wrong." She gave him a sidelong look. "Besides, as godparent, the responsibility of keeping a watchful eye on him falls also to you."

Atherton shuddered dramatically. "I was assured that the purchasing of a silver tankard for the christening covered the full extent of my duty."

"Well, you were misinformed," Emmie told him roundly. "If there is any danger of young Teddy persecuting maidens in the future, then we shall need all the help we can get keeping him in line."

"You think I would be helpful in reining in his excesses?" Atherton asked with a lift of his eyebrows.

"Certainly, I do. I have already heard several times a firsthand account of the lesson you taught him not to be careless with his personal possessions."

Atherton looked confused for a moment, then he groaned. "Not that wretched dip pen!" he exclaimed.

"The mother-of-pearl one he took to school."

He shook his head. "He will never forgive me for that."

"I am sure he would," she said kindly, "if you were to replace it, say on his next birthday."

Atherton spread his hands wide. "Alas, I am not even sure when that is!"

"Do you know," Emmie said thoughtfully, "that is the first thing I have heard that makes me disapprove of you in the role of godfather."

He opened his mouth, then closed it again. "Oh, very well," he said, sounding goaded. "I will find it out and henceforth celebrate the date with all attendant pomp."

"Now *that* is a good deal more like it."

He gave her a considering look. "I begin to see you are a woman to be reckoned with, Lady Faris."

She smiled at him, reclaiming his arm. "I do my poor best."

Jeremy appeared at this juncture, warmly welcomed his friend, and then bore off Emmie into the empty hallway which was now mercifully free of Good Works members. "You can hear the music from here," he pointed out. "Let's lurk about here for a while out of everyone's earshot."

"This is not very host-like of you," she said with a smile as he took her into his arms and they started to waltz.

"It's your fault, you put me quite out of patience with hosting after kissing me in that exciting fashion earlier."

"I know," she laughed, her eyes returning to the repaired fan which dangled from her wrist. A sudden frown marred her countenance.

"What is it?" he asked quickly.

"I hope Lord Atherton does not try to seduce poor Caroline Halperston."

"I thought you said she needed some excitement in her life?"

"Well, yes, but not that kind of excitement!"

"Never mind about them. I fear Gervaise is a lost cause. Let us concentrate our efforts instead on raising Teddy as a responsible young man with proper feelings. A real Fernando."

"Alas," Emmie mocked, "Teddy is already a lost cause, for he is quite the biggest rogue in Penarth." They glanced over to the drawing room, through which door they could plainly see Teddy coaxing Pinky into dancing with him in the center of the room.

He laughed. "Very well, then, imagine a daughter."

"Whose daughter?"

"Ours."

"You want a daughter?"

"I find I do, very much in fact."

Emmie considered this. "I hope she would inherit your looks."

"And I would hope she inherits yours. I already have one child in my image," he said, glancing at Teddy, who was now leading Pinky about the floor.

"Or you might get your spare at last."

"If it's a boy, I will also be very pleased," he confessed. "How about you?"

"I, too, will be happy with either. Shall we slip away to the conservatory again, husband? It looks so wonderful in there with all the glass reflecting the Christmas tree lights, and that new circular 'borne settee' that Mr. Penrose was so clever as to find for us."

His smile grew. "Tempting, very tempting, Lady Faris, but I don't know. We need to be back here at ten o'clock to stand on the staircase and make our Christmas toast together with all our guests."

Emmie wondered if he had made a conscious decision to exorcise the very last of the bad memories of that fateful night at the Hawfords' with such a toast, or whether it was a happy coincidence.

Suddenly, something that had been tickling at the edge of her memory unfurled. "By the way, whatever happened with Charlie Symonds?" she asked on impulse, dimly remembering some words of Lord Atherton's from their wedding day.

Jeremy stared at her. "Who?" he asked at last, but she had a strong suspicion he was playing innocent.

"Lord Atherton told me to ask you about him," she answered truthfully.

His expression wavered between astonishment and annoyance. "Oh, he did, did he?" he asked wrathfully.

"Not tonight, but at the wedding. I forgot all about it, until he mentioned that he had given me some helpful clues and it popped back into my head."

"I think I need to have a quiet word with Gervaise!" Jeremy muttered under his breath.

"Whatever was it?" she prodded. "I vaguely remember a Mr. Symonds from my debut but…"

"Mr. Symonds said something once that I took exception to, at a party over a decade ago."

"Oh?" Emmie was intrigued. "What was it?"

"He intimated that he was going to ask a certain someone to dance."

"And?"

"That person belonged to me at that time. She still does."

"You knocked him down?" she guessed. "For *that*?"

"I did."

"Good grief."

"Ballentine?"

"Yes?"

"Shall I give you a little something else to remember me by?" he asked quite casually.

"Yes, please."

Scorching her with the intensity of his gaze, he bore her off in the direction of their new conservatory.

THE END

I do hope you enjoyed this story. If so, perhaps you would be kind enough to leave me a rating on Amazon, Goodreads, or Bookbub.

Join my mailing list for a monthly newsletter and updates by visiting my website: www.alicecoldbreath.com

Upcoming books from Alice Coldbreath in 2025

A Most Forgettable Girl

Cheerful Gunnilde Payne is hiding a bruised heart behind her bright smile. When her friend invites her to spend some time away from her provincial home, she jumps at the chance. Distraction is just what she needs to forget the sad disappointment of her childhood sweetheart getting betrothed to another.

All is going well, until Gunnilde overhears herself rudely dismissed by two knights as "nice, plain, and utterly forgettable." Poor Gunnilde is mortified, but as soon as the thoughtless words left his lips, someone starts to notice she has plenty of charm after all.

Other series by Alice Coldbreath you may enjoy:

THE VAWDREY BROTHERS SERIES

Book 1 – **Her Baseborn Bridegroom**

Lady Linnet Cadwallader has been raised a helpless invalid in her own castle. Brought up to believe she will "never make old bones" she lives a quiet and lonely existence, hiding away her excessive freckles and red hair from a world that believes her to be hideously misshapen and ugly.

Until one day her uncle arranges a marriage of convenience for her, a marriage in name only with a young puppet groom…but Sir Roland does not show up. In his place turns up his baseborn brother Mason Vawdrey. And dark, forceful Mason is no one's puppet.

Things are about to get interesting at Cadwallader Castle. And Linnet is about to discover that maybe a golden leopardess does not need to change her glorious spots.

More books from the Kingdom of Karadok by Alice Coldbreath:

THE BRIDES OF KARADOK SERIES

Book 1 - **Wed by Proxy**

Thrice wedded, but never bedded, Mathilde Martindale has long lived in the shadow of her indomitable mother, and meekly done as she was told. Until one day, she decides to become mistress of her own destiny and leave the royal court to find her own path.

Married by proxy, Lord Martindale has never even met his bride of three years. Wed as part of a peace treaty, he bitterly resents the mercenary wife who cares only for wealth and prestige. And then he meets her.

Book 2 - **The Unlovely Bride**

Lenora Montmayne leads a charmed life as the most beautiful woman at King Wymer's court, surrounded by ardent admirers. And then disaster strikes. The red pox sweeps the summer palace at Caer-Lyoness, and Lenora's fair face falls victim to its ravages. Without her looks, what does Lenora have left to her?

If ever there was a knight the crowd loves to hate, it's Garman Orde. Even his own family despises him. Then one night a heavily veiled lady offers him an extraordinary bargain. And he finds out that Lenora Montmayne was never just a pretty face.

THE VICTORIAN PRIZEFIGHTER SERIES

Book 1 – **A Bride for the Prizefighter**

Mina's well-ordered life is thrown into disarray when her father drops a bombshell on his deathbed: she has a brother she never knew of. Not only that, he is on his way to rescue her from the collapse of their school under a mountain of debts.

A wild journey across the country later, Mina finds herself thrown at the feet of the brutish William Nye, prizefighter and owner of a disreputable inn, The Merry Harlot. Respectable Mina is appalled to find herself obliged to wed this surly stranger!

Forced to draw on reserves of inner strength she never knew she possessed, Mina uncovers perilous secrets and bravely carves herself a new life at the side of this man as she proves herself a more-than-worthy partner for the prizefighter.